SIX

GOODBYES

WE

NEVER

SAID

CANDACE GANGER

SIX GOODBYES WE NEVER SAID

WEDNESDAY BOOKS
NEW YORK

First published in the United States by Wednesday Books,
an imprint of St. Martin's Publishing Group

SIX GOODBYES WE NEVER SAID. Copyright © 2019 by Candace Ganger.
All rights reserved. Printed in the United States of America. For information,
address St. Martin's Publishing Group, 120 Broadway, New York, NY 10271.

www.wednesdaybooks.com

Designed by Anna Gorovoy

Library of Congress Cataloging-in-Publication Data

Names: Ganger, Candace, author.
Title: Six goodbyes we never said / Candace Ganger.
Description: First edition. | New York : Wednesday Books, 2019.
Identifiers: LCCN 2019012709 | ISBN 9781250116246 (hardcover) |
    ISBN 9781250237088 (ebook)
Subjects: CYAC: Grief—Fiction. | Interpersonal relations—Fiction. |
    Obsessive-compulsive disorder—Fiction. | Social phobia—Fiction. | Anxiety
    disorders—Fiction. | Racially-mixed people—Fiction. | Orphans—Fiction.
Classification: LCC PZ7.1.G3547 Six 2019 | DDC [Fic]—dc23
LC record available at https://lccn.loc.gov/2019012709

Our books may be purchased in bulk for promotional, educational, or
business use. Please contact your local bookseller or the Macmillan Corporate and
Premium Sales Department at 1-800-221-7945, extension 5442, or by
email at MacmillanSpecialMarkets@macmillan.com.

First Edition: September 2019

10 9 8 7 6 5 4 3 2 1

For the broken hearts,
& punched-out souls,
& grief-hollowed bones,
& muddled minds,
In the darkest hours,
Fighting for the light.

AUTHOR'S NOTE

Hello, dear reader.

I think it should be known that, while *Six Goodbyes* is a work of fiction, I share the many characteristics, fears, and pains, in both the delicacy of Dew, and the confused ferocity in Naima. Please let this brief note serve as a trigger warning in regards to mental illness; self-care is of the utmost importance. And while I hope *Six Goodbyes* provides insight for those who don't empathize, or comfort for those that do, I also understand everyone reacts differently.

Dew's social anxiety is something I, and many others, struggle with. We carry on with our days and pretend it's not as hard as it feels inside. Others can't quite see how much it hurts but we *so* wish they could. Naima is the most visceral interpretation of all of my diagnosed disorders combined. Her obsessive-compulsive disorder (OCD) and related tics, her intrusive thoughts, her utterly devastating and isolating depression, her generalized anxiety disorder (GAD), which makes her so closed off from the world, and her post-traumatic stress disorder (PTSD) from losing the biggest portion of her identity—those are all pieces of me. Very *big* pieces. They don't define me, but it would be misleading if I didn't admit they sometimes, mostly do. I'm imperfectly complicated like Naima. And though I've written extensively on both my mental illnesses and living biracial, between two worlds—never enough of one or the other; always only half of something and never whole or satiated—I often still feel misunderstood. Hopefully Dew and Naima's stories will provide a little insight as to what it's like inside their heads, and inside mine.

Both Dew and Naima want to hold on to the roots that have

grounded them in their familiar, safe spaces. But once their meta-phorical trees are cut, and all the leaves shielding them from their pains have fallen and faded away, not even photosynthesis could bring them back to life. Those roots, Naima and Dew feel, will die off, and everything they had in their lives before will, too. There are many of you out there who feel the exact same way, but I assure you, Dew and Naima will find their way—they will grow new roots that flourish—and you, my darlings, will, too.

Thank you for reading, and may *Six Goodbyes* serve as per-mission to speak your truths—the good and the painful.

Here's to another six airplanes for you to wish upon.

SIX GOODBYES WE NEVER SAID

ANATOMY OF THE FLOAT PHASE

When someone like Staff Sergeant Raymond K. Rodriguez leaves to fight for their country, the rest of you wait, counting down the days until the next arrival, and the next leave—because there's little breathing in between. You check the empty mailbox, hold your phones like bulletproof vests, and bargain with whoever you pray to that your fathers and mothers and sisters and brothers don't come home in a box. *No one* wants to be in the FLOAT phase—*Fallen Loved Ones Awaiting Transfer.* Not knowing when the body of your loved one will arrive on American soil wrapped in ice. So you can release that pang you've been holding on to, only to replace it with a new one. So you can stop pacing in fear, and hold on to something else: acceptance.

When you're in a military family with an active service member, death becomes something you prepare for. You talk about tradition, honor, dignity, and death at the dinner table. A black sedan becomes a symbol of someone's sacrifice. If one drives near, grieving begins before you know who to grieve for. But the thing is, Naima Rodriguez has been grieving as long as she can remember, because she's never gotten over being left in the first place. That's the thing about absence—it sinks into your skin, clinging to the bone until it's so much a part of you, you can no longer tell where it ends and you begin.

You are the *FLOAT* phase.

Only the dead have seen the End of War.
The rest of us carry it inside.

—PLATO

I hate everything about mascots.
Show your face already.

—NAIMA RODRIGUEZ

Voicemail

Dad

cell
May 3 at 7:33 PM

Transcription Beta

"Guess who's getting ready to come home and take you to Ivy Springs? That's right, Ima. It's happening. It's finally happening. Don't tell Nell. I want to surprise her."

▶ 0:00 |⎯⎯⎯⎯⎯⎯⎯⎯⎯⎯⎯⎯⎯⎯⎯⎯⎯ -0:10

Speaker　　　　**Call Back**　　　　**Delete**

Email Draft (Unsent)

New Message　　　　　　　　　　　　　×

To

Subject

I'm holding my breath
   Until you're standing in front of me
      Because we've danced this song
         So many times before

And I no longer trust
You'll do what you
Promise.
Just in case,
I'll count the hexagons.

NAIMA

Nell is a dingy yoga mat; the sweaty barrier between total chill-status and my shit reality (aka, my annoying stepmom and ru-iner of all moments) (trust me on this).

"JJ and Kam aren't going to believe how much you've grown since the funeral," she says on our long-ass 794-mile drive from Albany, Georgia, to Ivy Springs, Indiana. She *tap tap taps* her long, pointed fingernails against the steering wheel to the beat of what-ever imaginary song she's playing in her head. Probably some-thing disco or hair band. The radio is silent, always silent, when we ride together, but the second she speaks with that high-pitched nasally voice I loathe, I regret this necessity. I concentrate harder on the objects we pass so I can properly pinch my toes between them.

Tap my nose. Tap my nose. Tap my nose.
  Tap my nose. Tap my nose.
    Tap my nose.
      Click my tongue. Click my tongue. Click my tongue.
      Click my tongue. Click my tongue.
        Click my tongue.
          Flick my thumbnail. Flick my thumbnail.
        Flick my thumbnail.
  Flick my thumbnail. Flick my thumbnail.

Flick my thumbnail.

Flick.

Flick.

FLICK.

I continue with my sequence the length of the drive. Nell hates it, but I hate when she wears fingerless gloves in the summer, so we're even. Without my boring-ass stepbrother, Christian, to be my talk block—the dull cushion of conversation between Nell and me—(he left two days ago on a death star/plane to see his dad in NYC), the "spacious" SUV feels like I've been placed at a dinner table in a vast canyon and right across from me is literally the *only* woman I don't want to meet for dinner. Like, why can't I eat with the Queen of England or Oprah? I'm bound by my father's love for Nell, or whatever, but now he's gone, and I'm climbing the hell out of the canyon before she wants to talk about how big my naturally tousled hair is (a perfect mess), period cycles (semi-regular, FYI), sexually transmitted diseases (don't have a single one, thanks), or worse—my feelings (happily buried!). *Ugh. GTFO.*

The failing engine's hum, where the metal scrapes and churns with a whir, competes with Nell's increased tapping. I've missed too many objects, my toes rapidly pinching and releasing, to make up for what's been lost. But it's too late. My mind shifts automatically to a neon sign flashing WARNING! There's always a consequence to messing up the sequence. *Always.*

Counting is to time what the final voicemail Dad left is to the sound of my heart cracking open; a message I can't listen to. It'll become entombed in history, in me. My finger lingers over my phone and quickly retreats, knowing there's nothing he could've said to make this pain less. Nothing can make him less gone.

I look out the window to where my dreary-eyed reflection stares blankly back at me; Nell glides over the double yellow lines into oncoming traffic, violently overcorrecting just before we would have been hit by a semi. The sound of his horn echoes through the high-topped Tennessee mountains. Three thousand two hundred eighty-seven people die in car accidents every day. I Googled it. After I Googled it, I looked at pictures. And after I looked at pictures I went through the sequence. Car accident. Fatalities. My legs smashed up to my chest. Nell crushed into the hood.

"Sorry," she says; her voice rattles. "Make sure Ray's okay back there."

I turn to investigate the vase-shaped metal urn surrounded by layers of sloppily folded sheets (Nell did that) and one perfectly situated hexagon quilt (that's all me). The sun's gleam hits *U.S. Marine Corp* just so, and I'm reminded again that he's gone. *Gone.*

"*It's* fine," I say, refusing to call that pile of ashes "Dad," or "he." The urn arrived several days ago in a twenty-four-hour priority package. Nell saying, "No reason to waste time getting him *home*," and I was like, "What's *that*?" and she was all "Your dad, silly," and I was like, "Huh?" and she asked me if I wanted a banana-kale protein shake after she "got him situated." A big *hell no.* I immediately dove into a Ziploc ration of Lucky Charms marshmallows to dull the pain of conversing with someone so exhausting.

After he was transported in ice from Afghanistan to Dover, after they sorted and processed his things, after he was cremated, after the police and state troopers closed down the streets to honor him as we drove him through, after we had the memorial service, after we were handed the folded flag with a bullet shell casing tucked inside, after they spoke of his medals, and after Christian and I sat in disbelief beneath a weeping willow tree for three hours, Nell finally decided the ashes *should* go to his hometown in Indiana, after all. I didn't think she'd cave, but after one talk with my grandma, JJ, she did. If anyone could turn a donkey into a unicorn, it's JJ (or so she says). And so, it was decided—Dad, I mean *It,* was going home a unicorn.

"Let's stop for some grub," Nell says, wide-eyed. "Hungry?"

"Grub," rhymes with "nub," which she is. "No."

"Let's at least stretch our legs. Still a few hours to go."

"Fine. But no travel yoga this time."

She pulls off to a rest area a few miles ahead, exiting the car. I crack a window and wait while she hikes a leg to the top of the trunk, bending forward with an "oh, that's tight." After, she says, "Going to the potty. BRB."

I flash a thumbs-up and slink deep into the warmth of my seat, hiding from the stare of perverts and families. My foot kicks my bag on the floor mat, knocking my prescription bottle to its side. Dr. Rose, my therapist in Ft. Hood, said sometimes starting over is the only way to stop looking back. But what about when the past is all you have left of someone?

My gaze pushes forward to the vending machines. Dad and I stopped at this very place on *our* way to Indiana *without* basic Nell. He'd grab a cold can of Coke and toss me a bag of trail mix to sort into piles. If I close my eyes, it *almost* feels like he's here—not a pile of ashes buckled tight into the backseat. We'd play a game of Would You Rather to see who could come up with the worst/most messed-up scenarios (I usually won).

Would you rather wear Nell's unwashed yoga pants every day for a month?

Or call an urn full of ashes "Dad"?

Sometimes, he'd pre-sort the trail mix,

Leaving me the best parts (the candy-coated chocolate).

I am one-of-a-kind

Magic, Dad would say.

But he was, too.

A unicorn, I think.

Definitely not a donkey.

The more I think on it,

Maybe JJ could turn Nell

Into a unicorn,
Too,
But *no* magic is that strong.

Voicemail

Dad

cell
June 1 at 9:04 AM

Transcription Beta

"Open the door."

▶ 0:00 -0:03

Speaker **Call Back** **Delete**

Sent Email

No Subject

Naima <naimatheriveter@gmail.com> Jun 1, 9:07 AM
to Dad

If I open it,
Will you really be there
Or just a memory
From the last time?
Nevermind.

I see you,
The ghost
Outside my window.
<3

⏮ ⏭ ▶❚❚ ■ ● DEW GD BRICKMAN
DURATION: 10:49

*In today's forecast, sunshine early morning will give
way to late-day thunderstorms. I love the smell of
rain. It's the aroma of being alive.*

August Moon and the Paper Hearts—the band my parents opened
for—advise we speak kindly to strangers through song. I'd like
to think that's what my parents would've said, too. I can still see
my mother's chestnut eyes soft as she hums. From the tired
bones in her feet after long shifts at the glass-making factory
(after the band split apart), to the graying curls that sprang into
action when the beat hit her ears, she's frozen in time; a whim-
sical ballerina, twirling inside a glass globe to a tune only she and
I can hear.

"Let the music move your soul," she'd tell me. "Let it carry
you into the clouds, my darling."

She'd grab my hand, hers papered by the rough gloves she
was required to wear during her shifts, guiding me by the glitter-
ing moondust, while Dad watched on from the old twill rocker,
threads carved around his boxy frame. Our feet stepped along
invisible squares against the floor, round and round, until the
world vanished beneath us. We floated.

"You got that boy spoiled, Momma," Dad would tell her.

"Don't you know it," she'd reply, pulling me closer.

That was when the universe built itself around the three of us; vibrant wildflowers, dipped in my mother's favorite verb: "love." I wish I could remember the smell of her better. I wish I could remember what Dad would say. When I lose my breath in the thick of human oceans and panic, I wish harder.

My second set of parents, Stella and Thomas, are kind to me. Stella's eyes remind me of my mother's—two infinity pools, giving the illusion of boundless compassion—while Thomas's laugh is an eerily mirrored version of my father's. Sometimes, when Thomas finds himself amused, I catch myself thinking Dad is here. I can almost see him holding his bass guitar, doubled over from a joke he'd heard.

My sister, Faith, hasn't settled into this family yet, even after a year of fostering. She cries, punches her bed pillow—sometimes Stella; sometimes Thomas. Her wailing is incessant, scratchy, and raw. Sometimes I sit outside her door and silently cry with her. When you're taken from your birth parents, it doesn't matter how wonderful your new, adoptive, or temporary, foster parents are. They can be every warm hug you've needed, but if you're holding tight to the feeling of being *home*, you may find comfort in the cold, dark night instead. I did at first. After all the months with us, Faith is realizing the Brickmans *are* her *home* now, but she's still fighting to stay warm on her own, hoping her parents would somehow return.

"You can never know someone's pain or happiness until you've stepped inside their shoes," my mother would say.

"What if their shoes don't fit?" I'd ask. "If our lives are too different?"

"Find a connection; something similar enough that all the differences bounce off the table completely, like Ping-Pong balls. If we look past things that divide us, humanity will find a way to shine through."

No one should step inside my shoes unless they're prepared to understand the kind of grief that's whole-body and constant. It's quiet but deep. The same way Earth orbits the sun every hour of every day of every year, I miss my parents, and Faith misses hers.

Stella and Thomas try. They've searched our shoe collection. They've tried them on. And, just as Cinderella found her magic fit, they've managed to find a pair that fits in some way. Of the hundreds of thousands of kids in foster care, they placed an inquiry about me, they went through the classes and orientation for me, they did the home study for me—they adopted *me*. Same for Faith, however different our circumstances.

It makes no matter that Stella and Thomas couldn't conceive naturally. The foster and adoption process stole chunks of time they'll never retrieve, for a "special needs" boy—due to my age, "minority group," and "emotional trauma"—long past diapers and bottles and baby powder–scented snuggles. It was financially and emotionally draining for all of us involved, with no guarantee I would welcome them or they could love me the way my parents did. I didn't embrace them at first. I quite liked my previous foster family but they felt me only temporary. The Brickmans embraced me without hesitation, with a permanent kind of promise. It's the same kindness my parents would endorse. They gave me a home, a family, and a place I belong. And so, to every stranger along my path, I will be kind, too. Even—*especially*—the ones who'd prefer I didn't.

"Those are the souls who need compassion most," Mom would say. "The ones broken by the world, angry and afraid of trusting. You must remind them that they are not alone. Nothing can be lost in trying. Remember that always, my darling."

As I hear Faith shouting into her comforter again, I wonder how many have failed to try on her shoes through the near dozen foster homes she's been in.

I hear you, Faith.

I am you.

I think all this before my pre-planned path to Baked & Caffeinated—the coffee and bakeshop at which I've been employed a mere six days—with August Moon streaming through my earbuds. Today is my first scheduled shift, and if you could feel my heart beat, you'd assume it was about to burst (it very well may). Though Ivy Springs maintains a compact three-mile radius, it's my first time walking alone. For most, it's a relaxing walk. But, as my father would often tell me, I am not most people. The mere thought of the journey had me curled in a ball on my twin mattress for at least an hour. Beneath the covers, I gave my best, most inspiring pep talk about how, despite those voices telling me I can't do it, I can and I will and I'll be glorious.

Mom would always lift the blankets off the bed and sit next to me. "This, too, shall pass, my darling."

"And if it doesn't?" I'd say with quivering lips.

"It will. You are my corpse flower," Mom told me. "The largest, rarest flower in the whole world. Blooming takes many arduous seasons, but it is worth the wait."

The longer she's gone, the more I understand the layers she peeled off of me. With each one, my shine radiated a little more. Mom and Dad never saw my fears in black and white; people aren't made so simply. We're straddling a blur of gray.

The downtown café is fairly new to this small blip of town. Serving variations of roasted coffee beans, espresso concoctions, and freshly baked confectionaries you can smell for miles, Baked & Caffeinated is one of the few places people my age come. With school out for summer, the position of highly regarded cashier is a way to blend in slightly more than I stand out. When the manager, Liam "Big Foot" Thompson—college student and "organic medicinal specialist" (whatever that means)—barely glanced at the application I spent two long hours filling in, I'm not sure what prompted him to hire me on the spot, but there it was: an opportunity to slide into a new pair of shoes.

"Hard work reveals who people really are," Dad would tell me. "When the going gets tough, some hide and others rise."

I will rise, Dad.

One glance at the clock and I see no matter how I rush, the seconds tick by faster than I can keep up. I'm dressed in freshly ironed slacks, an ebony polo buttoned two-thirds of the way up (I was told this is appropriate), snazzy checkered suspenders, and the taupe fedora—feather and all—I *cannot* live without.

"I'm off," I tell Stella.

She sits at the kitchen table, a list of recipe ingredients in hand, peering over the bridge of her reading glasses. She pulls a ceramic coffee mug to her lips and sips her coffee with a slurp. It dribbles to the paper. "Ah, damn it!"

I step back, my hands gripping my suspenders as if they're bungee cords.

"Sorry," she says, standing. She squares her shoulders with mine and drives her stare through me. "I hope you have the best time." She pulls me near—an attempt at a hug that's strangled by her awkward, coffee-saturated positioning. "If you feel overwhelmed, take a deep breath, excuse yourself to the bathroom if necessary, and you can always, *always* call me. K?"

I hesitate, fear squirming between us.

She tips my chin up so my eyes fall straight into hers. Her eyes swallow me up in a bubble of safety, little lines spiderwebbing out from the corner creases that cling to my distress, fishing fear out of me, casting it somewhere else entirely. It's a trick Mom used to do, too.

"You're going to do great," she reassures. "Promise."

I nod, finally, and she releases me from her grip to deal with the coffee puddle. I watch her for a whole minute before she urges me out the door. I'm supposed to work on my time management. I lose time when my brain is knotted with worry. But how do you untangle something you can't even see?

Along my walk down the potholed sidewalk, my eyes carefully plot each step to not catch on a divot. The last time, I nearly broke my arm, the exact spot ridiculing me as I pounce over it with the light-footed pirouette of a cat. I'm so proud of this move, distracted by my obvious victory against that mean concrete hole, I run straight into someone.

"Oh, I'm so sorry," I stammer.

"Dude," a boy says with a heavy grunt. "Watch it."

I'm hesitant to make eye contact, but I do—Stella and Thomas have encouraged it—alarm bells blaring. The boy's eyes are narrow, brows furrowed. I replay last night's news headline in my mind—TEEN SHOOTS FORMER CLASSMATE AT GRADUATION PARTY—and fold as far down as my small frame will allow.

He rips his earbuds out, his face softening only slightly. I try to walk by, he blocks me. I move to the other side. He stands in my way here, too.

"Excuse me," I say.

"You should watch where you're going. It's a small town with shitty sidewalks."

"Yes," I stutter. "I will, thank you for the advice."

He presses his earbuds back into place and allows me to pass with the wave of his hand.

"Have a wonderful day," I tell him. My voice shakes, my feet moving faster than before.

Mom would say, "Chin up, eyes forward, not back," so I repeat this to myself, pretending she's here to ricochet these interactions into outer space. I'm still learning how to be my own hero. My deepest darkest fear is, maybe I never will.

I stand outside the bakeshop and stare up at the illustrated coffee mug on the sign. My reluctance holds me in the center of this busier than normal sidewalk. I remind myself I'm okay. The crowds won't harm me. I can breathe through it and the day will go on. It can and it will, because it has to. As the sweat accumulates beneath my hat, I think of Mom telling me "now or never," and open the door. The bell attached to the door rings as I breeze through.

"You're *so* late," Mr. Thompson says after I wind through the line of customers bunched near the counter. "I thought we said ten."

A quick glance at the time—ten seventeen—and my chin sinks into my chest. "Apologies. We did agree on that time." Dad used to say, "The only good excuse is none at all," so I swallow the ones rising into my throat and try to ignore the gnawing feel-

ing in my gut that makes me want to lock myself inside the bathroom to escape all the noise and people and smells and sounds.
My sensory dashboard is on overload. I imagine a little robot in a
white coat frantically working to calm each circuit board before
it fries. Poor fellow. His work is thankless and sometimes a complete and utter failure. I do my best to help by inhaling another
deep breath, exhaling through my mouth as Mr. Thompson
guides me to the space behind the counter where I'm to stand. I
fumble in the small space, as another employee, a girl in a long
flowy dress covered by an apron, welcomes me with a wide grin.

"Hey, newb," she says. "I'm Violet."

"Nice to meet you. I'm Dew." I keep a generous distance to
not make her uncomfortable, but she moves in close enough to
notice how well I've brushed my teeth (well enough, I hope).

"You have a really great aura. It's blue-centric with electric
swirls of pink. Very neon, man."

I respect her need for close proximity and we stand almost
nose to nose. "Interesting. What does that mean?"

Her eyes widen as if she's swallowing every centimeter of
mine. "You're highly sensitive, intuitive, and have strong mor-
als. Like, you're honest to a fault and can't seem to deviate from
it, even if it'd serve you better to keep your mouth shut. I know,
because I'm a *total* Purple. I can read your palms if you want."

I slip them into my pockets. "Perhaps later, after I've grown
accustomed to the process and routines here."

She smiles and allows me the space to breathe again as Mr.
Thompson waves me to a short stack of papers I'm to fill out.
"When you're finished with these, I'll have Violet show you how
to brew espresso shots for lattes."

I nod. "Sir—"

He stops me with a snicker. "Please—my dad is *sir* because he's
a dinosaur. I'm Big Foot."

My eyes confusedly scan the perimeter of this man who
is neither big nor seems to have larger than average feet. Perhaps
that's the irony. I decide I like it. "Mr. Foot," I begin; he stops
me again to remind me it's *Big Foot*, "I don't have a driver's license

yet, only a permit. My birthday is in a few weeks, though I'm not interested in driving a motor vehicle at this time. I also have some allergies that may restrict my duties outside of handling the register. I forgot to mention it when I applied."

He lays a hand on my shoulder. "I read the notes on the application. I have a little bro with some pretty gnarly allergies. We specialize in nut-free, dairy-free shit. It's my duty to represent the underrepresented, you know?"

I nod, relieved.

"If you're not comfortable with any part, I'll make sure the others know to step in. Wear gloves. Wash your hands. Take your meds," he pauses, looks me over, "you got meds, right?"

I nod again.

"I got you, bro. Let me know if you have a flare-up from anything, 'cause I've got EpiPens and all that jazz."

My posture relaxes a bit.

"It'll be all right. Come get me after V trains you on the espresso shots."

I nod again, folding my hands in front of me.

Local boy freezes in the middle of summer—tonight at 10.

"So, listen," Violet says, drawing me closer. "My best friend, Birdie, went through major crappage this past year, and I've learned how to be a better friend because of it. Apparently she didn't feel like she could trust me with her most important secrets, so I totally reevaluated my life choices and decided, with a cleanse, to start anew."

"Good for you." I stop to wonder why she's telling me, a perfect stranger, this.

"Point is, I know we just met, but as this new, improved me, I'm good at reading people. And it looks like you could use a little encouragement."

She pulls a notebook from the cubby beneath the register, the words on the front flap, *Book of Silver Linings*, catching the gleam of the fluorescent lights. I watch her fingers flip and fumble to a specific page. "Confidence grows when we step out of our comfort zone and do something different." Her mouth hangs open, half smiling, as if she's waiting for my reaction.

"That helps. Thank you."

"No problem. I think you'll be okay, Dew—what's your last name?"

"Brickman now, was Diaz."

"I think you'll be okay Dew-Was-Diaz-Brickman." With a wink, she packs the notebook away. "So you're gonna be a sophomore or . . . ?"

"Correct, you?"

"Only here for the summer, then off to pre-college; a year of exploratory learning."

"Where are you headed?"

"Caramel School of Massage and Healing Arts, about forty minutes from here so I can go home when I want. Do you know what you're doing after high school?"

The question strikes me as abrupt. I've thought about the future, but not in the context of who I'll be in it. "Undecided."

"I was, too. Don't stress too much. It's only the rest of your life." She laughs, but it's glaringly obvious it's not a joke.

I turn to the stack of papers, still unsure of which boxes to check, which address to write, what emergency contacts to state. My initial reaction is my old Indianapolis address, Plum Street, and my parents' cell numbers, which I've memorized. I have to stop myself and carefully think what is true today—a Pearl Street address in Ivy Springs, and numbers that belong to Stella and Thomas. It's a habit I wish I didn't have to break.

As I neatly write my answers, I look up to see a man reminiscent of my father, dressed in desert-camouflaged pants and a tan fitted T-shirt. He orders a large coffee, black, no sugar. I have a penchant for details. They're the difference between knowing someone in 2-D or 4-D. Violet pumps the fresh java from a carafe while the man slides inside a booth near the entrance. The large window lets the sun seep in, coating him in a sunshine glaze; almost angelic. Perhaps it's my dad inside my bones, moving my feet—he never passed a service member without thanking them for their service—but I find myself standing at the foot of this man's table.

"Thank you for your service," I say dutifully.

"Thank you," he says with a warm smile. "I appreciate that."

"Well, I appreciate you appreciating me, so I suppose we're at an impasse of gratitude." I grin, my hands tucked behind my back to fidget with reckless abandon.

He chuckles as his phone rings. "I'm sorry, but I have to take this."

"Have a great rest of your day," I say. "And thank you again."

"No, thank you—" He stops himself with a palm over the phone speaker. "We could go on forever."

Violet brings a steaming cup to the table. "This cup signifies my gratitude. Plus, you have a really great aura."

"Thank you," he tells her before his attention returns to his call.

The crowd has thinned out and I slink back behind the counter without incident. Violet joins me moments later. I study the way the man holds himself, strong and steady. I wonder who he's leaving, or coming home to. I wonder where he's been and where he calls home. I don't mean to eavesdrop. But his dutiful brawn, his voice, his presence, they almost resound in our small space.

"Sir," he says, shuffling in his seat. "I hadn't intended to—*yes*, sir. I understand."

A sudden, hard silence falls like a gavel, cutting his booth into before-and-after: the pleasantries before the call, and his tightened jaw after. He holds the phone steady in the air, parallel to his ear, before clutching it inside his fist. All the color fades from his face. I want to look away, I *should* look away. But one moment he's a floating warrior, levitating through fields of all he protects; the next he's human, weighted by a sharp blow of someone's brandished words, and I can't.

"I know that look," Violet whispers. "Heartbreak."

She says it like she knows the term well. I refrain from spilling how deeply I understand its etymology, my focus still attached to this man—a mere stranger I feel strangely connected to—if only because my story has had a few chapters that didn't end so well.

He dials a new number. His face contorts into different expressions, shaking the tightness loose to find some kind of smile.

"Smiling tricks the mind and body into thinking you aren't in pain," Stella taught me. As he forces his lips to upturn, mine do the same.

He clears his throat. "I just wanted to say . . . I . . . I love you. I wish I could stop time, you know? Of course you know. It's always about the time, isn't it, baby? We need to talk later. . . . Let me know when you and JJ are back from the farmer's market. I love you. . . . So much . . . Talk soon."

Violet sighs. "Man. I feel for him. And whoever that message is for."

I quietly decide I'll do my best to unearth his buried treasures in the event there is an answer among them—one I've been searching for since everything in my own life changed.

"We all have things buried so deep, it would take a dedicated search team to pull them to the surface," my counselor told me once. She said it after my parents died, when I first learned of the Brickmans' interest in fostering me. It was a time when I only felt the pieces of me that went missing. This man is missing something, too.

As the clock moves forward, I feel that pull of time passing. Like oars dropped in the ocean, I scramble to grab ahold. But, losing time doesn't change what's happened.

In tonight's top headlines, new Ivy Springs resident and soon-to-be high school sophomore Andrew Brickman finds something he hadn't intended during his first shift at Baked & Caffeinated: the crushing realization his parents aren't coming back.

NAIMA

Would you rather lose every item in your possession, or a lifetime of memories?

From the moment we enter the village township of Ivy Springs (too many nail-tapping hours later), we're greeted with light posts adorned with vibrant American flags, patriotic yard signs of thanks and memory, and red, white, and blue *everything* suited for the small town's upcoming Fourth of July celebration—the day we're to memorialize Dad. Surrounded by streets aligned with every last drop of my father, I'm both surrounded by him and absent from him in the same frozen breath. The word "hero" chokes me. My chest squeezes tighter, shooting electric tingles across my body. If it were a heart attack, it might *start* with this same tightness in the chest, coming and going with the added discomfort in my left arm or jaw. I could become nauseated, dizzy, and right here in the front seat of Nell's SUV, my heart could beat for the last time. This could be my final moment. Nell's clutching the steering wheel with white knuckles; she senses the same.

One breath. Two. Three breaths. Four. Five breaths, six.

"Look at that," she mumbles, pointing to the vibrant display of geranium, poppies, bluebells, and zinnias near the community garden. There's a crack in her tone; a thorny burr she swallows. My eyes swell, taking in the etchings of the place that created my dad; created *me*.

Last summer, when Dad came to stay at JJ and Kam's *with* me for a couple weeks—something he did to preamble another leave—we'd weave in and out of these same streets. Because of how many tours he'd been on, there were times I thought about what it'd feel like to navigate the path to JJ and Kam's without him. But I never knew it'd feel quite like this. *Hollow.*

Staying in Ivy Springs with my grandparents is how I always

imagined summer camp to be (without weird bunkmates), but with the added bonus of being near people who actually *get* me (humans who are *not* Nell). But here, without Dad, it feels like a dream.

A nightmare.

Someone should wake me from
Before
I die inside of it,
Only knowing
This life without him.

Voicemail

Dad

cell
June 13 at 9:36 AM

Transcription Beta

"I just wanted to say . . . I . . . I love you. I wish I could stop time, you know? Of course you know. It's always about the time, isn't it, baby? We need to talk later . . . Let me know when you and JJ are back from the farmer's market. I love you. . . . So much . . . Talk soon."

▶ 0:00 ───────────────── -0:47

Speaker　　　　**Call Back**　　　　**Delete**

Email Draft (Unsent)

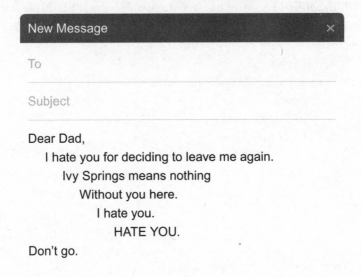

New Message   ✕

To

Subject

Dear Dad,
    I hate you for deciding to leave me again.
        Ivy Springs means nothing
            Without you here.
                I hate you.
                    HATE YOU.
Don't go.

⏮ ⏭ ▶︎⏸ ◼ ⏺ **DEW GD BRICKMAN**
DURATION: 11:31

*New this morning, local boy to take part in
downtown farmers' market while simultaneously
wishing he could be anywhere else. The weather
remains rightfully unsettled.*

Faith launches four glass apple-butter jars that Joelle—the warm-
est version of a cinnamon-scented hug I've ever seen—gifted us
the day we moved in next door. The glass shatters, covering a
good portion of our laminate kitchen floor. Thomas has left for
work at the water company while Stella kneels to pick up each
glass chip, palming them, smashing them into her skin like shimmering bits of glitter dust.

"Not today, Faith," she says in an exhausted huff. "Please."

I watch from the living room couch, where I've been given the task of safeguarding the remaining pieces of our farmer's market stand comprised of a canopy tent, folding card table, three bunched-up chairs, enough metal poles to start a revolution, and several cardboard boxes of Stella's handmade, lavender-lemon sugar scrubs and lotions. Faith plops into the empty space next to me, her arms crossed against her chest like a shield.

"Why did you do that?" I ask.

"Felt like it." She shrugs with a precise combination of carelessness and curiosity; an excellent execution of a girl pretending not to care, while her body language and darting eyes reveal she very much does.

"You know it's not helping your case," I tell her. "Stella's doing her best."

"Don't care."

I angle my body toward her slightly. "I think you do."

"What the hell do you know?" she grunts in a voice that so clearly lost all hope at such a young age, it could never be heard unless amplified by her own vocal chords at a volume and ferocity she can no longer control. She just wants a place to belong. *Don't we all?*

"More than you think," I say, calm.

Her eyes narrow into small slits, nostrils flaring. "*Ugh!* I hate this place, and I hate *you*." She marches to her room and the door slam that follows knocks a photo from the wall. The sound startles my bones awake.

Stella pops in to pick up the cracked photo glass. "Dammit. Why today? Why now?" She turns to me, rubbing the deep lines settled in her forehead. "Can you take that stuff to the truck?"

"Sure."

"If we're not out in five, assume the worst and save yourself." She follows Faith's footsteps and cups her mouth against the door. "We don't slam doors in this house. I'm going to need you to open up and apologize, please."

I haul the items to the pickup. Between trips, I catch snippets of Faith's colorful vocabulary that Stella's been told not to react to. Stella's usually gentle, but in Faith's refusal to open her door, her patience wears thin. The air constricts.

"That's it," Stella says, opening a junk drawer and lifting out a spare key. She breezes past, eyes glaring with a sparkling mania only Faith seems to conjure. She jiggles the lock loose. "Ah-ha!" she shouts with glee, closing the door behind her. Thomas would tell her to take a breath; to remember she's the adult, not Faith.

A quick glance at the clock shows we're late to what the *Ivy Springs Tribune* refers to as "A Weekday Summer Delight," though, as the shouting becomes more of an operatic song of sorts (with a possible cowbell ringing along to Stella's emphasized words of *GO; GO NOW!*), we may miss our chance to make our grand entrance as the solid, united front Thomas and Stella have worked so hard to build.

I'm reminded of the *one* time I shouted at my father. I'd failed an important math test, and while trying to calm me, Dad rested a hand on my shoulder. I shoved it off as quickly as it landed.

"You don't understand," I told him, tears building. "I can't do it. I'm not all you want me to be and never will be. I'm not you!"

He pulled his hand back, surprised at how loud I'd become— how disheartened. "Dew," he said, "you can do anything. I've witnessed it. Don't let one test derail your hard work. We'll get the help you need."

I'd stomped off to my room like Faith, but when the door slammed, I sat along the edge of my bed and sobbed—not because I'd failed, but because of how I treated a man whose only mission was to make sure I felt supported. After he died, that memory floated to the surface faster than most because it wasn't until I left my room, ready to apologize, that I saw him secretly buried in Mom's arms crying about how *he'd* failed *me*.

I never raised my voice at him again.

I wait in the small foyer, my hands tangled together, as Stella emerges, holding Faith by the crook of her elbow. Stella's long, fire-dyed hair falls in sporadic directions and heights. She's part triumphant warrior, part defeated parent.

"We're ready, aren't we, Faith?" Her breaths are short, but she manages a slight smile.

"Ready," Faith repeats, pulling her elbow back to her side. Once she's managed freedom, she pushes past me, through the door, and out to the truck, without us.

"I won't ask," I say.

"Better that way."

Once everything is secured, we pile into the rusted red truck like a hurried row of baby ducks. Our bodies press together in total silence. Faith's long, blond locks drape over my shoulder. I carefully knock them away, but she notices and does it again, testing boundaries. I wish Faith would accept there's nothing she can do that's bad enough for Stella and Thomas, or even me, to "send her back."

"The weather is pleasant," I say, breaking the silence. The lie soaks through my T-shirt.

"The weather is shit," Faith mumbles. Stella holds her gaze to the road, seemingly unfazed.

"People who swear have a higher IQ," Stella explained once in defense of Faith. "And they're proven to be sincerer than the rest of us. So, as much as it stings to hear 'fuck you and the fucking horse you rode in on' from a ten-year-old's mouth, we need to let her express the hell out of herself. Maybe then, she'll see we're not going anywhere."

"I hope people buy my scrubs," Stella says now, pivots. "You never know what kind of crowd a new town will bring. Especially one as small as this."

Faith remains quiet, her hand weaving in and out through the window's air, her fingers swimming through pockets of atmosphere with gentle fluidity.

"If only I had all that apple butter Joelle gave me," Stella adds. Faith's hand stills.

"Perhaps it's for the best," I say. "It could've been tainted. You wouldn't want to poison the whole town so soon after we move in."

Stella smiles. "That's what I'll tell myself."

"See?" I nudge Faith. "You did her a favor."

Her hand continues its journey of flight, and I know I've somehow unlocked the next level in her secretly guarded video game.

Breaking news: Girl accidentally smiles, may do it again in the future.

Soon we reach the parking lot across from a community garden—where fruits and vegetables are harvested by the local food bank for the whole town's use. Thomas said, "It's so no one goes hungry," something I know too much about. We had lost our already small, cold apartment and slept in our cluttered and cramped car. But the being hungry part was the hardest to explain—how you pray for bedtime to come fast so you can pass the time without feeling the pang. When things turned around and we could eat a complete, hot meal we didn't have to share, it stuck with me: baked chicken with vegetable medley. It's my favorite to this day.

"Maybe I should look into volunteering," I tell Stella, lifting as many cardboard boxes from the truck as I'm able.

"That's a great idea, Dew. Oh! There's Nancy," Stella says, pointing to the woman who runs the summer market. "You two head across, and I'll be there in a few."

She leaves in a rush, scurrying up to the small-framed woman in a wicker hat. Faith stands with her hands shoved in her pockets, while the boxes I'm carrying threaten to topple. It feels as if all the air in town has crowded in around me. Sweat drips into my eye, blurring my vision.

"What's with you?" Faith asks.

"Perhaps the weather isn't as pleasant as I previously thought."

"Like I said—hot as shit." She watches me struggle but offers no help.

"We'd better find our spot."

"I hate people. Why do *we* have to be here? She doesn't need us."

I tell myself to breathe; I'm okay. But the farther I walk from Stella's view, the more I wish to disappear.

"Right?" Faith repeats, more desperate than before. "We get in the way. At least, *I* do."

We cross the street where I stop along a brick wall and set the boxes to the pavement. While relieved at the lack of weight, I suddenly feel exposed. Like a raw wound still bleeding to the world. I take a step behind the boxes.

"Listen to me," I say. "That's not true. She appreciates when we help."

"I don't even do anything. I'm, like, a waste of space."

Though people are now passing with greater frequency, I take another breath and move in front of the boxes so Faith can see she is heard. She holds her arms tight against her chest.

"Never say that again," I say. "Stella loves you. I love you. You're a delightful use of space."

Her expression sours like the deflated fizz of a lemon-lime soda. Fists clenched, eyes shooting imaginary lasers through me. "Love is a lie."

Strangers weave in and out of our space. My body tightens.

"Love is a verb." My mother's face passes in a wisp. I reach for her, but she disappears before I can grab ahold. "Stella and Thomas may not always say the right things, but their actions prove they're filled with love for you. I hope someday, you're able to accept that feeling."

For a moment, the people surrounding us fade. I see the fear in Faith's eyes. Like if she lets go of all her grief, she's letting go of who she is, where she came from. I soften my stare. Her posture relaxes ever so slightly.

"You're pretty fantastic at a lot of things that have nothing to do with getting in anyone's way," I tell her. "Please know that."

"Such as?" She's standing on a cliff, precarious. I tighten my lasso.

"Throwing things. Shouting. Your tantrums are revolutionary. You could be a major league player or singer in a screamo band. We should all be so lucky to contain so much fiery rage in such a beautifully compact package."

"All of this is true." I get her to semi-sort-of laugh—another level unlocked—and temporarily forget the crushing sensation inside my chest. The sidewalk becomes busier with each passing second. "Are you ready?"

"Ready."

We make our way to where we're to set up our things. I may not be able to maintain eye contact with a perfect stranger, or win the game of Faith, but I am a farmers' market pro at sugar exfoliation and the art of a sale.

Stella arrives minutes later to pitch the tent. Faith finds relief in switching between Minecraft and funny cat videos on my phone while we set up in, quite possibly, the worst best space in town. Worst, because it's in the epicenter of the crowd, and best, for the same reason. Once everything is properly aligned, and customers begin to line up, Stella finds me huddled behind everything.

"What's wrong?" she asks.

"Nothing," I manage, but the word bubbles and burns against my tongue.

"Are these made with anything synthetic?" a woman interrupts, holding a jar of sugar scrub.

"All natural," Stella reassures her. She turns back to me. "Do you feel okay?"

"What is jojoba oil?" the woman asks.

"It's a moisturizer," Stella answers, a littler sharper.

She turns and moves toward me. The sounds overlap and compound. My eyes move from thing to thing in rapid succession. And my heart kicks wildly. Everyone, and everything, smashes me into a flat disc, unable to reinflate.

"Will the lemon extract irritate sensitive skin?" the woman asks.

Stella's eyes expand. She turns to the woman, slow. "YES. IT'S THE WORST FOR SENSITIVE SKIN. DO NOT BUY."

The woman frowns, setting the tub on the table. Stella refocuses on me, but I'm seeing many versions of her that flash in and out. Now, she's too close. I feel Faith's eyes, too. Everyone is watching me. My hands begin to claw at my shirt, as if ripping it away will unblock my tightened lungs. I abandon our tent and sprint to the corner of the general store. I fall to my knees in the nearby grass, and try to catch a full breath, but my lungs have revolted. Stella and Faith run after me. Stella kneels, too.

"You were doing so good," she says, fingers brushing the side of my face. "What happened?"

My words hiccup, tears explode from my lashes. *What happened* is, I want so badly to fit within this family. *What happened* is, my parents' death shot a hole through me that may never repair. *What happened* is, standing in a field, surrounded by a sea of faces, intertwined with me, standing in a cemetery, surrounded by a sea of faces. Everything, and nothing, are triggers all the same.

Faith kneels, too. "What's wrong with him?"

"Go back to the stand." Then reassures her, "He's fine. We'll be there in a minute."

Faith lingers, I look up and catch her fear-soaked eyes.

"Faith—*go*," Stella repeats. Reluctant, she does as asked, but turns back every few steps.

"Is he okay?" a woman asks.

Stella preempts the woman's movements by shoving her arm between us. She becomes my barrier. "Yes, thank you."

The woman goes. Through my erratic breathing pattern, Stella gently guides my eyes to hers. "Hey, *hey*—look at me, look at *me*. We're going to breathe together, okay?" she says. "Deep breath in," she breathes in, "and out," she breathes out, long and slow.

I try, and fail. The oxygen leaps in dotted attempts.

"Okay, listen." She presses her forehead to mine and hums the August Moon song—"Forever." I imagine my mother doing the same, the lingering scents of lemon and lavender intermingling with her rose oil. I close my eyes and breathe, forgetting everything around us.

Mom's voice breaks into the hum and Stella's fades into the background. I pinch my eyes tighter, forcing the stray tears down my cheek.

"Good," Stella's voice breaks in. "Again."

I breathe a full breath. And another. And another. Until she's hummed the length of the song. Then, she cradles me in her arms like Mom once did. I could argue my caseworker revealed these comforts, but aside from my inherited love of August Moon, they're things I've never said aloud.

I finally let my body fall slack. She releases me from her grasp. "That was embarrassing. I'm sorry."

"Oh, sweet Dew—you have *nothing* to be sorry for."

Nevertheless, my body crumbles in exhaustion. My panic attacks, the counselor explained, may come without warning, but the triggers are almost always related to my parents. PTSD, she called it, from the sudden loss of the only two people in my world. Inside the panic I'm not the ruler of my universe, but a prisoner.

"You wanna go home?" Stella asks.

I manage a slight nod. She ruffles my soft curls with a wistful gaze.

"You want me to drive you?"

I glance to Faith. The table is surrounded by people. She ignores them completely, eyes locked on me. "No," I say. "You need to stay. I'll walk."

She looks me over. "You sure you're okay?"

I pull myself up to catch a glimpse of my reflection in the store window. It's a shadow of who I was minutes before, but a survivor's shadow. "I'm fine. It's passed."

She tilts her head as if trying to decode my complex, and PTSD-altered, chemical makeup. "Can I hug you?"

"Please do." She wraps her hands snug around me, reminding me there is a space in which I'm unequivocally safe, and loved. *A verb.*

"Once we find a new therapist here, we'll find a way to make all this better. Okay?" I nod, but can't manage a word. She rubs the tip of my chin before jogging off to the tent. Faith is still fixated on me. No smile or frown. No wave hello or goodbye. She's just . . . there. I shove my hands in my pockets and keep my eyes to the ground as I walk off, because maybe I'm just . . . here, too.

The instant the judge granted the Brickmans legal custody of me, my parents' ghosts turned to dust that blew away with the wind. When new people surround me, especially in the name of trading my Diaz roots in to become more of a Brickman, I feel them come to life. It's an unmistakable pain only loss of memory could bring. Maybe someday, it won't hurt so bad.

Until then, I press my invisible Band-Aid into place, and sing August Moon a little louder.

For them.

NAIMA

Every turn of the wheel pushes us closer to our new, totally effed reality. As Nell slows the car to a crawl along Pearl Street, her eyes turn to the rearview mirror, where her fingerprints have stained the corners from adjusting and readjusting her line of sight—as if she's looking back at the ashes, trying to remember what he felt like sitting next to her—but the angle never feels quite right.

I do the same.

My brain knows he's not in that urn whether I'm taking my meds or not (turns out, this whole loss situation sent me into a seriously dark spiral and I *might've* locked myself in my room, and my therapist was MIA, so Nell made me an emergency appointment with the lady she sees, Dr. Tao, and I'm fine, everything's fine; it's fine) (Seriously) (FINE).

I'm not fine.

I count 279 seconds before we pull into the old gravel driveway, just as the church bells ring throughout—an Ivy Springs standard at 9:00 A.M., noon, and 5:00 P.M.—to see the full Rodriguez house in all its glory. Off-white siding with navy trim. JJ said it felt patriotic. Stained wooden fencing lines the yard with smaller areas sectioned off for Kam's prizewinning tomatoes. I once asked what made them "winners," and he replied "with love, soil probiotics, and a hell of a lot of cursing." It's strawberry season, meaning the stems are bountiful with the fruit I can't like no matter how JJ uses it. Jams. Sauces. Pancakes. Straight-up with sugar, no sugar, pie. They wonder how someone raised in Ivy Springs—Strawberry Capital of Indiana—could *not* love their beloved fruit, but I don't.

Dad didn't either.

The speed at which she's pulling in makes me want to scream. Stop or go, already. She puts the car in park and JJ and Kam appear beneath the doorframe Kam constructed, his long arm around her hunched shoulder; their bodies two solid masses of comfort and grief all mixed into one. They're trying not to cry because "crying doesn't help anything," JJ says, but their gleaming eyes say it all.

Nell releases a long, broken sigh from the driver's seat, looking back to the urn. JJ and Kam watch us. No one moves, and somehow, *this* makes sense to me. *This* is okay. Nell probably wonders what her life will look like when she leaves this car, and leaves Ivy Springs to return to Albany, where she'll pack up his things and move on with her life, without him. I'm wondering, too.

JJ rivals the pink flamingos one of the neighbors has perched in their front yard with her brightly printed neon leggings that cover her strong, muscular legs she earned by training for, and running, every marathon within a two-hundred-mile radius, and an oversize, matched tee that hangs off one bronzed shoulder. She dazzles beneath their high porch awning, just as I remember her from last summer, before I left them, and said goodbye to Dad, for the school year.

Kam cocks his head to find me when I'm gone, yet right in front of him. It's something he's done since I sat on his knee at five, worrying about how Dad would find his way home if he went so far away. He's in his usual summertime garb, complete with the button-up Hawaiian shirt Dad gave him for Father's Day one year, and the infamous cargo shorts with the bleach stain, further emphasized by the hideous black socks and open-toed-sandal situation I'd rather un-see. The front few buttons of his shirt—eight—pop out a bit more than they did last year, but the extra weight isn't *that* noticeable unless JJ mentions it (and she will), dragging him for not running alongside her for health's sake, when he'll inevitably argue he "doesn't have the time," and she'll call bullshit since they're both retired.

"Now or never," Nell says, hesitant. She doesn't move a limb.

"You need to lay off the Bieber references. It's not okay."

"Thought you were a Belieber."

I nearly choke on the fire she just shot into my heart. "Not even if I had to choose between him and licking a soiled boot."

"Graphic imagery. But—"

"I'd choose the boot."

"Got it. Adding that to my mental checklist of things you hate."

"You have one?"

"I knew when I met you, if I wanted to survive, I'd have to."

"Aw, so sweet."

"You got your meds?"

I pull the bottle and "shake it like a Polaroid picture."

"And the number for Dr. Tao in case you need anything?"

My fingers fumble the business card I'd bent in half when I pretended it was a greeting card that said, *Jesus Loves You! (Everyone Else Thinks You're an Asshole).*

She inhales deeply, her eyes focused on the awning that's tried, and failed, to welcome her the way it welcomed Mom. "Okay. This is happening. Let's get your dad inside. I'm sure they want to see him."

"He's ash," I murmur.

"Only physically."

"Exactly."

"*Exactly.*"

"What?"

"Okay. Let's go."

Would you rather be alone for the rest of your life?

Or only have annoying people surrounding you, forever?

That's a tough one I lament over. She swings the car door wide open while I remain. Stuck watching the back of her, tapping my nose six sharp times. That long, stringy red hair that swishes with her hips could be one thing I won't miss seeing. I can't un-scrunch my toes until we move past the still objects, JJ and Kam.

If I do,

    Life will keep going

      And I will be lost

        Somewhere in Tennessee

          Where we stopped

            So she could "potty."

(The bathrooms were nice, though)

Voicemail

Dad

cell
June 29 at 12:35 PM

Transcription Beta

"I know you won't have access to your phone while in treatment, but I wanted to hear your outgoing message. It's become a comfort of sorts. My greatest comfort. This place sure doesn't feel like home. It's hot, dry. Feels like I can't breathe sometimes. Anyway . . . I'll check in with the front desk, but [sigh] JJ, Kam, and I miss you so much.

▶ 0:00 |⎯⎯⎯⎯⎯⎯⎯⎯⎯⎯⎯⎯⎯⎯ -0:23

| Speaker | Call Back | Delete |

 **DEW GD BRICKMAN**
DURATION: 8:23

> *Clouds mixed with sun throughout a day that becomes transplanted Ivy Springs student's metaphor for life.*

I'm sitting in a hunter green chair across from my new therapist, Dr. Peterson, as we finish my first session.

"Thank you for speaking with me," she says, opening the door.

I exit, and she signals for Stella. They huddle together while I take the chair next to Faith.

"Did it go okay?" I'm hesitant to ask.

She forces her posture away from me.

"Same," I tell her. It's not a total lie. Whenever I get a new therapist, I have to rewind back to my origin story. That means starting from the beginning *again*. Peeling back the Band-Aids *again*. Tackling the strategies to overcome my obstacles *again*. There comes a point when I think, *Maybe this is a feeling I have to learn to live with.*

She turns a bit, adjusts. "I hate talking about any of it."

"Me, too."

She may not mean to, but she leans into me, her shoulder grazing mine with the lightest of touches. I offer a sympathetic grin—a "we're in this together" kind of thing—and while she doesn't reciprocate, she doesn't have to.

"All right," Stella interrupts the moment, "let's go."

"Practice what we talked about," Dr. Peterson tells me.

I tip my hat—Dad's hat—the way he used to. *The showstopper*, he called it.

"She mentioned guiding you through a couple of exercises," Stella says on our way to the truck. "Did they help?"

"Perhaps if I practice them."

"Perhaps," she says.

"Perhaps," Faith adds, lacking her usual sarcasm. We both stop and turn to her. "What? You both said it. I wanted in."

Stella's eyes find mine. We share a smile and pile into the pickup.

"We're making a pit stop," Stella says, revving the engine. "Dr. Peterson gave me an idea that might help you, Dew, before we attempt EMDR therapy to work through your traumas."

"What about me?" Faith asks. "Can *I* get something?"

"Sure—within reason."

Faith smiles wide, knowing the last time that phrase was uttered, she walked away with a PSP 4 bundle and four games. I fold my hands together in my lap, paying close attention to the twists and turns. We end up downtown. Stella puts the truck in park.

"This is going to be one weird trip," she says confidently.

Faith hops out first and skips inside, happily ready to spend any cash Stella offers up, while my feet drag. Therapy drains me. It's like walking out of one version of myself and into another. Spaced, dazed, and rethinking every last answer I gave—like the one about the nightmares I've been having—it's possible to open specific veins while holding all the rest closed. If the wrong vein is opened, it's a virtual bloodbath. It's all I'll be thinking about until the next session.

The old store is a mishmash of rare bird wants and needs. Bits and bobs, odds and ends, this is where you go to find the thing-amabob, or doohickey within the menagerie of fever-dream aisles.

Faith abandons us to navigate the store by herself—something that's gotten her in trouble more than once—while Stella hums quietly behind me.

"Wasn't sure what all they'd have," she says. "But I'd call this place a win." She pulls a ceramic clown into the air and waves it in the direction of a pink flamingo attached to a metal yard stick nearby. "I mean, seriously."

I point to the row of "gold" watches nestled next to maxi pads that have been stacked into a triangle. "Can I just live here?"

She laughs and covers her eyes with star-shaped plastic sunglasses. "Only if I can."

I slip on a pair, along with a pink feather boa. "Guess this is home now."

"Who will tell Thomas about our fancy, new lives?"

I point toward a cardboard cutout of the infomercial guy who sells stain remover. "He seems trustworthy."

Stella laughs—with the kind of full throttle joy that makes you feel like you're the funniest person alive; so similar to my mother's, my father's, too. I instantly lose my smile.

Faith rushes through and stops. She's equipped with a tall stack of WWE magazines, a pine-scented candle, a plastic necklace, and a roll of pink Bubble Tape gum.

"What are you doing?" she asks.

"Better question," Stella replies, "what's with the wrestling stack?"

"I asked you first."

I'm frozen again. Stella reacts by swiftly removing her accessories. "Just messing around. Now you go."

"I fell into a *WWE Raw* trap. I need to learn how to do a full nelson STAT."

She nods along. "You've got a lot of stuff there. Do we need the candle?"

"If you want the house to smell like pine we do."

"I didn't say I wanted it to smell like pine."

"Didn't you, though?"

Stella's brows crunch together. She senses my sudden absence and guides Faith out of my space until I'm able to break through the invisible wall. "If you help me find the thing I came for, the house can smell like disgusting pine."

Faith sighs. "Fine." The two disappear out of sight while I try to shake Mom's laugh from my brain. But it's stuck; a record caught in a groove. My pulse picks up. To avoid a full-on panic, I frantically look around in hopes of salvaging a good afternoon with a good counselor, with a good mother person, in a good corner store.

As I'm about to lose control of my breath, I see it—a rare August Moon and the Paper Hearts poster, live from the Fillmore in San Francisco. My eyes alight. A magnetic force draws me in. Mom's voice echoes. "The Fillmore. An American dream. *Someday,* my darling, Dad and I will be more than an opener; more than a warm-up. *Someday.*"

I feel them inside the confines of this vibrantly colored poster, where I pretend their names to be. Pencil etchings of their outlines twirl between my fingers. There's a pinch in my gut.

"Dew," Stella shouts, "we're ready."

I find them at the register, poster in hand. Stella's eyes find it with quiet understanding. "Put it up there."

"Thanks."

She winks. "No thanks necessary."

We watch the items float down the belt. The cashier scans them one by one.

I pick up the item Stella laid to the front and hold it in front of her. "What's this for?"

"Dr. Peterson mentioned some things that could help with your anxiety in crowds. It reminded me of a project I did in college where I recorded my thoughts for a week. Like a live journal."

I study the small handheld voice recorder. It fits in my palm. There are several small tapes that go inside. "What's the point?"

"To pinpoint emotional obstacles so I could learn how to deal before they ruined me."

Faith leans in intently. "Did it help?"

"Didn't hurt."

I spin the small recorder between my hands, put it to my lip, and decide I like the feeling it gives me to hide behind it. "I'll try it."

"If you like it, I'll talk to Thomas about ordering a fancier version online. If it helps. At the very least, it's good practice for your future as a news reporter or weatherman, right?"

Faith's eyes are consumed by our interaction. Maybe she sees now, she's not the only one trying to find a place here. We're all looking for something.

Stella watches the total owed go up as items are scanned. She digs into her wallet and counts barely enough, a slight panic in her eyes, items still yet to be rung through. I dig into my pocket. Empty.

Faith reaches for the Bubble Tape and puts it back, and two of the four magazines. "I don't need these, I guess."

Stella grins, and I think—maybe the thing we're all in search of is right in front of us.

A SUMMARY OF NAIMA'S
MEDICAL HISTORY

The question that plagues Naima most often is the simplest and most complex. She'll never have the answer, because she's busy picking out Lucky Charms marshmallows from the first of six boxes, via an intricate system that resembles a meth lab setup. She assures her stepmother it's on the up-and-up, though it still remains to be seen. Naima's therapist in Fort Hood said Ray's continual absences triggered her generalized anxiety disorder (GAD), which triggered the obsessive-compulsive disorder (OCD), which also re-triggered another anxiety disorder, all resulting in massive dips of depression that would, at some point, come back up, only to dip way back down. It's a neat, inescapable circle, only disturbed by the wrong medications and, at times, questionable therapists for whom Naima rarely cut herself open and offered her pain to.

The petite doctor with sharp knobby knees never understood Naima's humor as a means to cope, which further separated Naima from healing. She often redirected to Nell's pain and sacrifice instead, which wasn't totally off-base, but nothing Naima wanted to unpack. When asked, "Why are you here?" Naima replied with "My dad's making me," and the good doctor said, "No, why are you here, *on this planet?*" and so Naima spent an entire month sobbing in her quilt wondering the same goddamn question—*"WHY AM I HERE?"*—because if there was a right answer, or something logical, or a reason for her existence, she didn't have it, other than, "My parents drank too much and banged. Nine months later—*voila!*" There's no mystery to her, or any other, existence. But the way the good doctor phrased it, like there *should* be a mystery to it, made Naima wonder how much she really understood about life (or sex, for that matter).

"What do you believe your *purpose* is?" was the follow-up question every week after. Dr. Rose would emphasize "purpose," like by saying it more pronounced, the reasons would become more obvious. Naima told her what she told everyone else: "To live a life worth remembering" (because she saw it in a book, or something). To which the good doctor responded, "And how are you taking steps to fulfill this?" and Naima stared through an irregular pocket of air for an unknown length of time before saying something like, "I've written to General Mills multiple times about the dissolution of Lucky Charms as we know it, so they'll replace it with an all-marshmallow version." She then confessed to having a life-hack conveyor belt built with a milk carton, pens, and a roll of drawing paper. She had to manually turn the belt via the pens with one hand, and *yes, it's a lot of work to go through just to watch the marshmallows move down the line, dropping into a separate bowl at the bottom, but it's exciting to watch and—DON'T JUDGE HER.*

"And how's the writing *thing* going?" Dr. Rose asked, her words dripping in judgment.

"They told me to stop or they'd forward to Legal."

After that, Naima clung to a different protest—Truvía, the sweetener. The commercial's song gave her migraines and a newly found hatred of singing and voices and people and life in general. They declined to respond to her emails, but at some point, the commercials stopped airing. Dr. Rose pointed out the obvious fact that Naima was diverting—something she'd become very good at—reminding her of the core issue at hand, saying, "It all circles back to your dad leaving." Naima, inevitably, replied with "It circles back to the fact that opossums can lie in a comatose state for forty minutes to four hours." The doctor asked what the point was and Naima countered with "How long is this session?"

The only time Naima heard any sense was when Dr. Rose told Nell there were reasons for the disorders and the things they caused Naima to do, no matter how odd or time-consuming those things appeared. They were not "quirks," but to Naima, a way to maintain control of *something*.

After Naima's suicide attempt, and Ray gone again, Nell worried something was "wrong" with the stepdaughter she never could get close enough to. She knew most people had anxiety-related disorders, but always felt like Naima's might be beyond her capabilities. She tried to help, and advocated relentlessly on Naima's behalf, despite Naima's continual protests.

Naima wouldn't dare tell her, or anyone, about the times she thought about sticking her fingers into an outlet or stepping in front of a semi, because she didn't think she'd actually follow through. They were just thoughts, but Naima feared the thoughts might someday become actions. For the moment, electricity scared her, cars scared her, pain scared her. Dr. Rose called these thoughts "intrusive," and changed her medication.

Pinch the toes between passing objects becomes snapping the fingers together between stoplights becomes scratching a forearm until it bleeds becomes clawing at the throat to let the air escape becomes counting the seconds she can't get back becomes counting everything with repetition becomes the thought that, should she miss an object or a snap or a scratch or a claw or a count, cut in like a knife to remind her of all the ways pain exists in life and death with flashes of wonder that become "what if" that become the anxiety that strangles her every breath that becomes the beat of her heart at full-stop becomes the day she could return to the past to tell her father, and mother, she's sorry because maybe she doesn't deserve to be here becomes the guilt becomes the nagging pull of an anchor dragging her to the very place she's most terrified becomes the death her father suffered and back to her mother and round and round until the end of time.

Every new place they moved, Naima started again, and when she started again, her tics did, too. And when her tics did, too, those thoughts became more thoughts, and more, until they piled up into places that only made sense in Naima's mind.

But maybe Dr. Rose is right (Dr. Tao in Albany, too, but Naima thought the clock that hung above her desk ticked too loud). Maybe everything does circle back to Ray leaving. Maybe Naima needs different medication and someone to talk to whom she trusts. Maybe she needs a more intensive form of trauma therapy to finally work through one of the greatest losses of her existence. Or maybe Naima should learn to get through life in a comatose state like opossums. Either way, she's glad the Truvía commercials stopped. Besides, she's moved on to a new commercial about psoriasis (all the touching grosses her out).

Except she's stuck on the thought
The Truvía thing could be a coincidence
And not from her (many)(many)(many) complaints.
To think this means
Her voice means less
Than she hoped it did.

NAIMA

JJ squeezes out all the life left inside of me and I think, This is it—I'm dying now. My ribs collapse against my lungs until I gasp, thinking it's the last breath.

"Let the girl breathe, Joelle," Kam says. He gently tugs at her arm.

"I just want to hold her." She stands back to get a full look, her tears seizing when I notice them. Kam's hands are full of wadded-up tissue. He sobs in the open, unafraid to hinder his pain. Behind JJ, I see the giant portrait of Dad in his dress blues, staring at me.

Nell's rushing in and out with my boxes cradled in her arms. She catches JJ's hand halfway down my back. "She's still not much of a hugger," she says.

I wrap my arms around JJ's small waist, laying my head to her chest. "I know," JJ says. "Makes me never want to let go."

Nell lingers beyond the door, almost longingly. "I wouldn't." Her voices goes quiet. Her face has paled, and beneath the same sunlight that favors JJ, a halo rests above her head. She almost looks approachable. Understanding. *Almost.*

I let JJ hold me until Kam offers to take the boxes from Nell. As he moves through the house at an Olympian sprinter's speed—something JJ would normally comment on—the three of us form this weird triangle of silence. All of us feeling the space where Dad should be.

The next item Kam fetches is the urn.

His movements have slowed, the metal cradled gently in his arms. He stops short of JJ, offering the cold object with as much care as he might his newborn son. Their foreheads meet, and for an instant, they're the only ones in the room.

"My baby, my baby," JJ weeps.

"*Our* baby," Kam cries.

Nell and I mutually decide they've earned this moment as much as anyone else and remain silent. One hundred twenty-nine seconds pass before they release their grip on the urn.

"Thank you for bringing him *home*," Kam says to Nell.

She nods. "It's where he belongs." The word echoes, and I wonder, Where do I belong? Ivy Springs is *home*, but something is noticeably absent from this small town, from me; more than Dad.

"Put him at the table," JJ says, stern. "In *his* chair." Kam nudges the urn tight between the table and chair to hold it steady. The four of us stare in disbelief at the very thing every one of us prayed could never be.

We dry our eyes and wipe our noses (I use the antibacterial sanitizer on JJ's counter after) and in seconds, shift to different positions. JJ to the stove, where she cooks to dull the aches. Kam to retrieve my stuff so he can hide behind objects instead of feelings. Nell in everyone's way because she's determined to be the ever-present sun around which we revolve. Dad in *his* chair, where he belongs.

Thirty seconds after Kam kicks open the bedroom door their eleven-year-old blond Pekingese monster, Hiccup, comes barreling toward us. With his grungy, greasy hair and short, stumpy stride, the little fur ball zips from point A to point B in—what he feels to be fast, but what we see is—slow-mo. He's panting through the charge. Nell backs so far into the wall, she becomes part of it, screaming and yelping rivaling Hiccup's stream of noise. They're essentially barking at each other and it's the best thing I've seen in *ever.* I want to snap a photo, forever marking the moment, but hear Dad telling me to give her a break. Reluctantly, I do.

"Hiccup—crate," JJ shouts with a damning finger pointed toward the door from which he escaped.

He ignores her, or doesn't hear the command (he's partially deaf in his right ear), chewing the hem of my pants with a non-threatening growl. I hold out a hand, hoping he'll remember my scent, or whatever, but no matter how many summers I've spent here, I'm a stranger.

"Crate!" JJ repeats. She's snapping her fingers, but his cataracts only allow him to see what's right in front of him, and right now, it's my leg. We play this shit game every year. Meanwhile, Nell acts like it's her leg he's after. Her knee is hiked up to her chest, her face turned inward, eyes scrunched tight. Her hair flies from left to right like a Tilt-A-Whirl. *Get a grip, woman.*

"Damn it—*Kam!*—come get the damn dog!" JJ screeches. She has a hold of his faux-diamond-encrusted collar, but he's had a taste of my pants, and he wants the rest of it. "GET YOUR ASS IN HERE!"

Footsteps pounce closer in a cheetah-like fashion. Without a word, Kam swoops an arm beneath Hiccup—who shuts up the second he's midair and carries him back to his crate. JJ dramatically wipes her forehead with an exhausted sigh. "Sorry, Nell. I've seen Kam run faster for the cinnamon rolls on Sunday mornings."

"It's fine." Nell pats her clothes smooth, as if Hiccup came anywhere near her, or her yoga pants. "Dogs don't like me."

"Smart," I mumble.

"What's that?" JJ asks, glaring.

"Nothing."

She swoops my hair off my shoulder and offers a vague smile. Our triangle of uncertainty resets. Nell moves in and attempts to do the same with the other side. I flinch.

"Sorry," she says, quietly.

JJ steps between us, my umbrella from the storm. "I'll take it from here."

Surprised, Nell trips on her words. "Oh, okay. I, uh, I guess I'll get going."

There's a pause. This is where I'm supposed to hug her goodbye. My feet refuse to move. A shadow cuts the space between us in half, an object that forces me to scrunch my toes.

"You know what? How about some food first?" JJ says, knowing neither Nell or I could move forward in this moment without her.

"Food would be good," Nell replies, relief blushing her face.

A small, barely discernible breath escapes me. Either I'm dying again, or I'm *home*. Sometimes it's hard for my brain to tell the difference. And while death is inevitable, home is where I don't have to pretend, or wish, or wait. I just *am*. But it also hurts in a way nothing else does. A paradox.

JJ and Nell ignore me and talk about a 5K JJ organized and plans to run in honor of Dad, and how Kam wouldn't run a race even if they offered a buffet at the finish. They share a laugh or two, but ultimately, the discomfort squeezes me like a juicer. I step outside from the constant buzz. Between JJ and Kam reminiscing about their time teaching at Ball State, Dad's path veering away from a similar journey once he met Mom, and Nell's stories about Christian getting into Stanford with a major that's somehow correlated with his "appreciation" for fine arts and humanitarian efforts (he actually means he's stoked to go to school far enough away that he can learn to do a proper keg stand), the noise makes me feel like I could combust any second.

Would you rather have Nell go to parents' weekend at college or have no parents at all?

I go outside to the garden that's brimming with—what else—strawberries, carefully stepping around the divots in the ground where Hiccup did his business. I lean down to smell the literal roses, when a sound beyond the fence catches my attention.

I lean forward, eye to the low hole Kam accidentally pierced in a bizarre situation he called "an epic battle with the drill" (I'm not sure who won). Through the space, I get a clear view of the vibrant green grass on the other side of the fence. It hadn't been more than dirt last I stood here.

I lean closer, my forehead pressed into the stained wood.

"Hello," a voice says. An eye meets mine from the other side of the hole.

Startled, I fall backward. "The fuuucck?"

"She means 'who are you' with a curl of the tongue—as if to judge before ever seeing past his cornea," the voice says. "Perhaps she should look deeper. Into the soul, where his light shines boldly."

"*Uh.*" I crawl back to the hole. There are solid black sneakers with toes wiggling against the tops.

"She continues to watch in anticipation of her fate," he says. "More tonight on *Dew's News at 10.*"

"What the hell are you saying?" My face is shoved up against the fence now, wishing the hole would expand big enough to see past this tiny picture of a person. "And stop tap dancing."

He doesn't reply, but instead, holds a recorder to the hole, blocking my view. The screen is aglow. He's recording this—*me.*

"Total invasion of privacy, dude," I say. "Like in an illegal way."

He moves the device and exchanges it with his eye. It's big

and bright, brown with gold specks and lashes long and dark. The pupil dilates, zeroing in on me. Hard.

"Dew, actually."

"That's not a name."

"Dew, short for Andrew."

"Whatever, Dewwwd." I stand to dust the dirt off my pants and turn to leave when he stops me.

"You have spectacular eyes," he says. "Out of this world. They're two shining constellations hovering over a planet that rotates through darkness. Well, I only saw the one. I assume there's two."

I take a step backward, feeling my cheeks streak with blush. I immediately deny myself the right to feel this way. "Why are you recording me?"

"I like interesting things."

"I'm the least interesting thing ever created."

"I report the facts. And the weather. But mostly facts. I saw you tapping your nose from my garage. *That's* interesting. It's why I tapped my feet. Similar to the way animals interact without words. You tap, I tap, Naima."

"I'm not an animal." I scoff, audibly. "Who told you my name?"

"Your grandparents entertain my presence when my parents are gone. They're glorious souls. You must be so happy to have them."

"They are, and I am. But stay out of my business. You don't know me."

He moves to stretch a hand over the top of the fence. "Then allow me to fully introduce myself so I may. Andrew Brickman. Pleased to make your acquaintance."

I ignore the gesture. "So you *live* there?"

"Yes."

My brows knit. "Care to elaborate? Like where you came from, what your story is, why you're stalking me?"

He finally retracts his hand. "In due time."

"You mean in *Dewwww* time." I snicker, and to my surprise, he does, too.

"Exactly," he says. "You're as charming as everyone says."

"Who's *everyone*?"

"A gentleman never reveals his secrets."

I walk backward, away—*far* away. "Okay, well, nice chat. DEWD. Later. Or not."

"Farewell, fair maiden."

My steps are slow as he continues speaking to himself.

"Lucky for us, Julie, this story ends on a positive note. Her eyes never abandon the empty space through the fence, the space where the odd boy stands. It's as if leaving him meant leaving her purpose, right there, in between the sunken grass where her heart lay by her feet and his tap to lift it back up to where it belongs," he says.

Uh. Who's Julie?

A grunt pushes through my lips. Or, maybe a smile. I immediately tuck it away so as not to get used to the idea that a boy like that may ever interact with a girl like me in that way again. When my feet are on the concrete, my hand on the door, he belts out one last thought:

"Meeting you has been my greatest pleasure. Thanks for joining us."

When I turn around,

   He's gone.

     And I wonder if

       I've imagined him,

         Or if he's imagined me.

Voicemail

Dad

cell
July 10 at 2:21 AM

Transcription Beta

"Hi, baby. The nurse said you're making
great progress. I'm so proud of you.
I've done a lot of thinking and this is it.
After this leg, I'm done leaving. Going
home for good. I love you."

▶ 0:00 |━━━━━━━━━━━━━━━━━━━━━━━| -0:14

Speaker   **Call Back**   **Delete**

No New Emails

⏮ ⏭ ⏯ ⏹ ⏺ DEW GD BRICKMAN
DURATION: 6:10

*In unusual news, boy suddenly understands the
phrase "manic pixie dream girl," fights hard to
dismantle his problematic feelings.*

Thomas and Stella scuttle around the kitchen to finish dinner, an
intricate series of moves designed to avoid each other's personal
space, as I rush in completely and utterly breathless.

"She's *home*," I say.

"Who is?" Thomas asks. He's still in uniform—navy slacks and a crisp white button-up shirt with mud caked to the hems—moving around me to arrange the table with our four plates and accompanying utensils.

"*Naima*. Naima's home."

They both stop and turn to face me. If it weren't for the sizzling pan and oven air vent, you could probably hear a pin drop between us. "Did you . . . introduce yourself?"

"Technically."

"After all you've heard about her since last summer, I know it's exciting, but Dew, give her time to settle in," Stella says. "She's been through a lot and may not want everyone crowding her." Thomas gives her a sharp glance. She immediately self-corrects. "I mean, *you've* been through a lot, too, which is why you'll understand her need for space."

"Yes, ma'am," I say, barely able to contain my glee. "I don't want to be a bother, but I think we can help each other."

"Don't force it. If she says leave her alone, do it. She'll make the next move if she chooses. Even though you mean well, no means *no*, okay?"

"Understood."

She redirects to dinner, scribbling notes along the margins of her recipe paper—she does this with every new meal she's looking to blog about. You don't become Lady Clean Cuisine, allergen-friendly food blogger, without trial and error—and a whole lot of adjustments.

"Faith, dinner," Thomas shouts.

"Ask her about the magazines," Stella whispers. "You'll get bonus points."

Faith stumbles in, eyes glued to one of the wrestling documentaries she's binged on all week. Dr. Peterson suggested leaning into our interests, whatever they may be, so Stella obliged.

"What are you watching?" Thomas asks, innocently enough.

"*Shh.*" Faith waves her hand at him, eyes locked on the screen's display. He looks to Stella for support.

Stella steps in. "Faith and I talked about finding a non-gender-conforming or all-girls wrestling team to join, didn't we, Faith?"

"*Shh.*"

"Sounds cool," Thomas says. He fills her plate and nudges it in front of her. "I was obsessed with 'Macho Man' Randy Savage when I was little."

Faith ignores him, her eyes darting across the screen.

"I wrestled in high school. Didn't love it. Apparently not the same as WWE. There's no chair throwing or animals involved. Just double-leg takedowns and a lot of spandex."

She forces the screen closer to herself.

He moves on and fixes plates for the rest of us. "Not sure about this chicken recipe. Smells weird."

I take a bite. It's bland and sort of earthy-tasting. "Delicious."

Stella smiles. "Thanks, Dew. Never know with some of these recipes that call for ingredients I have to scour the earth for. Like arrowroot. Who automatically has arrowroot?"

"We do," Thomas says.

She purses her lips with an eye roll in his direction. "*Because* of the recipe." Thomas winks. Her lips loosen into a smirk before she turns back to me. "Joelle said she'd have some apple butters ready in the next couple days. Maybe you can pick them up for me."

My heart skips a thousand beats. "I'd love to."

"Did you meet Naima's stepmother? Nell, I think."

"No."

"From what Joelle said, the poor woman tries, but Naima never took to her."

Faith looks up. Brows arched, stare screaming at us in some kind of deliberate way. We all catch it before she returns to the screen.

"I'm surprised we didn't run into them last summer," Thomas says.

Stella drops her fork so loud it makes a clang. Her eyes bulge in Thomas's direction.

"What do you mean *last summer?*" I ask. "Naima was . . . *here?*"

She sighs, heavy. "For a short time, *yes.*"

"Secrets and lies," Faith blurts. "Secrets. And. Lies."

"Why didn't anyone tell me?" I ask. My appetite suddenly vanishes.

Stella and Thomas connect through the small space, their stares speaking loudly as Thomas urges her to say *something.* "I wanted you to focus on you, Dew. Not get distracted. When you're distracted, you lose track of time. And when you lose track of time, you spiral. Think of what happened in the last school, why we moved."

"We moved because Thomas transferred jobs."

"To help *you.*"

I'm a bulletin board everyone's eyes pin to. It doesn't matter how right she may be, to what level of distractibility I'm capable of, or the depth of spiraling that's occurred. It doesn't matter how my parents' death and getting a new family changed me from the inside out. I chew on my words carefully before they cascade off my tongue. "What did you do—plan our days and nights around *avoiding* her?"

Her posture sinks. "I *may* have spoken with Joelle, who revealed Naima had her own issues to work through."

"So *I* would've been a distraction to *her?*" My words are heated, but I maintain my composure. "That's what you really mean, right?"

Faith eats her food slow, but quiet. Listening, watching.

"I didn't mean it like that," Stella reassures me, but her eyes avoid me. I hear a different truth between the syllables. The shame. The embarrassment of me.

I leave my plate and lift my recorder, pressing the button so it lights red. *"Breaking news: Local boy sentenced to an entire year without the chance of meeting his one true love."*

"Dew," Thomas says, "it's not love when you've never met. Love is—"

"A verb," I interrupt. My mother's face comes into view, fading before it's fully realized.

"I was going to say it's complicated, and if you're going for a forever kind of thing, it *should* be reciprocal. But *yes*—also a verb. Which is why you can't say you love someone without knowing them. True love happens *through* the verbiage."

"You say you love *us*," Faith says. "And you don't know me at all."

"That's not true. I know more than you realize."

They pull the silence near, in an obvious wrestling of what to say.

"Why do you think Naima is your true love?" Stella asks with caution.

I see Faith's hope hanging on whatever I'm about to say—as if I'm answering for the both of us, stepping into her shoes and mine, simultaneously.

"When I met Joelle, she had on August Moon," I say.

Stella sighs with understanding; an exhaled relief. "I see. You thought it was a sign."

I nod, try to avoid Faith's stare in case I've let her down, if my answers aren't relative to her own tornado of emotions.

Stella reaches for my hand. "Maybe it was, maybe it wasn't. But I understand what you're telling me."

I feel a little lighter when she continues.

"I'm happy you've met Naima, and I'm sure you'll be great friends, but for now, be considerate and remember she's still very much grieving. So again, if she asks for space, respect her wishes."

"Wow," Faith says.

I grow heavy again. "Excuse me," I say, abandoning my plate.

"That was messed up," I hear Faith add as I tread to my room and collapse onto the crisp coolness of my bed. "He's obviously looking for someone who understands that *he's* still grieving. Even I get that."

I don't believe in Instalove, to be clear, but I'm a disciple of signs. And this hasn't been instant—it's been a long time in the making, thanks to Sergeant Ray and Joelle filling in Naima's legacy portrait for me. The universe threaded Naima and me together long before last summer. I feel it in the places blotted out by pain. I imagine my parents twirling across our apartment floor, their smiles infectiously intertwined. I hold my stare on the twinkling particles and tip my hat. *Showstopper.*

NAIMA

"Who moved into Mrs. Langston's old house?" I ask.

JJ, who's adorned with an apron that looks like she's wearing a bikini on the beach, is salting a big pot of boiling water. "I take it you've met sweet Dew."

I walk over and lean my hip against the counter, propping my chin up on a closed fist. "What's his deal?"

With a slight smile, she swirls the water with an old wooden spoon, never fully turning. "What do you want to know?"

I shrug, holding back my eagerness to ask every question spinning circles around us. "I don't know. Where'd he come from?"

"You know where babies come from."

"No," I sneer, "where did they *move* from? People don't move here unless they have ties. Does he . . . have . . . ties, or?" She knows what I'm getting at, but she prefers when I'm direct.

"He's from the east side of Indy." She turns with her whole body and we're squared off. "Maybe you should ask your new friend."

"Ooh, what new *friend*?" Nell interrupts. Her suitcase-size purse is slung over one shoulder.

"Nothing, never mind," I say. JJ gently drops spoonfuls of dough into the water, carefully watching each one plump and float to the top. The secret Gi Gi (her mom) taught her was not to overmix, and to let it sit for ten minutes before boiling. While JJ was born into Puerto Rican cuisine like *mofongo*—fried plantains with pork—Kam, a Detroit boy at heart, was raised on American classics. Over the years, their cultures married, inviting a slew of menu mash-ups. These pillow-soft dumplings are the shit, and I'll likely devour them before Nell and Kam ever get the chance.

"She met one of the new neighbors. He's about your age, Ima."

Nell's eyes expand and though I keep mine hard-pressed to the boiling water, I feel her smile growing. "*He's* your age? That's great! You could use a friend."

"*You* could use a business you mind," I mumble.

"Naima Grace," JJ says with a stern flick of the spoon. It splashes me with little pellets of hot water.

"I could lose an eye that way," I say.

"Hiccup does fine with one good one. You'll be okay."

"You have no idea how many microbes are embedded into that wood."

"I do. That's why I use it."

"Disgusting." We share a brief chuckle. Sarcasm is the coping mechanism even JJ's good Lord would encourage. Nell's presence weighs it down. She slowly moves to put on her shoes, the ones with the strap behind the ankle, but can't get the flap to slide into the metal slot. Her struggle grows when it slips from her fingers entirely.

"I thought you were staying awhile?" JJ asks, half disappointed, half relieved.

"I'd better get back on the road," she replies, half disappointed, half relieved, her tone and cadence mimicking JJ's as if she hoped we'd beg. We all know she's going home to nothing.

"You sure?" JJ asks for good measure.

"Yes, but thank you."

She hovers in the doorway again (it's her thing), awaiting everyone's farewell wishes and hugs and kisses, and all the things I've not given her in the years she's been part of my life—seven.

With her hand on the doorknob she pauses. "A nice *boy* will be a good change, Naima. Maybe you'll have someone to hang out with all summer."

She doesn't even acknowledge my taste is in *people*—because gender is fluid—and if I were into any person, it sure as hell wouldn't be that kid. And because I can't muster anything nice to say, I choose silence instead.

JJ moves away from the stovetop. "Nell might be right. You two have a lot in common. Could be good for you."

"You and Mrs. Langston had a lot in common and you never wanted to hang out with her."

She gives me the look. "She's a thief. Stole my ceramic owl."

"You don't know for sure."

"Saw it in the old broad's window! Anyway, maybe you and Dew can help each other navigate, you know, life this summer."

My toes scrunch up and release. The smell of apple cinnamon slowly simmering on the back burner scents the room—a scent that always reminds me of being here—reminding me of all the times Dad told me things that *could* be good for me. Breathing is overrated. School is the worst. "Friends" don't get me.

"Doubt it," I mutter.

"Oh, I don't know, Naima," Nell interjects. "If you actually get to know someone, you'll see that letting people in isn't so bad. It helps us feel less alone, you know?" She stares wistfully out the window to the car.

"K," I say, "byeeee."

JJ steps between us, a wall of empathy directed toward Nell. "It's final. Stay, eat some dumplings, then go."

"Or, just go."

"Ima—enough," JJ snaps. When she snaps, it's not with a voice that stretches until it breaks, but a deep, assertive snip, as if she's cut the words straight from the dictionary's pronunciation guide. Each syllable slashes my eardrum, forcing me to stand at attention—just as she intends.

And without words, without a yes or a no, Nell falls into JJ's arms and sobs like I've never seen her sob before. JJ rubs the back of Nell's stringy hair, shushing and crying, too. I think about the way her fingers catch in pockets of tangled-up, matted mess from where Nell forgot to condition or overconditioned. I never remember which because I don't keep mental lists with her crap on it.

We're not a triangle anymore. They have merged into parallel lines, while I stand, perpendicular, alone. None of us talks about the reason we're smashed together, with the damn urn nestled in the table chair looking on as the guest of honor. They begin to talk of the days Dad's living body occupied the space, reminding me of the voicemail.

No. No. No. No. No. No.

Finally, after four minutes, thirty-six seconds (that feels like a lifetime), Nell tries the goodbye thing again, with more urgency to her tone. This time, I hope it sticks. This time, I hope she understands she has a home someplace else, where she's welcome to grieve, but not in the space I need to.

"I guess this is it," she says.

"Yep."

"But I'll see you soon?"

"Yeah, sure," I say, abruptly remembering some major things I've not seen. "Where'd you put my shoeboxes and flytrap?"

Nell hesitates. "I didn't see any of that."

My teeth grind. "What do you mean you didn't *see* them?"

"I didn't see either of those things. I got your big boxes from the front room, but I don't remember a shoebox or plant."

"It's not just a shoebox and PS is more than a plant. You asked me to put my things by the front door before we left. I did that. Where are they?"

I see in her eyes she's searching for the memory of what happened, with a sudden realization we've miscommunicated. "I meant the *back* door because I'd pulled the car into the garage."

"But I need them. *Especially* my shoeboxes. Six. There are six. I need them. Like right now."

"I'm sorry, Naima, I—"

"No," I interrupt, heat flushing my cheeks. "Just bring me my things."

Kam idles near. I see his hands waving through the air as if he's trying to swat the negative energy. It's as if he's, in his words, exerting his energy in a charette—a super-intense period of design energy—something he's done many times over the years, usually in bursts of creativity or inspiration. Dad said he designed the shed after discovering Mom was pregnant with me. Didn't sleep for days.

"You should've mentioned them sometime during the drive and I'd have remembered I hadn't seen them. Did you take your medicine this morning? You're on edge." Her voice challenges me, but in a way that suggests she'll back down if I challenge back.

"I'm *allowed* to be upset about something I care about. I'm *on edge* because you're still here. And yes—*this is me*—MEDICATED."

"Naima!" JJ snaps. She whips the wooden spoon she's washing on the counter with a *clack*. I can almost hear the germs writhing in pain.

"That was uncalled for," Kam adds, his voice far less threatening.

My hands have balled up; my knuckles rub against each other. I do what JJ wants me to—not what I feel. "Sorry."

"Don't apologize to *me,* child."

Nell sighs, disbelief glossing her eyes. "I never intended to ruin your life. I loved Ray, and I tried to take care of you, but I guess that was wrong, too. I'd better go." She slings her purse over one shoulder, and JJ blocks the doorway with an embrace. Nell wants more from me. I'm not sure I have it to give.

I take one step forward. "When you find PS, don't kill her because you're pissed at me. She doesn't deserve it."

"What's a PS?" JJ asks.

Nell speaks before I can answer. "She named her Venus fly-trap after me."

"Okay, so the *P* is for Penelope but what does the *S* stand for?" Nell looks to me, smug. "*You* tell her."

"Smellope." *Sorry, Dad.*

"Mature." JJ sighs, and Kam laughs but doesn't let JJ see, triggering a stray bark from Hiccup down the hallway. "What in God's high heavens do you have in a shoebox that's worth all this fuss?" JJ asks. She waits only three seconds before crossing her arms and I know I've waited too long to answer.

I mumble the answer.

"What's that?" JJ asks. She holds the spoon up to her ear. "Louder, please."

"MARSHMALLOWS!" My chin tucks into my chest.

Nell fidgets. The patience in JJ's voice has worn thin. This usually doesn't happen until I've been here a few weeks. *New High Score! Go, me!* "I only had one in the car."

She turns to Nell, points that spoon like a weapon. "Don't you worry about no damn marshmallows. I'll get her fixed up. You take care of whatever you need to."

"I appreciate it," she says quietly. "But I'll make sure you get them. Okay, Naima? Okay?" The second "okay" is a plea. She wants me to be okay. If I'm not, then what? And if she's not? And if we're never okay again, will we still be connected?

I nod, reluctantly.

"I'm going," she says. "I've done enough damage for one day."

"You did no such thing," Kam says. "We're all in need of some grieving time."

"Grieving time," she repeats, voice trailing. "Yes. *Time.*"

JJ rubs her hand over Nell's back and I can't take my eyes off the way her nails *catch and glide catch and glide catch and glide catch and glide catch and glide catch and glide.*

Nell turns to me. "Remember to take your medicine, and get enough rest, and do your deep-breathing exercises like Dr. Tao suggested."

She lingers, waits for me to hug her, but I don't. "I know you won't call, but you can text me anytime. If you want."

"I'll be on top of it." JJ squares her hands firm on Nell's defeated shoulders. Her movements are a series of choreographed movements she may have practiced in her head. "You're sure you don't want to stay through the Fourth? We have room."

Nell's eyes dart between us, her thoughts probably swirling. About staying in a house that was never hers, a place that could never know her the way it knows me, *knew* Dad. She can't be a stand-in.

Can't. Can't. Can't. Can't. Can't. Can't.

After a long pause, she speaks. "I have a lot to get packed up at the house. Ends to tie up. All of Ray's . . . matters . . . you know. It never ends." Her voice cracks. JJ pulls her in and again Nell sobs into JJ's shoulder. I study my nails and think of the last time I filed them or painted them without picking all the paint off. My hands are dry and scarred. I think on this, and this alone.

When JJ releases Nell, I glance to the dinner table and notice the chair the urn is in has been knocked slightly askew. My brain shouts to *FIX IT NOW.*

JJ grabs my forearm and gently nudges me to Nell. "Don't you want to tell her goodbye?"

"Bye." I can't look her in the eye, so I choose the top of her ear instead.

"Give her a hug."

"That's okay," Nell says. She doesn't mean it, I see. It's not okay. I'm not okay.

We're not okay.

I move closer. The world slows on its axis. Each step echoes. My feet are heavy like the marine's boots on the airstrip in Dover, and when I reach Nell, her arms open only slightly. They shake, fearful of my rejection, maybe, and it's weird, but I think I like this about her.

I unexpectedly lunge toward her, hugging as hard as I can manage. She hesitates to reciprocate my strange affection, but squeezes back. Nell and I—this woman I loathe—are trapped in an uncomfortable embrace that lasts approximately ten seconds. It's the longest ten GD seconds of my GD life. Nothing about it feels natural, but for the sake of giving her a semblance of peace before she goes, I give her all I've got.

When I peel myself away, all the tears that melted into JJ's shirt are on mine as well. "Thank you," she whispers, gracious. "Thank you, thank you."

JJ lays a hand on my shoulder. "That's my girl," she says quietly.

Kam stands far enough back he doesn't interfere. He's a maestro, listening to a symphony. Nell is satisfied enough to step beyond the door, *finally*, and we're free to redefine everything we know.

Would you rather hug Nell or swallow fire ants?

I think I'll paint my nails today. Something dark.

Voicemail

Dad

cell
August 14 at 5:00 PM

Transcription Beta

"I heard you're on your way back to Albany. I bet you're happy to be done with treatment. Probably not so much about going back to Nell, Christian, and a home you didn't have the time to settle into before all of this. Don't worry—I didn't tell Nell about your stay. As far as she knows, you danced the days away with JJ and Kam after I left. But if you want me to tell her, I will. Let me know when you've made it to the house? I hope school is better for you this year than it was in Ft. Hood. . . . I'm tired, Ima. I'm just . . . so . . . tired. I know you're angry with me. I'm sorry the summer wasn't everything you hoped. I'm just . . . so sorry."

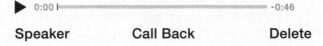

▶ 0:00 |━━━━━━━━━━━━━━━━━━━━━━━━| -0:46

Speaker   **Call Back**   **Delete**

Email Draft (Unsent)

New Message   ×

To

Subject

I heard my phone ring
   But couldn't answer
      Because you still don't
         Understand how I feel

About you leaving
Again
After you swore
You wouldn't.
I'm not okay.
Don't tell
Nell
A thing.

◄◄ ►►| ►|| ■ ● DEW GD BRICKMAN
DURATION: 03:25

*A weatherman's philosophy, according to Dew: The
sun sets the tone for a day while the stars set the tone
for a dream.*

I don't mean to startle her while she's bent over, crying in the
rose garden, but I could tell she needed someone to hear her.

"Are you okay?" I ask.

"*Oh,* I'm sorry—I didn't know anyone was out here," she sobs.
"Fine. I'm fine."

I walk around the fencing to where their gravel drive meets
ours. "Ma'am?"

She looks up at me. "You met Naima."

I nod with delight. "She's such a treasure. And you're?"

"Penelope—Nell—Ray's, uh, her step, um. Just Nell."

"I'm Dew. Lovely to make your acquaintance, Just Nell."

"Likewise." She dabs a tissue to her nose. "Can you promise
me something?"

"Sure."

"I know it's a lot to ask from someone you've just met, and

Lord knows she doesn't *want* anyone's help—because she's stubborn as hell—but maybe you can humor me and make sure she gets along okay? She'd kill me for asking, but I need to know, for *me,* she'll be all right when I go."

I smiled. "That's the very thing I promised Staff Sergeant Rodriguez."

She blinked away her tears. "You knew Ray?"

"Ordered his coffee black, no sugar. Said Naima is fiercely independent, but like a house of cards, may fall apart with the slightest of moves."

"Accurate," she says. "What else did he tell you?"

"She loves hard—*if* you can make it past the intricate obstacle course she's set up around her heart. She's headstrong and fiery, but delicate and breakable. He said she feels in color; when she's angry the colors fade translucent. And despite her confidence, there's always a voice reminding her she doesn't belong. So she's always searching, she just isn't sure for what. He described her as a paradox not meant to be solved, but one worth trying to."

She leans in, awed. "*Wow.* That sounds very much like the Naima I've tried to know for years. But I never fully succeeded."

"He said she's hardest on the ones she cares about most. Maybe you're one of her favorite people, but she wouldn't dare tell you because it'd mean admitting she needs you."

She perks up, a glimmer radiating in her eyes. "He said that?"

"He did."

She steps a little closer, clutching the fabric of her shirt. "Thank you for telling me. I never know."

"Never know what?"

"Anything. I've been on the outside of Ray and Naima since we met. I've learned to accept it, but it hurts, you know? I love my son, but I always wanted a daughter. But Naima, she loved her dad and never wanted another mother. It was a permanent impasse. Maybe she can find some peace here. With the people she wants to be with instead of the ones she's stuck with." She looks away to draw in a deep breath. "Sorry. Don't mind me. Just sorting through my feelings. It's not your problem."

"I don't mind," I tell her. "I like speaking with you. You're kind. I hear it in your voice."

She forces another smile. "So, you work at the bakeshop here in town—is that where he got coffee?"

"Correct."

"You've been here how long?"

My head hangs. "Approximately one year."

"And you didn't meet Naima then?"

"We did *not* meet," I say. "Only Staff Sergeant Rodriguez. But it *feels* like I've known Naima as long."

"That's strange." She thinks on it, seemingly lost in a string of silent conversations.

"I agree."

"You didn't see her outside, coming or going—anywhere?"

"I did not."

"It was nice to meet you, Dew, but if you'll excuse me . . ." She marches back to the door and I suddenly fear I've done something wrong.

AUGUST MOON AND THE PAPER HEARTS: "FIRE"

The very afternoon Staff Sergeant Rodriguez spoke of his one and only daughter's ability to befuddle the hearts of all who knew her, Dew Brickman skipped home to the sounds of August Moon and the Paper Hearts streaming through his earbuds with a renewed sense of purpose. However wrong those feelings, he clung to them with all his might, singing along to the words his mother and father sang to him every day of his life, until the last day of theirs.

> *You're crackling fire, dark can't break,*
> *Lemon drop moon, sky won't take,*
> *Saltwater waves, pain you ache,*
> *Burn, lava fire, neon stake.*
> *Burn.*

NAIMA

Seventeen. Seventeen. Seventeen. Seventeen. Seventeen. Seventeen.

So far, the "celebration" of my seventeenth year on this burning Dumpster fire of a sphere hasn't been great. I have a web-shaped rash on the back of my hand from all the scratching and the walls of my throat are slowly smashing together so all the air around me is wasted and I'm pretty sure my pulse is, like, impossibly slow for a living human, but by the time anyone notices *anything* about me, I'll have decayed. I've put a lot of thought into it, as my therapists are acutely aware. And there's currently this endless knock at the door. It's GD Nell and now she and JJ are whisper fighting.

"What the hell happened last summer?" Nell asks, louder. "And why didn't anyone tell me?"

JJ tries to shush her, but her whispers grow louder, too. Nell's hands shake, cupping over her mouth, and JJ is confessing the thing we hoped to never tell. She turns to me. Kam, too. *Busted.* I look away and let JJ take the hit.

"She's fine," JJ says.

"I knew something was up but couldn't figure out what it was. Tell me."

JJ sighs. "She came to us and said she needed help and didn't want anyone to know, so we got her help, and that was that."

Nell's eyes threaten to bug out of her head. She rushes up to me. "You were struggling and I wasn't there. You can't keep things like this from me—you can't. You *can't*."

I feel her fear in my bones. It's the same fear I had when I took those pills, not *wanting* to die, but not sure how else to stop the pain. How to stop my head from spinning out of control into a dark place I couldn't see my way out of.

JJ places firm hands on Nell's shoulders. "It's my fault. Ray and I thought—"

"*Ray* knew? And didn't tell me?"

Kam intervenes now. "He knew because he was here."

Her eyes are desperately piecing things together, a time line of events. Things that didn't make sense to her last summer because we lied.

"She was fine. If she weren't, he would've told you."

"She wasn't *fine,* Joelle. She wasn't fucking *fine.*" Nell's finger is pointed in JJ's face, but she steps backward, slowly making her way out.

JJ stands in the doorway, watching. Kam rests a hand on her. "She's right," JJ says. "She should've known."

I interject, "It had nothing to do with her."

"But it did, Ima. It did, and you know it."

I watch Nell struggle to settle behind the wheel. She's sobbing into the open air. Maybe we should've come clean sooner. She knows I get really dark, and fast. It's intense, all-consuming. After I nearly died, I did what Dad called "the mature thing" and told them I was scared. That my depression was sucking all the air from my lungs, and I needed help: serious help. *Yes,* Dad leaving again triggered it, but ultimately, the chemicals in my brain had misfired and I still hadn't learned to cope. There's no mystery around my stay at the treatment center. I had dark thoughts that scared me, and wanted to get better. We just didn't want Nell involved.

I didn't.

Last year, I had Dad to keep me level and Nell to mess with my level. As long as he was home, it worked. She's not the *total* worst, and I'm "lucky" to have her, or whatever, and she was actually kick-ass in her own annoying way. But she wears a crocheted beanie and fingerless gloves in the heat of the summer, for Christ's sake. *No.* Like, doesn't she realize how many germs reside on the fingertips alone? Little pads of bacteria on display.

But there's always a strange lump in my throat when I leave her for the summer. It's not like I *need* her—but maybe she needs me. Or maybe that's another lie I tell myself. And maybe I didn't want her to know because it'd be another reason she wouldn't understand *me*. Another *thing* in our way. More problems she can't solve. She'll tell you it's my avoidance of "normal" things like cereal additives and white-on-white cake. I'd argue she's both of these artificial things, so no—I don't want "normal."

Instead of unpacking, I find my glossy poster of Rosie the Riveter (which is actually Beyoncé dressed as the iconic image of Rosie) (because, Beyoncé) (known henceforth as Bey-Ro) that's been folded and refolded more times than I can count, smoothing the edges with the side of my palm. As I look into the mirror at the fierce badass-ness staring back at me, I line my eyes thick with black-winged liner—bottom rims, too—swipe on red lipstick (NARS Velvet matte pencil via Dragon Girl), and rummage through my random barrettes and things until my fingers clasp the very symbolic item I need right now. I tie the red paisley bandanna into my hair like Bey-Ro to wave off Nell, this time with a twinge of regret. She waves back, however it drags.

"Are you *trying* to make a statement with that?" she'd always say.

"Yes," I'd argue.

"Feminism ruined conservatism, you know. Now women are expected to work *and* take care of the kids without a single complaint. It's too much pressure. You'll see when you're older. Being independent isn't that great. Believe me. I went through that phase, too."

"Equality isn't a *phase,*" I'd challenge. "It's a basic human right." I loved tightening the knot while holding eye contact until she broke. She always backed down, cheeks flushing crimson across the apples of her otherwise fair palette.

"I didn't mean . . . I just meant . . . oh, never mind." I enjoyed when she retreated because it meant I was heard. *See, Dad—I will not shrink.* The way she argued, I always felt like she never believed her words. Like someone branded them into her. At the core, when you cut all the shit, she was okay. More than okay. She cared if I lived, and packed my crappy lunches, and offered to tuck me in even after I'd yelled at her for something random.

I run up to the back door, hoping to go through this series of familiar motions one last time.

Only, she's gone.

Voicemail

Dad

cell
September 9 at 3:33 PM

Transcription Beta

"Ima! Just wanted to know how school went. Make any new friends? Nell says

Christian and Caroline have both
gotten into Stanford. I bet they both
said "babe!" right? Call me back. Love
you."

▶ 0:00 |▬▬▬▬▬▬▬▬▬▬▬▬▬▬▬▬▬▬▬▬▬▬| -0:14

Speaker　　　　　**Call Back**　　　　　**Delete**

Email Draft (Unsent)

New Message	✕

To
_____

Subject
_____

Nell said if I applied myself
　　I could be like Christian
　　　　And go to a good school
　　　　　　And prepare for my future
　　　　　　　　As if I'm just sitting here
　　　　　　　　　Wasting time
Until you're home.
I guess
She's right
Because I can't see
Past this moment,
Let alone the rest of my life.

⏮ ⏭ ⏯ ⏹ ⏺ **DEW GD BRICKMAN**
DURATION: 5:51

Top story: Local boy's virginity exposed—tonight on Dew's News at 10.

"Today, Venus and Jupiter's alignment are perfect for new beginnings," Violet says between espresso shots. The sparkle from her silver metallic winged eyeliner is bold enough to speak on her behalf. "*Harmonious* is how my astrologer put it."

I can barely hear through the milk steamer. I keep my distance after witnessing the way the nozzle sprays in all directions. It blows like a freight train's emergency whistle and her voice carries with it, rivaling both its volume and urgency.

"What's your sign?"

I shrug. I'm holding a gallon of almond milk and a bottle of non-dairy whipped cream, awaiting my chance to lay them next to her. "My birthday is August twenty-third."

"Ooh, a Virgo! You *definitely* read Virgo to me. I should've known." She pulls the milk, letting it splatter, to get a full glimpse of me. "I guess I can see it." The door rings, a line of customers forming. "Virgin."

"Pardon?" I shout.

She laughs to herself, and—*finally*—shuts off the steamer.

"YOU'RE A VIRGIN!"

My face blushes every shade of crimson on the spectrum. The room quiets, except for small bubbles of conversation and giggles between customers. I hand her the milk for the next drink and return to my designated spot. "Your astrological symbol is the Maiden—she represents purity and innocence. It's an Earth sign, meaning you're motivated but can make people anxious with your energy."

She pours the milk into the brewed espresso shots, creating a beautiful splintered heart with the milk foam that drips from the spout. I study her. She's so comfortable in her skin, the discom-

fort of others almost doesn't register. I wonder what it feels like
to know yourself so intimately that you're allowed to just *be.*

"Doesn't sound like me," I say. "I mean, the motivated part."

"You're also inquisitive and observant, honest, and unwavering in your support of something, or someone, you care about.
Very avant-garde. Totally unorthodox. Basically, you're an original, Dew-Was-Diaz-Brickman."

"Amazing—how do you know all this?" She turns the steamer
wand on for the next drink, leaning back so I can hear her ex-
tremely loud, incredibly close words.

"I'M A VIRGIN, TOO!" She says it with a slight wink, or
maybe there's espresso dust in her eye, and the line of coffee-
obsessed faces snicker in a more obvious manner. However red
my face blushed previously, the heat strengthens.

Violet is void of a filter. I feel a twinge of envy and a pang of
intimidation. Who am I to be in the presence of someone so un-
apologetically bold? I want to match it, but I am too fearful I
never could.

I look up to find the source of a particularly harsh laugh—
from the very same fellow I bumped into on the sidewalk: Dodge
Teagarden. Violet explained he's a transplant from Boston who
likes medium mocha lattes with no whip, and will be a senior at
East Clifton High. I've tattooed those details into my brain, hoping we can find common ground. Violet uses her eyes to delicately urge me to put my MP3 recorder out of sight.

"Can I help who's next?" I ask with a nervous crack. When
Dodge makes his way to the counter, towering like the Eiffel,
he lays a five and states his order, medium mocha latte, as expected.

"Yes, sir," I say. "Four dollars and fifty cents, out of five?" The
drawer refuses to open. I slap it with the edge of my palm. I
would love to report working around people has eased my social anxieties, but it would be a lie. There are times standing here
only emphasizes everyone's stares. Like now. Dodge's impatience
is assumed, his eyes frowning. I swing a hip to the drawer. The

computer beeps, the screen freezing completely. "Violet," I say with a nervous laugh. "Help."

"Be right there," she says. "Let me get his milk steaming."

Stella once told me working through anxiety is a lot like figuring out the perfect recipe for her blog. "You have to needle with the parts that aren't working, and accentuate the ones that are. It's all about self-editing."

Dodge huffs, his arms crossed tight. He decides now is the best time to make direct eye contact, and I find myself falling into the center of each iris. Two endless pits of darkness I can't seem to look away from. I'm falling, falling, sweating, falling, until Violet squeezes between me and the counter to reset the computer.

"You hit the wrong key," she says with a warm smile. "Should restart in a sec. Sorry, Dodge."

"No worries," he tells her with a crooked grin. When he drifts back to me, and my inability to look away, the smile vanishes.

Violet rushes to concoct the perfect drink, setting it on the counter in front of us. "This one's on us. For the delay." She pushes his five back, at which his face becomes alight.

"Thanks, Vi," he says as he heads out. Relief washes over me. If I were to walk in Dodge's shoes, I wonder what I might find. If his days are spent in such anguish, it's all he can do to wake up each morning. Or if, as Violet says, there are some people in life that have a bad aura no matter what. Regardless, I refuse to write him off as a flat, 2-D character with nothing but a few bad lines for no good reason.

"Thanks," I say.

"Anytime, Dew-Was-Diaz-Brickman." She winks again, and this time, I'm sure of it.

Breaking news: Boy imagines having friends, may actually have one (or two if Naima will allow it).

THE ORIGIN OF NAIMA

"Naima" by John Coltrane.

When nineteen-year-old Josephine threw up her Egg McMuffin in a McDonald's parking lot, Ray had this song playing on their car stereo. She looked up at him as she wiped her chin and said, "I'm pregnant and we're naming her Naima," to which Ray replied, "WUT?" and after they cried and cursed a little, he said, "What if she's a *he*?" Josephine smiled and said, "Naima will become Naiman, and it will be lovely." When Ray reminisced about his one and only (with no offense to Penelope), Josephine always used the word "lovely," which made Naima envision her mother visiting with the Queen, drinking tea at high noon. She likes tea, and high noon. And she forever wishes she could hear her mother say "lovely" just once.

Ray would tell Naima how often Josephine listened to that Coltrane record, and Naima always got caught up in semantics, asking, "WTF is a record?" forcing Ray on a tirade about the evolution of music that grew from a record player to a cassette tape and so on, joking that someday, we'd hear the music in our minds. He made it sound mysterious and magical—two words he also used to describe Naima *and* her mother.

He said "Naima" calmed Josephine when she felt the pains of growing a baby. It empowered her to bring a child into a life surrounded by love—despite an overwhelming resistance from Josephine's parents. She was too young, too smart, with too much potential to sacrifice for anyone. Josephine fought for the life of Naima, and the life she wanted with Ray. Sounds "lovely," doesn't it?

Except Naima came into the world the day her mother left it, and that is the very essence of Naima's heart—existing because of, and in spite of, loss.

As she grew older, Naima would find the courage to listen to the song her mother treasured. It reminded her of all her parents deemed worth protecting, never knowing it was her existence that would forever change the lives of many. Everything Naima is, ends and begins with the love between her parents, and the ultimate sacrifice both have made, for different reasons. Never ask her about her name.

The day before Naima got the news of her father's death, she forgot to count the tiles in the bathroom, just as the day she was born, she didn't have the slightest concern for counting the seconds her mother had left in the world.

Because she forgot to count, they are dead. Or

Maybe it's because

She *did* count.

And so, she can't ever forget to count.

And she won't forget.

So nothing else bad happens.

There are ninety hexagons.

Never ask her about her name.

NAIMA

My "room" is in the finished basement, next to an old washer and dryer (because they refuse to buy new, working ones). This means, because JJ does seventeen thousand loads of laundry a day, I get zero privacy. I do get the privilege of listening to the continual knocking sounds from whatever's broken that they refuse to fix. So, there's that. I think it's JJ's way of checking on me without being obvious but *HELLO*—THIS IS SOOO OBVIOUS BECAUSE NO ONE DOES THIS MUCH LAUNDRY EXCEPT MAYBE INMATES SENTENCED TO LAUNDRY DUTY!

I'm sprawled out on an air mattress the size of a toddler's bed. It's the same one I sleep on every summer. It knows the curves of me before I even lay my head to its lumpy ridges. When Dad stays . . . *stayed* . . . he took the upstairs couch to give me privacy. He forgot about JJ's EFFING LAUNDRY ADDICTION, or he totally knew and didn't want to be the one she snooped on. Probably that.

The upstairs door—the third Kam cut from a wooden block and varnished—is slightly askew, in case I "get scared" or whatever, so I hear the latest podcast streaming from JJ's laptop. Every few sentences, Hiccup barks to remind us that he's still here.

Would you rather bark as your only means of communication or never speak again?

As a women's and gender studies professor at Ball State for over twenty years, JJ's more Beyoncé or Rosie than Bey-Ro put together. Even in retirement, girl power, equality, and women's rights saturate her every breath. When I was little, I was afraid she'd see me only as broken parts—that I could never be strong like her. Next to her, it's easy to feel inferior. No matter how fly I feel, she's that, and more. Without a mother, I learned by watching *her*. It's her voice that never shrinks, and if mine does, she helps me find it.

Back in Texas, when I felt uninspired, I'd do some online stalking to read her work. It's everywhere. Her words made, *make*, me want to fight for something, but I've never been sure what that something is.

Kam paces near my entryway, his six-foot frame holding a thick book in hand—no doubt one of JJ's latest creations—mumbling an occasional "Amen to that." JJ's last book didn't sell well, but her first was a "near overnight success" (this phrase is a myth, BTW), bringing her voice to the world in ways I couldn't imagine. This is the book of her heart. The one, she says, poured out of her soul; the very thing that made her want to be a better human. When she speaks about her life, her passions, it's hard to remember how much she's lost, too. Her mom a couple years back, a sister years prior. Never knew her father. Always questioned her existence—an unspoken truth we share.

At every pass, Hiccup nips at Kam's heels, tugging on the backs of his dingy white socks. His slobber is thick, leaving a string of mucus. I gag—like physically gag. Kam reads on, cradling the spine between his palms as if the book were a newborn babe. Hiccup is a boundless ball of energy on my last GD nerve and it's only day 1. He will legit never die and if he does, he'll haunt my nightmares, tearing holes in all my pants. The moment I think it . . . I miss Dad so much, it's a wallop to the gut and I'm being sucked from the universe into a place with no oxygen. I look to my phone, think about the last voicemail, and leave it be. A star in the sky; untouchable.

The time is 10:53 P.M. EST.

I close my eyes. Toss to one side, and the other. Musk and detergent scent the air, and the knocking between the washer and dryer tubes echoes into an infinite black hole. I look up, there's Dad. I look left, right, there's Dad, too. Pictures of him, memories inescapable. Seeing him at every angle forces me to think, and I don't want to think—I want to *not* think. It's hard to think of Ivy Springs without Dad. As much as it feels like home, being here is an evergreen reminder of his absence.

For a solid fourteen minutes, I debate the pros and cons of moving back to Nell's in Albany versus staying—something I never thought I'd wager. The winning bid comes when the dryer stops and the banging stalls. Kam has moved to another room. Hiccup, too. And it's quiet and my thoughts are all I have to hold on to. Except for the podcast.

I take one last look at Dad, *I miss you,* and drag myself up the stairs to the kitchen table, where JJ's hunched over her laptop with a steaming mug of tea. Her hair is wrapped in terry cloth, and she's dressed in floral pajamas and a ruby robe. When she sees me, she pushes the third chair out—because Dad, *it,* is still in the second chair—and points for me to sit.

"Tea?" she asks. "It'll help you sleep."

Tea is never just tea. It's an offering.

"Okay." The smell of chamomile twists into the remaining scents of apple and cinnamon from the apple butter she concocted after dinner. She boils water in her rusted antique kettle—the one Gi Gi gave her—while I strain my ears to hear what's being said through her laptop's small speakers. The voice cites excerpts from an essay by former President Obama called "This Is What a Feminist Looks Like." In it, he says he raised his daughters to know their dad is a feminist because "that's what they'll expect from *all* men." The words ring out, clanging against Dad's urn. It's as if he's saying "preach!" right along with Mr. Obama. Without realizing the consequences of the choices he made (moving, marrying Nell, joining the military, even being there for me), I see how Dad did the same. Maybe it was how JJ and Kam raised him, the way they've raised *me.*

As the podcast goes on, JJ hands me my mug. Inscribed with *I Donut Care Right Now,* it's the mug I always drink from; no other. My hands are wrapped tight around the ceramic as I sip. She's nodding along the length of the audio, a slight smile rising from the corners of her lips when something strikes her, and I find myself doing the same. When it ends, we're connected by the silence that follows.

"Oh, honey," she says, "that was *something.* If all men were feminists, we wouldn't be in this political nightmare right now."

My eyes connect to the urn. It shines brightly beneath the kitchen lights and I can't look away.

She grabs my hand and I don't let myself pull away. "He loved you so much," she whispers, her voice breaking apart. The same way I have.

I take another sip, letting her hand fall to the table. My eyes don't abandon the urn—Dad. *God,* it's so weird. Like, seriously, why hasn't anyone moved it/him? But it kind of feels okay. Almost like he's here, but not.

She follows my stare. "Not really sure what to do with him . . . *it* . . . just yet. I can't seem to . . . move the damn thing. I can teach college honors classes, run ultramarathons, and open the damn pickle jar without help, but with every fiber in my being, I can't move that urn."

I nod, and take another sip.

With the room quiet, she does the same.

We alternate without another word spoken as we sit with my father, enjoying our tea. This is normal; everything's normal.

Come home. Dad, please.

Voicemail

Dad

cell
September 20 at 3:57 PM

Transcription Beta

"How is school so far? Hanging in there? Taking your medicine? Going to therapy? Nell said she overheard a call you made to Dr. Rose. That you said you don't trust Dr. Tao. You deserve some peace in your heart, so please reach out to someone, anyone. I need to know you're okay. And baby—could you stop returning my letters? I thought we were past that. Love you."

▶ 0:00 ▬▬▬▬▬▬▬▬▬▬▬ -0:21

Speaker   **Call Back**   **Delete**

No New Emails

◄◄ ►►Ⅰ ►ⅠⅠ ◼ ● DEW GD BRICKMAN
DURATION: 6:01

*In today's top stories, virgin Virgos make great
friends, not so great espresso.*

Lady Clean Cuisine never explains the inner workings of building a recipe from the ground up. Not the way my mother did. While Stella is content scribbling, tasting, and editing a dish until its near-blog-worthy perfect, Mom baked by feeling her way through a recipe. In the chaos of burned Baked & Caffeinated shots and brownies alike, this is all I can think about. Big Foot says customers complain, that I need to remake drinks if the shots are burned, and I should toss a batch of perfectly okay (however burned) brownies in the garbage. He tells me to speed up, to stop wasting time. There are too many steps, too many things happening at once, making beverages shouldn't be so difficult—especially when I've been making them for two summers now—but like most things I've found, everything is difficult.

Everything.

"You need to relax, man," Big Foot says during my break in the back room. His brown hair is pulled back into a low bun, sparse strands dangle in his face, begging to join the rest of the hair. "You smoke?"

"No," I say.

"Then do some yoga or puzzles. Something to settle those nerves." His Converse sneakers are kicked up on the small desk that lines the break room wall where the motivational bulletin board resides, shouting slogans like *You're better today because of what you endured yesterday.*

"If you're ever interested, I own a dispensary," he says.

"A *legal* one?"

"Not *technically*."

"Cool." My fingers fumble in my pockets to be sure the record function is in the Off position. I've recorded entire conversations entirely by accident. I'd hate to be an accomplice in drug-related activity without my parents' permission.

While Big Foot, who's become the equivalent of a campfire storyteller in this small space, tells of how steep the start-up costs are to get a dispensary approved and opened and thus, why he's found his clientele don't mind he's unlicensed because he's "helping them and that's what matters," I overhear Violet taking an order so I peek around the corner.

"Thank you so much," she tells Dodge. "You know, you have beautiful eyes."

He blushes, unaware Violet is the most open soul he'll ever meet. Her compliments range from the mundane "cute shoes," to the unbelievable "you have the greatest personality I've ever known in all my lives." I've yet to see a single one mean anything more than a way to make someone's day a bit brighter. I feel for Dodge when his posture shifts, as he leans farther into Violet's zone.

"I was going to say the same about yours," he says cunningly.

"They *are* the windows to the soul."

She brews a perfectly caramelized shot then turns the steamer on to froth the milk.

"Your windows are great," he yells through the steamer's ear-piercing hum.

"Thanks! My ideologist, Althea, diagnosed me with allergies by looking into my irises. Said they were inflamed."

"Was she right?"

She shuts the steamer off, accidentally yelling over the silence, "IT WAS THE ESENTIAL OILS—" She quiets, giggles at the sound of her voice. "I was allergic to the oils she used *near* my eyes. Anyway, here's your mocha." I lean more into the doorway as Dodge takes the drink, lingering in Violet's ethereal glow.

"Anyway," Big Foot concludes the story I've blocked out, "I'm lucky he survived or I'd have been charged with more than a misdemeanor, you know?"

Reluctant to nod, as I clearly missed a big chunk of his criminal history, I smile. When I turn back to Violet, Dodge has left and she's helping another customer. "I better get back to work," I say.

"Good dude." He flashes a thumbs-up. "Just chill out when you're busy. Breathe. It's all good, cool?"

I nod again.

"I'll be here if you need anything."

Violet refills the espresso beans when I drift back through.

"Mr. Dodge seems to have a thing for you," I say.

She appears confused. "No way."

"Way. Don't you notice the way he looks at you compared to me?"

"No?"

"There's an obvious difference, I assure you."

"Maybe he doesn't realize he's doing that."

"Or maybe he likes you. It's not beyond the realm of possibility."

She thinks on it, tilting her eyes up at the ceiling. "Interesting theory, Dew-Was-Diaz-Brickman. But I'm not interested."

"Not your type?"

"I don't have a type. If you're a living, breathing soul, *that's* my type. Although, some of the dead have captured my heart as well, so who knows? I'm open to all possibilities." She smirks, wipes her area clean. A vision of vibrant reds catches my attention through the storefront window. My eyes follow.

"You okay?" Violet asks.

"I want to be with you in the colors." The words to an

August Moon song quietly pour out of me, but I don't intend to direct the words in her direction. They come as effortlessly as each breath.

"What did you say?"

"Nothing."

"Classic Virgo." While she runs a cloth beneath scalding tap water, I excuse myself to the bathroom and lock the door. I stand in the damp corner, near the double-pane glass window, rewinding through my four-thousand-hour audio file until I locate the exact sound byte I need to hear, to validate the emotion I'm feeling.

"I don't know how to leave her again," Staff Sergeant Rodriguez says the day before his final departure. "I'll have to send a red balloon every day to make this one right."

I stop the recording. *The colors.* I'll give them to Naima (yes; *classic* Virgo).

NAIMA

It's after midnight. I count the seconds. The ceiling tiles. The sounds outside my window. My fingers grasp at the tightly wrapped silk kimono I've laid atop the rest of my things. I drape it over my pajamas, taking in the soft sheen with each pass of my hand. You should *never* wear silk when it's seventy million degrees out, but I need to. Dad sent it after his brief stint in Japan a few years back. It's my "favorite."

No, but really—it's gorgeous and I appreciate the culture, which is why I prefer to *not* appropriate. But I also hate the way the fabric feels on my skin (it's a textural thing I can't get past; like cotton balls = *ew*). Like, I seriously loathe silk. It's the equivalent of a boa constrictor squeezing me into a dizzied state of reality, making me wish it would end already. And don't even think about raising your arms or bending forward because this shit will rip right around your delicates.

Would you rather let a boa constrictor squeeze you to death or walk around in a revealing item of delicate clothing the rest of your life?

Dad *never* acknowledged my size. Not that he was ashamed— I don't think weight was ever a factor in how he viewed me. I'm fat. Not pudgy or plump. Not thick or curvy. I was born with gorgeous, insulated layers. I'll likely always have them and I'm good with that. Handing me something three sizes too small wasn't his way of trying to change me. Maybe it didn't occur to him because I'm just *me*. And anyway, when I look in the mirror, I see my worth. I'm capable, strong, fierce. I'm a goddamn beautiful powerhouse not to be fucked with. You don't have to be thin to love yourself (fact), and I *love* my body, for the record.

It's my mind I take issue with.

I don't know how long I sit touching the silk. Moving feels wrong, so I don't. The hands on the clock climb forward, *tick-tock, tick-tock*, but I don't worry about the seconds lost. How does anyone move forward with the passage of time after something like this? *I wish I knew.*

The time is now 12:47 A.M. EST.

I finally stand and walk toward the full-length mirror hanging on the back of the small bathroom door. My steps lull. I don't see *me*. I pay no attention to the kimono. And in this dim lighting, my perfectly frizzed hair bleeds into the background. It's as if every last part blurs, except the details of my face; the places that most resemble Dad, Mom, too. I'm not looking at myself. I'm looking at my parents, two planets who collided into one another until I burst into the world.

My chest pangs, heart ripping down the middle. I tear off the kimono, leave it on the floor, and collapse onto the mattress with my face buried in a pillow. The moment of impact, I'm startled upright by a muffled crash. The culprit—a hanging photo of my parents—is nestled in the middle of the kimono. I grab the last of my marshmallows in the Ziploc I've hidden beneath my pillow and chew them slowly, savoring the sugary sweet calm that washes over me; trying to ignore the enormity of the picture before me.

I am seen.

I wake with JJ and her scarlet and gold-plated flower earrings dangling over me. The plastic laundry basket is tucked beneath her arm with literally three garments in it (which is *not* enough for another load). She smiles.

I pop upright. Well, let me be clear. When I "pop," it's a slow, grumbling, Frankenstein rise to life with an underlying hatred of all things in my path. Mornings will never, *ever* be my thing (and she knows this), but let's assume, for the sake of the argument, I do, in fact, "pop" like a damn firework.

Pop. Pop. Pop. Pop. Pop. Pop.

"Good morning, sunshine." She hands me a porcelain mug full of liquid as dark as my soul. My fingers reject it.

"What's the matter?" she asks, offended.

I point to the words *Proud Dad of a U.S. Marine*. Third tour, he took three bullets. It was a Thursday when Nell got the call. You never forget dates attached to pain. They're with you for the rest of time. A few days after, Kam sent a text holding up this mug he bought himself as a way of praying without falling to his knees. Like if he had the mug, Dad had to get better. JJ said he drank everything from it. Coffee. Soup. Tea. Took it with him to the garden. Into town when he met his friends. It became his bulletproof vest. It's *his* vessel of hope.

JJ's eyes bulge. She pulls the drink back toward her. "I—I'm sorry." She drops the laundry basket to steady the mug in her shaking hands. Her fingers want to reject the mug now, too.

The liquid sloshes against the sides, streams of coffee dripping over.

I "pop" up to my feet (an actual "pop" this time). "Give it to me."

She's frozen, caught in an invisible net. I'm trying to free her, but her eyes remain as large as they are mournful. Dad is gone and he's not coming back. Every moment is a new realization, and we'll never escape it. Grief will hold on to us with both hands if we let it. JJ's resilient and brave. All the things I'm not. I don't know how to be that for her.

I don't know how. Don't know. How.

I carefully pry her fingers from the handle, and sip. Inside, I'm screaming, fighting not to go through these motions, but for her, I must.

Her eyes peer down. She's slowly reeling in the state of panic I'm so familiar with.

"Mmm," I say, pushing past the discomfort. "I love black coffee."

I hate black coffee.

She watches me strain to guzzle the disgusting drink down. "That hits the spot."

It doesn't hit the spot.

Every sip I take, I imagine Kam's lips in the very same spot. My brain screams for me to stop.

"Joelle," Kam yells from the top of the stairs. It snaps her attention away from me. "Where's my straw hat?"

"Probably wherever you left it last," she shouts. Her head is tilted, but her eyes stick to the mug. "Decades in planning, development, and architecture, and he can't find a damn hat."

"Wow, that helps." Kam's footsteps trail above, from one side of the house to the other, clomping a wallop with every stride. We hear him speaking to the walls about possible places it could be. Something about the yard. Hiccup carried it off. Could even be on his head if he'd check (it's not the first time).

"I swear," she says, "why do I have to be in charge of *every-thing*? Go find your own damn hat. I know where *my* hat is." Her ramble fades. There's not only a tense silence between us, but this coffee mug and everything it represents. If I lower it, we'll have to acknowledge the power it has. I hold it steady, a barricade, instead.

The clock's hands are all that can be heard. Eventually—when Kam's footsteps approach this side of the house again—JJ breaks our formation and lifts the laundry basket to her waist. "How about belated-birthday pancakes. Vanilla flavored, no syrup. *Right?*"

Much like Nell's "okay," the emphasis on "right" seems as though she's searching. For acceptance, compassion, or maybe just someone to remind her that even though life is abysmal (I heard the word used in her podcast) (I'm not completely sure I used it right, but whatever), some things are still fine.

We're still fine.

Fine.

"Three stacks of two," I tell her.

She breaks through the barrier of grief and smiles.

"I remember." The silence doesn't last. She yanks the mug from my hands with a sharp tug. "Give me ten minutes to get it ready."

She sees the picture on top of the kimono and strolls over for a closer look. With a weighted gasp, she picks up the memory and holds it to her chest. I look away. If a heart can break apart more than once and survive, it's mine; it's hers. Every second she stands there, I feel the tears she's holding back. I give her time to think about the faces in the frame before clearing my throat to pull the moment away from her. She rehangs the photo, rubs one hand over the surface as if to say *goodbye*, and makes her way to the staircase.

It's there that she waits, and I don't know if she's scared to move forward, or if she knows I am. To go through the belated-birthday pancakes without Dad means something. It's not just another breakfast, like that wasn't just any mug. Everything means something different now.

Kam interrupts this interaction of nothingness. "Found my hat," he says, "it was where I left it—on the coatrack with the other hats. Imagine that."

"Want me to throw you a damn party?" JJ replies.

"Could you?" he quips.

"Might not be the party you're thinking of."

She follows him up, and together, their voices fade. It's like I'm watching these scenes from a seat in a movie theater. Every conversation playing out the way it should, every ending wrapped in a bow, whether it should be or not. I keep thinking Dad's going to call my name and tell me the pancakes are ready.

But he won't.

One. Two. Three. Four. Five. Six.

The numbers don't take.

So I try again with more emphasis.

ONE. Two. THREEEEE. Four. FIVE. Six.

Deep breath in, and out.

And in.

Where everything is locked away.

Especially the feeling that anything good

Could ever be

Again.

Voicemail

Dad

cell
September 29 at 2:36 AM

Transcription Beta

"You always loved fall. Is it getting
cooler there yet? It's still warm here,
but temps are dropping slowly. Should
be close to report cards, right? God,
I've lost track of time. Remind me how
to focus on the seconds again. Remind
me. Please. [inaudible]"

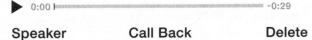

▶ 0:00 |▬▬▬▬▬▬▬▬▬▬▬▬▬▬▬▬▬▬▬▬▬▬▬▬▬▬ -0:29

Speaker   **Call Back**   **Delete**

Email Draft (Unsent)

New Message   ✕

To

Subject

I do love fall,
     Dad,
          But it's not quite cool enough,
               Dad,
                    Report cards are out next week,
                         Dad,

But Nell already knows
I'm failing math,
Science,
Social studies,
English,
And life.
    If you want to count the time, start with now.
      It's all we're guaranteed.
        Now. Now. Now. Now. Now. Now.

⏮ ⏭ ⏯ ⏹ ⏺ DEW GD BRICKMAN
DURATION: 5:30

*Today's forecast is partially sunny with late-day
woo-ing in the Blue County areas.*

Dr. Peterson is impressed with my progress, but suggests there's more work to do. She tells Stella I'm not working through my grief, but suppressing it. But I can't recall a pain I haven't acknowledged. I tell her I miss my parents, but that I'm aware of Stella and Thomas's devotion. I've admitted to having dreams where I'm the one who died instead. I say these things, and I manage.

Today, as I was leaving her office, she said, "Life isn't easy, Dew," but it wasn't her voice I heard.

"Life isn't easy, Dew," Dad would say as we struggled to stay warm in our compact car. "But you find a way to dance in the rain. It's part of the journey." His eyes twinkled even as he covered me in layers of cable-knit sweaters while I laid in the backseat. Mom would give a half-broken smile and say, "You two are my joy," and somehow, even on the coldest night, with the emptiest of stomachs, it was all okay. I'm trying to figure out what this means for me now—who I am, if not Andrew Diaz; my mother's darling, my father's heir.

Stella pulls me aside after my appointment and asks what I've divulged about Naima to Dr. Peterson. I shrug. Honestly I don't recall, but she grows visibly frustrated.

"It's a safe zone," she reminds me. "You should say whatever you need to." Her sentence ends as if she's asking a question, but I'm not sure what. The conversation ends abruptly, not another word spoken about it until breakfast the next day.

"I'm really happy you've spoken to Naima," Stella says mid-chew.

I look up. Faith's watching a new documentary on her phone, about Rick Flair, aka Nature Boy, her eyes as glued to this one as the last. She's been saying "woo" since the beginning (he's apparently known for it), though none of us is sure how to react. To compensate, we *woo* in return and pretty soon, everyone is *woo-ing*.

"Did something happen I don't know about?" Thomas asks. He worked late last night and missed dinner. Lately, he's missed most key conversations and activities. Breakfast, the occasional dinner, and bedtime are the only opportunities in which we can bundle up our stories like a net full of butterflies and set them free. He works hard, picking up extra shifts where he can, so Stella's not stuck counting change at the general store again and instead has proper time for Faith and me. I love this about him, but it also leaves our interactions as big, uncomfortable info-dump boxes we have to unpack in a brief amount of time.

Stella shakes her head, cuts her specially designed Lady Clean Cuisine gluten-free, dairy-free waffles with a fork and knife. "What *haven't* we done to help, Dew? What else can we do?" She looks up at me wistfully.

My brows scrunch as I cut my stack into pieces. "I don't know what you mean."

"You're still mismanaging time and—"

"Hold up," Thomas interjects. "Could you fill me in here, Stel?"

Agitated, she sighs deep and dramatic. "I want Dew to feel like he can open up to Dr. Peterson, but if he doesn't feel we're doing enough—that *we're* not enough—I feel, I don't know, betrayed? That's not the right word. Hurt, maybe? Definitely frustrated when we've done everything possible to give him a better life." Her words fade as she catches my surprise.

"He knows how much we—*you*—do for him," he says in my defense. "They both do."

"That's not what Dr. Peterson told me."

"I thought my sessions were private," I say.

"You're a minor; not only can she tell me what's going on, I can sit in on the sessions if I choose."

I drop my fork, unaware my words could be used against me.

"So that's how you know about me mentioning Naima."

"What does this have to do with Naima?" Thomas asks.

Stella turns to him with a snap. "You *know* what. She's all he's talking about. He's hyper-focused on a girl he doesn't know as a means of, in Dr. Peterson's words, 'redirecting his pain to not deal with it at all.'"

My face streaks with flushes of cherry-bomb heat. "I've barely mentioned her."

"That's not what Dr. Peterson says."

Faith pauses the documentary, tosses the phone to the table. "Naima was locked up last summer. That's why she doesn't want you to love her."

"Where did you hear that?" Thomas asks.

"Stella and Dr. Peterson talk *really* loud. *Woo.*"

I angle my glare at Stella. "What does she mean, 'locked up'?"

Stella straightens her posture, stumbling over her words. "Not *locked* up—that's *not* what I said." She looks to Thomas, who shrugs. "She was in a treatment center for her anxiety and depression." She fidgets in her chair. "She was . . . suicidal."

"So?" Faith challenges. "Everyone needs help sometimes.

That's what you always tell us." The guts on this kid are the guts I wish to have.

Thomas nods along, proud.

We all await Stella's next explanation. Our eyes wiggle with anticipation as she juggles it around her mouth before speaking. "I was afraid she'd somehow . . . influence your progress. Or you'd influence hers, becoming so intertwined with each other's grief, you'd both be swallowed up by it. Like *The Virgin Suicides* or *Romeo and Juliet*."

Faith laughs. "Virgin. *Woo*."

"Stella, come on," Thomas says. "Not the same thing. At all."

She relaxes only slightly. "Suicide pacts are a thing, so is suicide contagion. There's research on the Domino effect of mental illness at that level. Or substance abuse they'd get into—to numb the pain together."

"Give these kids some credit. They can help each other. Who better to talk to than someone who's going through similar things?"

She sighs, hiding her face from us. "You're right," she says, a crack in her voice. "When Dr. Peterson said Dew talked so much about Naima, I panicked. I just want him to be okay."

He lays his hand on hers. "You're a good mom to worry, but he'll be okay."

"Mom" rings through, sizzling my ears like a branding iron. "Let me get something clear," I interject. "You didn't want me to meet Naima because you *assumed* her problems would become mine, or mine hers, unfairly *assuming* we'd decide to destroy ourselves or take our lives, *together*? And I'm not to even mention her because it interrupts my healing. That's what Dr. Peterson suggested, that's what you're telling me?" I hold my gaze firm. Faith, in total domination, does the same.

Stella nods with a tinge of regret.

"Like Thomas said, maybe it would've been beneficial to know someone was going through things—*really hard things*—like me. So I could feel less different from other kids; from you."

My blunt comments leave her taken aback. "I know." She sighs. "I was wrong."

"You want me to break through some magical barrier with my grief, but disallow me the chance to do what might help. Do you see the irony?"

"I do."

"*I* sure as hell do," Faith blurts.

"So, it's decided," I add. "Because you officially made us star-crossed lovers without my permission, it only seems fair I'm allowed the chance to decide whether or not she's imperative, or detrimental, to my progress."

"He's right, Stel," Thomas says. "You meant well, but we can't interfere like that. He's almost an adult and he's in therapy, doing the best he can. Let him learn to sort stuff out on his own unless he asks us for help. Faith, too."

Tears fill her eyes. "I only want to protect you from more pain. That's all I wanted. I'm sorry."

With the sigh of a thousand lifetimes, I soften my stance, and immediately, Faith does, too. "I agree with Thomas. You are a good mom; but you forget we had lives before you." The words float between us, pausing in the air like a new picture to hang on the wall.

Her tears blossom until they burst from her lashes, streaking her cheeks. "I get it."

Thomas pats her hand until she calms. Faith watches this unfold, carefully pressing her eyes between her screen and us, hoping to go unnoticed. Perhaps she's not witnessed a family in this light. One that smashes into pieces but finds their way back together. Perhaps she's waiting to release a full breath when she knows, whatever this is, it won't change anytime soon. I did the same.

The table is quiet. We all eat in peaceful unison except Faith, whose attention is fully on the documentary. The glow cast from the screen illuminates a joy we've not managed to evoke, and for the first time since we've become a family of four, it actually feels pretty darn close to home. *Woo.*

NAIMA

When I *finally* settle on an outfit suited for small-town life that screams "*Please* don't talk to me" (a pair of printed leggings and a black tee with a skull and crossbones), I finger-comb my unruly curls with my favorite jasmine-scented pomade and slap on a fresh coat of Dragon Girl red to head upstairs, where JJ and Kam are sitting at the kitchen table with their hands clasped as if waiting on me for an intervention. As soon as my feet hit the top stair, Hiccup pounces from the living room couch to catch me, chewing bits of cloth from the bottom cuff of my leggings.

"GO TO HELL!" I snap, trying to shake him loose. The little shit breaks skin beneath the leggings, burning a memory of Dad through my focus. He said those words when Hiccup nipped at his feet. But *I've* never said them. *Why now?*

"Hiccup—fetch." Kam, who's wearing the hat he'd "lost," tosses a chewed-up stuffed cat toy—Hiccup's favorite—to distract him long enough for me to find my seat at the table, though we all know it's only a matter of time before he searches for another pant leg to gnaw.

"Dad" is still at the table. There's an actual place mat and utensils in front of him/it and I'm not sure if they're messing with me, or if this is us. As if the loss redefined our very beings to a strange and absurd state.

I slide into the chair next to him. "What's up, Dad?"

He doesn't answer.

"Cool. Same." I Googled "cremation," to be sure this isn't a panic-inducing scenario, and know the kiln destroyed all the bacteria and microscopic organisms in Dad's body. He's as sterile as he's ever been.

I feel JJ's eyes, but she refrains from commenting.

"Your leg okay?" Kam asks.

I feel the sting of blood. "Yep."

"What do you two have planned today?"

A newspaper is sprawled out in the center of the table. The headline references the Fourth of July memorial, citing a "local fallen hero." I stare, unblinking.

"Farmers' market day," JJ answers. She shoves the paper out of view, replacing it with my plate of pancakes. Three stacks of two. Like every year. Always three stacks of two. Not two stacks of three. Not one stack of six. Not even three and three. It has to be exactly the same as it has been before. There's no other way.

"Might head into Baked & Caffeinated for coffee after," she adds.

"Sounds fun," Kam replies. He cuts his single stack into quarters, piercing a fork into one whole pile, and I think there's no way that'll all fit into his mouth, but it does and I can't stop watching him.

"I don't want to go there," I say.

"Why not? You love their coffee."

I hate their coffee. "Don't feel like it."

"Listen here. We have plenty of time to grieve," she says. "Today is for celebrating Naima. *You.*"

"That's what you said when I got my first period. You're not going to make me wear all those beads and do a 'dance of the goddesses,' are you?"

"*That* dance was specific to the female reproductive system, *not* a birthday. My mother did it for me. It's a rite of passage."

"Right," I say. "My bad."

"You should've seen the dance she made me do after my colonoscopy," Kam jokes.

JJ smacks her lips, protective of the comforting rituals her grandmother performed. "Gi Gi taught me to do whatever cleanses the soul." She pauses, clenching the paper in her fist.

Kam swoops in, grabs the paper and lays it next to the urn, pushing time forward. Everyone needs that person. The one who sees you stuck between the minute and the hour hands of your most painful moments, and reaches out for you. JJ's shoulders relax.

"The annual dance-off will cleanse all our souls later," Kam says. "I've been practicing so you'd better bring your A-game."

"Dude, JJ's in better shape than everyone in Ivy Springs."

"*Psht.*" He waves the comment off. "Your moves are tired."

My body tightens. "We can't do it this year. It doesn't feel . . . right."

The tradition began when I was old enough to understand Dad's absence. JJ and Kam would bring out Dad's old boom box, crank up whatever mixtape or CD he'd left behind, and we'd challenge each other in the middle of the living room. I didn't forget Dad was gone, but for a short time, it didn't hurt as much. My grandparents carried it over into every birthday, in hopes they could preemptively soothe my lonely soul. Watching them dance gives me life.

They look to one another, silently deciding who'll handle this one.

"We're doing the dance-off. Unless you're afraid of losing," Kam adds, jabbing his elbow into mine, and forming an L with his thumb and forefinger.

I force a smile, but it hurts.

Hurts. Hurts. Hurts. Hurts. Hurts. Hurts.

The kitchen air goes stagnant, and all six of our eyes fall to the urn. The space where the place mat sits untouched.

Infinitely untouched.

"Eat up," JJ breaks the silence. "We'll leave in a bit. And this afternoon, we'll go to your favorite restaurant and have all the breadsticks you can handle. Just enough to make you lose the dance-off."

My fork streaks the pancake stacks, knocking them over one by one. My father's in an urn. There isn't room in my thoughts for the farmers' market, or pancakes, or anything else.

JJ lowers a hand to the tip of my chin and angles it up. Faint traces of flour are splattered on her shirt, and she smells of maple. "Your birthday. That's the *only* thing we're going to think about today. The *only* thing."

Her eyes consume me, tears stopping themselves before jumping off. JJ pushes a smile. *Here we are; this is us.* When she finally abandons me to clean up the mess in the kitchen, I turn toward the urn and imagine myself falling between the etchings. For six seconds, I'm part of the urn, too. And maybe that's where I feel most like myself.

The farmers' market is usually one of my *favorite* rituals. Nell might not get the other parts—the reason I need six red balloons (to make six wishes, of course), or why I have to count everything, or why I use sarcasm and blatant disgust for her as a means of coping with all the things I hate about myself. It has nothing to do with her. I decide this is another thing I like about her— how she ignores the very real fact that I do, in fact, like her (but don't you dare tell her). As for JJ, she carries a longer list.

At the market, she lets me have as many cheese samples as I want, and she doesn't ask, "Isn't that enough?" and she doesn't make a crinkled-up face when I try all the lotions, or ask if there's a hand-woven oven mitt in a different color because the orange and green didn't "feel right." She lets me be. It's the way of the Rodriguez house.

The way of *me.*

My phone buzzes.

Penelope-Smellope: *Are you okay, really?*

I hesitate to text back; there's nothing I can say she'll believe.

Me: *I'm fine.*

As I pretend to eat the pancakes by tearing pieces and moving them around, my phone buzzes in bursts as if it's just now come to life, reminding me of one last gift I left before parting ways.

Penelope-Smellope: *Well, good. Also, WHAT IN THE WORLD IS ALL THIS GUM DOING ON THE WALL BESIDE YOUR BED???* ☹☹☹

That she even texted this is why there are now three things I like about her.

(If you tell, I'll cut you.)

Voicemail

Dad

cell
October 6 at 4:11 PM

Transcription Beta

"Thought I'd try to catch you. Maybe
you've joined an after-school club (not
likely) or you're plotting the new
revolution (*totally* likely)? It's late here.
Nell is worried about you. Said you
haven't been leaving the house, or your
room. Please let her, and me, know
what's going on and how we can help.
Anyway, used my sweet app to have a
burger. It's pretty cool. I can order
from some of our favorite places back
home and have it delivered all the way
out here in the desert. Even got a pint
of cookie dough ice cream. Reminded
me of our Sundays at Baked &
Caffeinated before someone bought it
out and rebranded into somewhere
Nell might go, am I right? I miss those
nights. I miss you. . . ."

▶ 0:00 ▬▬▬▬▬▬▬▬▬▬▬▬▬▬▬▬ -1:11

Speaker   **Call Back**   **Delete**

Email Draft (Unsent)

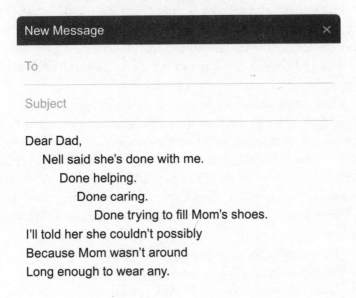

Dear Dad,
    Nell said she's done with me.
        Done helping.
            Done caring.
                Done trying to fill Mom's shoes.
I'll told her she couldn't possibly
Because Mom wasn't around
Long enough to wear any.

|◀◀ ▶▶| ▶|| ■ ● DEW GD BRICKMAN
DURATION: 03:11

*Coming up: Girl finds comfort in pro wrestler, boy
struggles with the fact that he encouraged it.*

I dump a Mason jar full of dollar bills and coins I've saved onto
my bed. I confessed to Stella and Thomas my plans regarding
Naima and, surprisingly, they didn't try to talk me out of them.
I tuck a five into my pocket right as Faith drags in, her big blue
eyes as tearful as I've ever seen them.

"What's wrong?" I ask, jumping to the space in front of her.

She lengthens her arm to show the still frame of Rick Flair,
frozen on her phone screen.

"I don't get it," I say in my most comforting tone.

Her brows furrow, anger balling inside her small but mighty fists. "He was adopted and his parents *hated* wrestling. If Nature Boy couldn't make his parents proud, how can I—HOW CAN I?" She grabs my shirt collar and shoves me back and forth until I'm woozy. As I said—small but mighty.

Once I pry her sticky fingers from my shirt, she collapses, burying her face in the threads, howling as if she's lost her best friend. Alarmed, I guide her to the bed, very aware she's *never* come to me, for *anything*. She's never sat on my bed. She's never let herself cry in front of me. This, my dad would say, is a defining moment. Where we can choose to do the same thing, expecting a different outcome. Or, we can do something brave. I choose to be brave.

"First of all, I want to thank you for being here."

Her eyes bulge. "We're not on a damn talk show."

I backtrack, and rephrase. "Thank you for coming to me with this. I take my role very seriously and assure you that whatever is said in this room is between us."

"Yeah, that's what Dr. Peterson, the traitor, said."

"She's a trained professional. I'm merely your brother." The word hangs in the air between us. It's stifling. She doesn't know how to respond so I offer my pinkie. "I will not repeat a word you say."

A hint of smile pokes through. She wrangles my pinkie—nearly breaks it—and prepares to release the floodwaters.

I allow her enough space; she can't physically react without fully turning. "You are not Rick Flair. You're far more special than that sexist womanizer, I assure you."

She growls.

I adjust my posture. "Let me start over. You already make them proud. There's nothing you can do they won't support and adore."

"Don't lie to me."

I forget how young she is. Navigating the same fears and traumas as me, only years earlier. She looks to me for something concrete; something my parents would've told me, or Stella and Thomas, something to help me sleep at night.

"Okay, I'll give it to you straight."

"Please."

I glance at the August Moon poster, song bursting through the air. A vision of my parents manifests, they're looking on. They nod to me. "It doesn't matter who you make proud, as long as you find peace within yourself. Make *yourself* proud. What does *Faith* need to be happy?"

Her tears cease. She looks to the phone, and back to me with a devious smile that borders on terrifying. "To make grown men beg for mercy. I want to wrestle, and I want to be good—the best."

I arch an eyebrow, and my fingers fumble through the money left on the bed. I scrape together enough to fund what she needs. "Then you're going to need some costume supplies. In the name of Nature Boy and all his gender-biased, questionable-fashion glory. It'll at least give you the confidence to see you already are the best."

She beams. There is no hug, no pinkie grab, and no words. There are times when words can't fully capture the heart of the story. I look to the poster again and marvel that everything my parents were is still part of me.

As Faith runs out, *woo-ing* through the house, I realize I may have awakened the beast. Whatever I've done, I sing a little song, and say a little prayer, and preemptively ask for forgiveness, just in case.

RED BALLOONS

Every birthday Ray was gone, he arranged for Naima to receive six red, biodegradable balloons. Each represented a wish he had for her, and once she released them into the air, the wish remained in her heart, even if it didn't come true. Naima knew the balloons were only a symbol of what her father left behind, but there was always a part of her hoping that when one went astray, it might float back down to earth with her father attached (a childish wish, if there ever was one).

Because news of Ray's death came the very day of Naima's seventeeth celebration of life, she's vehemently opposed to any balloon, red or otherwise, for the duration of her stay on this planet. The problem is, just because a balloon isn't present doesn't mean she can't wish for things.

Or that they won't come true.

NAIMA

Church bells ring, clanging against township walls, bouncing in through every crevice of this old, two-story home. Dad used to close his eyes to hear them. Said the sounds filled the empty spaces in his heart. I'd ask, "What empty spaces?" and he'd tearfully smile and point up to the sky to reference Mom. This once, I do the same, hoping for the same peace, but I'm still empty. The God I know hasn't responded to any of my texts, deletes my voicemails—my God has blocked me on social media. If Dad were here, he'd laugh at that, but he's not.

He's not.

Not.
  Not.
    Not.
      Not.
        Not.
          Not.

After we eat (and I've re-formed what's left of my three stacks into even layers), the sun splashes through the clouds against the grass, heat clinging to my neckline, where I feel the curls spring to life. As I walk, I hear that vague sound of annoyance I'd heard the day before, only this time, I know enough to keep moving.

"The glorious songbird buzzes along, wondering where all the nectar has gone," the voice—of Dew GD Brickman—says in a gross, unpleasantly pleasant tone. If there were ever a spring to a voice, as opposed to a step, he has it and it needs to stop.

I attempt to order my feet to move along, but they're curious, tricking my brain into thinking there's something worth stopping for. I shout into the void, politely but firmly, asking them to go, but they're planted in the yard like disobedient children.

"She pauses, a sunlit goddess against the dreary backdrop of all those who've soured," he continues.

I look toward the hole in the fence, where the voice is echoing like a bullhorn. "What do you want, man?" I ask.

He hides between fencing slats so I can't see his face, or even his eye, in full view. It would be romantic if we were in a dumb rom com. Girl meets boy with hidden, mysterious face. *Bam!* Instalove! Until she discovers he doesn't actually have a face, but is a giant Lucky Charms additive instead. She breaks his heart immediately, because no respectable girl would date an additive. Too basic. Marshmallows all the way, or nothing at all. If you're not on this side of history, bye.

"To observe, respectfully."

"Whatever." I sigh. "I don't have time for this weird shit today." My feet decide to cooperate, letting me take the steps backward I'd taken forward. I have to land in the exact places I did before, or I'll have to redo everything.

Hiccup, the SOB, barks at the back door, scraping his little mud-covered paws all over the window to get outside. It interrupts everything. Dew GD Brickman. My thoughts. My feet. Time. He's all I can focus on—that furry face, cataracts gleaming against the sun, tongue falling out of one side of his mouth.

"He's so majestic," Dew says. "Like a canine god."

My shoulders hunch. "Do you see the same dog I see?"

"I do."

"Maybe *you* have cataracts. Also, you should be polite enough to ensure proper pronouns before declaring the title of 'god.' You don't know how the dog identifies."

He snickers.

"I'm not joking. Don't be ignorant."

"Apologies. I'll ask next time he chases my ankle. What are your preferred pronouns? I don't want to make *you* uncomfortable."

Quietly impressed, I meet his eye contact. "'She/her.'"

"Wonderful. I'll make a mental note."

JJ opens the back door to let Hiccup out to do his business. "Don't mind me," she says with a wave. Hiccup's feet hit the yard, and he immediately wants back inside and repeats the same actions in reverse. Maybe me and the damn dog have more in common than I thought. My feet let me continue on my path so I can put Hiccup back where he belongs (in hell) inside.

Dew raises his voice over the barking. "When she walks away, her heart anchors into the earth, forcing her to turn around."

I don't smile, don't turn. Because that's precisely what he wants from me.

What I want from me, too.

I retreat to JJ's car—a less-than-roomy Beetle—where I'm

alone with my thoughts and a grand view of the empty back alley. The car smells of cardamom and roses, and filling the two cupholders are equal parts spare change and gum wrappers, likely Kam's doing. Lost in decrypting the mass of different types of gum wrappers, I'm startled by a face in the rearview where JJ's *Marathon Granny* chain hangs. My body turns, at which the strange boy, Dew, waves, so I spin back and slink into the seat. *One. Two. Three. Four. Five. Six.*

I look again. He's gone.

As I'm turned to one side, I'm frightened again—this time by JJ swinging the driver's door open. "Lord," she huffs, tossing her suitcase-size bag into the backseat. "Thought I'd never get out of there." Her movements are slowed as she catches a breath— something I'd think a runner wouldn't experience but hell if I know. "Ready?"

I nod, trying to ignore the shadow quickly approaching. "Go, *gooo!*" I say, helping her turn the ignition.

"What are you doing?" She slaps my hand away.

"We have to go."

She's puzzled, stopping to figure me out. I reach for the keys again, she slaps again. "I'm getting to it. What's the rush?"

Tap. Tap. Tap on her window. I point. To *him.*

She rolls the window down with a smile. "Hey, there," she says. "How are you, babe?"

This close, too close, I see him. Dressed in a black T-shirt (like me) and loud pants (like me), and one of those taupe fancy fedoras with the feather in the back (so not like me; *ew*). His wide eyes and freckled Latin skin mirror mine. He notices me noticing these things, so I slouch toward my window, before my thoughts are heard, too.

"Can't complain. How are *you*?"

She leans into him as if it'll keep me from hearing her response. "I don't have an easy answer for that."

He removes his hat, lays it against his chest, revealing his lightly curled mop of dark hair. "I expect you don't."

"I hear you've met Miss Naima."

He bends to see me, and I see him, and we see one another in the bounty of the light, or whatever. "I've had the distinct pleasure, yes. She's as wonderful as you've said."

"Ugh," I groan.

"Ima!" JJ snaps.

I turn my head away completely.

"I appreciate her unfiltered honesty," he says. "It's refreshing. If she were a news clip, I'd be riveted."

"She doesn't mean anything by it," JJ replies, as if I'm not even here.

"Yes, I do," I blurt. "I mean a lot of things by it."

He laughs over JJ's massive eye roll. "Staff Sergeant Rodriguez was right."

I snap to attention. "Excuse me?"

"Aside from your grandparents, I've also spoken with your incredible father."

I suddenly choke up. "When the hell was that?"

"Last summer. Before he left."

"Last summer . . ."

Last summer. Last summer. Last summer. Last summer. Last summer. Last summer.

My fists clench, and it's suddenly too hot, or maybe too cold. My skin is chilled with sweated-covered bumps and I realize I'm panting. The air flew out of me at the mere mention of Dad, or last summer when I lost all my shit after he said he was leaving— again—and I ended up on suicide watch in the psych ward. Last summer was the worst of my life. Last summer was the end of all things as I knew them. Screw last summer.

"We'd better be on our way," JJ says, resting a hand on my leg.

My eyes are searching, filling to the brim with tears, as I recollect every conversation I avoided, every call I ignored, every voicemail I saved that may have been about this very scenario.

"I'm running behind as well," he mutters, placing the cap back on his head. "Something I'm supposed to be working on."

"Okay, sweetheart," JJ says. As she begins to pull away he chases the front bumper with urgency; it's as if he lost his air, too, and is on the cusp of finding it. "I forgot to ask—do you like strawberries?" he shouts with a strained voice.

I don't answer, can't answer, don't want to answer.

"For the fruit or against?"

I shrug. "Who the hell cares?"

He smiles. There's a deep-set dimple on the right side. Catches me off guard but I try not to let it. "*I* care. Very much so. Indifference is a lack of enthusiasm, so I'll take that as being on the cusp of *for*. Does that sound right?"

"*Okay!*"

"Okay." He seems pleased. "Noted. Maybe you could use a little good fortune."

"*Whoa,* dude. You know *nothing* about me. Not about last summer or my dad or whether or not I'm indifferent or what I could or couldn't use, so take about three thousand steps back."

"Apologies. It feels like I've known you since last summer because I heard so much about you. I realize it may not feel the same for you." He steps back two giant steps and I wonder why not three? Or four?

Or six? It should always be six.

"Makes me wonder why I haven't heard of you." Now the passion ignites throughout the tone. I can't help it. I feel like I've been set on fire.

JJ cuts in, razor sharp. "You'd have had to actually answer calls, or read your dad's letters, to know the answer to that."

Burn.

"And if you'll remember, you weren't here but a few days."

I cower in my seat, raise the proverbial white flag.

"I didn't mean to cause a problem," he says.

"You're no problem here," JJ says. "We'd better be on our way, though."

He lays his hat back on his head, a slower, more deliberate sadness with the movement. I did that, I caused whatever he's thinking about or feeling now. And though I don't know the *dewd,* I'm having a hard time accepting that he knows me.

"Have a good day," he shouts as we back out of the drive.

"Tell Stella to come take some of this apple butter off my hands for her stand."

He bows again, waves us off. "Will do," he says before JJ's window goes all the way up.

I giggle under my breath. My brain forces it out of me before I explode into splatters. "Will do, *DEW.*"

"Naima . . . ," JJ says. "That's enough." *Is it, though?*

I pull out my phone to make a note, hoping to break the pressure of wanting to speak it aloud again. My fingers punch the keys frantically, *six times.*

Will do Dew Will do Dew Will do Dew Will do Dew Will do Dew Will do Dew

It only feels slightly better because the words are still hanging on my tongue. I bite the tip until it bleeds, letting one quiet *will do Dew* slip. I'm relieved once it's out of me, but JJ's noticeably more agitated. This is how summers here go. Just as with Hiccup, it takes time for us to find our footing, whether Dad's here or not. Because with JJ and Kam, there's no hiding in my head. They see me—like *really* see every layer.

Usually, by the time I'm ready to leave this old house, to start a crappy new school year with Nell and Christian and Dad if he's not overseas, we'll have found some kind of "normal." I'm only just feeling it: This is it; the only normal I'll have.

(Will do, Dew)

As we pull away, this boy stands in one spot watching us fade and I feel this tugging. Not in my stomach, like when I think of missing Dad, but in my heart.

"That boy's had it rough," JJ says, rounding the corner of another patriotically decorated road. All the reds, whites, and blues aligned on every light post.

"What do you mean?" I ask, reluctant.

She angles her glare toward me with a smirk. "Never mind. The Naima *I* know won't want that mess up in her head."

She's right. I don't.

And so I decide here and now I won't.

Apply another layer of Dragon Girl red, and another.

Scrunch my toes between passing objects

Stop thinking of the first day at my new school.

Others said I was odd; outcast to fend for

Myself

At a time

I felt

All alone.

So I tell myself *maybe I'll give him a chance.*

Besides.

A girl reserves the right

To change her mind.

JJ taught me that.

Voicemail

Dad

cell
October 31 at 11:55 PM

Transcription Beta

"Did you dress up for Halloween? We had a small party here but nothing like the ones Nell throws. Did you at least try to talk to people or did you hide in your room and count hexagons while talking to PS? I know the answer because I already spoke with Nell. If you don't at least try to work through these things, they'll always control you. Eh, what do I know? For the record, I love who you are. So don't change. But also, change a little. For your sake, and mine. Oh, and I'm sorry Christian dressed as that clown from *It*. I told Nell not to let him, but I guess that didn't matter."

▶ 0:00 |▬▬▬▬▬▬▬▬▬▬▬▬▬▬▬▬▬▬▬▬▬▬ -0:48

Speaker   **Call Back**   **Delete**

Email Draft (Unsent)

New Message   ✕

To

Subject

I legit almost killed Christian
   When he snuck into my room
      With that damn Pennywise mask
        But Nell followed
           To trade all my candy for
              Crap homemade granola
Which turned
My priorities
Faster than she could say
"But it's for your health."

⏮ ⏭ ▶❚ ◼ ⏺ **DEW GD BRICKMAN**
DURATION: 7:16

Later on Dew's News: *Ridic City is not an actual location but a state of mind (because life is ridiculous at times).*

"You're sure about this?" Stella asks on her way out the door.

I adjust my hat. "Positive."

"Okay," she says, one foot still inside. "And I can't give you a ride?"

"I'd rather walk. Gives me time to go over my plan."

Her eyes dissect me. I stand taller. "Come on, Faith," she shouts.

Faith barrels out of her room wearing a fall pleather jacket—one of Stella's old fringe items—that's been covered in multi-colored craft feathers. "Ready."

Stella's eyes nearly *boing* from their sockets. "What's . . . *this*?"

Faith flips her high ponytail back behind her shoulder. "I'm reinventing the Rick Flair style. You can call me Nature Chick."

"*But*—" Stella's eyes narrow, but I stop her with one flick of the hand.

I lean down to Faith's level, where the glitter blots over her lids. "How do *you* feel about it, Nature Chick?"

"Pretty damn good." She's beaming. And though Stella may bite her tongue until it bleeds, she manages a smile and urges Faith out the door. "All right, then. Let's go."

"*Woo.*"

Before the door closes Stella turns with a desperate whisper. "Nature Chick?"

"Dripping with misogyny, I know. But she likes it, so we *must* support her."

"Must we?"

"We must."

"You're too good for this world," she says, closing the door behind her.

When I see the car pull out, I begin my walk to Baked & Caffeinated, avoiding the buzz of the farmers' market crowd. August Moon and the Paper Hearts serenade my every step. Images of Dad thumping his bass guitar alongside August and Mom sharing the mic flash before me. Except, it never happened. The duo, aptly named Phil & Al, who were mere openers for no-names, aren't on my playlist. Everything vanished when they died; long before their lyrical jazz and funk-rock beats could make it to a record, cassette, disc, or SoundCloud. They never made it to a recording studio after leaving August Moon, so all that's left are memories of what Phil & Al longed to become, but never did. They were an almost—an unanswered calling. I fear that is all I'll be as well.

The metal bell rings when I step inside, but there is no space to maneuver through. My heart thumps.

"Excuse me," I say, pushing past the line of customers. "Sorry, excuse me."

My stomach bunches when I turn back to see the maze I've created swiftly disappearing behind me. I close my eyes near the register to take a full breath, a count of ten, to ward off the little pulses starting in my hands. Once they pulse, my whole body shakes, and that's when my version of Earth is launched into space, smashing me into the oxygen-free atmosphere.

"It's okay," I tell myself aloud. "You're okay."

"Who's okay?" Violet asks. Her lips shine a glossed shade of magenta I find oddly calming.

"I am."

"Yes, you are," she says with a smile. She brushes up next to me with her patchouli scent. I freeze, still focused on the faces as she hands a customer change. Instant regret takes over. I should've stayed home, where it's safe. Away from the bodies that multiply on top of me.

"What's up?" she asks. "You're not on the schedule, are you?"

"No. I need advice."

"*Ooh,* sounds serious."

I follow her to the espresso machine, where she brews multiple shots without so much as blinking. Her hands move like a seasoned ballerina's feet.

"I want to do something for a girl, and—"

"*WHAT—A GIRLFRIEND* AND YOU DIDN'T TELL ME?" She lets go of the shot, knocking a row of them over. She grabs my hands, and guides me into a dual jumping situation with her ear-piercing squeal.

I pull her hands down, forcing the vertical movements to end. "Not a girlfriend—*friend.* She's going through a rough time and I want to do something nice."

Customers become noticeably agitated, as we've boxed ourselves into this quiet moment alone.

"You should totally get your palms read together," she says. "It's so romantic. Well, except that time me and Navian Raj went and the psychic said one of us would die, but she couldn't tell us who, so he spent our entire sophomore year avoiding me in case I 'brought him down' with me, but I didn't die, and he's still alive, so—"

"Violet," I interrupt. "Did you drink coffee?"

She points to the cubby where three cans of Red Bull stand. "Not supposed to have them but life is short and *OMG,* the psychic was right."

"Can I order?" a customer interjects.

"So sorry, sir," she says. I stand next to her as she cashes the man out, then remakes the string of shots she dumped. She cups her hand around her mouth and musters all the voice between her chords. "Big Foot, I need youuuuuu!" It comes out grumbly, somewhat monstrous, with a gurgle at the end. I'm guessing that's the Red Bull working.

He emerges from the back with his hair looking as if he'd been laying down in a pile of garbage, leaving me to wonder what he actually does on those "breaks." With tired, squinted eyes, he waves. "Hey, man. You're not on."

"Just came in to say hi."

"It's Ridic City in here. Want a shift?"

The faces blur into a blobby mess. "Can't. On my way to something."

"No probs."

"Sorry, Dew," Violet says. "Maybe you can text me how I can help later. When we're less busy."

"I . . . don't have your number." It's the first time I've muttered those words to anyone, let alone a girl.

She rushes over for a pen, grabs my hand, and writes her number on my palm. "If you decide to get these sweaty things read, erase my number so she doesn't connect us."

"Okay?"

"Seriously." She points with a stern face.

"Later," Big Foot says with his fingers shaped into a peace sign.

"Text me," Violet repeats the exact instant one of the blurred faces I pass becomes crystal clear: Dodge. He's not smiling. I try to move faster, but the bodies hold me still, at his chest level, where I see the threads of his tee have come loose. He peers down, his warm breath blowing in puffs.

"Hey," I say as cool as possible.

Someone backs up, shoves me into him before I catch my feet. He pushes back and I knock into the crowd, falling to the floor. An older woman helps me up.

"Are you okay, hun?" she asks. Everyone stops to look at me. *The showstopper.*

I remove my hat and smooth my curls. "Fine, thanks."

"You okay, Dew?" Violet shouts from beyond. I manage a shaky thumbs-up.

I turn to Dodge, shivers slithering through me. "I'm so, *so* sorry. I didn't mean to."

He looks away, pretends I'm nothing but a ghost. Perhaps I am. Maybe that's what I've been all this time. As soon as a path to the door opens, I leave as fast as I can.

Mom used to say, "Kindness can manifest in the most unorthodox of ways; like with the layers of a person, you have to peel back the outer blanket to get to the good stuff."

Dodge Teagarden offered *some* form of kindness whether he meant to or not. He could have hit me. He didn't. I look through the window, my reflection mirroring his, and we catch eyes as he moves to the register to order his mocha latte.

Maybe he's in need of a friend, too.

THE GOOD FORTUNE OF
STRAWBERRY CAKE

When Andrew Brickman was an infant, the neighbors' door, directly to the left of Phillip and Alejandra Diaz's studio apartment, always smelled of strawberries. Alejandra—who dropped out of high school at fifteen so she and Phillip could care for her ailing *madre* by day, while sneaking into twenty-and-over clubs to play music at night—smelled the sweet aroma twirling through the hallway, up, and into her nose as she fed baby Andrew. She always connected the smell with happiness and good fortune, because the neighbors always appeared happy, seemed a little better off, and smelled of strawberries. Alejandra decided if she could make strawberry cake, her family, too, would have good fortune.

On the afternoon of Andrew's third-to-final day with his parents, Alejandra, and her sidekick Andrew, finally perfected the strawberry cake. And though Andrew should be angered at the mere mention of strawberries after that fateful day, he chooses to embrace the good fortune that came along with them: *He* wasn't in the car when they passed. A strawberry cake, to him, is the epitome of luck; a serendipitous taste of being alive.

NAIMA

The radio streams through the ride into town. I can't say if I prefer the silence with Nell or gospel and NPR with JJ. With Nell, I can think of new ways to annoy her, but with JJ my choices are learn or pray. Neither will do right now. We zigzag across the small, pear-shaped town, and, at the flags that line every last house my stare drifts out of focus. I don't know where his voice comes from, *Dad,* but it pierces through my mind so clear, it's like he's right here on the console between JJ and me, nestled over the spare change and gum wrappers. My fingers find my throat, clawing at the skin to break free from the sound of him. I count to rid myself, to forget.

One. Two. Three. Four. Five. Six.

I can't run from it. The memory of the day we got the news.

"What kind of cake did she get?" Caroline—boring-ass Christian's loud-ass girlfriend—said from the kitchen. I overheard everyone gathering in my honor, but couldn't remove myself from counting the hexagons. I hadn't heard from Dad, and hadn't received my balloons. I knew—*I knew*—something had happened.

And it happened because of me.

"White on white," Christian replied. My face scrunched up at the audacity. Why would he think "white on white" is a thing people say? I stood from the bed and thought about stomping out and correcting, but Nell raised him and that's why he is the way he is. I could already hear their responses. Caroline—the six-foot private-schooled art major with bad bangs—would be like "Whaaatt?" like some cliché trope, and Christian, another walking cliché, with his dumb haircut and too-skinny skinny jeans, would follow with "Dude, chill; not *everything* is racist," after I schooled him on sensitivity and being a person of color in this world.

He forgot, often, I'm only partly white, and that foul-tasting jokes ignite my inner Hulk. That's exactly how the conversation would go, I decided, because they've never been anything but 2-D characters to me, and that's the way I prefer it. Everything *is* racist when you're a little darker than your white family. If I can't escape microaggressions about my hair, my body, my *anything,* they shouldn't be able to escape their own unclaimed privilege.

Would you rather invite boring-ass Christian and loud-ass Caroline over for a white-on-white and vanilla discussion or pull all your teeth out with pliers?

"Happy birthday, Naima!" Caroline shouted, poking her head in my room. Her hair swung into her mouth. My gum lost its flavor, but I waited to add it to the gum wall until she left.

"Thanks, lady," I muttered just as Nell might. That word echoed—*lady lady lady lady lady lady lady.*

She stared. "Ready for cake?"

"Yep." I feared part of Nell had ingrained itself in me and I obsessed over it, wishing I could redo this moment or erase it altogether.

"It's the best part of any birthday, am I right?"

"Uh-huh."

I tapped my foot against my quilt's hem six times directly in the center of the hexagon. Of the six, I was slightly off center on the third, so I started again. It was at this time, approximately 11:13 A.M. EST, Nell pulled into the drive and exited her vehicle with a cake and balloons—the balloons Dad was *supposed* to send.

She had a solid grip on the balloon strings, but the wind picked up in gusts. It wasn't supposed to be windy, but it was; it's one of the first things I thought when I stepped outside. The balloons floated high above her, colliding into each other from the angry air pushing past. Panic rushed through me in tidal waves. Cue "End of the Road," an old song by Boyz II Men. It was playing on the radio Christian had turned on in the kitchen.

Before my thoughts caught up, before I could connect the stars in our constellation, I ran from my room and out the front door to grab ahold of the balloons, but I was too late. They fought with all their might to be free. I leapt forward, fingers outstretched, but the wind was too strong. *Then. I felt it.*

The weightlessness of the balloons as they untethered from her grasp. She let go, and I let go. I counted the seconds it took for life to unmute between my ears—*seven*—and I wished it had happened one second earlier. Nothing settled. We unsettled. Life unsettled. As I reached from the tips of my toes, I attempted to chase those six red balloons. *Always six, always red.*

Minutes later, when the balloons became distant red dots in the sky, my eyes pulled back to Earth, where this unexplainable series of circumstances suddenly tied together. A dark vehicle—a sedan—crawled alongside the curb, past the other cars. The wheels slowed to a stop in front of our house. The balloons—Dad's wishes for me—levitated up, between the clouds, where they disappeared forever to float somewhere beyond my vision, somewhere Mom had gone.

And then, I knew. Somewhere Dad had gone, too.

And I counted. And I counted. And I counted. And I counted. And I counted. And I counted.

Let me inscribe my wishes, I said,
   Fill them with helium, I said
      And set them free, I said.
      And out of nowhere,
         That goddamn Truvía song played in my mind.
         But not before "End of the Road."

The cross streets near downtown Ivy Springs are lined with various local vendors from surrounding counties, and there are a few I pull myself out of bed for each year. While it might seem strange to someone who doesn't know me—"how odd for a girl who's just lost her father to be merrily skipping [for the record, I'd never skip] around downtown Ivy Springs, sliding silken flowers behind her ears, and tasting all the samples"—but this is *my* version of normal: avoidance on every level. Literally. My therapist said, out of four unique styles, I have an avoidant/dismissive attachment personality—meaning I'd rather keep to mydamnself than rely on anyone else. Somewhere along my journey, I learned it hurts too much to seek security and fail to receive. Dad would totally understand and approve, but he's not here, which is why attachments and connections are worthless to me right now.

The moment I think it, *Dad's dead*, my brain flops. With a toothpick in hand, I'm suddenly acutely aware of the crowd. The noise goes from buzzing to full-fledged commotion. I turn for JJ, but she's lost between swaying bodies and heat—*my God the Midwest and its sweltering June heat.*

I catch a glimpse of myself in an elephant-ear trailer's silver exterior to see my Dragon Girl lips have smeared and bled across my face. What the hell kind of horror show is happening? More important, why is Nell *still* texting me about the gum pile? Like, let it go (the irony here doesn't escape me).

Penelope-Smellope: *I've been scraping gum off for 2 hours.*

Penelope-Smellope: *Just how I wanted to spend my day.*

Penelope-Smellope: *Was this because I asked you to chew your gum quietly? How did this happen? Where did I go wrong? How would Ray handle this? Help me help you.*

I clasp my phone tight, as a hand grabs at me. My reaction is to swat at whoever's touching me (they're lucky I didn't do the chokehold Dad taught).

"Oh, dear, I didn't mean to scare you," a woman—about JJ's age with earrings that don't rival the size of Earth—says. "You're Ray's daughter, aren't you?"

My limbs hang heavy. I attempt to nod but the movement dizzies me more.

"I'm sorry for your loss, sweetie. He was such a good man. We're thankful for his sacrifice."

Was. Was. Was. Was. Was. Was.

"Thanks." I pull away.

Another hand spins me around. "Your father was a hero. We owe him our freedom."

Was. Was. Was. Was. Was. Was.

"Thank you . . . ," I say again. This time the words trail. The heat rises, coating my cheeks in a discomfort I can't escape. If this were a page from a magazine, I'd pluck the scissors from JJ's junk drawer and cut myself out.

More hands grab at me, pull at my arms, spin me in circles to see them—*I see you; do you see me?*—to repeat the same sentiments. Everything they offer is in the past tense. They're all sorry. They're all saddened. They're all grateful. For who my father *was.*

Was. Was. Was. Was. Was. Was.

I'm trapped in a sea of apology and patriotism and I'm thankful, but I don't need a new reminder every second. In a matter of mere minutes, I've been surrounded. My head spins and my vision blurs in and out. Tightening lungs try to breathe in and expel but they're working overtime, getting little oxygen where it needs to be—my brain.

My limbs feel weightless, swaying, pulling me under.

"JJ?" I shout; *think* I shout. Maybe it's a whisper. Maybe it's in my head. She's somewhere I can't see. A tingle shoots through my feet, straight up into my head, before I fall back, crumble to the concrete. Now all of these strangers are patting my back, rubbing my hair—*don't ever touch my hair*—asking if I'm okay, if I need some water, if I want something to eat, a cracker, maybe? What I want is to scream. To yell as loud as the sky will carry; I want my voice to pierce the atmosphere with such force, the skin will fall off everyone's bones. *That* is the pain I'm holding, ready to break free. Not here, though. I'll swallow it, again, so everything can be fine; it will be fine. *FINE.* I'm not fine. I *was* not fine.

Was. Was. Was. Was. Was. Was.

"Naima?" I hear from beyond the swell. JJ rushes toward me, a winning sprint across the finish if I ever saw one, through the pack that's formed a trench around me. I'm trapped on this stretch of road where corn dog sticks lay at my feet. They are the moat, and I am the castle, trapped inside myself, only able to view what's happening through the clear box surrounding me.

I can't.

"JJ." My voice is quiet. The burn of her name forces it back down my throat. Her hand finds my back. Long, gentle strokes remind me of the times I cried into her as a child. When my attachment style leaned more on the secure side and I knew I could trust. I let my body fall into her loving hands, but the feeling in me has gone. People are mere colors and shapes, vaguely waving in and out of my tunnel vision. "Maybe she needs to talk to someone," I overhear. "Or medication." And the loudest: "She needs her parents."

"Can you give us some room, please?" JJ removes one hand to swat the flies and those flies step back. Not six feet, but two. They've all hushed to whispers, and even the music playing over the loudspeaker calms. I hear them. *She lost her Dad. Poor thing. I can't imagine all she's been through. Lost her mom, too.* But the one I hear most, the one that rings louder than the rest, is something I hadn't realized until an ignorant bystander who knows nothing of me said it.

She's an orphan.

Voicemail

Dad

cell
November 19 at 7:27 AM

Transcription Beta

"I've been told there is a chance I can come home for your birthday in May. I know it's early and I don't want to say too much until I'm sure, but I want to give you something to hope for. We all need a little hope. There are days I'm not sure where mine went. Where does it go? I asked the chaplain that very question and you know what he told me? Hope never leaves *us—we're* the ones who abandon it. So don't abandon it, Ima. Hold it like a balloon string and never let go."

▶ 0:00 |━━━━━━━━━━━━━━━━━━━━ -0:30

Speaker   **Call Back**   **Delete**

Email Draft (Unsent)

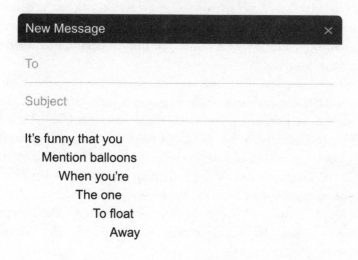

It's funny that you
    Mention balloons
        When you're
            The one
                To float
                    Away

⏮ ⏭ ▶⏸ ⏹ ⏺ **DEW GD BRICKMAN**
DURATION: 3:03

Breaking: Indianapolis boy intrigued by deathly strawberries, swiftly learns lesson.

"Your arms?" my mother asked, pointing, after I tasted a bite of strawberry cake. English, her second language, broke apart back then. She caught on to most parts but got stuck inside others. Splotches. Radish-red splotches. She ripped my clothes off in a rush, and ran a cool bath. The water never fully heated anyway, so when she turned the knob all the way right, the tub filled with icy water. I remember the burn. From the tips of my fingers to the very bottom of my feet. Mostly in my mouth. I tasted *fire*. Mom threw in handfuls of oatmeal and a splash of milk as she cried, "*why why why,*" running through the small space to understand what had happened. We didn't have a house phone or cell, so the only way to contact Dad was to knock on the good-fortune neighbors' door for their phone, trek to the pay phone down the road, or take a bus to tell him in person because he drove our only car.

It was almost dinnertime, so Mom decided to keep me in the water until he arrived. I sat there, my skin shrinking, while she searched the kitchen for an answer to my reaction. I hadn't gone much to doctors, so she couldn't have known about my food allergies. It wasn't until I went into anaphylactic shock that Mom burst through the door with my dripping wet body in her arms to beg the good-fortune neighbors to call an ambulance.

I don't remember much about what happened after, except when I awoke, my mother was in tears at my bedside. "What happened?" I asked.

"I didn't know," she wailed. "You're allergic. *Milk.* Eggs. Nuts. Dairy. Even *strawberries.*"

And so the good fortune and happiness others could find would not be the same for me. But I still can't help but believe in the good fortune of strawberries. It was a risk, but the night Staff Sergeant Rodriguez first told me about Naima, I decided she deserved the good fortune my mother, father, and I didn't.

Just in case, I keep an EpiPen handy. Stella and Thomas have intricate instructions from my doctor about how to use it, and what to do if I'm having a reaction. This is also the story of how Lady Clean Cuisine came to be, and why our food and general way of being are sometimes separate from those of the world.

And sometimes, why I am.

NAIMA

I rub my eyes to clear the blur. JJ kneels next to me. "This is my fault. You're not ready."

I think on the string of carefully constructed sentences. *Not ready.* How do I become ready? Are you ever? She brushes a stray curl from my cheek, cradling my face in her hands. The sun gathers around her, darkening her features but illuminating the rest. Reminds me of photos of Mom—my heart stops again—and Dad, now, too. I hold my stare as long as my lungs inhale, silently thinking *breathe* six times.

"I'm fine," I lie. "I want my cheese now."

She releases her hands and helps me to my feet. "Not too fast."

My head deflates as if I'm the one who's been filled with helium. Sounds gradually fill in, and faces clarify.

"Should've eaten your damn pancakes. Blood sugar's probably low." JJ's voice is calm, soft. But there's fear in the way she pauses between words. As if seeing me this way reminds her that I will always struggle with my mind; it will always scuffle for control. The point is that I never let it keep me down for long.

She reaches deep into her giant sack of a purse and hands me a bottle of water. I take a swig. It's tepid, all the minerals heated through. We're interrupted by another bystander, a tall man wearing an electric-blue apron. He abandoned his stand to offer me a small paper cup filled with liquid.

"Here, drink this," he says. His shadow is as long as the town clock is tall. It bends with his every breath. His hands shake the cup in front of me as if gesturing a ball I'm to fetch.

I shove the cup out of my personal space with blunt force. "You might've drugged it."

"Uh," the man stutters, "I promise you, it's not drugged."

"You probably drank from it. I don't want your spit in my mouth." The sun is in my eyes; his shadow moves, slinking behind him. Dad said you can see a man's truth in his eyes, but I can't see. "Also, stranger danger, and all that jazz."

His face scrunches up in wrinkled layers.

Most of the people have gone on with their lives. The music is turned up, and the whispers have grown to full-throttle conversations. A few still linger and can't believe Ray Rodriguez's daughter could be so rude to a kind stranger. *Gasp!*

JJ steps between us and grabs the cup, sloshing the water onto the tops of my feet. "Thank you so much." She catches the weight of me when my feet threaten to tumble.

"Just trying to help." The man reluctantly goes, his eyes turning back every few steps. She pulls me into the open pocket beyond the crowd. We pause somewhere between the general store and my favorite—Paint the Sky—the place Dad and I took a few classes together. I try not to notice, but the sign hangs above us; if there ever was a literal manifestation of Dad plus a sign, it's here. Like, right *here.*

"People worry," she says. "You can be a little nicer about it."

"I don't feel like being nice."

"I know." Her nails dig into my arm when she grabs ahold. "I don't always feel like smiling in church when Hattie Gillespie tells me my hips have widened since retirement, but I damn well do. Kindness matters. Not only when it's hard—*especially* when it is."

A giggle escapes. "*She* thinks *your* hips widened? Has she looked in a mirror?"

JJ's grip lightens, and she smiles, too. "Listen—it's not gonna be easy. It's just not. If we acknowledge our right to feel like hell, for as long as we need to, maybe others will give us a little more breathing room, you know? Then, they'll be kind, and you'll be kind in return, and round and round we go." Her eyes dazzle me, remind me this pain isn't only mine.

I nod.

"We can do this next week," she says. "We don't have to be *here* if you don't want to."

"It's tradition. You said it yourself." When she says "here," she doesn't mean the farmers' market, but "here" as in the sinking grief. And I get it, I do, but it feels like there's no way out of it. I'm so out of my body, I imagine a red balloon moving with the crowd. I close my eyes, shake the idea from my mind. It's gone. *Magic.*

"It's fine," I say, quiet, "can we walk?"

She reaches for my hand; I take it and together, we walk.

We find a steady rhythm floating between stands. It's okay, she's okay, I'm okay—*we're okay.* We finally reach the cheese stand (i.e., the most glorious spot in the whole market), but JJ leads me to a different tent. I see the cheese, fingers reaching, but can't get to it. Everyone takes the samples held by toothpicks. One by one, they disappear. I try to contain the panic, but JJ's guiding me to this sugar-scrub stand and all I want is to break free from her shackles and get a few cubes before they're gone.

Gone. Gone. Gone. Gone. Gone. Gone.

"Ima!" JJ forces my attention to the petite woman standing behind a long table covered with sugar scrubs that smell like weeds and sour fruit. Her long, fire-spiraled hair climbs down the length of her black tee, which says, BABES UNITE. I'm pulled toward her magenta cat's-eye glasses framing her perfectly angled face, to her nose pierced with a metal ring, down to her matte ruby-red lips. "This is Stella," JJ adds. "Dew's mom. And Faith's. Have you met her?"

"Nope," I manage.

"Can I hug you?" the woman asks.

I hesitate. "I mean, I hate germs, but *okay?*"

She walks around the table and tightly wraps both hands around me. Like, she didn't even consider how terrible I feel. I imagine shoving her off, into traffic—intrusive thought alert!—but distract myself with the off-kilter pattern on a passing woman's shirt. Her chin folds into my shoulder as she sways us back and forth. JJ takes a step backward to allow us the room to do whatever this is.

I abruptly push her away. "Actually, I'd rather not touch, thanks."

"Oh," she says. "*That's* what you meant by the germ thing. I'm so sorry for imposing."

"She's not much of a hugger," JJ adds.

"Neither is Faith. I completely understand."

Faith flashes a thumbs-up from Stella's shadow.

"I know words don't help much, but I'm very sorry about your dad," Stella says. "Very, very sorry."

I force back my urge to shout, instead lowering my voice to a throaty growl. "You're right. Words don't help."

JJ grimaces, so I look away as Stella's hands cup over her mouth, eyes watering the way condensation builds with early morning dew *(DEW!)*. I turn to JJ. "Can I get my cheese?"

Her jaw falls agape, hand firmly on one hip. Like *I'm* the one making this weird. "Hang on a minute."

"I'm sorry," Stella says, moving back behind the table. "I don't want to make you uncomfortable."

"It's all right," JJ says. "She has strong opinions, especially when it comes to germs and cheese and most everything."

Stella chuckles. "I respect that."

There's a lull in the conversation. My thoughts return to the hands still stealing the cheese—*my cheese*—across the way.

"What are you two up to?" she asks us.

"Celebrating the birthday we missed," JJ answers. "Just turned seventeen."

"Dew's sixteenth is in August. What do you like to do for your birthday, Naima?"

The question catches me off guard. All the birthdays before, I'd have run down my list of usual preferences: wishing on six red balloons, sorting and counting my marshmallows, going on whatever adventure Dad pre-planned, eating white cake with vanilla frosting (*not* white-on-white), eating cheddar jack cheese on a toothpick, going to Tuscany Grove for breadsticks, and winning an epic dance-off battle.

I shrug. My fingers begin to pick, toes scrunched, eyes flitting from thing to thing. *It's starting.* I survey all the ways out of this moment. It's the suffocating feeling that creeps back; invisible walls closing in from all sides.

She and JJ lock eyes. "So," Stella interrupts my sequence, "maybe you could come over sometime."

"Why would I do that?" I don't mean to say it.

"Dew doesn't have many friends that I know of, and he's struggling, and I was hoping . . . maybe . . . I don't know. I'm sorry; it's not my place." Her voice fades as a customer approaches. "I'll be right with you," she tells them.

"She'd love to," JJ interjects.

"I don't want to—"

JJ's face sharpens, along with her words. "We'll talk about it later."

"So much for consent, am I right?" The words shoot fire, singeing off every hair on their bodies.

"*Oh, no.*" Stella sighs. "Don't do anything you don't want to. Please. Forget it. And don't feel guilty. You do what's best for you. Forget it, *please.* Dew will find his own way. I shouldn't put that on you. *Especially* now."

JJ tries to smooth it over. "We'll let them sort it out. They're almost grown and probably don't want us meddling."

"You're right about that," I add.

She turns her neck in my direction and I know I'm pushing the boundaries. My mouth clamps shut to keep further incriminating words from marching out. She's the one who taught me these things; shouldn't she be proud or something?

Stella smiles. "I get frustrated. He's had a hard time adjusting in town, and the kids at school weren't very kind last year. But, if you know Dew, he doesn't let anything get to him, at least on the surface. But it gets to him. He only wants a friend and can't seem to find one. What a lonely place to be."

"Breaks my heart," JJ says. "Kids can be so cruel."

"Not only kids."

"Shame."

"I hoped Ivy Springs would be more accepting than it's been. His recorder makes him a standout, but he's always been outside looking in. It's hard to watch. I feel helpless."

My features soften. I try to stay silent, but can't. "Why *does* he have that thing anyway?"

She sighs again, heavy and long. "His therapist suggested different things that might help him cope with social anxiety and I remembered how much my recorder helped me in college. Plus, he loves pretending he's on the news. It's sort of his thing. We understand not everyone gets it or accepts him as he is."

"Being recorded is a violation of my rights," I blurt. "And it's weird as hell."

"Ima!" JJ cries out. "I know what you're trying to say, but remember to word things with *kindness* and *compassion,* okay? I'm sure he means no harm."

I shrink. "Being recorded without permission *is* against the law, isn't it? It's intrusive to stand outside, minding your business, only to be interrupted by him narrating my every move into some machine. I don't want to be on *Dew's News.* I didn't give him permission." The irony of intrusion pulses through my veins. As if I've never been *that* to everyone around me, simply by existing with my exhausting routines. I won't admit our similarities aloud, but I'm beginning to see more of *me* in him.

Stella thinks on it. "I never thought of it like that. I've been so focused on helping him get better. I certainly don't want you to feel violated. *God*—what an infringement on your personal feeling of safety."

I relax my tightened posture as a way of saying thanks.

"Honestly, if he knew it made others uncomfortable, he'd feel terrible and probably stop using it. Even if it set him back."

"If it's helping, let him be," JJ says. "Maybe just mention he should ask before using around Naima, which she'll have no problem deciding for herself. He'll move on when he's ready.

Might even end up being a top anchor on WTHR someday and we'll say we knew him when. Right, Ima?"

They both look to me with different expressions. JJ with a *you'd better agree so we can move on,* and Stella pleading *please say it's okay.* They refill the cheese tray across the street, so I nod.

"You're too evolved, Ima girl," Kam often says. But I can't help how fast the awesome moves. I just follow.

"It's settled," JJ says in her professor tone. "Do you need more apple butter? I've got so many in the cupboard, Kam's threatened to set up shop on the side of the road."

"I'd be happy to take them."

"Have Dew come over to get them later."

"Thank you for being so kind to us. Makes this small town feel more like *home.*" Stella touches JJ's hand, lets it linger, and releases. Vomit rises up into my throat. Think of all the micro-organisms swimming around. "It was lovely to meet you," she tells me. "Thank you for your honesty."

Lovely. Lovely. Lovely. Lovely. Lovely. Lovely, Mom.

"She can't help herself," JJ jokes. They chuckle as I'm pulled off toward *another* effing stand that's *not* the cheese stand. I try and *I try and I try and I try and I try and I try* to be good with perusing all this crap I don't care about, but at some point, I snap. I break away and sprint to the only place that will make this day better—the cheese stand.

"Do you have any cheddar jack?" I ask politely, and with a level of kindness JJ would praise.

"Just sold the last of it," the man says.

This is fine. I'm fine. Everything's fine. *

screams forever into the black hole I'd like to fall into

Voicemail

Dad

cell
November 24 at 6:33 PM

Transcription Beta

"Happy Thanksgiving, baby girl! I hope you're . . . [sigh] . . . okay. Be sure to give thanks to Nell and Christian for taking care of you. I know they're not your *preferred* company, but they care. You haven't answered the last few calls, and, well, remember when we'd sit along the edge of the bed and breathe together until you relaxed after an attack? [undecipherable] [coughs] I was hoping you'd count the breaths with me. As you can hear, it's kind of noisy and, well, most of the time it doesn't bother me, but others, well, I was hoping to hear your voice right now. Nell . . . she's great . . . but she doesn't understand. I've been rubbing the worry stone you lent me—thank you—and writing in my journals to distract myself. I might be home sooner. I hope. [undecipherable] I'm . . . thankful . . . for [undecipherable]" [no signal]

▶ 0:00 |———————————————————— -1:27

Speaker   **Call Back**   **Delete**

Email Draft (Unsent)

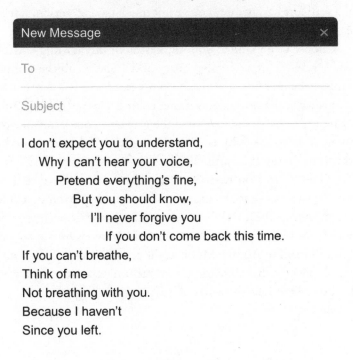

I don't expect you to understand,
   Why I can't hear your voice,
    Pretend everything's fine,
     But you should know,
       I'll never forgive you
         If you don't come back this time.
If you can't breathe,
Think of me
Not breathing with you.
Because I haven't
Since you left.

⏮ ⏭ ▶❙❙ ■ ● **DEW GD BRICKMAN**
DURATION: 1:19

*Today's forecast had a sudden shake-up. Storms
unexpectedly headed this way. Take cover.*

After purchasing one red balloon from the general store, I am
forced to follow the swell of crowds on my journey home. I'm
careful to sneak past the tent where Stella and Faith could blow
my cover. Stella's waist-deep in sales while Faith stands near the
back shouting at the air while kicking and punching at nothing
in particular. I melt into the shadows.

If you are hoping to understand why I'd go to such lengths for a soul I've barely met, you've not much paid attention. Kindness is something you choose each day.

"Choose to be kind at your darkest hour, my darling," Mom said, "and you already rule your world." She'd rub the dimple in my cheek and kiss the curls atop my head.

I glance at the time: I'm running behind. *Again.* I wish I could rewire my brain to manage time the way everyone wants me to. If you were to ask why time is my nemesis, I'd have to lie by omission. To say the truth aloud—that if my parents had left a few seconds later on their way to pick me up, they'd still be alive—reduces me to an angry, unkind me. My parents would hate knowing their only son can not let go of how time stole them from him, that it's what fuels him. It keeps him awake at night, humming August Moon as the seconds tick by. The only way to avenge what time took from me is to take time from myself, burning it into the ashes of my parents' effigy.

I am fire.

NAIMA

We are stopped by an old friend of Dad's on our way to the car. Her name is Constance McGreevy and she's carrying three cloth bags overflowing with produce and bath salts. She sets the bags on the ground, tugs at my shoulders and studies my face, uninvited. "I'm sure you hear how much you look like Ray, but you're all Josephine."

The time is 2:17 P.M. EST. Exactly six weeks ago, I aged another year, whereas seventeen years in the past, I came to life. Four pounds, three ounces, and two months premature, I rapidly surfaced, a mass of dense caramel curls, colossal pale green eyes brimming with apprehension, and a heart pleading for acceptance in a world I'd soon find excessive fault with.

In the backseat of an old green Camaro, Dad said, I shot out of Mom's body like a cannon. I wasn't expected yet; at their ages, I hadn't been expected at all. Mom had a difficult time carrying due to her diabetes, and I didn't make it easier (story of my life) by arriving so suddenly; breach at one point, with the umbilical cord tangled around my neck at another. My father, equally as young and terrified as my mother, would prove to be the one who'd ensure my healthy delivery, despite the mess it'd make in the car he'd worked so long to afford. I was created in unsettled form, between Mom's family, who couldn't accept her decision to keep me, and the financial burden Mom's medical needs placed on my parents' relationship so early on. Every molecule of me twinkled and electrified into this force so unstoppable, even Mom couldn't survive me.

I'm told once I came out, Mom called me Butterfly; said to fly far and free. Except it was *her* time to fly far and free. By the time Dad got us to the hospital, doctors couldn't save her, but they saved me. I became Dad's reason. To laugh and cry, love, and to hope. But mostly, to go. Because when I look at myself, I've always seen Mom.

He must've, too.

This would prove to be the origin of my internal restlessness and the punch line to every bad joke Nell made when Dad left on another tour. To make herself feel better, she'd say, "If you could look a little less like her, he'd stay." What I wanted to tell her was, "If I looked a little more like you, Nell, he'd still go."

Because you are *not* Mom.

Never could be, no matter what you do."

Not that I remember any of it.

Except that I became her *Butterfly*.

And so when it comes time

I will fly.

And I will do it looking like Mom. Josephine.

Just like *me*.

The ride back to the house is quiet. The radio is off and JJ's conversation stifles. We're both soaking in the grief, pretending we aren't a big, tangled mess.

She finally breaks the silence. "I didn't know what to do when Constance said that."

"I know."

"She came out of nowhere. I couldn't find the words to make it stop."

Her hands clutch the wheel so hard, her knuckles have lost all pigmentation.

"It's fine."

"It's not fine," she says. "It's not . . . fine."

I look out the window and pretend to fly away. Up into the sky, out of the galaxy.

She clears her throat, diverts entirely. "Do you want to say something at the memorial?"

"About what?"

"Whatever you want."

My stomach lurches. "No."

"*Okay* . . ." We round Pearl Street as she takes a long, thoughtful sigh. "A few years before retirement, there was this one young lady who's always been in the first couple rows during class. One day, I noticed she moved to the last row. Couldn't take my eyes off her. It distracted me the entire lecture. When she tried to sneak out, I asked if I'd done something wrong. She was one of my best students, genuinely interested in the syllabus. But that day, nothing. She was a different person."

I move my gaze from the window to JJ. "What happened?"

"Her mom died. And she let the loss define her. Never sat in the front row again; barely passed the class. If we don't find a way to cope with the grief, it'll strip us of living, ourselves."

I pause. "I get what you're saying, but I'm not talking at the memorial. I can't."

She sighs again. "If you change your mind—"

"I won't." Before any tears fall, I turn back to the window. Moments later, we're in the driveway. Neither of us reach for the door handles. Her words catch inside her throat as she tries to speak. I feel Dad's absence right in this car, more than I have since we left Albany. My hand tenses on my phone, the sweat pooling, making me cringe at the feel. It's as if Dad's calling from beyond, though I know I wouldn't answer.

Would you rather get a call from a ghost or a call from your worst enemy (Nell, obvs)?

JJ angles toward me; I'm frozen. "When I brought him home from the hospital, he didn't cry, didn't fuss. Just had these big old eyes—like yours—and a head full of curls—like yours—and I could tell he had a heart too big, too open, for the world—like yours. He was special from his first breath. All parents say that, but he really was."

It's too quiet with the ignition off. No hum of the engine; only our breaths and thoughts weaving in and out of each other.

"Even after losing Jo, and his heart was ripped in two, he said the same things about you," she continues. "That you brought her back to life. I know he's here. I *feel* it."

"Nah. He'd give me a sign." My throat strains.

She lays a hand on my leg. I flinch, but her hand stays. "The signs are everywhere, if you're looking."

My jaw is clenched, fighting to argue against her nonsense (because I don't usually win), but in my entire life, I've never felt my mother's ghost hovering or the chill of hairs standing on end. Those in the afterlife avoid me, much like the living.

"Pennies," she continues. "Lights flickering. Something misplaced. His voice out of nowhere in a memory—that's Ray. I believe it, and you should, too. It brings me comfort to know he's with us."

I want to say something—*anything*—but before I can, she points to the floor where a dull penny lies face-up. I pick it up, rub the edges between my fingers, and wonder, hope, Dad can hear me when I think, *If you're going to leave money, please let it be in hundred-dollar-bill form*. The coin fell from JJ's purse, I'm sure. She wants me to believe in something I'm not sure I can.

Twenty-three seconds pass before she opens her door. "We're gonna keep on with our day. It's what Ray would want—that penny told me so."

She smiles, shuts the door, and goes inside while I wait. For three minutes, forty-seven seconds—until the silence hurts. If I could grab ahold of it, smash it against the concrete—if only to watch the destruction—I would. The quiet lets my thoughts fester and accumulate. Until I can't sit here another second. Sitting here feels wrong. Sitting here means I'm alone.

I swing the door open, the heat washing over me like a tsunami. Before I go, I lay the penny back on the floor. I don't want it. *I just want you, Dad.*

Voicemail

Dad

cell
December 11 at 5:01 PM

Transcription Beta

"I guess it's the holiday season. Nell says you haven't told her what you want this year, which isn't like you at all. Where's the detailed list with proper buy links? There must be something you want (and don't say for me and Nell to divorce because it's not funny a second time and I might start to think you're serious). You know what I want? Remember the Christmas before I met Nell and I was feeling down and in a lot of pain? You, JJ, and Kam wheeled me around Ivy Springs and we went door-to-door singing— but not Christmas carols. We sang our favorite hip-hop and rock songs, and everyone who opened their door was confused but it made us laugh. That's one of my favorite memories because we didn't need anything but each other. That's what I'm missing tonight."

▶ 0:00 |━━━━━━━━━━━━━━━━━━━━━━━ -1:11

Speaker   **Call Back**   **Delete**

Email Draft (Unsent)

New Message	✕

To

Subject

I remember that Christmas
   It was the happiest
      I'd felt in a long time.
         Because of your injuries,
I was so sure
You'd never go back.

And then you met Nell.
And you went back.
And I've never loved Christmas
Again.

⏮ ⏭ ⏯ ⏹ ⏺ DEW GD BRICKMAN
DURATION: 2:22

Local boy to make a friend if it kills him.

Naima finally emerges. She appears more tattered than before. "The princess returns empty-handed," I say with delight. "This leaves the boy to wonder, what *is* she looking for exactly?"

"*Ugh*. Not now, Dewd," she says. "Ha-ha. *Dewd*."

Her feet are swift, but I keep up. The longing to step inside her shoes hits me hard. "Did you have a suitable time at the market?"

She stops near me. "Is this *you* talking or the recorder? Because maybe you could ask me before putting my voice on tape forever."

I shove my eye to the hole. "I hadn't considered that disturbing fact. I'm sorry. It's just me. *See?*" I refrain from telling her about my chat with Stella, though my trusty mechanical friend is still nestled in my pocket. I'm not quite ready to let it go.

"Well, 'just me,' you should consider other people's feelings and I *didn't* have a 'suitable' time at the market. I had a shit time. It was shit. *LIFE* IS SHIT."

"Oh," I say. "I'm sorry. If it makes you feel better, I often feel the same."

"Whatever. It doesn't matter."

"Of course it does."

"Why do you care? You don't know me."

"That's one version of this story."

She's quick to move away. "My life isn't a *story* to entertain you."

"Of course not. But you're a chapter in *mine*."

"Stop recording me before I call the po-po."

"It's not on, I promise. I just . . . I need it close by. It helps me breathe."

She makes a grunting noise—it shouldn't sound sweet, but does—and moves farther away from my sight. "K, well, good luck with that," she says, flashing her middle finger. "By the way, you smell like mother-effing strawberries, which I've decided I'm against. *Puke*."

I gently pull the recorder from my pocket, with a devious smirk if there ever was one. "In today's top stories, the magnificent creature is light on her feet, but not in her heart, marred by the cruelest of fates. The boy only hopes to one day change all that. She just has to learn to trust him. He only asks for her friendship, nothing more."

As she disappears inside the house, my chest feels full of heavy pains that pull and stretch. I put my recorder away. "I only need a friend," I mumble. *Please*.

NAIMA

"What was that about?" JJ asks when I walk inside. Hiccup barrels through the hallway, zigzagging toward me.

"Just—" I stop. JJ's bent over the sink crying and pretending not to. I never know what to do when people cry. I walk up to her and awkwardly *tap tap tap tap tap tap*.

She sniffles, wiping away her own tears, with her own tissue, but won't look in my direction. There's a knock at the door.

"Can you get that?" She turns the faucet on to mute the sound of her sniffling.

"Sure," I say with one last *tap*. My brain hates me for not following with five more. I tap my own shoulder to even things out. I'm careful to avoid the dip in the floor, off center near the kitchen. If I do these things, her tears will cease, Dad will rise from ash; everything will be sunshine and rainbows. Hiccup follows, nipping at my heels until Kam appears from the bedroom to pull him up.

"Didn't know you'd be back so soon," he says. Hiccup quiets, stares at me with the one good eye. "Thought you'd enjoy the afternoon out."

"Wasn't feeling well," I say.

My hand is on the door when he stops me. Hiccup growls. He smells of a Caribbean vacation. Mangos and coconuts. "Is Grandma okay?"

I look to the kitchen, knowing what she'd want me to say—*she's fine*—but can't. To lie to Kam would cause me to combust or something. Must be all those years of ordering people around on the construction sites where everyone did as he said, without hesitation.

I avoid with a shrug and he knows. "Got it." He retreats to the kitchen and wraps an arm around JJ, setting Hiccup on the floor. The faucet still runs, but she falls into his chest, her face masked by the fabric of his shirt. He lets her sob, as much as she needs. He sobs, too. Hiccup sits quietly at their feet and waits; grieves with them. *Canine god, indeed.*

I only watch for a second—it's their moment, not mine—before opening the door to no one. Another thick blanket of warm air smashes against my face. A single red balloon bobs, its string tied to the mailbox. The mail truck pulls away—two hours past the usual 12:14 EST route.

I lift the package addressed to me, and slide my nail beneath the flap. My heart stops. For three whole seconds, I'm dead.

A rubber band wraps around a stack of letters—letters addressed to me via Albany, via Fort Hood, too. All returned back to Dad when I refused them.

In case of death, send to Naima Josephine Rodriguez at the address of Joelle and Kameron Rodriguez, Ivy Springs, Indiana.

Voicemail

Dad

cell
December 25 at 3:09 AM

Transcription Beta

"Merry Happy Feliz Holidays! I don't expect you to be up spying on Nell as she fills yours and Christian's stockings (trying to keep the magic alive), but when you're up, could you call me? I'd like to talk to everyone. You, mostly. I had a strange dream last night. Your mom came to me and asked how you're doing and I didn't know the answer. It's bothering me. I couldn't go back to sleep. Call me?"

▶ 0:00 ━━━━━━━━━━━━━━━━━━━━━━ -0:27

Speaker   **Call Back**   **Delete**

Email Draft (Unsent)

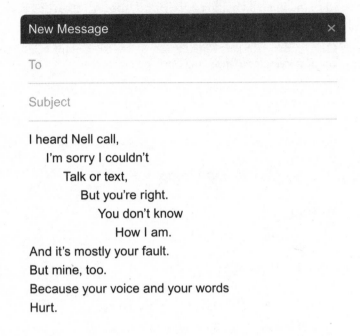

I heard Nell call,
    I'm sorry I couldn't
        Talk or text,
            But you're right.
                You don't know
                    How I am.
And it's mostly your fault.
But mine, too.
Because your voice and your words
Hurt.

◄◄ ►►| ►|| ■ ● DEW GD BRICKMAN
DURATION: 3:59

*Storms to pass quickly, humiliating experiences to
stay.*

From the safety of my bedroom window, I have a straight shot
of Naima as she pulls the balloon off the mailbox. Her fingers
lift the thread, the red latex bobbling high above, almost breathing in and out with her. From this angle, her reaction is shrouded
by shadows, so I can only hope in holding a tangible memory of
Staff Sergeant Rodriguez, she feels him soaking up the atmosphere like a phantom sponge.

As my hand lingers on the ribbon curtain, I glance at Violet's number smeared across my skin. Before the faded numbers wash away, I punch the information into my phone, accidentally hitting Call as I save. I cancel immediately, but an instant later, my harmonic-waves ringtone erupts.

"Hello?" I ask, hesitant.

"Who is this?"

"Andrew Brickman."

Violet sighs. "*Jesus,* man. Don't call and hang up like that. Thought it was the ghost I met through a séance last week. I do *not* need to deal with that today."

"I didn't mean to make you paranoid. My finger slipped as I saved your number."

"Oh, so I'm an *official* contact now?"

"Of course."

"Sweet. I'll save you, too. I mean your number. Not you— you don't need saving. I don't think. Do you? *Gah*—now I'm rambling."

"I don't mind. I quite like it when you ramble." My cheeks heat through with a prickling sensation.

There's silence and I'm not sure what to do. My mouth hangs open in search of a transition, but I come up empty.

"Well, Dew-Was-Diaz-Brickman," she says, "I'm still at work so I'd better go."

"As I said, I didn't intend to speak, but what an unexpected misadventure this has become."

"It sure has." Her breath hangs between the receiver and my ear. It has a crispness to it I can almost feel on my lobe, like the times she's leaned in to whisper, pulling my hairs straight up and out.

I should say something. I should. I can't seem to.

"We were already astrologically connected, but since we're contacts now in the most ceremonious of ways, can I call you later?" she asks.

My skin erupts in goose pimples. "That would be lovely."

"Cool," she says. "Very cool."

"Okay, well . . ."

"Hold on," she shouts with a muted fuzz—a hand over the receiver. "Big Foot's crying about the steamer being clogged. You know what happens when he's frustrated with technology."

"He turns on the oldies station and reminds us of 'the good old days' even though he wasn't born yet."

"Exactly. *No one* wants to hear that shit today."

"Then I shall let you go."

"Later."

She hangs up. I hold the phone in this exact position for some time, almost completely forgetting about Naima and her balloon. I move back to my spot near the window, but she's gone. A mere blip.

"You have the whole world spinning like a top at your fingertips, my darling," Mom would say. "How you decide to partake is up to you. Be an active participant—don't sit around and wait for life to happen. *Make* it happen."

I let the curtains drop to a close and pull out my recorder before the moment passes me by—a historic moment never yet achieved in the life of my two shoes. I press Record, and I smile.

> *Breaking story: Boy has actual conversation with a girl and doesn't completely blow it. But give him time. He will.*

NAIMA

As unimportant as it might seem to an outsider, knowing I did see a red balloon bobbing and weaving through town relieves me.

I haven't had vivid hallucinations like that since last summer, before my medication soaked through.

As I flip through the stack of familiar mail, dates of days past, I remember every time I checked the mailbox and received a letter. It hurt. It hurts still. I wish I could rip them open. I don't. Seeing them reminds me of chances I had and wasted. Words Dad wanted to share that I rejected. Because he left. The pettiness eats away at me. Maybe I'm not human. Maybe I'm a fatal flaw; something Mom should've never carried to term. Maybe I did curse them like I always felt I had.

I count sixty-six letters, which I know is *not* a coincidence. JJ and Kam rustle in the kitchen. I'm not ready to talk. Quickly I run down the basement stairs and lay them aside. From the pile of blankets, my fingers trace the hexagons on my quilt. I count ninety, always ninety, and I need to see ninety and the balloon hangs here, watching. JJ and Kam move, their footsteps pounding above. If they come down, they'll ask questions, wanting answers I don't have. *Why didn't you open them? Why did you send them all back? Why? Why? Why? Why? Why? Why?*

I'm spiraling, *I know*. The balloon bobs. I search beneath my pillow for my anxiety medicine, popping a small pill into my mouth. Swallowing hurts, the threads of my quilt hurt. *I* hurt. I think about texting my therapist but can't seem to move from this spot where all I want is to feel those damn threads and count the damn hexagons until the damn medicine saturates my veins. Sometimes it helps. Others, I'm left obsessing over why it didn't.

The first letter Dad sent this last tour, I held it to my chest. I sat on the edge of the bed with it for forty-three minutes. I couldn't open it. I don't know why—I just couldn't. It somehow felt like his last words. At the time, he explained why his leave was postponed, that he'd miss my birthday. I didn't want another excuse because it didn't matter. I'd already been in the intensive treatment program most of the summer, so I *should've* been able to read the damn letter. I was better, right? My brain was chemically operating on a "normal" level.

Not completely.

Through all the sessions and exercises and meditations and soul searching, one vein closed completely. I hadn't intended for it to go this way in exchange for my so-called healing, but he was the primary cause. The only way to get through his absence was to erase him. I ignored his calls, deleted his voicemails, deleted his emails, and returned his letters. To punish him.

I'm sorry.

Voicemail

Dad

cell
January 1 at 12:03 AM

Transcription Beta

"Wish you'd have talked to me on Christmas. And could you stop sending my letters back? Read them, Ima. I'm trying here. Will you ever *not* be mad at me? [inaudible] Oh yeah. Happy New Year. Here's to better times ahead. For the both of us. Not the way I wanted this to go. [sigh]"

▶ 0:00 |▬▬▬▬▬▬▬▬▬▬▬▬▬▬▬▬▬▬▬▬▬▬| -0:14

Speaker   **Call Back**   **Delete**

Email Draft (Unsent)

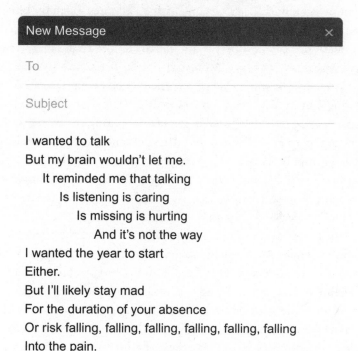

New Message   ✕

To

Subject

I wanted to talk
But my brain wouldn't let me.
   It reminded me that talking
     Is listening is caring
       Is missing is hurting
         And it's not the way
I wanted the year to start
Either.
But I'll likely stay mad
For the duration of your absence
Or risk falling, falling, falling, falling, falling, falling
Into the pain.

⏮ ⏭ ▶❚ ■ ● **DEW GD BRICKMAN**
DURATION: 5:07

*Update: Local boy did not learn lesson involving
deathly strawberries.*

I bake an infectiously pink strawberry cake with the most delightful of surprises baked inside. A dash of sugar here, a smidgen of
vanilla extract there, I've forced my childhood incident far from
my mind in hopes of conjuring up a little good fortune. I heed

my sensitivities, baking a slightly alternate version of my mother's fortune cake with Lady Clean Cuisine's allergen-friendly blueprints as my guide. I know better than to taste the rose-colored confection, but the smell is as saccharine as I remember. The aroma sparks a vision of Mom twirling in her sundress beneath the kitchen light while Dad says, "Smells good enough to eat, Al."

She'd hum August Moon and lovingly stir with the wooden spoon passed from her mother, my *abuela,* tasting the batter with her fingertip. Even if the cake failed her and became an underbaked lump, or a not-sweet-enough rectangle, or a flat disc that neither resembled strawberry pink or a cake at all, she'd look at me with a shrug and say, "All we can do is try, and sometimes that has to be good enough."

The first time the cake came out picture perfect, she cried. Her hand over her mouth, she'd looked to Dad and said, "Good fortune is on the horizon, Phil. I feel it in my bones." He'd walked up behind her, gently turning her toward him. "It's already ours."

My mother's recipe for strawberry cake was a pint of fresh strawberries, two eggs, a cup of flour, half a cup of sugar, a quarter cup of milk, a stick of butter, a dash of cinnamon and nutmeg, a pinch of baking powder, and a heart bursting with love. My *abuela* died not long before she perfected the cake, so when Mom stood over the countertop mixing away, it was her way of saying hello, goodbye, or the hardest sentiment between them—*I'm sorry.*

I'm careful as I mix the ingredients together, my allergy-friendly substitutions lined in a neat row. Though, there is no adequate substitute for strawberries (if you ask me), so I close my eyes and say a prayer before sliding a pair of latex gloves over each hand. Stella owns a wooden spoon similar to Mom's, and I decide it must be a sign of luck and use it, too. It's not long before the splotches form on my forearm, dotting a trail up and down the length of my bicep, to my chest, and through the length of my legs. Each one burns more than the last. I do a double-check of the ingredients—an accidental splotch of strawberry juice has found its way to my skin. I tell myself it's fine. A small price to pay.

While the cake bakes, I flip through Faith's wrestling magazines. The pageantry is quite impressive. A melodramatic soap opera with a sprig of good-hearted brutality. I can see why Faith sees a piece of herself between the glossy pages. Even if Stella and Thomas don't.

When the timer beeps, I pull the sweet-smelling cake from the oven right when Stella and Faith return. I lay the good-fortune offering on a pad on the countertop to cool, nearly dropping the entire thing on the floor as the heat melts through the pot holders.

"Ouch," I say, letting the pan drop into place.

Stella lugs boxes from the market into the room, while Faith—still in her Rick Flair feathered jacket—struts in angrily. Without so much as a word, she stomps off to her room and slams the door, knocking a photo to the floor.

Stella blows a wisp of hair from her eyes with a sigh. "It's been a long day with Nature Chick."

"I see that."

"Smells good in here. What's cooking?"

"Strawberry cake. For Naima."

She pauses, nods along to the beat of the silence. "You didn't eat any?"

"No, ma'am."

"And you wore gloves? I know it's overkill, but just in case."

I raise my hands, still gloved.

With boxes lined around her like a fort, she looks about in dismay at the house, an organized mess. Clean clothes unsorted. Random books and items splayed across the floor and tables. If you ask her where something is, she can tell you. If you look for it yourself, good luck. "How about we go out for dinner after therapy? I'll have Thomas meet us."

We're interrupted by Faith, pounding against her bedroom walls. We abandon the good fortune of the room and lean our heads toward the sounds.

"Did . . . something happen?" I ask.

"With Faith, something *always* happens. I don't know what I did. We talked one minute, and the next, she was *this*."

"What were you talking about? Before she became angry."

She hesitates. "I said Rick Flair isn't the best role model for a young girl. Because he's not. He's a sexist rage-a-holic with a penchant for the spotlight. Not exactly what I'd like her to aspire to. What about Maya Angelou? Dian Fossey? Oprah? A strong *female,* you know?"

"There are plenty of female wrestlers, even Rick Flair's daughter. Maybe she needs to connect with something we can't understand."

"I don't know, Dew. I'm trying to be what she needs, and it's never right."

"Maybe you're not meant to be."

She crosses her arms, fatigue evident in her expression. "How do you mean?"

"She's obviously going through something that requires a different perspective. This isn't your fight to win. It's hers." I signal for her to lean in. "Listen to what she's saying."

Through the thin door that doesn't shield more than a breath of air, Faith's not cursing out Stella. Instead:

"In order to be the man, you have to beat the man," Faith repeats. "You're the man, girl. Do the damn thing." She thuds something against the wall, scaring us back slightly.

"I don't understand," Stella says, exasperated.

"She's hyping herself up for a ring fight," I say.

"*Oh, God.* She wants to *be* Rick Flair."

I hold back a chuckle. "I don't think so. She just wants to be in charge of her life. After everything she's been through, she's looking for an outlet to give her back the power."

Stella's eyes soften, understanding any miscommunication isn't because Faith hates her, but possibly because she doesn't and she's clinging to anything she can to remind her she can have a say in her own life. And right now, that say happens to manifest á la Rick Flair.

"My MP3 player helps me. This is her thing. It's incredibly weird and offensive, and has nothing to do with what kind of parent you are. Let her have it."

She ruffles the curls that hang against my forehead. "You're pretty great, you know that?"

"So I've been told."

Another thud startles us two steps back. Faith's voice volume cranks to high. "I'm a stylin' profilin' son of a gun!"

Stella rubs the crease between her brows. "I'm gonna have to watch that damn documentary, aren't I?" She sighs.

I smile. *"Woo."*

NUMBERS AND DEATH

Salmon-colored poppies inconsistently situated on a pair of leggings Nell changed into after news of Ray's death. Forty-seven on the front, bits of jade foliage positioned in between. Naima wondered, *Why not forty-eight or fifty?* Nell broke her thought into segments with a muffled whimper, and as she looked up, Naima accidentally stumbled into her gaze. It was there that she saw it: heartache mixed with disbelief. She quieted, directed Naima to the two men—a marine and a chaplain—standing guard near the driveway with Christian and his friends. With a silent nod, Nell pointed, and the movement of her shaking finger cut the air between them; this is when Naima remembered what she said to herself about Ray the day before she attempted to take her own life. *I'll always be a ghost to him.*

Ray would tell her thereafter that people *can* change at the slightest crinkle in their world—just as he had after Josephine passed. But maybe he hadn't changed for the better, if leaving was all he'd ever be capable of. Ghosts are all Naima believes she has left. She'll wonder, if she'd caught the balloons when Nell struggled that day, or if she did what she did every year, or counted the hexagons again, or if she hadn't been born at all, things would be different now. But she'll never know what else to do, to fix a thing. That, to her, is worse than death. So she counts. And counts five more times.

Because when Ray died, he was on his *sixth* tour.

NAIMA

"Who was at the door?" JJ asks, coming down the stairs. I shove the balloon beneath the quilt but it flies out almost immediately.

"I got . . . a package," I say.

"From who?" She sets an emptied laundry basket on top of the dryer and moves closer. She spots the balloon. "Where'd that come from?"

I hold up the yellow envelope that contains the letters and let her see for herself. She pulls the stack and reads Dad's note, hand clamped over her mouth to hold back a wail. When she sees the letters addressed to me, her disappointment is clear. It's a look of "What did you do now?" and I turn away because she's right. What *did* I do now?

"You didn't open even *one*?" she asks.

I shake my head, avoid eye contact.

I expect her to scold me, but instead she lays a hand on mine. "I guess we don't all know how we'll react until it's our time to."

I nod.

She wipes her tears away and straightens her posture as if to say *moving on.* "Reservations set for dinner at seven."

She pauses for a beat, eyes a bit drearier than they'd been this morning. "Get ready in a bit, then."

Her face remains unchanged, but she doesn't ask about the balloon again as she goes to, mostly likely, tell Kam what I've done—er, *not* done. The thought of wasting the very thing that holds me back, more *time,* makes me ill. The balloon moves freely in front of me while the letters stay in the spot JJ left them. That's where they'll stay until my mind decides they can move. Not now, maybe not ever.

For now, I find my bandanna and tie it around my head. Searching the playlist on my phone, I press Play on an old Run-D.M.C. jam—"It's Tricky"—to dance out the rest of my nerves. "There's no better medicine than a good time," Kam would say.

And so I turn the music up.

And let my arms flail

As the balloon rises to the ceiling

Where it kind of dances with me.

And in the weirdest way,

It *does* feels like Dad's here.

Even though
I know
That's not a real thing.
Is it?
Ugh. Never mind.

Voicemail

Dad

cell
January 22 at 10:47 AM

Transcription Beta

"So . . . I won't be home like I planned. Something . . . came up. I can't go into specifics, but I'm okay. It's something I *have* to do. I've already talked to Nell, but she thought it'd be best if I told you myself. I know you're going to be angry, and I don't blame you. I promise—I'll be home in time for your birthday. If you don't want to talk directly, can you write me a strongly worded letter about how you're feeling? Give me all you've got. I just need to know you're okay. *Please*, Ima." [lost signal]

▶ 0:00 |━━━━━━━━━━━━━━━━━━| -1:11

Speaker   **Call Back**   **Delete**

Email Draft (Unsent)

> ### New Message   ×
>
> To
>
> Subject

A strongly worded letter
    About how I feel
        Could never do
            The thing
                I need it to
                    Like bring you
Home.

⏮ ⏭ ⏯ ⏹ ⏺   **DEW GD BRICKMAN**
DURATION: 6:48

Coming up on Dew's News: *The introduction of
Ivy Springs' newest wrestling sensation.*

Dr. Peterson is not happy with me. The strawberry cake pulled her down a spiral. I should've known; I felt it coming—an unleashing of sorts—because I've become so good at answering questions exactly how she'd want me to.

"By focusing so much on Naima's pain, you're avoiding your own," she says. "This is the redirecting reaction we've discussed."

I look down at my hands folded in my lap. "I don't know what you mean," I lie.

She leans forward in her rolling chair and removes her glasses.

"I think you do." She stands and takes the empty space next to me. "I'd like to try the exercise we've been avoiding."

My body instantly tightens. The excuses were easy, in the beginning: "I can't because I'm not ready. I don't feel well. Let's do it next week." After weeks of intensive therapy and the start of this exercise I couldn't finish, she and I both know it's time.

She tells me to close my eyes and imagine a memory that's caused unpleasant feelings. A situation that didn't end well. My parents try to shove their way into the limelight, but I hold them back. Dig deeper. For something, anything, else.

"Tell me what you see," she says, calm.

My eyes strain to stay closed. I pinch them tighter. "The lady comes to my school. She says my parents have died." I pause, still blocking chunks of time from that day; the worst day.

"Go on."

"I get in her car and she takes me to an emergency shelter. She says she will find a place for me to stay, and I ask her, 'Forever?' 'That's the end goal,' she says, leaving me in an unfamiliar place with unfamiliar people. I stand in the corner where it's quietest but even there, it's not so quiet."

"How do you feel in this moment, Dew?"

I choke on the words. "Scared. I want to go home. I want my mom to hold me. I want my dad to tell me it will be okay. No one tells me it will be okay. I'm alone. I play August Moon the whole night through, and pretend the day didn't happen."

My fists clench as tears fight their way through my lashes. She lays her hand on mine and tells me we're going to begin the story again, only, I'm to edit the memory in a way that flips the script.

"Tell me what you see this time," she says.

I inhale, deep, exhaling until my lungs deflate completely. "The lady comes to my school."

"What happens next?"

I think. Try to summon a new ending, but I struggle. This is the part that always catches me. The part I don't want to remember.

"Think, Dew. Who is your hero in this scenario? A caseworker. A teacher. A friend, maybe. Someone who enters this memory and saves you from feeling the pain. Who do you see?"

"The lady breezes past me. It's not my fate that's changed on this day. I look to the drop-off to see our car waiting for me."

"Where are your parents?"

"In the car. Alive."

"And what do you do when you see them?"

"I run to them and slide into the backseat. It's warm. They turn to look at me, and I feel okay."

She pats my arm and hands me a tissue. I'm calm now. A strange serenity flowing between my thoughts. In the silence before she summarizes my session sheet, I try to think of that day again, with the original ending; the one that hurts. But I can't recall. My only feeling is the warm backseat and the twinkle in my parents' eyes, and while still burdened with a deep sorrow, I also feel a little more okay.

I open my eyes to see Dr. Peterson's smile. "I'm proud of you. I know that was tough."

I nod.

She moves to her laptop and punches in her thoughts. "We still have work to do, but I think you just had a slight breakthrough. EMDR will hopefully help you 'rewrite' a lot of memories so they hurt a little less."

I sit, quietly reflecting, wondering why it's been so hard to confront this memory. She turns seconds later, before I'm directed out.

"But I also think, it's time for you to visit your parents' graves and say goodbye."

I trip over my words. "I can't."

"You have to, to get past the rest of what's holding you back."

She urges me out before I argue, and calls Stella over to whisper about me.

Faith waits in her usual corner chair, her feather jacket draped over her shoulders like a shrug. She looks up from her phone. "I was hot."

I sit next to her and pretend I don't notice all the glue bits hanging off the cloth, or that I'm emotionally drained and see-ing those glue bits might be the only redeeming thing about this day. "It *is* summer. I bet even Rick Flair wore a tank every now and then."

She huffs. "I have a reputation to uphold."

"Right, sorry."

She redirects her attention to her phone.

"How'd it go today?" I ask.

"*Meh.*" She pauses. "Actually, not bad." She pauses again, but doesn't look up. "What about you?"

My shoulders are square, almost relaxed. "Same."

Stella waves us over. "Sounds like you two worked very hard today. I'm so proud of you both." She squeezes us, and though Faith tries not to smile, I see it, and I smile, too.

Stella glances at Faith repeatedly before finally getting a sen-tence out on our drive—the sentence she's probably been prac-ticing after speaking with Dr. Peterson.

"If you want to work on your swing, Rick taped a string in the doorway and practiced punching toward it until it didn't move," Stella says with a shaky voice. "So you don't *actually* hit someone, you know? Takes a lot of practice. And hard work. But his daughter did it. You can, too."

Faith looks up, beaming. "I can do that."

"I've been thinking, maybe we should work on your wres-tling name, something that's more *you*. And I can have my seam-stress create a jacket unlike *anyone* else's. Don't be a recycled version of someone else. You deserve something special and unique. Like you."

The air between them grows thin. "I'm not good at any of it," Faith says. "I just think wrestling's cool."

"You're great at throwing random fits," Stella jokes. "WWE would be thrilled to have someone like you."

"I concur," I say. "You were born for this, Faith. I've never seen you so lit up before. My mom used to say—" I stop myself, glancing at Stella. "Never mind."

"What would she say, Dew?" Stella asks with the same warm smile my mother would've offered.

"Chase light like a firefly in darkness," I say. "That's what she would say."

"Sounds like she was a great mom." Stella reaches over and squeezes my hand.

It stings and heals all at once. "She and Dad would've liked you and Thomas."

"Found it—found my new name," Faith blurts out.

"Well?" I ask, relieved at the distraction. "What should we call you?"

Her hands spread wide, a fist nearly knocking the tip of my nose, letting the jacket drop from her shoulders as if she's been reborn. "Faith 'the Conniption' Brickman: Greatest Wrestler You've Not Met Yet."

And just like that (but not so quickly, actually), we went from three separate pods within a larger pod to a family, and all that was needed was a little good-fortune cake.

NAIMA

"More breadsticks?" the waiter asks. He looks from the empty basket to my plate that's covered in all six of them.

"Please."

Kam laughs, scraping the last bit of Alfredo sauce from his plate. "You're gonna turn into a breadstick."

"I hope so."

"Let the girl eat what she wants," JJ says, dipping into her salad. "It's her day."

"I didn't say it's a *bad* thing. I've been storing carbs for years.

Grandma might say it's made me more *a loaf*. Get it? Instead of *aloof*." His chin is perched out with a smile.

The waiter grabs the breadbasket, obviously uncomfortable. "I'll bring more bread."

"No, baby," JJ says, shaking her head at Kam. "Just *no*."

"That was wrong," I say. "You need to work on your grand-dad jokes. You're scaring away the workers."

"I'm funny. Like the one about not making my own sandwich because I hire contractors to do it. You two just don't appreciate *sophisticated* humor."

"Like the knock-knock joke where I said, 'Who's there?' and you disappeared, then ran back in to tell me it was a ding-dong ditch?"

"What's wrong with that joke?"

"First of all, it's not funny. Second, it's not funny."

JJ laughs. "Third, it's not funny."

He slumps. It's not that we're *not* close, Kam and I. Sometimes, he reminds me too much of Dad. He feels it, too. His posture practically shouts, *I am a third wheel!*

"*Ray* thought I was funny," he says.

There's a lingering silence as he drags his fork in the air like a magic wand, maybe wishing for Dad to be here with us. JJ grabs his hand, gently changing the tide. "I hate that shirt," she says. "Why do you still wear it?"

He chuckles, pulling at the fabric. "Because it gets a rise out of you."

She smiles and the corners of his lips pull upward as their hands intertwine. I stare at the empty chair next to me, remembering the nights Dad would swordfight me with his fork for the last breadstick, swallowing the lump that's formed in my throat.

The waiter returns with a fresh stack of bread. I pull the first breadstick from the top and lay it in front of the empty seat. Six breadsticks for the four of us. Like always.

Would you rather give up breadsticks or give up sleep?

We eat and we laugh and JJ talks of the 5K she's training for and Kam talks of a new development in Clifton he wished he could take over. We don't talk about how much it hurts to pretend we're not hurting.

After dinner, we stop by the grocery store—the one with the giant mural of a garden on the outside wall—in the next town over so JJ can pick up the cake she ordered—a time-honored tradition I'll inevitably complain about (another time-honored tradition).

"Be right back," she says.

Kam and I stay behind. I want him to let it be silent, but he's not one to keep quiet. JJ says it's a way of managing his own anxiety. Like the quiet will swallow him up, and to prevent it, he talks.

"How are you *really* doing?" he asks, soft.

"I don't know," I say. I find a piece of bread between my teeth and obsess over trying to unstick it with the tip of my tongue.

He clears his throat. "Dinner was good. Loved my Alfredo. Cooked to perfection."

I say nothing.

"Weather was nice today. Little humid, but nice."

With a sigh, he goes for it. "So you got some letters from Ray."

I say nothing.

"He must've really wanted you to read them if he kept them all that time."

Time. Time. Time. Time. Time. Time.

He elongates the last word, until it soaks into the air. I think about the letters.

Kam adjusts. "Put any thought into what you'll say at the memorial?"

"I'm not speaking."

"Why not?"

"I don't want to."

He processes. "Might make you feel better. To talk about it."

I hold my tongue. "It'd make me feel better for Dad to be alive, in this car, with us."

His head drops. "I know, babe."

With an awkward shift, he does it—he asks the thing you shouldn't ask. "Are you taking your medication?"

"YES!" I snap.

"I didn't mean to upset you. Just thought, *hell,* I don't know. Heard Nell mention it. And after last summer, well . . . we worry, is all."

My eyes scan the lot. "Where is she?" I mumble.

"You're all we have left of him," he adds, voice trembling. "I want you to be okay."

My eyes water as JJ exits the store.

All we have left of him. All we have left of him. All we have left of him. All we have left of him. All we have left of him. All we have left of him.

On the tips of her toes, she balances the boxed cake and several plastic bags against the car's body—like Nell did the day the Casualty Notification Officer (CNO) told us about Dad. A thousand flashbacks flicker through my memory in bursts.

Groceries.

Cake.

Balloons.

Counting.

Sedan.

Dad.

Gone.

Voicemail

Dad

cell
January 27 at 9:55 PM

Transcription Beta

"One. Two. Three. Four. Five. Six. That's how many times I've called today. I'm starting to think you don't want to talk to me. [laughs] That was a bad joke. I'm still hoping to be back for your birthday. Still hoping. *Hoping.* Guess I'll count the stars again."

[lost signal]

▶ 0:00 |━━━━━━━━━━━━━━━━━━━| -0:19

Speaker   **Call Back**   **Delete**

Email Draft (Unsent)

New Message   ✕

To

Subject

I wanted to answer
　If only long enough
　　To tell you what happened
　　　At school today
　　　　When Georgia Westbrook

Called me a depressing pig
But I didn't cry
And didn't kick the back of her knees
Like I imagined.
Instead, I did something you taught me.
I told her "I wish you the best"
And walked away (with my middle finger up tho).

⏮ ⏭ ▶❚ ◼ ⬤ **DEW GD BRICKMAN**
DURATION: 3:32

*Ivy Springs doctors urge residents to be on the
lookout for stray eyelashes—an often under-
estimated but deadly predator.*

"Just a burger, not cooked in butter or oil, lettuce and tomato on the side, no fries, broccoli if you have it," Stella orders for me.

The waiter scribbles the intricate ask as Faith stumbles over her order of chicken tenders—not from the kids' menu, the adult menu. All eyes are very much on her vibrantly situated general-store feathers, including the waiter's.

Thomas holds his hand over his mouth with the slip of a smile shining through. "Does anyone want to talk about Faith's incredible style?"

Faith's lips curl.

"I'm serious," Thomas says. "I love it."

"We decided, with Faith's sudden and intense interest in wrestling, it'd be a good idea for her to pursue it," Stella says. "Dr. Peterson thinks it might help her work through some of her anger and aggression, while fostering confidence. It gives her a healthy, semi-healthy, *kind of* healthy—maybe not *the best* kind of healthy, but it's what we're working with—outlet."

She leans into Thomas close enough for me to hear while Faith stares at her phone. "It's about giving her some control back in her life, so let's get on board here."

"Got it," he whispers. "I can't wait to see your moves, Faith."

"Faith, phone away, please," Stella says.

With a grunt, she does as she's told and pulls a packet of crackers from Stella's salad plate to eat.

"What about you, Dew?" he asks. "How was your day?"

"Dr. Peterson said he's making great strides. And he baked Naima a strawberry cake," Stella answers. "Isn't that nice?"

"Lucky girl. Explains the splotches on your arms. You didn't eat any, did you?"

"No, sir," I say. "The strawberries exploded a bit. It's fine."

"Do you have any Benadryl?" Thomas asks Stella.

Her face quickly flushes to colors of worry. "At home. Do we need to go? We can go."

"No, it's okay," I say. Beneath the table, my fingers secretly scratch the rashes that I'd forgotten. The mention of them sparking more irritation.

"I feel terrible. I didn't pay enough attention to how bad you look. Does it burn?"

"No."

"Does it itch?"

"Only slightly."

She scoots from her chair abruptly and surveys each table's customers, asking if they might have any allergy medicine. Like a modern-day drug addict. She bothers five tables before a kind woman provides me with an antihistamine tablet.

"Thank you!" Stella cries. She puts the tablet in my palm and urges me on. "If it doesn't help right away, I'm using the EpiPen and calling an ambulance."

"I baked the cake hours ago. I'm fine. *Really.*"

"Don't bake anything like that without me again. Just in case."

She hovers over my shoulder until I've swallowed the pill. As if the minute it's in my system everything will vanish and I'll be magically recovered. The waiter returns—everyone's eyes sewn to my every gesture—and he's nearly afraid to interrupt our strange silence.

"Your food will be out shortly," he says.

No one says a word until, out of nowhere, Stella blinks an eyelash from her eye, into her eye. She struggles to fish it out, eyes watering, nose full of snotty discharge. Now she's the one who could use an antihistamine.

Thomas moves in to help. She waves her hands around from the sting. "Ow, ow, ow!"

When he pulls the eyelash onto his finger, he holds it out and tells her to make a wish. She closes her eyes and blows a little too hard. The lash floats up, and out, straight into Thomas's eye. Now, Stella works to pull the lash from *his* eye. They're both flailing, tears streaming, and for the first time since we've been a complete family, Faith and I hold our bellies to contain our laughter. The muscles tense, I'm bent over, nearly crying, in the best way possible.

This is insanity. *This* is comical. *This* is our family, a complete pod, however lacking in spaces. And it's splendid.

NAIMA

"Tried to be as quick as I could," JJ says, fighting for a breath. For someone who runs marathons, the plight of running in and out of a store quickly for my sake has her winded. "Damn cashier wanted to tell me about this mole she found, and spiraled into why she's divorced. In her words, it's 'because that son of a bitch can't keep it in his pants.' If I had to hear that mess, so do you."

As she glides into her seat with a wink, my bandana pinches at the base of my neck. She settles, seems to feel the tension that morphed after she'd gone. The quiet in the car forces JJ to cut in.

"What happened in here?" she asks.

Kam's stare is angled out the window.

"Babe?" she pokes. His hand cups his mouth. JJ turns to face me. "Ima, what happened?"

I shrug, and stare at the floor.

"Someone tell me what the hell is going on." Her voice trembles.

Kam lays a hand on hers. "We miss him." He's so quiet; I don't remember a time his voice barely carried in this way.

Her wide eyes soften with waves of sadness. She pats his hand. "Me, too."

She turns back to me. "You okay?"

I barely look up, hands folded tightly in my lap so as not to pinch, pull, claw, or scratch. I don't nod or shrug. I can't seem to do anything. She watches me struggle for a solid sixty-three seconds, before she nods, eyes welling with tears, and turns forward.

Kam breaks the silence. "Did you tell her about the bench yet?"

"Kameron," JJ says with a sigh. "Can't tell you nothin'."

"*What?* She should know."

"It was a damn secret."

My hands free themselves, letting me pull myself forward into their conversation. "What bench?"

Kam starts to explain, but JJ cuts him off. "Kam designed a bench that'll be installed in the community garden next to the cherry blossom tree. It'll have Ray's name on it."

"That's great," I say. "Dad would've liked that."

"Nell said you used to sit under a cherry blossom tree for hours in Albany; a willow in Fort Hood, too. We figured maybe . . . maybe it's where you prayed, or thought about your future, or talked to yourself about Ray. Maybe this could be where you can talk *to* him."

The air escapes my lungs and I audibly gasp. "Nell told you that?"

Kam turns, too, and they smile at each other. JJ takes this one. "She tells us more than you think."

"Doesn't sound like anything she'd do."

JJ quiets and Kam takes over, like the well-oiled machine they've always been. "She cares about you. About how Ray being gone affected you, how it affects you now. She was really upset with us for not telling her about last summer. I don't blame her."

JJ holds up her phone, illuminating the screen. "She's been texting me a lot since she left, asking how you are—she didn't want to bother you."

"What do you tell her?" I wonder about the letters, if she knows, too. But I can't bring myself to ask.

"Same thing you would. I say you'd be better if she'd send the flytrap and those damn shoeboxes already."

By the time we get back to the house, the sky begins its slow decent into darkness. Summer nights in Ivy Springs are like a first kiss: warm, electrifying, and surreal. They meander, enjoying every last taste of the sun's kiss before finally letting the moon take hold. I couldn't paint a better picture than what this small village already is. Where every other place I've been is watercolored, Ivy Springs is thick, bold strokes that take you aback the moment you arrive and keep doing so until you've left the township limits.

I sit on the back stoop. JJ and Kam let Hiccup out to relieve himself, and leave him out here to bark, while they take over the kitchen with the music turned up (probably to drown out Hiccup). They slice the cake and put each piece onto Gi Gi's antique dessert plates—the ones passed down through generations—and

I let Hiccup back inside where he won't interrupt my lingering thoughts on those letters. He immediately scratches at the door directly behind me until Kam removes him, and puts him elsewhere (thank you).

The time is 8:11 P.M. EST.

I look up to the sky, wondering if Dad can see me from way up there. He used to stand far enough away that he could lift his finger to make it appear like he was holding the moon on the tip of it. He'd say, "Isn't is beautiful—an entire sky on display just for us?" I'd argue the whole world could see the same thing, and he'd reply, "Maybe you and I are the only ones looking up." As if the whole galaxy spontaneously generated from nothing, stars twinkling just for our view. "Right here, right now. The constellations shine and stars die, and our moon glows. *For us.* It's really something, if you believe."

I don't know how he did it, but I believed.

Believe. Believe. Believe. Believe. Believe. Believe.

He'd tell me when he was far off in another country, he'd look up to that sky made for us, and pretend I was looking, too. I lose myself in moonlight and memory, just as a car pulls into the driveway next door. Dad's voice is interrupted by the voices of the Brickmans. They're carrying on about someone using a middle finger to wave at someone else. I don't pull Dew's voice from them, not that I try.

I crouch down to overhear without being seen, crawling toward the hole in the fence's slat. When I peer through, I see this beautifully connected group of people. It reminds me of something Mom, Dad, and I could've had.

Could've.

I don't remember the last time I felt that happy, *free.* I long for it, my fingers reaching out, wishing they could spare a dusting of their joy, if I promise not to waste it. I'm staring so hard; I don't feel the small tears until they find my lips. The salt is all I taste.

As they disappear into their house
　　I collapse into the grass.
　　　　I repeat to myself, six times
　　　　　　My name is Naima Josephine Rodriguez.
　　　　　　I am my mother's daughter,
　　　　　　　　I am seventeen years old.
And I miss my father
So much
I could die
Of broken heart syndrome
Here and
Now.

Voicemail

Dad

cell
February 14 at 11:15 AM

Transcription Beta

"Will you be my Valentine? Word has it
I'll be home in May just in time for your
birthday. You heard right. I'm coming
home. *Home*. I love you. [cries]"

▶ 0:00 |━━━━━━━━━━━━━━━━━━━━━| -0:13

Speaker　　　　　**Call Back**　　　　　**Delete**

Email Draft (Unsent)

New Message ✕

To

Subject

Are you serious?
  Are you?
    Are you?
      Are you?
        Are you
          Coming home?
Home.
Home.
Home.
Home.
Home.
Home.

⏮ ⏭ ▶⏸ ⏹ ⏺ **DEW GD BRICKMAN**
DURATION: 0:54

At the top of tonight's top stories, water is some-
times thicker than blood, depending on your water.

Faith confesses having seen me use my middle finger, promising
to use it in her wrestling act as she's having a "conniption."

"I've done no such thing," I argue. "I'm a gentleman."

"Did, too," she says with a snap of the tongue. "During the
farmers' market that first day. You went to scratch your face

while talking to that tattooed eyebrow lady when she was mad but used your middle finger. You couldn't do it to her face so you pretended there was an itch but I saw it."

I gasp. "No."

Stella's laughing. "You *can* be a little passive-aggressive, Dew. We need to work on expressing your anger in a healthy way. But, to be fair, I know who Faith is talking about and I think I did the same thing."

"Well, she wasn't very kind," I confess with a smirk. "She said my hat was 'unflattering.' I wanted to say the same thing about her eyebrows, but I refrained."

"I knew it!" Faith elbows me like a sister I've had my whole life.

Perhaps she is also the fire August Moon speaks of.

After dinner, we pile into the pickup and make our way through town. The windows are down, warm summer air flowing through, and Thomas follows closely behind. In this moment, you could look at me and see past the layers of grief, you could walk in my shoes and be content. In this moment, I hear Mom singing August Moon, how "without the sky, there'd be no moon," which feels appropriate.

As Stella turns up the radio dial and sings at the top of her lungs, getting Faith to join in, too, I look between them and see a whole new sky. It's not where I started, and not where I'll end. But for now, I'm home. *Home.*

THE BEGINNING OF THE SHOEBOXES

After Naima's suicide attempt in Fort Hood, one of her therapists suggested a long list of coping mechanisms to replace the ones causing her harm. Naima didn't quite take to any traditional techniques—group therapy with other military kids, dual sessions with Nell via the Military Spouse Network, meditation, yoga, prayer, grounding, visualization, breathing, journaling, exercise, and use of a worry stone—despite her exhaustive attempts to make use of them. Therapy was not a one-size-fits-all, and because Naima took great pride in embracing all that made her unique, it took great effort to find the thing that could be hers and *only* hers.

It would come by accident, on a day that involved Nell purchasing a pair of shoes an anxiety-ridden Naima refused to wear, and the arrival of groceries that Christian left on the countertop at a time Naima felt particularly famished. She hadn't intended to begin a new ritual, but once she'd picked out nearly half the Lucky Charms marshmallows from the box, she needed a place to hide them for when Christian burst through the door. She didn't want him to catch her doing yet another strange thing she couldn't explain. So she stuffed the marshmallows into Ziploc bags and hid them in the one place no one would find them: the shoebox.

Naima never knew something so absurd could bring her so much fulfillment—particularly when Christian discovered his Lucky Charms was a lifeless box of bland additive cereal, void of marshmallows. That satisfaction, and that alone, is the very reason Naima continued the tradition, eventually finding relief during times of chaos, such as another move, another goodbye, and another loss.

Little did she know that hundreds of miles away, Andrew-Phillip-Diaz-Soon-to-Be-Brickman had his own hurdles to overcome. After the loss of his parents, and no other family to care for him, he'd find himself in foster care, awaiting someone kind enough to take in a boy who'd lost so much of himself he could barely speak. The Brickmans would have to peel Andrew back, layer by layer, uncovering the sweet boy they knew him to be. He wouldn't find solace in shoeboxes or marshmallows, but in a sheer fascination with the news and how reading a headline might give him authority over his own life—and the life he lost when his parents had floated into the clouds.

NAIMA

As soon as I walk inside, eyes still damp, I'm presented with a small plate. My vanilla cake with vanilla buttercream frosting rests in the center. JJ turns the music up almost as loud as her speakers will allow—loud enough that Hiccup joins in by barking.

A podcast streams in the background, talking of relationships through the ages, and JJ turns to Kam, who's licking frosting from a fingertip, a smattering dressed over his upper lip, and says, "If Ball State faculty could see you now. What a splendid sight."

JJ dances across the floor, plate in hand. She takes a bite between moves, and I can't help but smile. I taste my cake—it's so good—but refuse to dance. That feels wrong. The urn watches us from the chair, a plate directly in front of it, for it, *Dad,* to celebrate me. My smile drops. I want to focus on how much it hurts, but JJ and Kam won't let me.

Kam dances around me, snapping his fingers to the beat. He's wearing the ankle weights he says will "keep Hiccup from biting," though, from the bite marks, Hiccup sees them as new toys to chew through. He's adorned with a hot-pink sweatband around his hairline that reads, *Born to Shake What My Momma Gave Me*—no doubt one of JJ's running headbands. It lures another smile from me, and he grins.

From the outside, we are normal; we are *okay.*

"I almost forgot," JJ says, lifting the contents of the plastic grocery bags into view. "Happy belated birthday." She sets a single box of Lucky Charms on the counter, and another, and another, and three more after. All six are in a perfectly straight line, reflecting everything I am. She slows her movements, hands folded in front of her as if to say—*Is this okay?*

"It's everything," I say.

"I've got a shoebox and some baggies, too. We'll get you set up."

"Can we not call them 'baggies'? I'm not a dealer."

"That I know of." She elbows me, taking a cue from my body language not to hug. I don't feel open; I'm closed off, imprisoned. The urn suddenly becomes my entire focus. Why hasn't he been moved? *It's not okay. We're not okay.*

"We getting this started or what?" Kam shouts through the music. JJ raises her finger to shush him. I see it from the corner of my eye. It silences him immediately. He shuts the music off and they stand here, soaking in the silence with me. All of our eyes are on the urn.

The time is 8:47 P.M. EST.

"Ima," Kam begins. JJ shakes her head and his lips tighten. In a way, it feels as if us standing here is a salute to Dad. The flag's crisp angles and vivid colors folded into a perfect triangle that are on display, too, represent the parts of me I cling to—the parts that *have* to stay an exact way—while the part beneath, the wooden box with the U.S. Marine Corp emblem, is everything else. Out of sight, tucked away, however disheveled. I would stand here forever if I could. With the cereal boxes lined up between me and the urn, I find a strange comfort. But only in this spot, right here, right now, where a knock at the door erupts at the exact moment a burst of creation spontaneously generates.

Somewhere between my life, and his death.

Voicemail

Dad

cell
March 3 at 1:24 PM

Transcription Beta

"[sigh] I didn't want to say this on a voicemail. I don't have much time to talk but wanted to tell you before Nell does. I won't be home for your birthday in May after all. They need me to stay a little longer. I'm sorry, Ima. I wish I could fix it, but it's my job. I won't do another tour after this. We only have to make it through a little while longer, and I swear—I'll make it up to you in Ivy Springs as soon as I can. Promise. Read the letters. I'm sorry, baby."

▶ 0:00 |▬▬▬▬▬▬▬▬▬▬▬▬▬▬▬▬ -0:22

Speaker   **Call Back**   **Delete**

Email Draft (Unsent)

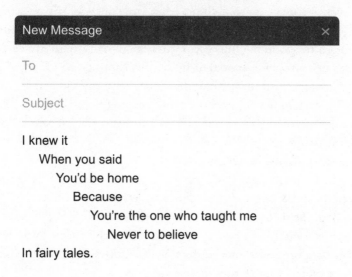

I knew it
   When you said
      You'd be home
         Because
            You're the one who taught me
               Never to believe
In fairy tales.

◄◄ ►►│ ►││ ■ ● DEW GD BRICKMAN
DURATION: 6:05

Boy mixes allergies with ashes, has delightful reaction.

Kam invites me through the front door. "Hello there," he says, searching my still slightly rash covered arms. "Are you okay?"

"A minor allergic reaction. I've made something I'd like to give to Naima, if I may." I balance the strawberry cake on top of the cloth Stella made me drape over my skin (in case I came into contact with the ingredients again).

"I hope you're all right?"

"I took some medicine. It's fine." I struggle with the weight of the cake. My arms have never had much more than skin over the bones—something kids at school have pointed out as a means of picking on me, or something—but I'm okay with my outsides. My arms remind me of my father's. Long and thin but strong enough to scoop me into them. Just as I'm okay with my care-free curls and wide-mouthed smile, like Mom's.

He shuts the door behind me. "They're in the kitchen."

I'm careful not to drop my creation, stopping directly on an uneven pivot. I'd love to walk farther, but the placement of Naima stops me.

"Why are *you* here?" she asks.

"Ima," Joelle says, studying the cake, her eyes devouring the perfectly pink frosting with delight. "What do you have?"

With the pathway cleared, I move closer, pushing a row of ce-real boxes out of the way to make room for this marvelous, ter-ribly dangerous (for me) confection. Sprinkles from the top fall to the table. "I made this. For her."

"DUDE!" Naima cries. "Watch the GD boxes!"

"Apologies."

"Isn't this the nicest thing?" Joelle compliments.

"It's strawberry cake," I say. I avoid making direct eye contact. "My mother's recipe."

"Now I get it," Naima says. "Strawberries." She doesn't appear impressed.

"You are so sweet," Joelle fusses. "Let me cut you a slice. Join us."

I back away. "I'm allergic."

"All those times I sent food over, no one said anything."

"We didn't want to be rude. My parents and Faith *love* your food. I certainly loved looking at it—I just can't *eat* some of—"

Naima interrupts. "What's on your arms?"

I hold my fists out, reveal the splotches now barely evident along my arms. "It's a lot better than it was a few hours ago."

Joelle's jaw falls open. She rushes to me to get a closer look. "You poor thing! Are you okay?"

"I'm fine."

"Why would you bake for me if you *knew* you'd have a reaction?" Naima asks. "That's, like, a suicide mission."

Among their eyes, and the heat of the light, and the kick of the allergy medicine, it all puts a tad too much pressure on me. I pull out my recorder and instantly calm. Though Dr. Peterson has suggested weaning me off of its use, I find comfort in the way my fingers wrap around the shape of it. "He offers the girl a gift of good fortune to signify her future. Perhaps it's not what she envisions, from a person she wants nothing from, but hopefully, it's everything she deserves."

"*Whyyyyy* do you do that?" Naima asks. She knocks the recorder from my hand while Joelle's back is turned. My mechanical friend tumbles to the carpeted divot. I envision him screaming as he falls, reaching up for me to save him.

"It's easier than talking directly to you," I say, losing all confidence. "To anyone. I don't mean to make you uncomfortable, but it helps me redirect my own discomfort, if that makes sense."

"Well, stop. It's weird."

I pick up the recorder, but leave it at my side. "Perhaps weird is my preferred aesthetic. It keeps people guessing."

Her face is frozen in a confused manner. "You're winning, then."

"What's with all the Lucky Charms?" I ask, pretending Joelle didn't already tell me they're Naima's absolute favorite.

"Nun-ya."

It draws my smile bigger. The mystery of it feels more profound than she's prepared to reveal.

"Why are you looking at me like that?" she asks.

"You're really pretty up close. More than that one eye I saw through the fence."

She blushes—*I made her blush*—and it feels like an electricity shoots through me. "Yeah, I know," she says. "I don't need anyone to tell me the facts, bruh."

My attention veers to the shiny metal peering at us from the chair next to her. "Is that . . . an urn?"

"What of it?"

"Why is it sitting at the table . . . like a person?"

"Why *not*?"

"Fascinating."

There's a really long silence when I choose to commemorate this exact moment by grabbing my recorder again. So I don't forget any detail of it. "May I?" Before she answers, I go on, "She invites death for dinner, hoping it will either stay or take her when he's finished. Tonight at ten." I'm not finished, not at all, but she knocks the recorder from my hand *again*—this time, harder. It flies into the hallway right when Joelle spins around.

"What are you doing, Ima?" She's balancing a large cardboard box filled with apple-butter jars on her thigh. Naima refuses eye contact with either one of us. Kam, who was well within my sight line, approaches. His posture angles down toward her. "Saw that," he whispers. "Not okay." She leans back in her chair as if being in his line of sight makes her uncomfortable. Or, perhaps, being in mine.

"It's not okay; he keeps recording me."

"These are general observations," I say. "Not specific to you."

"You're talking about me, in front of me."

"Semantics."

Her lips thin and tighten. "Care to mansplain anything else? Like, tell me what it's like being a woman in this world because I have no idea."

"I, uh . . ." My voice putters out.

Her eyes magnify, so I break the tension. "You received a package earlier. Was it important?" I can't seem to stifle the smile bursting through.

"Are you spying on me?"

"No."

"Wait," she says, "did you leave the balloon?"

"Your father spoke of your love of them once. I hoped it'd brighten your day."

"Stop talking about my dad like you knew him—like you know *me*."

I lose my words, a sudden sense I've done something terribly, horribly wrong. "I'm sorry. I didn't mean anything by it."

"You say that a lot. Don't you have somewhere to be? Like, not *here*?" she snaps.

"I'll help Dew with the box," Kam says, taking the box from Joelle.

I witness a strange silence among the three of them and decide it's not my place to stand here a minute longer.

"Come on," he says in a comforting tone.

"Have a nice evening," I tell them. I don't look at Naima, but I feel her eyes on me. She's trying to figure me out, I know. I've felt it before from far meaner people. Beneath my breath, quiet enough Kam or Joelle can't hear, as I pass, I feel it my duty to tell her something I can't seem to hold on to any longer. "Whatever was in the package, I suspect Staff Sergeant Rodriguez had something to do with it. I hope it helps."

She doesn't stop me from going, and she doesn't ask how I'd know. It feels like a time, like Stella said, when I should allow her the space to grieve. I'm trying to understand that notion, but I suppose, in the desperate need for someone to understand my own grief, perhaps I'm dragging her down with me.

Kam walks me to the door, where I take the box off his hands. "Thank you for your help, sir."

"You're welcome." He pauses. As if he has something more to say. Something heavier than he could carry within the walls of their house.

He clears his throat. "JJ pulled me aside earlier and told me she thought you'd left the balloon. Timed it with the mail. That Ray likely planted the seed in your head."

My stomach lurches. Maybe I *have* done something wrong. The very thought of it triggers my heartbeat to skip a little faster.

He lays a hand on my shoulder and I calm. "Naima may not understand your kindness, but we see it."

"It was nothing," I say.

"Andrew," he continues, "considering what she's been through, what you've been through, it was a very kind gesture. Your parents would be proud. Stella and Thomas sure are."

He leaves me here as I tear up, my fingers fumbling inside my pocket, and I realize I've been recording the whole time. I don't tell him how many times I plan to listen to the clip, but I hope he's right.

NAIMA

"I get that you miss Ray—we *all* do—but don't take it out on Dew. *None* of this is his fault." JJ's finally grown tired of my antics. I want to give an excuse for treating him the way I have, but I don't. "So he left a balloon. It was a nice thing from a nice boy who wants to help you feel better. Leave it at that."

My teeth grind. Maybe if he understood how symbolic red balloons were to Dad and me, he wouldn't have done it. They're ours. And I don't know where his hands have been. What if the portion of string I grabbed on to had anthrax? I can feel my throat closing in on me.

"You two would get along if it were any other time."

The letters. The letters. The letters. The letters. The letters. The letters.

The thought of this strange kid waiting for Dad's letters to arrive so he could run over and attach a symbolic balloon to them is beyond me. What reason would there be to do this to someone (other than to torture me)? I want to scream, and punch the wall, and rip that dumb smile off Dew GD Brickman's face until he tells me why he did this—*why?*—and I can't breathe, so I abruptly stand from the chair, shoving it into the table in one angry motion.

"Can I take a walk?" I ask. My breath is hot, my knuckles clenched at my sides. Thoughts of Dad's last voicemail overcome me.

"Walk? It's nearly nine o'clock."

"I need some air. Please?"

Kam returns, catching us in this silent standoff, which seems to be the only thing we're good at. "What's up?" he asks.

JJ leans back against the sink, arms crossed. "She wants to go for a walk. At night. Alone."

"I hate people," I say, "it's the best time for a walk—no one's out."

The look in Kam's eyes changes. He turns his back to me, leans over to JJ's ear and whispers something I can't hear. A minute later—fifty-seven seconds, actually—he turns around.

"Go," JJ says. "But take your phone so I can keep track."

When my feet move toward the door, they follow with a peace offering—a hug. Their arms tie around me like ropes, knotted and firm. I wiggle, try to pull away, but the harder I fight them, the tighter they squeeze. Whenever I try to run, this is what they do. To show me they're here, that they'll always be here; steadfast and unwavering, even when the rest of my life is an island crumbling into the ocean.

I don't say another word about the letters. It feels like they're only mine; between Dad and me, like the galaxy created just for us to see.

We stay locked in this embrace until I get a glimpse of the clock.

The time is 8:59 P.M. EST.

Not that it means anything because time is now irrelevant.

Nell texts me a link to a story about Dad. I shouldn't read it, but I do. The focus is on the specifics. The details of what happened. I don't want to know the *how*. What does it matter *how* he died if dead is dead is dead is dead is dead is dead? I suppose it matters if it were something profoundly absurd such as death by flashlight or death by ladybug. I'd been raised to understand my father's possible death would be important to our country in some patriotic way, heroic, but to me, he's just . . . gone.

Nell, and a lot of others, think it matters—the *how*. Nell always thought a lot of stuff mattered that didn't. The way my hair lies, the choices in clothing I made, the path I veered violently toward to piss her off.

The day the sedan pulled into our drive, she asked the CNO about the *how* and wanted to shout it from the rooftops, as if Dad would hear and glide back down from above. The words "with honor" bounced between the walls. She persisted so he respectfully instructed her to call the Casualty Assistance Call Officers (CACO), who could give her the gory answers she sought. It was an extra step she *had* to do, though I wished she hadn't. If he'd died by a ladybug, would it feel any less traumatic?

I think of the sequence, the *how* with Mom, for Dad and Nell's paths to have crossed. *How,* if Mom had lived through my birth, Dad wouldn't have joined the military, maybe. *How* he wouldn't have been shot on his third tour, probably. *How* he wouldn't have needed physical therapy, where he'd meet this stranger, this woman obsessed with clean eating and boutique clothing pop-up shops like Lee Lee Rose in her living room, who had a kid my age who's nothing like me; *how* he'd decide she could fill the void Mom had left in both of us. *How* it would be good for me, for us (not realizing how many of those pop-ups I'd have to partake in) (too damn many). That's a lot of *hows* that didn't create an entire galaxy from nothing. It merely interfered with a system already in place.

I heard Nell on the phone after. After the CACO call, when she spoke to people from her "just in case" list—those to contact "in case of Dad's death." We had it pinned up on the inside of the cabinet for months, but pretended not to notice it. I noticed, always. As she spoke in one long incoherent ramble, I kept my ears pinned back from the noise. I couldn't help what I heard. Pieces of the *how* uncovered. She pressed and pressed.

How Dad stepped on an Improvised Explosive Device (IED).

    How it alerted his platoon allowing them to take cover.

        How proud we should be of all his years of bravery.

        And we are.

            But not without the anger

That selfishly comes with losing him.

So, really,

This article doesn't say

Anything I didn't already

Know, but wish

I didn't.

Voicemail

Dad

cell
March 19 at 1:11 PM

Transcription Beta

"Thought I'd try back while I have the chance. You're mad I'll miss your birthday—I get it—but I'll be back to take you to Ivy Springs. That's something I'll make happen. I swear it. Nell's been worried about you. Said you came home crying from school but didn't want her to know. What's going on, Ima? Is someone treating you bad? Tell me and I'll take care of it. But I know if there's something to take care

of, you're the girl who'll do it yourself.
Am I right? Maybe I'm worrying over
nothing. Tell me it's nothing. Is it
nothing?"

▶ 0:00 |▬▬▬▬▬▬▬▬▬▬▬▬▬▬▬▬▬▬▬| -0:37

Speaker   **Call Back**   **Delete**

Email Draft (Unsent)

New Message	✕

To
_____

Subject
_____

It's not nothing
    But I don't want to bother you
        Or Nell by telling you
            The things that have happened
                Almost every day
                    Since school started.
It wouldn't change anything
And I don't really care what
Those girls say.
They don't know me
And I don't care
To know them.

◄◄   ►►| ►|| ■   ●   **DEW GD BRICKMAN**
DURATION: 3:38

Breaking: Bath time isn't age- or gender-conforming, but makes a great slogan if you say it right.

Stella runs me a warm bath, sprinkling oatmeal into the basin. It smells like the cookies Dad loved; the ones Mom often burned; the ones Stella's edited for allergens and bakes proudly.

As I'm waiting, I replay Kam's words on a loop, and imagine my parents standing in front of me. My vision of them is translucent. They're fading. They don't say a word. Dad wears this fedora, and Mom wears this August Moon T-shirt. It's how I last saw them. Before the lady showed up at my school, when my life was in one, compact piece. My fingers rub along the underneath of the hat's rim, the way Dad used to when he was thinking, or reading something important. There's an indent in the fabric where he pressed the hardest, the spot of fabric his finger and thumb touched most often. I touch it, too.

Faith practices hitting a string we hung in her doorway, occasionally missing and slamming a fist into the wall. It knocks into my wall, to which she follows with "sorry." I sit and contemplate the plotline of my life. How I got here, the steps that had to happen for me to sit on this bed, staring at an August Moon poster, while listening to my sister shout wrestling slogans. I'm deep in thought when my phone skids across the bed, vibrating. It's Violet.

"Hello?" I ask.

"So how'd that thing go you never asked me about?" she asks.

My hands shake. I try to steady them.

"As expected."

"Is that good or bad?"

"It remains to be seen."

"What are you up to?"

I can't tell her I'm nearly seventeen and awaiting my bath. "Nothing. You?"

"Just got off work. I picked up another shift because we got so effing busy."

"That's a long day."

"I should've known. My horoscope said, 'Today is a day for action,' so it's my fault."

"What did my horoscope say?"

"Let me look." There's a long pause as she fumbles with her phone. I anxiously await, still reveling in the fact that she's called me at all. "K, ready?"

"As ready as one can be."

"It says, 'The universe has a surprise arranged for you. You won't see it coming, and you'll be caught off guard, so be prepared for *anything*.' Wow, okay. I'm spooked, are you spooked?"

"Should I be spooked?"

"DEW—YOU SHOULD BE SPOOKED."

"It's settled, then. I'm spooked."

"But seriously," she says, "what surprise do you think it means?"

"This phone call was a surprise, so maybe this?" The line goes dead. "Hello?"

"Yeah, no, I'm here. You just blew my damn mind." She laughs to herself, mumbling something about how she should've thought of that.

"I suppose astrology doesn't have to be big, life-changing things for them to be accurate."

"Who said me calling isn't a big, life-changing thing?"

That blushing thing happens again. This time, I think my jaw numbs, too. I feel my nerve building, stacking upon itself to do the thing—to ask her on a date. I open my mouth, fully ready to commit to this other big, life-changing thing when Stella interrupts.

"Dew—bath's ready!" she says. I quickly cover the receiver as if it can rewind time and erase it completely.

The silence lengthens. And lengthens some more.

"Guess I'll let you go," she says. "You work tomorrow, right?"

I slap my hand over my eyes, mortified. "I do, indeed."

"Enjoy your bath." She laughs, and I laugh, but I'm dead now.

When I hang up, I lay my phone next to the recorder. And suddenly it isn't an August Moon song that fills my ears, but Faith barreling in from the hallway.

"Dew! Dew! I did it—I have a new catchphrase," she says.

"Give it to me."

"'Bath time, baby.'"

NAIMA

I walk along the quiet sidewalk, stumbling on a large boulder used as a monument that celebrates the loss of someone else who's been lost. I kneel next to it, wishing I'd folded up the first of the letters to read here, beneath the streetlamp. Something about it feels right enough. Mosquitos bite into my legs and arms. I swat and continue on, unsure of where I'm going, remembering only where I've been.

The history of me.

I pass a group of girls my age. I've seen them in passing over my summers here. They laugh and I wonder. If changing schools matters. If people really change. If I'll always feel like the out-lier. Our old neighbor, Mr. Powell, watched our life-changing news from his window. He didn't hide from sight, probably re-lieved it wasn't about his wife who deployed before Dad. They talked about the drive to Dover Air Force Base, where we'd be reunited with Dad's remains. The word slipped and we could tell it wasn't meant to be used. The officer grew visibly anxious, backtracking his words to clarify in a more respectful manner. But I'd already heard it—"remains." As if the rest of Dad had been abandoned somewhere. And, I suppose, it had.

He was in the FLOAT phase, a fallen loved one awaiting transfer. While I died somewhere in between

Courage and cowardice.

Darkness and light.

Forgiveness and condemnation.

Rising and fading.

Forgetting and remembering.

And all that happens

Before death.

I remember these things with such an ache in my chest, I don't know where I've ended up until the light startles me out of the past. Baked & Caffeinated is lit from within, booths and tables full of all of Ivy Springs enjoying the same treats Dad and I used to. I press my hands and face to the window to peer inside at the smiles, pretending I'm still in there, too.

When I let go, I don't see a penny, but a different sign of sorts.

HELP WANTED

Feeling the sign between my fingers, I'm sick. A cold sweat, rumbling stomach, and dizzied haze encompassed around everything I see. If I move, the weight of me could fall over on the sidewalk, where I'll become part of Ivy Springs forever.

My phone rings but I ignore it. JJ and Kam want to hear my voice, to know I'm "okay." I can't answer. I let each ring go to voicemail, again and again. Just like I did to Dad.

I pick up my phone to see a barrage of new texts.

JJ: *Tracking you but call if you want to be picked up <3*

Instead of replying, I decide to take myself on a tour of all the spots that mattered to Dad and me. Leaving Baked & Caffeinated, I walk half a block down to Paint the Sky. One class, we painted the constellations. Another, it was the sunrise. I didn't realize then that he was reminding me he'd always be part of my world. In swirls of canvas color.

I don't stay long. The town feels a little too empty. I start toward the place the memorial will be—where the bench will sit next to the cherry tree. But I can't. Instead, I turn, and head home. Or the closest thing to it. My finger lingers over the voice-mail file from Dad. I want to hear his voice but I can't.

Would you rather listen to something that will break you, or always wonder what words may have been?

My feet pick up the pace, following the route I'd taken summers past. Somehow carrying me back to Baked & Caffeinated instead. People stroll through the glass door with ease. The simple act of going in, or going out, seems impossible to me. I do this five more times. My feet grind into the pavement, protest my indecision.

I hold my breath and force myself inside, expecting an explosion or confetti or something so huge, I'll wish I'd never come. But once I breeze through that same glass door, there is nothing. I find myself at the counter, tapping my nails against the marble.

"Can I help you?" A guy, probably early twenties, asks from behind the counter. I didn't see him last summer, but last summer is a place I've come to rewrite memories from, not a well from which I can pull concrete truths.

I freeze again and I hate it. *Like, please don't talk to me and please read my mind and please be my friend but one last thing—don't be my friend.*

"Ready to order?"

My mouth opens, but I'm silent. Another employee, a girl dressed in a spaghetti tank and long, billowy skirt, rushes over to whisper into the boy's ear. Her hair is adorned with a twisted metal halo, sculpted flowers along the sides. There are whispers and fingers pointing and waving. Maybe toward me, maybe not.

My vision blurs in and out so I can't be sure. Pressure crushes my every thought. I stare, blankly, at the riddle. He leans over the counter.

"You all right?"

I find my balance and courage. "I want to apply for a job."

"Sweet sauce." He pulls a page from beneath the counter and lays it flat. A line forms behind me. From here, I can see the booth Dad and I sat at every Sunday. I liked it because it was the farthest from the front door, closest to the counter. It's always good to know your exits. I hadn't been inside since the last time he was with me. I stare longingly, imagining our imprints still there, laughing over coffees—his black, no sugar; mine sugar, no coffee. No one sits there now. The booth is empty.

Empty.

"You want to fill it out now and then we can chat?" he interrupts my thoughts.

I look to him, and to the empty booth again. My mouth remains closed.

One long minute passes. Maybe two. I don't know how much time. *I don't know.*

"Do you want some water?" the girl asks. "It's pH-balanced."

I fight through the feeling of everyone watching and listening, pulling myself out of it. "No . . . thanks."

The walls box me in; there are too many people. It's hot. It's cold. I should've left before my feet crossed the line. I could redo. I don't know how long I stand here. I can't count with everyone watching and I can't touch my throat and I can't flick my fingers so all I can do is sprint through the door.

My legs have never moved so fast. Arms pump, lungs struggling to catch any air, I run and run and run and run and run and run, avoiding all lines, cracks and splits and bumps and rocks, until I collapse at the base of the cherry tree. It already feels like this spot belongs to me. I sit in a shadow where they've sectioned off the dirt—the place some of his ashes will be buried—and catch my breath. I hadn't really looked before, or maybe I didn't

want to. It's surreal to see it, to know this is the end of everything. And as the application crinkles between my hands, maybe
the beginning.

I hate the start. Start. Start. Start. Start. Start.

Of new.

Voicemail

Dad

cell
March 25 at 2:40 AM

Transcription Beta

"I can't stop calling. I know you won't
answer, but still. I call. Nell tells me
you've been struggling. I'm so sorry,
baby. Wish I was home."

▶ 0:00 |▬▬▬▬▬▬▬▬▬▬▬▬▬▬▬▬▬▬▬▬▬▬ -0:15

Speaker   **Call Back**   **Delete**

No New Emails

⏮ ⏭ ⏯ ⏹ ⏺ DEW GD BRICKMAN
DURATION: 6:21

*Update from an earlier story: Adorbsville is not an
actual place either.*

Violet has ahold of my hand. I photograph the feeling, the way
she delicately cradles the underneath, the smoothness of her
skin. She says there are four major lines: heart, head, life, and
fate.

"You have a water palm," she says. "You're sensitive and emotional."

The store is empty, and has been for hours, so we've been
spending our time smashed together on the back countertop with
a gluten-free brownie between us while Big Foot mans the front.
She says it's like the movie *Sixteen Candles*—aside from no cake
or birthday or really anything else.

"Never seen it," I tell her.

She gasps. "Blasphemy, Dew-Was-Diaz-Brickman. Everyone's seen it—it's an eighties cult classic."

I shrug.

"*Say Anything?*"

"Like what?"

"No—the movie. Tell me you've seen that one."

I don't answer. She understands this as my confession, and
pulls my hand closer to her.

"Tell me about my fate," I say.

"Having a water palm mean's you're special. Not everyone
does." She angles my hand, looks a little sharper. She points to a
deep line cutting through, with intermittent breaks along the
path. "Oh, this is interesting."

"What?" I audibly gulp.

"See how it breaks and comes back together?"

I nod, my heart racing.

"It's a sign there's a bigger force at play. Something that might wreck your world—multiple times, even—but you'll find a way to persevere."

She lets go and my hand drops to my side. "Pretty deep, right?"

"Indeed." I dizzily walk away, contemplating.

"Does it sound like you?" She chases me, grabs ahold of my hand again to show me the lines, compared to those in her palm. "See how different our lines are? My fate line is short. It means compared to someone like you, I'll be seen as a free spirit and I can go from thing to thing without stressing too much about it."

"Sounds accurate enough." She elbows me and follows me to the utility closet, where I grab the broom.

"Can I ask you something personal?"

"Sure."

"Why are you always late? Today it was twenty minutes, yesterday seventeen. You don't seem like the slacker type, or the dude who's okay with people being upset with him. What's the deal?"

I grip the top of the broom. "I have a weird thing about time. It gets away from me."

"But, like—and stop me if this sounds too rude—people who are consistently late are *usually* avoiding other issues. Is everything okay at home?"

I hesitate and she backs off. "I'm sorry. *Totally* not my business."

I decide to peel back another layer. For me, this time.

"Being on time reminds me that my parents are gone. I guess there's a part of me that's decided being late is safe—because if they had been late, they'd still be alive—and so I'm always late. I don't know what *that* says about me."

Her eyes well and she leaps toward me, wrapping her arms around me, snug. I drop the broom. "I'm sorry," she says. "I wasn't expecting you to get that deep. Thank you for trusting me with something so painful."

"It feels good to say out loud. I never do, really. I'd rather pretend it's part of someone else's life while I move on with mine. It's easier that way."

"My dude," she says, "you sound like my girl Birdie. Eyes forward, chin up, don't think about it, don't talk about it, don't acknowledge it. Because the second you do, you'll combust. I get it. I'd probably react the same way."

We share a long, silent stare that borders on too long. When she lets go, I feel a release of sorts. Like I've been submerged underwater for a long time, and suddenly, I can breathe again.

I deviate from the awkward as I pick up the broom. "We've been working together long enough. You should know something about me other than my love of August Moon and the Paper Hearts."

"Yes, *please*. A girl can only take so much."

"My mom and dad were part of their band for years, then became openers for other bands before they . . . nevermind. I could listen to them every second of my life and it wouldn't be enough."

Her head drops. "Damn you, Violet," she tells herself. Then, looking up at me: "I don't mean it that way. The music isn't bad, it's just that, it's all we've heard and . . . you know what? I'm going to stop talking now."

"It's okay. Not everyone understands why I have to listen to them. How the melodies remind me of the good times. Even when life felt unbearable, I still had my parents through the music." I feel a little too exposed. To fill the space, and avoid eye contact, I begin to sweep the floor around us. "Tell me more about you. Why are *you* always perfectly on time?"

"It's strange, but I have a weird thing with time, too. Ever since Birdie's little brother was in that accident, I'm almost afraid of it. The way the fates lined up for such a horrible thing to happen kind of haunts me. Makes me wonder how much control we even have. Over anything, really. Maybe me being on time is similar to why you're late. Somewhere in me, I've decided it's safe and so, I'll always be on time." She winks, but there are more tears she's holding back.

"I get it," I say. "I'd probably react the same way." Now I wink, but it's more like my face contorts. I play it off by pretending a bug flew in my direction.

She asks more about my parents, how they managed to birth someone so "awesome," and something about my adoption, when I hear *that* voice.

"Sorry about before," the voice says. "Running out of here was weird and inappropriate, and I'm kind of working on it but kind of failing. Please don't judge me."

"No judgements here, friend. It's cool," Big Foot replies. "I get anxious in new situations, changes, when storms roll through, and when there aren't enough Oreos in my Blizzard. We all have our things, you know?"

"True . . . so I don't have a rèsumè or anything, but I like baked things and the smell of coffee," she says. I inch my way to the edge of the doorframe to see Naima standing before Big Foot. I retract my body as far back as possible, my ears opening like satellites.

"Are you available for random shifts—evenings and weekends?" Big Foot asks.

"I have no life, so yes," she replies. "As long as it's a schedule I can rely on. I don't like last-minute changes. I'm not that person."

"Minimum wage to start but there's tips and room for advancement. Free coffee drinks and one allergen-friendly brownie or cookie per shift."

"Don't really need the money but I like free stuff and judging people from behind a counter."

"When can you start?"

"Not this exact minute, but, like, tomorrow."

"Cool bones. Sounds like we have a deal."

"Awesome Sauce City."

"Come about an hour before we open for training." He hands her another stack of papers. "Fill these out, bring your social security card, and an ID if you have one."

She doesn't smile, doesn't really do much of anything. "Welcome aboard," he says. "You're about to get Baked *and* Caffeinated. Get it?"

"Unfortunately."

I lose my grip on the handle. The broom falls to the floor with a loud *crack*. I'm now completely, and utterly visible, as if every layer has shed, leaving me here in the nude.

"You okay, Dew?" Violet shouts from somewhere deep in the back room.

"*Dew*—GD—Brickman works here?" Naima asks with a razor-edged tone.

"You know this fedora-wearing mini-muffin?" Big Foot asks. "Isn't he Adorbsville dot com? Legally, I'm not supposed to say that because, you know, the Me Too movement and sexual harassment and such, but I'm speaking the truth. He's a mini-muffin and anyone who says otherwise needs their noodles cooked."

She doesn't laugh. Actually, she appears angrier than ever before. As if I've ruined a perfectly smooth sweater by tossing it into the dryer.

"I don't need the job *that* bad," she snaps. The bell on the door dings as she storms out.

He turns to me, confused. "I take it she doesn't like mini-muffins or Adorbsville dot com."

Violet joins me as I shrug, but I'm beginning to understand: Naima's problem has nothing to do with love or friendship, and everything to do with her inability to deal with how she *might* want to be friends with *me*, too.

NAIMA

On my way out of the dumb bakeshop, I nearly trip over an object—a recorder that looks like Dew's. I keep ahold of it so JJ can walk it over ('cause I'm not gonna). If it's trash, that's where I'll put it, hoping the sweet raccoons will find it and record their little nose boops and hijinks.

Would you rather boop all the animals or be a sad, lonely soul?

I still have the first saved voicemail from Dad, and I've been playing it on repeat while avoiding the last like the plague (side note: if the plague hit, I still wouldn't listen to the last voicemail).

"*Naima . . . you don't hate me. I know . . . I should've been home by now. . . . I'm frustrated, too. . . . I promise I'll be back soon. Once you're settled in Indiana, I'll call. And honey . . . I love you. Never forget that.*"

When I get back to the house, I replay his words without a care as to how long it takes for me to seal his voice into my subconscious.

Again

    and again

        and again

            and again

                and again.

After the sixth time, I remember I've also saved a voice memo for hard times where he says, "Butterfly," but it cuts off. *If I'm really a butterfly, Dad, let me fly away to wherever you and Mom are.*

If only long enough for me

To say.

I'm sorry.

Despite the tics building inside my bones, I force myself to grab the necessities: six packs of gum, my phone, charger, headphones, a Ziploc of marshmallows, and the stack of letters I've yet to open. Is there not a piece of Ivy Springs that Dew is absent from? I don't want to live next to him, work with him, or take anything—like Dad's letters or balloon—from *him*, but there has to be a sacrifice somewhere.

And anyway, Dad would understand if I didn't stand up to speak at the memorial, he would, he would, he would, he would, he would, he *can't*. I dump my balled-up things into a plastic grocery sack pulled from a drawer full of them. The handle nearly breaks when I try to free a single bag from the bulk. There are other groceries—eggs, milk, and various crackers and cans on JJ and Kam's counter. Instead of putting them away, labels facing out, everything aligned just so, I leave them. There's no time; never any time.

Time. Time. Time. Time. Time. Time.

My fingers form a devious point at the front of me. These things matter to me because these things I have control over. I will leave that strawberry cake on the table. I will. I will leave it. Right there. With the anthrax-laced ingredients. With the urn watching over. And I'll avoid JJ and Kam's questions about where I went, or why I'm not speaking at the memorial. I can't.

Can't.

The next day, I'm in the basement staring at the letters when Kam tiptoes down. I barely notice him until he's right next to me. I could hide everything, again, but don't.

"Are you going to read them?" he asks, taking a seat where the balloon still hides beneath the covers. "He probably sent them in the hope you'd find comfort."

"I'm not ready," I say.

He sighs, dragging it out as if he's taking the extra time to consider his next move. "I probably wouldn't be either." There's a pause. "I haven't been able to drink out of my favorite mug. Can't even seem to help JJ move the damn urn."

"Maybe he arranged for you to get letters, too."

"Even if he had, I'd do the same thing you are. It's too soon to think of the past, a past where he was alive." He lays a hand on my shoulder. "But I hope you didn't give Dew a hard time about the balloon. He meant well."

I chew my bottom lip, fighting my argument back.

He stares at the letters before standing to go. "We love you. I hope you know your dad did, too."

I tap one foot just to the other side of the floor, and back to the inside. Six times. JJ shouts from the top of the stairs.

"Time to get to the church to help the girls set up."

Seven.

I start over.

Tap tap tap tap tap tap.

"You coming with us?" she adds.

"I'll walk down in a bit," I say.

Presence lingers. "It'll be okay," she reassures.

Footsteps finally fade, Kam's too. Hiccup is, thankfully, crated. I hold my glare on the letters, fingers itching. I take a breath and pull the first from the stack, sliding my nail underneath to open the flap. It suddenly feels as if I've waited too long and I can't read it fast enough. Until his handwriting strikes me dead. Here he is, right there, in that old ink and faded paper. He says he loves me, he misses me, he's sorry he's gone. But the part that almost breaks me, as if he knew our intent today:

Go to the church. It's the only place you'll find the peace you've been looking for.

After a while of staring into the void—at least an hour and eighteen seconds—I grab my grocery bag full of things, and walk in the direction of the church. There's a fund-raiser in the basement for the Paxton boy—Benny, I think. Last year he was hit and nearly killed by a drunk driver in Clifton, the town over. The Paxtons have been there before, JJ says, but I wouldn't remember. For me, it's been a long, *long* time.

Along the multi-block journey, I think of my fifteenth birthday when Dad, JJ, and Kam drew perfectly pointed arrows in neon chalk on the sidewalk. My feet decide to follow the memory without asking. The arrows alternated in color; a pattern. I

couldn't have known there would be a splendiferous pattern—
something my feet could fall into without worry. The small details are important. They matter. Dad knew that.

Pink blue yellow orange.

Pink blue yellow orange.

Pink blue yellow orange.

Pink blue yellow orange.

Pink blue yellow orange.

Pink blue yellow orange.

For once in my life, my clumsy feet paid no attention to the
sidewalk cracks or the time or how many windows were on each
building or how many objects I passed that required my toes to
scrunch. There was lightness, like someone new inhabited my
mind. Maybe it was because Dad was alive, so whether I followed
the arrows or not, the universe was intact; constellations still in
formation.

When I was young, I thought the church was a castle where
the princess of Ivy Springs lived. JJ and Kam would try to bait
me inside on Sunday mornings. For a long time, the church
bells and sky-length spires frightened me. It never felt like a safe
place, one of comfort. It felt, to me, as if the moment I'd step
inside, my soul would be sucked out of me. TBH, I still feel
this way.

As I walk through the community garden, hand-planted by
JJ, Kam, and the urban youth organization they helped establish
on the outskirts of Indy, I know I shouldn't be so consumed with
my own grief. This event isn't about me. I move closer to the
church, envisioning the arrows drawing past the roundabout,
through City Hall's paved courtyard path, to a large castle/church
on the corner of Market and Franklin Streets. The spires seem
to reach the moon. I lift my hand, pretend to stretch as far (and
also look stupid AF).

I pause. My breaths shorten into wisps. The sight of the enor-
mous building pains me; the memory pains me. I've spent my
life avoiding this place, going out of my way not to see it. And

here I am, standing at the helm of the only building in Ivy Springs that Kam didn't build or have a hand in building via his architecture-laced family. The only building that holds both my mother's and father's faces both dead and alive.

I have no place here—no right. People are in and out of the big wooden double doors. I turn away so they don't speak to me. I'm slow up the steps where the imaginary arrows end abruptly, my fingers tapping the doors.

As I stand with my plastic bag at my side, something keeps me from going straight in. Not a breath of wind or physical barrier. My feet have burrowed into the ground. Trying to protect me. But what if I don't need protecting this time? What if everything I need is just beyond the door? Still, the only real echo of memory I have—something I was way too young to remember, but have been told about all through my life—stands in my way.

Mom's funeral.

Voicemail

Dad

cell
April 20 at 7:14 AM

Transcription Beta

"I called Principal Maynard. I want you to know, in case anyone gives you any trouble today. I think we should talk about moving schools. He gave me the impression this has been going on longer than you, or Nell, have let on. I wish I could do more, but I can't if you

don't talk to me. If anyone messes with
you again, go straight to the principal.
If you won't tell me, please tell Nell or
JJ or Kam. We're trying to help."

▶ 0:00 |▬▬▬▬▬▬▬▬▬▬▬▬▬▬▬ -0:33

Speaker   **Call Back**   **Delete**

Email Draft (Unsent)

New Message   ✕

To

Subject

You didn't help me by calling
   The school.
      It only made those girls
         Come after me
Harder for
Getting them in trouble.
I want to change schools
I want to move in with JJ and Kam
As soon as possible.

⏮ ⏭ ▶⏸ ⏹ ⏺ **DEW GD BRICKMAN**
DURATION: 2:49

*Tonight at 8: Boy attempts to fly his plane against
the wind, may fail.*

I can't find my mechanical best friend. I've been sitting along
the hem of my comforter, watching the seconds tick by, retrac-
ing my steps. All night, Faith's voice carried through my wall,
shouting phrases and slogans, hoping another might stick. I covered my ears with a pillow, but it offered no consolation. I tried
humming Mom's favorite song, but the words wouldn't scroll.
All I could think about was the recorder. Even as Stella and
Thomas prepare to attend a fund-raiser at the church, waiting
for me to make my grand entrance beyond my bedroom door, I
sit, and I stare, and I think.

I text Violet in haste, positive I've erased entire blips of time
like a sort of disassociative disorder as a way to cope.

Me: *Did you, by chance, happen to see my recorder anywhere?*

Violet: *Like, the phone you're texting me from?*

I pause, my fingers lingering over the letters. It isn't the time
to explain.

Me: *Never mind.*

Violet: *You want today's silver lining to help you deal?*

Me: *Sure.*

Violet: *Okay—this is my favorite Henry Ford quote so hold it close:
"When everything seems to be going against you, remember that the airplane takes off against the wind, not with it." Does that make your situation
any better?*

Me: *It actually does. Thank you* ☺

Violet: ☺

A knock at the door pulls me from this cycle of time-wasting.
I drag myself to the mirror, run my fingers through my hair, and
practice my smile until it reads "believable."

I open the door to see Joelle with a palm opened. "Did you

lose something?" My recorder is dirt-covered and wary. "Hiccup tried to bury it in my magnolias. Hope it still works."

Before I muster a single coherent word, I fall into her, arms wrapped snug around her small waist. "You have *no* idea how grateful I am."

She gently rubs the back of my head while shushing, and it reminds me of Mom. I suddenly feel sick with sadness.

She peels me back. "You're gonna be fine, you hear?" A finger tips my chin. "With or without that thing. I know it."

"Yes, ma'am."

"And with Naima," she hesitates, "give her time."

When she steps away, I tell myself it's over, *I'm okay.* Following the shape of Joelle to her car, I watch from the window. She and Kam slip away, on with their day, and I wonder where Naima slipped to. I glance at the clock. I'm perfectly late. I press Record on my recorder and I feel it. As if tattooed along my fate line.

If the airplane flies against the wind, so will I.

NAIMA

Why did I come? When I release the breath, I halt all other thoughts by shoving the doors wide open. I half expect the angels to sing or birds to fly down around me but I guess that's *not* real life? Whatever. When my eyes flutter open, the beauty of the stained glass sets in, warmth of the golden oak pews radiate, and the beam of light, that almost feels as if it were created straight from the heavens, shines just for me. I think about texting Dr. Tao for affirmations (*you're a bad mamma jamma*). But like all the other times I think of doing something, I don't.

I take it all in. I walk slowly down the long aisle, between the passing people. A few ask how I'm doing. I ignore them. JJ is directly to my left, but I avoid even her. Because I have no memories of Mom, every last piece I hold of Dad rushes in. His laugh, his smile. The comfort, strength. The last time he hugged me. The last time he told me to "be brave," and the last time I ever felt safe in my entire life. I remember it all. *I remember. Everything* except *anything* about Mom.

No matter what I do, how I try to fill the empty space of Mom, *I'm still empty.* How can you miss someone you've never known? Being in this place, just like all the times JJ tried to convince me to join her and Kam here, reminds me—not of all I have—*of all I've lost.* And those things are lost because of me. I did that. All of it.

One. Two. Three. Four. Five. Six.

At my school in Albany, a group of girls who controlled almost the entire grade called me selfish, said everything wasn't about me. That I was obsessed with making the world stop to see me count or scratch or hop over a divot or talk about the headlines that kept me up all night. Said I wasn't worth the air I breathe. That no matter what I did, I'd only ever be broken and pathetic. They said it's why Dad left. They'd known me a total of four weeks and knew this about me. Some of the last thoughts I had about Dad were "stay gone forever."

So my brain says, *Maybe they're right.*

Molecules collide inside me—every last twinge of pain—until they suddenly combust. In front of everyone, right there in the center of the aisle, I fall to my knees, and as the light holds me down, I bellow a shriek louder than any I've ever created. It births in the deepest pit of me, and rises, my voice breaking into shards as I release it. People stop hovering over the family they're meant to hover over and run to me, the selfish one who can't seem to find her way out of her own bits of broken mind long enough to hover with them.

"Is she hurt?" a woman asks.

"What happened?" another interjects.

JJ pushes through. "I got her." She shoves my bag out of the way, kneels, and pulls me into the warmth of her. Her arms wrap tightly around my head, so I can't see all the eyes pressed. I don't stop my tears; I let them fall fast and hard, right here beneath the giant cross. I cry and I pray and I pray and I cry like I never have in my life. I don't know if anyone outside of our universe hears me, if it matters, but somewhere in this building, in my heart, maybe Mom and Dad do.

I wish I could be unborn so you can live again, Mom; so you'd never have left and died, Dad.

"I hope she's okay," I hear. When I squint my eyes, it's the faces of the parents we're here to support. *They're* comforting *me.*

As JJ rocks me, shushing into my ear, Dad's voice chimes in. On my birthday every year, when we'd have to remember my life is here because of her death, he'd say, "*You* didn't kill her. She wouldn't want you to feel guilty—she'd want you to soar on without her. *Butterfly.*"

Reverend Mills—the very same who baptized me and my father; the very same who was present when my father was delivered to the Blue County cemetery for his memorial service—rushes in and crouches down. "Can I pray with you?"

I look up, barely holding the sight, and nod. We bow our heads and pray.

My thirteenth birthday, I refused Dad's letter for the first time because I was mad he'd left again. He tried to tell me how important this would be; that to pray might set me free. No matter how many times Dad told me, I never felt it, never believed him.

Never.

Never.

Never.

Never.

Never.

Never.

I pay no attention to the time, or those surrounding us. I forget this is a carry-in fund-raiser for a boy who almost lost his life. Maybe it's the way the light hits or the emotion of all before me, but when I open my eyes, just barely, I see something shiny beside JJ's foot—a penny. Finally, for the first time in seventeen years, I forgive myself for being alive. *I love you, Mom. Thank you.*

Even if,

I don't deserve it.

Voicemail

Dad

cell
May 10 at 10:09 AM

Transcription Beta

"[sigh] Ima . . . I need you to know, I'm sorry for missing your birthday, for not being there for you. For *everything*. Take care of Nell and Christian and always remember that [call ends]"

▶ 0:00 |======================= -0:24

Speaker   **Call Back**   **Delete**

Email Draft (Unsent)

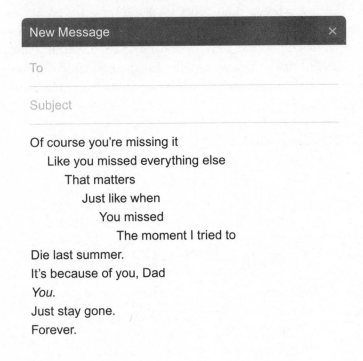

New Message   ×

To

Subject

Of course you're missing it
    Like you missed everything else
        That matters
            Just like when
                You missed
                    The moment I tried to
Die last summer.
It's because of you, Dad
You.
Just stay gone.
Forever.

⏮ ⏭ ▶⏸ ⏹ ⏺ **DEW GD BRICKMAN**
DURATION: 4:01

*Coming up: Run-in at local church causes quite a
stir for one family.*

At the church, Stella, Thomas, and Faith sit along a plastic-covered
table with plates full of various potluck foods. Faith is wearing
the general store's feather boa, a cowboy hat, and sunglasses
shaped like stars. I hold the umbrella I brought—there's a chance
of rain—and pin it to my side like a protective battle sword.

The flap is torn, and the latch you'd normally push has a strange malfunction where it pops upright without warning, but it's one of the first things Thomas gave me, so there's no other I'd rather have.

"Wasn't sure if you'd make it in time," Stella says, watching the cat video Faith shares with her. Their faces are consumed with the screen's brightness.

"I had a small altercation with life."

"What happened?" Thomas asks.

"I misplaced my recorder but Joelle found it in her garden."

"How'd that happen?"

"Your guess is as good as mine."

"I'm glad she found it. We could've bought you another."

"Dr. Peterson wants to wean me off it. She thinks I rely on it too much."

"I think it's helped. Think of where you were before it. Now you have a job, and you're in a full church, without so much as a panicked sweat."

I consider her words. "You're right. But so is Dr. Peterson. I need to learn how to cope without it."

Thomas pats my back. "I'm proud of you."

"We all are," Stella says. "And of Faith."

"Yeah yeah yeah, everyone's proud of everyone," Faith says. "We got it."

I casually scan the historic church that's filled with a rainbow of faces. Mary from the general store. Louis, who sits on the bench near the community garden I pass on my way to work. Enrique from the bank. But no Naima.

"She already left," Stella says with a smirk.

I pretend to act confused. "I don't know who you mean."

"Sure."

"She had a major breakdown," Faith interjects. "Screamed real loud. Everyone checked on her and she was fine. It was weird."

"Was she hurt?" My blood pumps a little harder. As if whatever happened, happened to me.

"No," Stella says. She signals for me to come closer, so she can whisper. Joelle and Kam are approaching. "The church must've reminded her of her parents."

Now that she's said it, I realize the stained glass resembles similar etchings from the church where my parents' funerals were held. My stomach drops, melting into a puddle along the taupe-carpeted floor. "Is she . . . okay?"

Joelle interrupts, hands intertwined. "So glad you all made it," she says. "And happy I was able to brighten your day, Dew."

"Thank you again," I say, though I can't manage to hold my smile. Thoughts of Naima wrenching in pain are all I see.

"Heard about the new fence that's going up in the community garden," Thomas says to Kam. "If you need more volunteers, let us know. We'd be happy to help. I know Dew's interested in helping, aren't you, Dew?"

My eyes fixate on a carpet thread that's come loose. I'm unable to move them.

Kam holds out a hand to shake. "I appreciate any help we can get. It's been a long time coming. The zoning alone was somethin'."

"Oh, Lord," Joelle says. "Don't get him started. We'll be here all night."

Faith sighs loud enough for everyone to drop the conversation.

"And you, Miss Thing, you look marvelous," Joelle tells her. "Very fancy."

She tosses her boa back and decides now is a perfectly good time to practice her latest catchphrase on actual people. "Gonna mop them boys up."

Their eyes bulge.

Stella swoops in. "She's decided to be a wrestler. This is her shtick."

"Now, that's something," Kam says.

"What's your stage name?" Joelle asks.

"The Conniption."

Joelle slaps Kam's back as she erupts with laughter. "You'll have to let us know when you have a match or meet or whatever it's called. We'll be there doing whatever wrestling fans do."

Faith offers a thumbs-up, her attention diverted back to her phone.

My attention drifts. Violet stands near the front of the church. She's dressed in a sunny yellow romper, her hair swept up in a loose bun as she converses with the parents of her friend, Birdie. A gleam across the floor catches my eye.

"Excuse me," I say.

As I lean over to pluck up the shiny penny—Joelle told me it's a sign someone above is watching—another hand reaches out.

"Found it first," the voice says. He looks up and a wash of red coats his face. Dodge. He drops the penny and backs away. In here, he looks like someone else. Long hair sideswept and clean. Crisp shirt tucked into smooth pants.

"You know the Paxtons?" I ask.

"Everyone does."

Sweat forms beneath my fedora. I tuck my chin to my chest and lose eye contact as he towers near. Not another word, not another breath in my direction. He shoves past and leaves the church altogether. So, I do the thing Mom wanted me to. I think of stepping inside his shoes, and I follow.

NAIMA

I can't stop thinking about what Bess Paxton, the mother of the boy who was hit by the car, said before I left the church.

"Grief will kill you if you let it. Some things are out of our control."

It was the way she said it. I could feel the gratitude of life in her words, but also the heavy sorrow within the context, that her son survived, albeit with a traumatic brain injury. There's acceptance in her cadence. She's right.

I'm in control of nothing.

Rounding the corner from the memorial spot, I'm mere doors from Paint the Sky. I've already thought of all the words I could use with those letters, *PTS*: Pass the Shit, Peasant Trash Soap, Pit-Tee-Stain, Please Talk Softer, and my favorite, People Tell Secrets, because I'm living it now. The historic row of buildings in the heart of downtown represent a time and place most of the world has pulled away from. The sun is at its brightest, hottest; heat bounces from the old brick and mortar. The orange flames lick the top of my head, revealing a long shadow in front of me. When I reach the steps to the shop's door, I relive the memory of a package that once sat there; a package meant for me.

I peer inside the window. It's now empty as their hours have become by-appointment-only, but the space I can see reminds me of the year Dad missed the father-daughter dance in Fort Hood. He promised he'd be home to take me, but at the last minute, couldn't. Nell and Christian offered to take me, but no—I was so upset I painted all the words I could think of (the not nice ones) onto the paintings he and I made together. When he made it home, he saw, and I could see how much it hurt him. But I didn't care. He'd hurt me first.

Months later, when he was gone and I was here for the summer, I received instructions to come to this very spot for a belated birthday present. I didn't want to, but my curiosity got the best of me. He somehow planned for a box to be here when I was, and inside was the gown I wanted for the dance he missed. And I looked into this very window, through the muted shade to the reds, blues, and greens that flickered onto the floor. The colors don't sparkle now; the room is dark and empty.

That day this happened, a strobe light ignited, spinning a rainbow of colors across the shiny wooden floor in starry-eyed fashion. The floor revealed tape, formed like arrows, stopping at an

X in the center—the place where the tables were usually situated for paint class. I stood in that spot for a few minutes when a song burst through the speakers—"I Hope You Dance"—and out of the shadows, Dad appeared in his dress blues with his hand out, asking me for the dance he missed. It was the kind of thing you'd only see in movies.

I, inevitably, accepted his offer because, let's be real—he was always gone and I *wanted* to be near him—but then I complained about how sweaty touching hands was, and about moving in circles, and how pointless dancing was, and he asked how I could ever get close to anyone if I couldn't even dance with him. My tongue twisted and spit the fire of "We're not close. You're never even here!" To which he responded, as he always, always, always, always, always, always responded, with, "I'm here *now*." But *now* is gone, forever.

> *For prom begins at half past eight,*
>> *Just go inside; don't hesitate,*
>>> *Will you give me one more chance,*
>>>> *To offer you this one last dance?*

Now I only see the prom he'll miss; the wedding I might have. Any children I may conceive. Every career ladder I'll climb. I place my hand on the doorknob, part of me wanting to believe he'll walk out of the shadows like before. I've not danced with anyone since (dance battles with JJ and Kam don't count).

I let go.

Voicemail

Dad

cell
May 19 at 1:02 PM

Transcription Beta

"Couldn't sleep last night. Can't wait to spend time with you in Ivy Springs. It's all I can think about. We'll do all our usual things. It'll be like old times, but better. As soon as I can—even if it's through the school year. Promise. I miss you."

▶ 0:00 |━━━━━━━━━━━━━━━━━━━━━━━ -0:11

Speaker   **Call Back**   **Delete**

Email Draft (Unsent)

New Message   ✕

To

Subject

I wish I could tell you
    How many times
        I've counted the days
            Until I see you
                But in my heart
                    I don't believe
You'll actually
Show.

⏮ ⏭ ▶⏸ ■ ● DEW GD BRICKMAN
DURATION: 1:55

Storm warning: Ivy Springs weather to take
another unexpected turn, mechanical casualties
expected.

I remain ten steps back. A magnetic force drives me in his direction despite my stomach tangling into a million tiny knots. Perhaps I don't believe Dodge's hate has something to do with me. I sense a kindness—one he's not ready to confront—and wonder if I should step into his shoes, peel back a layer. Or maybe ask how he's feeling. I don't mean ask in a way that prompts a generic "fine," but to ask and really listen to the answers.

Dodge walks with his head down, avoiding eye contact with those he passes. I do the same, to commiserate, empathize. We're near the community garden when he stops abruptly.

"Why are you following me?" he asks.

I consider not moving or speaking, as if it might coat me in an invisibility cloak.

He turns and clomps toward me.

"Oh, hello," I say. My body crumbles.

"What do you want?"

"I, uh, I just wondered, um . . . ," I step back, my shoes catching on a sidewalk crack. I tumble backward into the cinderblock wall of the garden. My recorder falls from my pocket, out of reach and into pieces, and the umbrella shoots open like a burst of lightning. The metal knob at the top of the folded canopy lashes Dodge in the cheek. He stumbles, holding the sting in his palm, with a brief glance of heated rage. The events unfurl in slow motion. Dodge wipes a bead of blood from his cheek and looks at his hand. I fold tighter, wait for him to hurtle toward me. The recorder is stuck on Play, sounding a loop of tape.

"Your parents would be so proud proud proud proud . . ."

My heart beats wildly as everything around us silences.

Dodge flinches so I close my eyes and await his blow. It doesn't come. There's a light tap on my shoulder that pings one eyelid open. His hand lingers at my eye level to reveal my recorder's pieces. The tape is jammed; the only way to force it to stop is by breaking the plastic surrounding it. As I strike the concrete with my mechanical friend, a guttural scream echoes somewhere inside. Tears slide down my face; there is no stopping them.

"Are you okay?" Dodge watches intently, his eyes now commiserating, empathizing with mine. I feel him stepping into *my* shoes, peeling off my layer.

I open my mouth to say something profound, something my parents would've said, instead only managing a nod. He turns to walk away. It's not much, but somehow, it's enough.

NAIMA

I round the corner to see a figure moving away from another bunched-up figure on the sidewalk. The one cowering is Dew, by the design of his ridiculous fedora.

"What did you do?" I shout at the boy leaving.

He stops, turns around.

I run, not caring if I'm hitting cracks or divots, and I don't count how many steps. I slide between the two, and as the boy's empty hand raises again, something happens that never has before. I don't flinch. Eyes open, chest straight and proud, I stand here, prepared to take a hit meant for a boy I don't even like. It's for all the *me's* and *him's* of the world. For those who've been picked on for being ourselves.

"Naima, wait," Dew says.

I react swiftly, grabbing the boy's wrist, and with a rapid twist, all my weight is on top of him, with his arm and wrist bent behind him.

"Mercy!" he shouts. "MERCY!"

The Krav Maga moves Dad taught me, but was sure I didn't pay attention to, must've stuck. "Apologize," I order, tugging tighter.

"Naima, stop," Dew says, pulling himself upright.

"APOLOGIZE TO HIM."

The boy fights to be free. "Fine—let go! Let go! I'm sorry!"

I hold on, enjoying the rush of power streaming through me. This is for all the girls that called me a whale. For all the whispers about my hair. For all the damning stares they thought would break me. For all the people who've called me "crazy" instead of knowing me at all. I hold, then, as the adrenaline drops, let go.

He rubs his wrist as Dew rushes between us. "He didn't do anything to me. I tripped."

My laugh bellows. "Yeah, okay."

"He did," the boy says. "I didn't touch him."

"Hi, yeah, so you can go, thanks," I tell him, redirecting to Dew. The boy goes, hesitant in his steps. He rubs his red wrist, rounding the corner out of sight.

"Why did you do that?" Dew asks.

"I've had enough of this shit. Some people never change. At some point, I have to do something or it'll go on forever."

"This wasn't about you."

I frown. "Excuse me for helping."

"No, I mean, thank you for stepping in. You're a true ally and I appreciate that. But he honestly didn't cause me any harm. It was an accident."

I step back, shoving my hands in my pockets to pinch the fabric. My feet remain on either side of the sidewalk crack now. "Maybe he'll take it as a preemptive threat so he doesn't mess with anyone in the future. He'll fear I'm always waiting in the wings ready to strike if he steps out of line."

Dew takes off his fedora and holds it to his chest as he glances to the broken bits of recorder. "No," he suddenly cries, stuffing the bits into his fedora and pockets. "It's okay, Dew. It's okay. It's okay," he tells himself. "You're okay."

I lean down. "Maybe we can fix it."

He's inconsolable, sobbing into the pieces.

"I hate this thing, but it's only a recorder. You can get a new one."

He's shaking his head. "You don't understand."

I grab ahold of his hand to settle it. "I counted thirteen seconds since you took off your hat. My dad just died. I cried when my stepmom forgot my marshmallows. I *so* get it. More than anyone else. You knew that before we met. Give me some fuckin' credit."

He calms, finds my eyes. Realization flashes across his face. He stands and brushes off the dirt from his clothes. "I'm so embarrassed."

"*You're* embarrassed? I just wrestled some asshat—for no reason, apparently. Like a common day vigilante, an Avenger. *Damn.* I should be the new Dr. Strange to fix this time issue."

There's a lingering silence where our breaths connect—multiplying germs and all—and in an odd way, it brings a wash of calm over me. Dad used to tell me, on the days I'd come home and lock myself away after someone stole bits of my confidence, to look at people as mirrors. He said we could see the good and bad parts of ourselves in others. In Dew, I'm starting to see both.

Would you rather befriend an enemy or become one?

"So what were you doing anyway?" I ask, annoyed. "Stalking is a whole other conversation we need to have."

He gathers his thoughts. "No, nothing like that. I left the church and was on a stroll to the levee."

"Someone—JJ or Kam—probably told you to make sure I'm okay."

"No, I assure you. It's a matter of being in the same place at the same time, purely by coincidence." He hesitates. "But I did hear something happened. I suppose there's a grain of truth."

His thick curls flop over his forehead. His head is smaller than I remember and I wonder if that's why he covers it with a hat. I assume he's wondering why my head is so big and why I don't cover it with a hat. In my imaginary conversation, we come to an impasse.

"Are you . . . *okay*?" he asks, emphasizing that word again.

"Aside from almost kicking that guy's innocent ass, terrible. You?"

"To be frank, I was having a rather stressful morning." His voice dips, losing its usual cheeriness I hate.

"Who's Frank?" I can't help myself. "J/K. Why was it stressful?"

"I misplaced my recorder and cried for an hour before Joelle found it."

My feet kick at the ground. I refrain from confessing I had it, thought about listening to what was on it, but decided to keep it mum. Hiccup located it before I could give it back. It's the dog's fault, really.

"You don't need it," I say.

"My insides tend to disagree."

I study his face, the way his eyes twitch, the way he bites his lower lip after finishing a word, and it feels like he *is* me. Not always, but in this moment. I decide to do something Dad would've: offer grace.

"I know the feeling."

"Thank you for stepping in. I *could've* been in danger and you'd have saved the day." With his fedora still clinging to his chest, he offers a slight wave and walks away.

I watch the back of him. He's so alone. A star falling from the sky without a single planet to catch him. I start to wonder if it might not be so bad to fall right along with him.

"Wait," I say.

He turns, not hopeful, not much of anything except a shell of the kind boy I spoke with before.

"Can I come?"

He smiles. Lifts his fedora full of broken recorder to his mouth. "The princess finally sees the frog for his full worth, while he's always seen her for hers."

"Now it's just sad," I say.

His shoulders slump until a plane passes overhead, pulling his attention. "There goes another one. We'd better hurry."

"What?"

"Are you joining or not?" He signals with an inviting wave of the finger. "I'll let you have the first wish."

I don't know what it means, or where we're going. It doesn't matter.

He says I get a wish, and I know exactly what I'll wish for.

Missed Call

Dad
cell

May 23 at 4:59 AM

Saved Voicemail

◁◁ ▷▷ ▷❙❙ ■ ● DEW GD BRICKMAN
DURATION: 3:33

Breaking: Insides exposed on Ivy Springs levee;
prepare to evacuate.

Few cars drive past as we slink into murky twilight. The feeling of being on a roller coaster as you hit the peak of the climb and catapult into the descent—that's what my stomach feels like. We head to the levee, where benches hang by metal cables connected to the trees. She sits first, and I follow, allowing her enough space that a whole other person could manifest between us. The river water glitters from the slow-burning sun as the moon begins to reveal itself and the stars brighten their celestial patterns.

"Look up," I tell her.

"Why?" she asks.

"To make a wish."

"You know falling stars are dying, right? Wishing on them is morbid."

"Not on a star; an airplane."

"Did you hit your head?"

"No, did you?"

"No."

"It's settled. No one is injured."

We sit awhile in silence. Her body angles back to search me over, head to toe, before her gaze drifts to the endless blanket of sky. I let a grin slip through. The sun eventually slinks away, few aircraft taillights evident.

"There's one," I say.

She finds it, holds its movements steady, and what she's wishing for, I suspect it's something I wish for myself. When she blinks to a different section of sky, I know the wish is finished, and carefully pick through the jumbled words in my brain before speaking.

"Do you have a significant other?" I blurt. So much for my sorting process.

"Rude," she says.

"I'm only trying to peel back your layers."

She guffaws. "Gross. Please don't."

"Oh," I say, the disappointment ringing through. "Don't you need a friend?"

"Nope. I'm good."

"What a lonely path to walk." *I should know.* I fidget with my fingers. We idle in the silence that expands in size.

"Staying mostly friendless works for me," she adds. "I'm not bothered by it. Just want to clarify."

"Understood." It feels as if she's punched a hole in my chest and ripped my heart in two.

"Do *you* have a significant other?" she asks, mocking.

"Never."

"Never? As in *ever*?"

"As in *ever.*"

"How is that even possible?"

"No one's ever taken an interest, I suppose."

"Sad." She loses the sarcasm, adding a touch of emphasized sympathy.

Our conversation stalls. I feel slightly too confined by the open space. I pull my recorder pieces into view and pretend my mechanical friend is still intact. "The two sit inches away, but worlds apart. Her heart isn't written on her sleeve, but remains safely tucked away for the right moment, with the right person he hopes could someday be him."

She leaps from her seat with her hands out in front of her. "STOP! It's not even functional!"

I lay the pieces aside. "I'm so used to the way people react to me, it's easier to hide behind something."

She sits with a heavy sigh. "I get it, but there has to be a less creepy way."

I search the sky again, lost in the dotted stars coming to life.

"Why'd you move here, anyway? There's nothing here."

I hold my tongue.

"Hello?" She waves her hand in front of my frozen gaze.

"Stella thought it sounded like the perfect place for a fresh start when my issues at school didn't resolve, so Thomas transferred jobs."

She fidgets. "I've heard parts of the story, but not that."

"Do *you* like it here?"

"It's a nice town."

"But do you *like* it?"

"As much as one can, I guess."

She searches for what to say next. There's never an easy transition in discussing how I came to be with Stella and Thomas. Some expect me to tell them bluntly. When I told Violet, my words flowed so easily—but now, I can't seem to say even the most basic of facts.

"I know your parents died," she blurts. "I'm sorry."

My lips tighten. I fight that choking feeling back so as not to burst into tears. "Thank you."

"Do you feel like Stella and Thomas love you?" she asks.

"I do. I'm just not sure I know how to love them back the way they deserve. I feel guilty for that. Do you feel loved?"

"Sometimes. I don't deserve it, though."

"Unequivocally false. We're all deserving of love and compassion."

Her attention snaps to me, as if I've said something she hadn't considered, before wavering back to the sky. "Another plane."

I watch the way she pinches her eyes shut, her lips moving words in silence.

"Let me ask you something," she says, "would you rather . . . always have to say everything on your mind, or never be able to speak again?"

"Do I get to use my recorder?"

"Ugh," she groans.

"I can't imagine *never* using my voice again so I guess the first one."

"I'd argue you already do that." She elbows me in jest.

"Touché."

"Would you rather wade through a mile's worth of dead bodies or shit?"

"Dark and rather disturbing."

She shrugs. "Choose wisely. Our potential friendship will ride on what you say."

I contain my smile. "I feel like you'd rather move through piles of the dead, but I'm not sure why, so I suppose I'll follow in your footsteps. That's what friends would do."

She looks to me with a smirk. "I would've chosen the shit. We're so not friends now, you weirdo."

"Understood."

SKY FULL OF WISHES

When Dad was home, he'd shake me awake and carry me outside whatever house we lived in at the time. While I was in my dreary state, he'd grab my hand and point at the big canvas of sky while I'd complain in a sheepish voice that I couldn't see what he saw and I begged to go back to bed, but he'd insist, point to a spot in the sky and say his wish out loud, and as he opened his palm, a shooting star would fall in the distance. I'd clap in awe of his trick while Nell would stand in the doorway, never getting what it is we saw. Dad would whisper, "The sky is full of wishes." I used to think he was magic, invincible. I think the balloons believed it, too. I can't help the sinking feeling in the deepest pit of my stomach as another plane vanishes in the distance. Or maybe it's a star, falling, dying.

I think I've just let Dad go.

If you wish on a falling star, it's said that whatever you've put your heart and soul into will crash-land somewhere under the Northern Lights. If you wish on an airplane, as Dew's father suggested, your heart and soul are guaranteed to be momentarily in flight, landing safely in a designated wish zone, where, Dew imagined, airline employees sort wishes into bins with the luggage. Some wishes would make it to their owner's hands, while others—the goodbyes we never said—would be lost in transit. I have six. Dew was still waiting on the right plane to carry a wish so big, it needed extra cargo space. Because saying goodbye swallows the whole sky.

NAIMA

He points up as another plane passes overhead. The engine's roar is faint but the light of the fire trailing behind leaves a smattering of dust. I think of all the reasons I could never fly on one, and how big they are but also how small, while Dew closes his eyes, his lips muttering something I can't hear.

"What are you doing?"

"It's an extra-special wish."

As soon as he says it, I flash back to the night Dad created a falling star from his palm like magic, and it becomes crystal clear. Dad lied.

I'd wished on an *airplane,* too.

"So, what did *you* wish for?" I ask.

"I can't tell or it won't come true."

"Whatever. I bet it was something dumb. Like a new fedora."

"I *like* my fedora."

"That makes one of us." I smile and see he is, too. "You should always wish in multiples. To increase your chances. Six, *always* six."

"Why six?"

I stumble on my words. "Never mind. Do what you want."

We sit for a while in the warm air and silence. I can't count the seconds or claw at my neck. I feel okay. After watching the planes, the stars and moon, I feel Dew's stare. When I finally turn, he's just . . . staring. Big honey*dew* eyes, full of hope, or something like it.

"What?" I ask.

"You're like a beautiful painting, perfectly executed."

I laugh nervously. "What a freakin' line. You're full of those."

"You don't even see the air of beauty that precedes you. Like your soul is on the outside. You wear it, but pretend it's lost, forgetting others can see it."

Uhhhhhh . . .

"What are you doing after high school?" I ask to break the wall of awkward.

"I'd love to be a news reporter, but I'm not sure I can get out of my own way long enough to be on camera. It's too much to figure out right now."

"Ain't that the truth. Why are we supposed to have our entire futures mapped out before we get to vote? Like, get off my case, SHARON."

"Who's Sharon?"

"No one. Well, everyone. Like the world in general."

"I see. Where do you think life will take you after graduation? Will you stay in Ivy Springs?"

"*God, no.* Being here hurts. I've got my sights set on becoming a combat medic. So I can save the wounded in the field. No one will die on my watch. Not a GD one."

"Sounds like you'll be stepping into Staff Sergeant Rodriguez's shoes."

"More like beside them so they aren't blown off in the first place." My voice strains.

His eyes cast up to the planes, a slight twinkle rivaling the stars. "I bet your therapist fully supports this goal. It sounds curative."

"*Ah,* you see, me and therapy have a long, sordid history."

His eyes find me. I feel the weight of all he's carrying but pretending not to. "I understand your apprehension. Sometimes it takes trial and error to find the right person you feel safe enough to open up to."

I interrupt, the words unable to wait. "Maybe my heart is so broken, there's no cure. I'll just live with the grief every day for the rest of my life and nothing will make it better. *Nothing.*"

I swipe a tear that broke loose before he sees. "Anyway, I technically have my stepmom's lady, and I tell her things. But I don't feel any better."

"There'd be no moon without the sky."

"What?"

"My mom used to tell me that. As in, there'd be no joy without the pain. Perhaps all of this is a preamble towards something so fully realized in its greatness, you won't see it coming until you find yourself hurting a little less."

His words, however dumb, fill my heart with a bubbly fizz in the places where cracks had formed. I'm weightless. Neither of us knows how to transition worth a shit so I just go for it. "Let's move on."

"Have you given up on your dream of working at Baked & Caffeinated?" he asks.

"Didn't want the job."

"Because of me."

I hesitate. "Wow, full of yourself much?"

"I'll quit if you ask me to."

"Won't change anything, honestly."

"It may not help, but I work with this girl Violet—she's close with the Paxtons—and she told me this quote: 'When everything seems to be going against you, remember that the airplane takes off against the wind, not with it.' It helped shift my perspective a bit. Accepting life will be hard and messy sometimes, but knowing I'll find a way through it is the most difficult thing."

"Sounds like you have a thing for Violet."

He blushes. "We're friends."

"You're really dedicated to this friend thing. Ask her out. I bet she'll say yes."

He gives a small, secret smile. "Perhaps I will."

We watch a few more wishes pass us by. Plane lights fading in the inky sky.

"The package was full of letters I returned to my dad," I blurt. "He set them up to be mailed in case of his death."

"Oh." If there were an invisible string, his mouth holds one end and my ears, the other. "May I ask why you returned them?"

"He promised he wouldn't leave again. And he did."

He turns toward me, lays his fedora to the side. "I didn't mean to upset you with the balloon. My only intention was to brighten your day, but I overstepped. It's not my place to insinuate myself into your life."

"That's the realest thing you've said all damn day. My stepmom tried to handle the balloons once, and only once. The day they told us he died. Maybe it's not connected, maybe it is. It's *our* thing." My body tenses, flashes of Dad whooshing in and out.

"I didn't realize."

"Obviously. Like, get over yourself already. It's not about you." The irony bites through my lips.

"*Oh, Naima,*" he says with a profound sense of shame. "I never intended to cause you to feel this way. In my quest for friendship, I hadn't considered how my actions made *you* feel. I'm *so* sorry."

I stand abruptly. Something inside, the place where anger had only fizzed and bubbled in the cracks, now feels like shards of glass stabbing through. "I'm gonna go."

He stands with me. "Let me walk you."

"Take a GD hint, Brickman."

As each foot deliberately stomps the pain away, his voice fades. "Thank you for saving me."

I stop for a breath to muster all the strength I have left, and run. All the way *home*.

One. Two. Three. Four. Five. Six.

⏮ ⏭ ⏯ ⏹ ● **DEW GD BRICKMAN**
DURATION: 2:37

Late breaking on tonight's Dew's News:
Germs collide.

"He *wanted* to tell her he was sorry, that she isn't alone. That if anyone in the whole universe can understand, it's him. He's been under much duress since his first separation from all he knew; no one can tell, though, as he wears a suit of glee. He sees himself in the girl, even if she'll never see him in return."

I say this into my recorder, or what's left of it, my eye peering through the fence hole to where Naima sits on the back stoop. She listens, before reluctantly walking to the hole, where her eye moves into view. Swirls of green reflect against the moon glow, making them nearly translucent. We stare through this small space that transports us somewhere else entirely. Another city. Another state. Another galaxy, where the plane lights flicker at our disposal.

"Please forgive me," I tell her. "I'll leave you to deal the way you deem fit."

She sighs. "I don't know how to process losing my dad. You remind me of that."

"I only wanted to help."

"Sometimes help is not helping."

"Can I ask you something?"

"Dew," Stella calls, "are you out here?"

"One minute," I return. I knit the words together with care. "How do you say goodbye to someone when you're not ready to?"

Her vision drifts. "I don't have an answer for that, as you can see."

"I miss *them*." It slips, sits between us.

"I know. I miss *him*."

"I know."

Her eye finds mine again. She clings tighter to the fencing, her long lashes rising and falling with mine. My heart is aflutter; a butterfly flapping its wings against my rib cage.

"Come closer," she tells me. Her lips move to the opening. "Kiss me."

"What?"

"If you want."

I have no time to consider whether I do or don't. The dream of her is a swirl of vivid colors. To muddle the paint is terrifying. I press my lips to hers with the fencing against the rest of my face. It's a lukewarm feeling, a flat piano key. There are no fireworks or explosions. With airplanes buzzing overhead, wishes lost, we pull back at the same time. The colors fade slightly, bringing me back to earth, where I'm grounded.

"That was . . . ," I begin.

"Awful," she blurts. "*Totally* read you wrong."

The silence lasts forever. "We'll politely agree to forget about it," I say.

"Yeah, that'd be . . . cool," she says. "So, I'm gonna go."

I'm not way up in the clouds, not searching for wishes on planes. *I'm* the wish; the plane. My heart is absent of flutter when she steps away, taking me back to a birthday party I once attended. When Spin the Bottle began, someone rigged it so the most popular girl—Willow Jenkins—would have to kiss me. She declined with jovial, disgusted laughter. I spent the remainder of the party in the corner, watching everyone else move along without me.

Naima's almost to the door when she turns. "I decided I'm taking the job."

"Wonderful."

"Never speak of this or I'll cut you while you sleep."

As I walk inside, I'm greeted by a smile plastered on Stella's face as she puts clean dishes into the cupboard. Thomas dries first and hands them to her. They're a well-oiled machine and clearly look as though they know something I don't.

"What?" I ask.

"Nothing." Her smile grows.

My shoulders hunch. "You saw?"

She snickers. "I didn't *mean* to eavesdrop. Or see what I saw."

"Don't worry, there won't be any more of that. It wasn't very good."

Thomas leans in. "Some of them aren't. But one day, you'll find the person that makes your heart explode. *Fireworks.*" He winks at Stella.

"So I hear." To disrupt the discomfort, I drop my fedora onto the center of the table. Pieces of the recorder clang together in a mountain of useless plastic and tape.

"What happened?" she asks.

"There was an unfortunate incident."

They both stop what they're doing, eyes expanding. "Did someone hurt you?" Thomas asks.

"Nothing like that."

"So, what, then?"

"I tripped while following someone. He could've hurt me if he'd wanted to, but Naima stepped in and put him in an arm-lock. Turns out, he didn't hurt me, and my recorder was sacrificed in the process."

They look to one another, and to me. "Wow," Thomas says. "That's a lot to unpack. Good thing for her being in the right place at the right time."

"Wait," Stella say, "why are you following people? We've discussed this."

I kick my feet around. "I sensed he needed a friend."

She throws her hands on her waist and tilts her head in frustration. "You have a big heart, and I know you mean well, but you can't follow strangers around. And while we're at it, remember, you can't record people without their permission. It's for your personal use only."

My fingers find the pieces. "No chance of that now anyway."

Faith barrels in, stopping to peer down at my recorder-filled fedora. "What happened?"

"He broke his recorder," Stella says.

Faith's mood shifts as she rushes off, returning seconds later draped in her feather boa, with star-shaped sunglasses and a wand of sorts. "Tell me who it is." She punches one fist into an open palm. "I'll handle it."

I lay my hand on her shoulder. "That's very kind, but everything is fine."

"Random girl next door can protect you, but *I* can't?" she cries.

"That's not what I mean."

"I'm just as strong as she is. STRONGER." She kicks a leg straight out.

"You absolutely are, but my point is Naima shouldn't have gotten involved in the first place. It wasn't necessary because I wasn't in danger."

"Whatever." She throws her boa and sunglasses to the floor, waving her wand as if banishing us to a faraway land, and runs to her room, where the door slams behind her. Another picture frame falls to the floor, cracking the glass.

"That didn't go well," I say.

"Welcome to the phrase I mutter after most conversations," Thomas jokes.

They continue to buzz around me but I'm stuck to my recorder's pieces.

Stella shoves a flyer in front of me. "I found an amateur girls wrestling team. Tryouts are tomorrow."

"I'm scared for anyone in her path," I say.

"We all are," Thomas says.

I collapse into a chair and spread the pieces in front of me like a puzzle. One by one, I line them up as if putting together the broken bones of a friend. The recorder represents so much more than the duty it served. It's me: shattered, but in this light, all smashed together, good enough.

NAIMA

I brush my teeth six times, gargle mouthwash, and say a little prayer for kissing Dew GD Brickman. I plead temporary insanity. Must've been some weird virus in the air that turns brains into zombie mush. Once I'm content with the slaughter of the germs, I find myself flipping open every letter, laying them into view. One is a collection of musings I'd written during a dinner out with Dad. I didn't know he'd noticed, or that he kept any of them.

The dinner was his way of making sure I felt included. Suddenly there was this whole new family I didn't feel a part of. One Dad would leave me to figure out, without him. Chill bumps coat my skin as I scour over my deepest, darkest thoughts he'd been privy to. Things about Nell. About him leaving.

Who I am.

My hair's never straight enough or curly enough. Mom was too light, Dad too dark. I'm never who people think I should be.

In school, I'm asked the same GD question—"What *are* you?"—by some new group of mean girls every year, as if "what I am" defines my existence. People think the question doesn't burn, but it does, it has, it will. I like my curly hair. I like my body. I like my broken skin with freckles and markings. I like me—I'm the perfect blend of Mom and Dad, JJ and Kam, and everyone who came before, from all sides. So what does it matter to you, dear asker, *what I am*? The question undercuts my every attempt to find my place. Leave me be. *What I am* is not your concern.

Would you rather be the subject of regular microaggressions for looking different, even if you're happy with yourself, or be miserable, never having someone criticize your appearance?

Dad would say, "Ima, not everyone will accept you right away. As long as you accept yourself, the world will eventually follow." I knew he was right.

What are you?

I suddenly, overwhelmingly, have an answer and know the exact way to execute it. I'll conquer everything I've ever feared in the name of taking back my identity—of being made from Mom and Dad.

Also, I'm in the mood for cake.

Strawberry with rainbow sprinkles.

(And still, probably, anthrax.) ☹

◄◄ ►► ►‖ ■ ● **DEW GD BRICKMAN**
DURATION: 0:36

Boy, 16, realizes he's missing something, finds memory.

I sit along the edge of my bed, missing the feel of the recorder in my hand, when my phone buzzes.

Violet: *My acupuncturist sensed a new source of tension and I wondered if it's you.*

Me: *Me? How?*

Violet: *In your heart. I'm an empath so if you're hurting, I am, too.*

Me: *Then yes, your acupuncturist is correct.*

Violet: ☹ *Want a silver lining?*

Me: *Always.*

Violet: *You're crackling fire dark can't break.*

My hands squeeze the phone tight, tighter, tightest. I drop it to the bed. I glance at the August Moon poster, my thoughts spiraling down a long, winding path. I don't text her back, because maybe I'm not capable of being "normal" enough. Maybe the recorder is as close as I'll ever get and that's a stretch. Awaiting a new one feels like the string of days before my parents' funeral. Consumed with trepidation, I can't anticipate what's to come and even after, it'll never feel the same again. Maybe Violet shouldn't waste her silver linings on me.

The pieces of my recorder stare up at me. I've let them down, they tell me. It was my job to protect them, they say.

Like everything else, it all comes back to time.

Had I not attended the carry-in when I did, I wouldn't have run into Dodge, I couldn't have followed him, and this wouldn't have happened. With the caricature wolf staring at me from the August Moon poster frame, I stand to look in the full-length mirror. My posture slinks, my eyes have visible bags, and my hatless head reveals my curls have been smashed flat.

Mom's voice drifts through my ears, her hum of song streaming through. We're in the car on the way to school the morning of. Windows down, sun peering over the horizon to mark the start of the day.

"Goodbye, my darling," Mom said.

"Have a great day, son," Dad said.

If I'd known those were the last words I'd ever hear them say, I'd have remained in that car with them forever. There's a picture on my nightstand of the three of us. One of the few things I have left of before. It remains untouched, covered in dust, with August Moon's howling anthem behind the glass. With my recorder lying helplessly behind, and memories faded in front, and my hat out of reach, I see myself—like *really* see this boy they call Dew. And how infinitely empty he is.

NAIMA

Before Dad began a tradition of giving me challenges to gain "prizes" and conquer my fears or whatever, I was terrified of balloons. The way they bobbed and weaved, mocking my panic, felt ominous enough that I hid when he began bringing them home on my birthday. He would blow them up himself so they'd scoot across the floors, chasing me.

This was before his second tour. My memories of it are only bits and pieces, the rest diluted with things far more important (literally everything else). Dad accidentally popped one beneath his giant boot, and I ran screaming to my bedroom, where I buried myself beneath the hexagon quilt and counted. Moments later, I felt a tap. My eyes peering out, I saw Dad had dragged up his feet from the floor, as if scared, too. He told me there was hot lava we had to skip over if we wanted to survive, pointing to the red sea of balloons dragging along the edge of the bed. He'd asked, *Would you rather die from hot lava invading your space or get injured from trying to escape it?*

I was skeptical but it was the perfect metaphor for living with mental illness and how complex it can be to manage. I hated balloons and didn't think I could ever believe otherwise. But Dad hopped off the bed, over each balloon, into the hallway. He laughed and held his hand out into the air for me to join him.

"You have to jump through the lava if you want to be free," he said. "Even if it hurts. *Especially* if it does."

I was so scared of what might happen if a balloon grazed my toes. But there was this look on his face, asking me to trust him, so I did. I pushed my body out of the comfort of my bed, letting my toes drop between the bare spaces, until I reached him. He grabbed my hand and pulled me into him.

"I'm so proud of you," he said, hugging me tight. "You are the bravest girl I know."

Brave. Brave. Brave. Brave. Brave. Brave.

Eventually, that shaking, terrified feeling went away. Or, maybe it morphed into other fears. But after that day, I knew the balloons wouldn't hurt me—even when they popped. If this story says anything about my father, it's that he always knew I was capable of things before I ever did.

At the beginning of last summer, though, something shifted. I don't know if it was the air, the earth, or me. Dad promised not to leave and he went anyway. I only wanted him to tell me he'd stay, and mean it. But he always left. *Always.*

I think we all know I won't ever be a combat medic. My heart wants to, to erase dad's death. Maybe to understand why he always left. My mind tells me to follow a different path. If I can't conquer my fear of life, how can I surround myself with death?

I scour the letters spread out in front of me. Dad challenged me so I could persevere with, or *without,* him. So that someday, I could be courageous (like with Dew). By encouraging prayer and meditation to reflect on all I had, not what I lacked. By learning forgiveness, no matter how I struggled. By passing down family stories so I could understand who I am. But I've never fully learned how to live. Maybe I'll dig up my memories of those things he challenged me with, where I tried and failed, or didn't try at all, and do those moments over, better, as a means of rewriting who I am.

Oh, God.

Oh . . . God . . .

I get it now.

While I wrapped myself in my hexagon cocoon,
He was showing me
How to be the *Butterfly*.

⏮ ⏭ ⏯ ⏹ ⏺ **DEW GD BRICKMAN**
DURATION: 3:03

Today's top stories: Go Magic! Craze taking over the town, most still don't get it.

"Go Magic!" Violet says. We're playing a card game during the last ten minutes of work. It's been a virtual ghost town all evening thanks to a Summer Nights Festival just outside of Ivy Springs.

I look at my cards, baffled. "I don't understand the rules."

"It's like Go Fish, but instead of fish, you have magical powers, locations, and people. If I ask you for the Isolated Desert or the Demented Skull and you don't have it, you say, 'Go Magic!' See?"

Big Foot interrupts, turning the OPEN sign off. "Go home already."

"You sure?" Violet asks. "I can stay until ten."

"Nah. Go do rebellious-youth stuff. That's way more fun than playing," he stops to look at our cards, "whatever the fuck this is."

"Leave Go Magic! alone." Violet tosses her cards onto the stack and gathers her backpack, which doubles as a purse. "It's revolutionary as far as card games go. We're starting the next trend. You're a part of history, man."

"I didn't realize," he says sarcastically.

"You want me to leave as well?" I ask for clarity. "Or only her?"

He stops to stare, blank-faced. "Yeah, man. Go."

"See ya," she tells Big Foot.

"Good night," I say.

"Don't do anything I wouldn't do," he says with a sly smile. I follow Violet into the night as he locks the door behind us. He cups his hands over his face to get a clear view of us beneath the light before waving one last time. We wave in return.

"He's so funny," she says.

The air is stagnant. Warm and unkind. My fingers pinch the inseams of my pockets, where my recorder should be. I unknowingly walk her to her car, mindlessly going wherever she goes. The scent of sugar and espresso lingers behind her.

"Are you parked here, too?" she asks, spinning around to face me.

"I don't have a car."

"Oh, right. Forgot. Need a ride?"

"No, thanks." I fight the arguing voices in my head and take a deep breath, running the line: *Will you go out with me?*

Before I spit it out, she says, "I've been meaning to ask, do you wanna hang out sometime?"

"I, uh . . . ," My heart races, pulsing through my pressure points. I'm sure she can tell.

"If you don't want to, it's cool."

"No—I do. I was going to ask you."

She laughs. "I knew it. My horoscope told me to expect the unexpected."

"Wouldn't that mean you *didn't* know I was going to ask you out?"

"The opposite—because *you're* the unexpected, see?"

I don't. "I do."

"Glad we're on the same cosmic page."

"Okay, well, if you're interested in attending a youth amateur wrestling tryout tomorrow, I'd love to have a plus one."

"Ooh, *that* is unexpected. Did *not* see that wild option coming."

"Is that a yes?"

"I'd love to. I'll text you?"

"Okay." I back away, letting her slip into her car.

Her voice rings through the open window, "*Wait.* I forgot to give you something."

My footsteps ingrain themselves into the river of white rocks, crunching with such grit I almost feel powerful. "Give me something?"

The slight wave of her finger draws me near, and just like that, the moment I lean in, she grabs me by the collar, then pulls back ever so slightly.

"Is this okay?"

I nod haphazardly, and she kisses me. *This* time, it is as soft and warm as I imagined it to be. A perfect piano note that sings. I am not grounded, but floating into the stratosphere, becoming a plane for others to wish upon. *Fireworks.*

NAIMA

Shortly before the second to final time Dad left, my room became a haven for flies. We were months from leaving Ft. Hood for Albany when a swarm sought me out and bounced against the windowpane. We don't know how they got inside, or how they knew that beyond the window was *home,* but I think they found me for a reason. In the beginning, I'd crack open the window, wave them out, but they'd just come back. It was as if they were running from something on the outside or maybe they knew I was. I'd wash my hands and scrub and scrub and scrub and scrub and scrub and scrub but I never felt, feel, clean enough. At some point, they'd fall into a dead heap near the window. I couldn't move the bodies. I felt such guilt, I just couldn't. *Wouldn't.*

"It's disgusting!" Christian screeched.

"What's *wrong* with you?" Nell would ask on repeat, the word "wrong" echoing. I never saw it as *wrong.* Especially not in the way she said it (such disgust).

It was hard being the judge, the god of the room, to make the decision for them to go or to stay. I wrestled with being left alone versus setting them free and I know how it all sounds but I'm not a sociopath or anything—I'm just no good with decisions (add it to your mental list).

The next day, four days before Dad left, was a Monday, and I remember because we had gym that day at school and when I undressed in the locker room, a Skittle fell out of my bra and I thought, *When did I have Skittles?* because the answer was literally NEVER so this whole scenario threw my entire day off. Anyway, that Monday, I came home from school to find a gift on a small stand near the window—a Venus flytrap. As I examined the bug-eating plant, Dad appeared in the doorway. "Now you don't have to choose whether they live or die," he said. "Mother Nature will."

I turned to him and smiled. "I'm naming her Penelope-Smellope."

He chuckled. "I don't think Nell would appreciate you naming a fly-eating death trap after her."

"I don't appreciate being the fly she wants to eat." The instant I said it, I knew why I couldn't move their bodies—because *she* (Nell) wanted me to. Dad cleaned up the flies and sat the plant, which I renamed PS for code, on a perch next to the window where the sunlight hugged her leaves. He didn't leave, even when Nell griped about the plant and tried prying him from my room. He counted the hexagons and made me forget about the Skittle incident, or how that rich bitch Emily Green shoved me into my locker "by accident," and at lunch, Emily's BFF, Casey, tripped me on my way to the trash can, and how days after this, he'd be gone.

But now I don't remember Emily or Casey (other than what royal pains they were). Or all the things Nell would yell in the days to come as I let the flies accumulate. I only remember the way Dad looked inside the doorframe after proving, even when I felt like the most invisible thing in any room, he saw me.

Until his image disintegrated into nothing.

No New Voicemail

⏮ ⏭ ⏸ ⏹ ⏺ **DEW GD BRICKMAN**
DURATION: 4:40

Boy saves local girl from humiliation, humiliates himself for the cause.

As I dress to meet Violet at the old-movie-theater-turned-rent-a-space where Faith's tryouts are, I replay our electric kiss—*Go Magic!*—in a foggy daze. It's unlike anything I've felt before. I find myself tracing my lips, pretending to feel hers pressed against

them again, and maybe the feeling will fade, but maybe it won't.
I work to straighten my bow tie, which refuses to straighten,
when there's a light tap on my door.

"Come in," I say.

I gasp when I see Naima. "What are *you* doing here?"

Her hands are nestled in her pockets. "Your mom, uh, Stella,
let me in. I met Faith. Total badass. Bet she'll kick all them wrestlers' asses."

I feel the need to rip my bow tie from the collar. To pull the
comforter up over the place where my head lies at night. To stand
in a way that doesn't reveal my giddiness over Violet. Her eyes
wander, studying the *where* and *why* of every item placed.

I stand tall, hands folded in front of me, but the passing time
shouts at me. "Is something wrong?"

"I don't know if it's *wrong,* but I thought a lot about our conversation. I think I have an answer that might help."

"You need a reliable sounding board?"

"*No*—I need help." Her voice shrinks at the mention of such
a weighted word.

"What help could *I* possibly offer you?"

She fidgets with my bed comforter along the same hem I do.
"Not exactly sure yet. But something pushed me out of the house
and over here."

She stands before me, delicate with the heart she's pulled from
her chest. "I'll help however I can."

Her eyes are mournful. "Cool, cool. Is now good, or . . . ?"

I clear my throat, which is suddenly dry. "Violet's meeting me
at the tryout."

Her eyes expand, a smile forced through. "Good for you.
That's, um, that's awesome." She rushes toward the door.

"Wait—you don't have to go yet." I look at the clock, the lie
eating at me.

She can tell. Dad always said I'm not a good liar.

"This was a mistake," she says.

"Come with us to Faith's wrestling tryout."

She watches the time pass, before pulling the door open. "I . . . I have somewhere to be. Have fun on your date." The door slams behind her, the sound of a picture falling to the living room floor.

"Wasn't me this time," Faith yells.

I linger, dissecting what happened, but Stella calls for us to go, so with one last glance in the mirror—and a crooked bow tie—I go.

Violet is seated in the stands when we breeze in. The auditorium smells vividly of sweat and nacho cheese. She's avidly cheering for whoever is on the mat, waving a small pompom that reads *Clifton H.S.*

"So you're the Violet we've heard all about," Stella says after checking Faith in on the floor. "I remember seeing you at the carry-in for the Paxtons."

"Nice to meet you. Your auras are electric," Violet says, grabbing one each of Stella's and Thomas's hands. "And would you LOOK at these lifelines?"

They exchange confused glances before retracting. "Thank you?" Stella says. They sit behind us and promise not to be a bother, but I can feel their attention pouring over our every interaction. I turn once and Stella's grinning. I turn to the other side to see Thomas smirk.

I decide to ignore their loud whispering about "how cute we are" even if she's "a little too old" for me, and focus on Faith, who paces behind a rickety metal chair beyond the mat. She's wearing all of her gear, but as she's only just noticed, no one else is dressed this way. She lays her boa on the chair, removes her sunglasses and jacket.

"I'll be right back," I tell Violet.

"I'll be here."

One glance at Stella, who's still grinning, and I swerve through the row toward the space Faith has claimed.

"What are you doing?" she asks.

"Helping you."

"I want to go home. This isn't the wrestling I thought it'd be."

I lean to her level so only she can hear. "I never thought I'd utter this question, but what would Rick Flair do?"

She shrugs, her arms and legs stitched together as if to hide even further.

"You *know* he'd go out there in his fancy clothes, saying all sorts of ridiculous things no matter what anyone else thought. He *owned* it. You should, too."

"But everyone's looking at me. I want to puke."

"They're jealous they didn't think of it. You're an icon."

She's still hesitant. I have to do the big, brave thing if she's to believe me. I reach for her things, put her sunglasses on my face, drape her jacket and boa around my shoulders, raise my arms in the air, and yell, *"Woo!"* Everyone stops to stare, Violet included, and even though I'm screaming inside, I hold my pose. For her, my sister.

Violet stands, the only person applauding. Stella and Thomas join her, the three of them our own little section of hope. Faith's light beams through the entire auditorium, her fire reignited. Shoulders square, she pulls her things from my body and situates them back onto hers. Within minutes, she transforms from Faith to the Conniption right before my eyes.

I turn away but then she tugs at me, spinning me around and falling into me. Her small but powerful hands wrap around my waist, and I feel her final layer fall to the floor. "You're a great brother, Dew."

I hold back tears and squeeze her back until she releases me and says to "go away" so she can " concentrate."

"That was seriously too cute," Violet says when I return. I ignore all the other staring eyes. "Her aura changed the second you started talking to her. You two must be really close."

Thomas pats my shoulder. "That was great."

"There's hope for us yet." Stella sighs with relief.

As they call the Conniption to the mat—this once frightened, angry shell of a girl who didn't speak to any of us our first week together—I don't only see my sister. I see *me*. We're both hanging on the best we can, hoping it'll amount to something: A family who loves us for who we are, despite what we've been through. People who stop looking at us as broken or damaged, to just ourselves, blemished but true.

The ref spouts off—tells her to remove her accessories, per the non-WWE rule book—before giving Faith and her partner a start. Though disappointed at first, she abides, using those feelings to do the double-leg takedown and half nelson Thomas taught. Violet grabs my hand. The crowd erupts in cheers, and only after Faith is accepted onto the team do I realize they're not cheering for me and Violet. *Fire*.

NAIMA

A few days later, I only know it's morning by the quick start of the washing machine. JJ is shoving wadded-up balls of fabric into the abyss. She looks over her shoulder between each until our eyes meet.

"Good morning, sunshine," she says. "I should say good almost-afternoon. And forget I mentioned sunshine."

I grunt, or something. My eyes don't spring open. Instead, they're glued to the lashes, interlocked and clinging not to part. I catch a glimpse of the clock.

Eleven-thirteen A.M. EST.

My body pings upright. Sleeping this late means breakfast has passed, which means I've lost half a day, which means I won't feel right until I start again tomorrow. I manage a nod to JJ because she's staring kind of hard. She's wearing a silk floral head wrap and big, dangling hoop earrings that rival the bangles clanging on her wrists.

"What'd you do last night? You got home so late, I kept tracking the phone to make sure you weren't in a ditch somewhere."

"I'm not a convict."

"I need to know you're safe."

"I texted in my mind."

"Not good enough, girl, and you know it. We have rules here."

I don't want to tell her where I've been going—the river to wish on planes—because it's between Dad and me, our secret spot now, not Dew's.

I grunt again, this time louder. "I need to get ready."

"Where you going?"

"Nowhere." I don't want to tell her this, either: that ever since I dropped by his house, Dew's been helping me overcome small fears so I can work up to big ones. I'm not dense; I know it won't "fix" me, or whatever, but it feels like the right time to test myself. To do something; anything.

"No secrets."

I slump over, defeated. "I'm meeting Dew."

Her face lights up and I feel instantly sick.

"When did this happen?"

"*We* aren't a *this*. We're friends. Actually, he's seeing the girl he works with."

Her arms cross. "How do you feel about that?"

"I'm not interested in him like *that* but I guess he's a decent human. We're on a trial basis while I see how this friendship thing goes."

She's cautiously happy, trying to conceal her smirk. "I'd expect nothing less from you."

"We're going to try some things Dad would've wanted me to do. Nothing major. I've been thinking a lot about everything he wrote and all the chances I missed to, you know, live. I want to make up for it. I just hope it's not too late."

She looks down at the scattered letters. "As long as you're still breathing, it's never too late." She squeezes my hand. "Just don't think it's a magic fix. You still need your medication, and we'll find you a solid therapist here, too. Maybe who Dew sees. But I'm happy you're feeling lighter. What's the first thing on your list?"

"The Ferris wheel. I have to start small, like I'm being reborn or something."

She pulls back. "You hate heights."

"I know. It's time I understand why."

Her face shifts from glee to something resembling pride. "Ray would be proud."

I smile, and a few minutes later, she retreats upstairs to let me prepare for this incredibly weird day with a boy I didn't care to know a few days ago. Once I've coated my lips in Dragon Girl red, my bandana is tight, and my EQUALITY MEOW shirt is smoothed, I run up the stairs. Hiccup chases me as soon as I step onto the landing, and instead of carefully moving over the divots, I run. I run, and I trip. I trip, and I fall. Into the kitchen chair.

And I forget.

  I forget.

    I forget.

      I forget.

        I forget.

          I forget . . .

About Dad's urn.

I see it fall like a flip-book. I reach, but the urn doesn't freeze in midair like it might in the movies. Instead, it hits the floor with such force, I swear the tiles shift beneath my feet. By the time everyone runs in, Dad's ashes are spread all over the newly remodeled floor. The dust blows up into my nose and mouth and I'm inhaling Dad and standing in him and the image isn't connected to my brain. JJ's jaw drops. Kam lifts Hiccup out of the war zone.

My feet dig into the floor but my heart races and races and

races and races and races and races. I feel a slight graze against my arm and jerk back only to see JJ's face. No one says a word but the grief has spilled from this container and we're collectively searching for the remaining oxygen, only there isn't any and we're going to drown.

Amid the silence, Hiccup howls in a way that resembles what I did inside the church, and I don't know if it's the look in his eyes or the mess I've made, or knowing Dad's body is all around me and not here in the same breath, but I push through everyone and run down the stairs to the pile of sheets strewn about. I find my quilt and gather it into my hands so I can feel the threads as I'm cocooned both literally and figuratively on the floor. I count. Ninety hexagons. There are ninety and as long as there are ninety, I will be fine. Things are fine. Everything's fine. FINE.

Not some full sixty seconds later, there's a knock on the front door. I hear muffled voices and the scatter of feet, and steps moving down this way. So I take a breath and five more.

"Are you ready?" Dew asks.

I shove the quilt away from me and spring upright and pretend what just happened, didn't. "Is Violet going?"

"Jealous much?" He smirks. Gross.

"Just wondering if I'm about to be a third wheel or if we're a bicycle type of duo." I get up from the floor and try to get us back up the stairs and out of the house before the incident catches up to me.

"She's working, covering my shift. So, a bicycling duo, I suppose."

"You did that for *me*?"

"We're friends. That's what you do."

Would you rather have a friend who does nothing for you or no friends at all?

Without letting him see how full that makes me feel, I pull at him. "Let's get out of here. Like, now."

He's drawn into the kitchen by the dust. "What happened?" he asks JJ, who's scooping the ashes into a dustpan.

"Naima tripped and fell into Ray, so I'm putting him back where he belongs. You know, the usual."

"Utterly fascinating."

JJ offers a sympathetic smile. "Go on. I'll get Ray back into his urn. It's fine."

I can't move.

"Go, Ima. It's really fine. You have more important things to do."

At the nod of her head, my eyes meet Dew's. "Let's go."

Somehow, it was like Dad was there, saying goodbye, and good luck, too.

No New Voicemail

◄◄ ►►I ►II ■ ● DEW GD BRICKMAN
DURATION: 6:52

Coming up at 10: Fair turns nauseating for two local teens.

There is a crowd all around us. A big one. The kind that swallows you right up until you no longer exist. I do my best to guide Naima through, though my chest tightens and tingles, too. There comes a point, between the shimmering metallic corn dog trailer and the claustrophobic ride section, we tangle inside the swell of the crowd. Waves of people swish past and through and around us in blurs of faces. I offer her my hand through an opening in the air. She takes it long enough to pull us into a strip of dead grass, then lets it drop.

"I'm not ready yet," she says. "I changed my mind." Her shoes dig into the dirt, twisting spirals in her small square footage of land. We're directly in front of the pink and teal elephant-ear trailer that smells of hot oil and cinnamon. And gluten. A lot of gluten.

"Can I help you?" a woman asks.

"He's allergic," Naima says.

"One, please." I slap down a few crisp dollar bills.

"What are you doing?" she asks. "You can't."

"It's not for me. Perhaps eating something delightful will help you relax."

"Oh. Thanks." She seems surprised. "Not gonna turn down free food."

I ask the employee to hand her the ear directly as not to come in contact with it. Naima tears off steaming bites, cinnamon sprinkling to the ground. Her mood changes almost instantly. She meticulously spaces out the bites, lines them up, and chooses which to eat next by way of an intricate internal system. We find a spot to sit on the curb behind the trailer, approximately three feet apart. The afternoon sun is harsh, striking straight through to the skin. I take off my hat to feel some nonexistent breeze and find no relief.

"So this is an official friend date," I say.

She stops chewing. "Don't call it that."

"A *date,* then."

"No, that's what you and Violet did. *This* is a hang."

"What's the difference?"

Her face sours. "Didn't we already have this conversation?"

"I'm joking."

I sit with my knees up to my chest, hands tied around them until she finishes her fried dough. When she stands, she procrastinates further still. I hold out a hand to guide her, which she takes. "Don't get used to this or anything."

"Of course not." We move through the fair like a couple who've been together a lifetime, knowing which foot to step forward first, so in perfect unison. I realize now, I don't know as much about her as I thought. Not in the way one should to call it *love*. Through her father's colorful stories, and Joelle's musings, I lost myself inside of a dream, forgetting she's a living, breathing girl with her own thoughts and opinions not swayed by what I, or anyone else, thinks. As her hand slides against mine, there's a vague pang inside my heart.

We make our way to a game of throwing Ping-Pong balls into small goldfish bowls. Little exhausted fish move about inside their confines.

"Would you like one?" I ask.

"One what?"

"A fish."

"You know these games are rigged, right? Besides, I don't like when people pay for me so often. It's sexist."

"Do you want to pay?"

"Not really."

"Do you want a fish?"

"Yeah."

I smirk and hand the man a five. In exchange, he gives me three white, dirtied balls (and yes, I realize how inappropriate this sounds).

She stands back, arms latched across her chest. "There's no way you'll win a—"

"WINNER!" the man shouts. He points to the center bowl, where one of my balls floats (yes, I hear this one as well).

"Fish for the lady." He hands her a plastic bag with a small, nearly lifeless goldfish inside.

She perks up more than post–elephant ear. "I love you already, Marshmallow the Second."

"Perfect," I say.

"Would you rather have a fish you can't pet that lives forever, or a cat you can snuggle that only lives a day?"

"What's with your dire scenarios?"

She shrugs. "It's *my* aesthetic."

"I'm starting to see the pattern. I'd have to say the cat. Better to have a full day of happiness. Life's short anyway."

"I'd take the fish, which sums up our differences nicely."

We move along, slowly approaching the Wheel of Doom. She falters in her steps. This time, *she* pays the attendant in ride tickets. "This one's on me. In case we die."

"Do you want me to hold your fish?" the woman asks, as enthused as one can be in 100-degree weather.

Naima holds it to her chest. "No way."

The woman takes our tickets and lets us inside, checking that the bar around our waists is snug, though Naima appears uncomfortable at the woman's slight struggle, whispering curse words beneath her breath as she tries to force the bar to latch over Naima's midsection. When it finally does, Naima's face is flushed.

"She had the strength of a small child," I say. "And this seat is too small." I neglect to mention there's a wide gap between the bar and myself; the possibility of my body flying into the sky is real. She smiles, only slightly.

"My size doesn't bother me until someone does that shit," she says. "Like, I know I'm not teeny tiny, but no need to make a big, dramatic scene over it."

"It was unnecessary."

"Fat phobia is a thing, and the funny part is, I get it most from grown-ass women."

"She's probably unhappy with herself. I feel bad for her."

"I wish I could see people the way you do."

"Give it time. You will." The ride begins slow, the air shifting as we move up. I hadn't much realized I don't enjoy heights until right now. She grabs ahold of my thigh, surely an instant bruise blossoming. Her eyes are closed, too.

"Are you okay?" I ask.

"My dad wanted me to ride this thing every damn year and I refused every damn year for good reason. So, no."

I don't tell her how terrified I am because this isn't my fight to win. Instead I peel her hand from my leg and let her squeeze my own hand as hard as she needs. The ride lasts an entire five minutes, during which we remain static in this position, only Marshmallow the Second's water sloshing between us. Finally, when she feels the slow stop-and-go motion of letting people off, she peeks one eye open, then the other.

"It's over," I tell her. "You did it."

"Hope you enjoyed your ride," the woman says.

"NOT RIGHT NOW, SHARON," Naima snaps.

I awkwardly laugh and pull her away from the dizzying scene. She holds her stomach, the color draining from her face.

"Wanna go again?" I say jokingly.

"*Hell* no. Take me home, Brickman."

"As you wish."

The walk back is quiet. She puts on a tough act, her exterior straight-faced and serene, but her fingers bunch the fabric of her shirt.

"K, bye," she says as we approach our dueling houses.

"Wait."

"WHAT, DEWD?"

"Can I have your number? To check on you later?"

"Just walk over. Don't make it weird."

"Okay, so maybe I'd like a valid reason to text you, just because. Friend stuff."

She lingers, a vague smile forming.

"Fine, it's—" She doesn't get the number out before vomiting on my shoes.

This is the friend thing I've been missing out on?

NAIMA

Marshmallow the First rests in peace in the memory box I was given at Dover during Dad's transport. I'm not sure what made me put the lifeless fish in the box. Maybe it was my way of burying the pain of missing Dad. But I'm wiping puke off my chin inside the bathroom when JJ asks about Marshmallow the Second. She drops him into a giant mixing bowl until we can get a proper tank. Dew helped me inside to JJ, for which she offered to buy him new shoes. He declined, stating he'd "forever have a reminder of his first friend date." I think I gagged again. After JJ helps me clean up, she guides me downstairs. Kam follows close behind.

"I take it you didn't have the best time?" she asked.

"It wasn't bad."

"What were you up to?" Kam asks.

I angle my head up. "I know JJ told you."

He smirks. "Just wanted to hear it from you. Eat too many fried Oreos?"

"Elephant ear. *Ugh.*"

"Isn't he allergic?"

"Oh, yeah. It was all mine."

"Now, that sounds good. I could go for one of those."

JJ smacks his arm. "Why don't you go get yourself one and leave us be?"

"I think I will."

"Wait—brew me some tea and fetch my laptop, would ya?"

"You talking to me or the dog?" he jokes.

JJ's face shrinks stern. "Please?"

He winks. "Sure thing, my love. Get some rest, Ima."

JJ doesn't say much else. She guides me to bed, where the letters remain scattered, tucking me in on all sides like Dad would do, and disappears while I settle. She pulls an old rickety chair from the junk room beyond the washer and dryer and sits in it to the side of me.

"What are you doing?" I ask as Kam hands her the laptop.

"Tea will be down shortly," he tells her.

"Thanks, babe." She offers him a peck on the lips and turns on the latest podcast. The intro speaks of gender inequality across the globe. How even poverty is sexist. I want to listen, but my eyes droop. I offer her one last look, giving into my drowsiness completely. "You can go."

"You think I'm just gonna leave you down here when you're sick?"

I sink into my pillow, and don't wake up until the next morning.

⏮ ⏭ ▶❙ ◼ ⬤ DEW GD BRICKMAN
DURATION: 1:30

In Dew's News *you can't re-use: Why one woman says dying young may have saved her life.*

"Dew," Stella asks, knocking, "you okay?"

"Fine," I say before hanging my head over the porcelain bowl.

"Maybe you're coming down with something."

"It's called Naima," I whisper to myself.

"Can I get you anything?"

My parents, I think. *A warm bath. The smell of strawberry cake. August Moon and the Paper Hearts. A way to reverse time.* "Nothing, thanks."

"Let us know what we can do," Thomas adds.

"Me, too," Faith chimes. After they've left, she lingers. A small shadow beneath the door crack. "Feel better." She finally walks away.

Once everything is out of my system, I collapse into my bed, where the sheets welcome me. My phone almost immediately vibrates.

Violet: *Your horoscope says there could be "twists and turns" so stay vigilant!*

Violet: *Also, hi.*

Me: *Hi! Question. Would you rather live for a thousand years without the ability to feel joy, or die young but be filled with it?*

Violet: *Totally the second one. Why live forever if you're miserable?*

Me: *Agreed* ☺

Violet: *How was the fair? Was she able to ride the wheel?*

Me: *She did, and then we both got sick.*

Violet: *Aww* ☹ *Anything I can do?*

Me: *Tell me there are better things in my future*

Violet: *There are better things in your future.*

Me: *Perfect.*

Violet: *How about I bring some essential oils, a healing crystal, and my ginger root tea.*

Me: *That sounds like better things to me*

Violet: ☺

Violet: *Be there in 20*

I lie back, my eyes buzzing with migraine pain. It's hard to reconcile feeling joy, because I'm struck with the reality of never being able to tell my parents about any of it. Still, dying too soon but living happily seems paradoxical, an irony of the fates. Maybe that's why I'm so drawn to it, and why my parents died when they did.

They were just too happy.

NAIMA

I wander into Baked & Caffeinated the next day. "Hey," I say, embarrassed. "I hope you're wearing different shoes."

He laughs. "Indeed. I put the others in a glass case to commemorate our day."

"You're gross."

"Naima," Violet says, stepping between us. She stands close, but I step back. "You're back."

There's an odd pause.

"We didn't get the chance to officially meet before, but I'm Violet. *Wow*—your aura reads dark. Almost black."

"Tell me something I don't know."

"What brings you in?" Dew asks.

"I called the dude and he said I can start today."

"I didn't realize you were serious."

"I didn't realize you aren't a total douche, but here we are."

"Let me get Big Foot," Violet says.

"Like a Sasquatch?"

"More like a human manager," Dew corrects.

"*Obviously*. What a name," I say. "What. A. Name."

We stand, awkwardly, waiting. It's a weird tension. Like we didn't just have a friend date.

Big Foot emerges from his shire. "Welcome to my humble abode that I don't actually own, but run like I do. Ready to get started?"

When Violet returns, I feel her eyes on me and I can't decide why. I check to be sure my shirt isn't riding up. That I don't have anything in my teeth. And I remember. Sometimes people don't need a reason to hate me. They just do. It's part of their makeup.

Hate. Hate. Hate. Hate. Hate. Hate.

"These two bad cats can get you trained on the machines after you fill out the paperwork. I promise not to call anyone an adorable mini muffin."

"Cool."

"Questions?"

"Seems pretty self-explanatory."

He raises his hand for a high five—which I don't do—and leaves me here, the third wheel.

"Naima," Violet asks, "you're going to be a senior right?"

"If I'm still alive." The moment I say it, the words repeat in my head.

If I'm still alive. If I'm still alive. If I'm still alive.

If I'm still alive. If I'm still alive. If I'm still alive.

"Sorry about your dad," Violet says. "Can't be easy losing both parents."

My face turns to Dew, heated.

"I didn't mean to say that," she says.

"It's okay."

Dew blushes so I change the subject pronto. He walks me through the basics of the store step by step. Turns out, it's not hard. Ring this shit up, grab that shit. Don't say "shit" to customers. Basically, cake (except for doing everything I just mentioned because my brain really doesn't want to comply).

Violet leans near him at a safe distance as if trying to figure out her place between us. I want to tell her there is no *us*. But the stifled conversation and avoidance of direct eye contact would make it sound like I was lying.

As customers come in, I watch Violet trace the lines on Dew's palms as she sits on the countertop. I swear there's a time or two she looks right at me while doing it, but my nerves are so bunched up, I'm starting not to know what's real. I'm there, wiping counters, refilling stock, and learning to serve customers with a knot in my stomach. My thoughts start to invade. They're persistent. They tell me morbid things. I want to ignore them but the next customer has a speck of food on his hand when he lays it on the counter. What if it's contaminated? He could poison me, and via everything I've touched, I'd contaminate the whole place. This is how contagion begins; this is how the world ends.

"Can I order?" a voice asks my back. Dew and Violet went to get more utensils and napkins and I was like "Does it require both of you or can someone help *me*?" and they both went. I'm wiping sweat from my brow.

When I turn, it's *him*. The boy whose arm I twisted. His expression sours in three seconds flat.

"No, you *can't* order," I tell him.

"Why not?"

"Because I don't like you. Once that's decided, there's no going back."

"Is there a manager or someone else I can order from?" he asks.

Big Foot runs out, an impeccable display of audio cues. "How can I help you?"

"She's refusing to serve me for no reason."

Big Foot turns to me. "Is that true?"

"This butt nut messed with your little mini-muffin."

Violet and Dew emerge from the back room. I don't want to claim they have "make-out" hair, but they totally do. Plus, her gloss is all over his chin. *Ew.*

Dew's eyes alight with fear.

"Did he hurt you?" Violet asks Dew. Her eyes zoom between the boy and Dew.

The dude's face turns to Violet, softens a little.

"No," Dew says. "I told you, Naima—he didn't touch me. I tripped. It was purely an accident."

They all stare at me like I'm the guilty one. I'm not sure why I've chosen this as my cross to die on, but here I am. Open and bleeding for a boy I wasn't even sure I wanted to know at all.

Big Foot spreads his arms like wings and tells me to "go hang" in the back, code for "Imma get a lecture." My blood heats, my fists clench. He gives the boy a latte, on the house, and pulls Dew and Violet aside to whisper something I can't hear.

By the time he makes his way to me, I already feel a shift in the air. He comes at me with a pseudo-mentor type of disappointment and tells me to take a seat.

"It's your first day," he says, "so we'll pretend this didn't happen. In the future, the customer is always right. If they're wrong, they're still right. Until they're wrong. Then, come get me so I can tell them they're right. Okay?"

I feel how scrunched my eyebrows have become but flash a thumbs-up to make this end. He's thrilled, instantly hopping around in celebration. "I knew you'd get it," he says.

A while later, Violet ends her shift early for an appointment with her "reflexologist," so it's just me and Dew. For two solid hours, we say nothing except what's necessary for me to do my job. Finally, I cave to kill the silence.

"What did Big Foot say about me?"

He bites his lip. Looks everywhere but my eyes.

"DEW."

"He spoke with Joelle. We're to give you a break since your dad died. To 'babysit' you. Those are his words so please don't shoot the messenger."

"Gah! Of course she told him. I wish everyone would let me forget for one second. It's not all I am. It's not all he was, either."

"I know."

I hug my arms tight to my chest as my invisible walls disintegrate. As if I've been put through fire, my shield melts so all that's left are my exposed insides. A flash of Dad zaps through my brain and I don't know when or how or why but *I cry. And I cry. And I cry. And I cry. And I cry. And I cry.* Dew guides me into his arms, but stops to ask if it's okay.

I nod through the pain. He holds me until I decide to let go. For 113 seconds. There are no customers, and Big Foot has stepped out back for his "herbs" and a garbage nap, or whatever. It's just us. When the last tear falls, he wipes it from my cheek and tilts my chin up. With a slight smile, it's the first time I see him. Not as some weird kid all up in my business, but as the person, Andrew Brickman. What the hell is happening to me? It's not okay.

He moves to change subjects, which I appreciate. "What's next on your minor adventure list?"

"Forget about it. It was dumb to think I'll feel better by doing those things."

He pulls back far enough to take in my swollen eyes. "Have you ever dance-walked through town?" I think of dancing at Paint the Sky and my chest pulses.

I take a giant step backward. "I don't like where this is going."

He unties his apron and wanders out back to retrieve Big Foot so the place isn't free to ransack. "Come on. Our shifts are over." With the door open, and the sunshine pouring through, he waits for me. I reluctantly follow. Outside, where dozens of people stroll by, Dew snaps his fingers. With a kick of the foot, he dances, and walks—dance-walks—down the sidewalk. His arms flail and fingers snap and he couldn't look more ridiculous—or *free*.

"Everyone's watching," I say, hiding my face.

"I know! I feel like I'm dying, but I'm working my way through it by not caring what other people think."

I stand back and watch how he gives himself over to the moves. They're terrible, and he should stop, but doesn't. There's a freeness radiating from him, and I know he's not free. He's carrying a lot, too. But I get the point he's trying to prove: I don't have to be perfect to find a glimmer of happiness, of hope that I can be okay.

I throw my head back and ignore all the voices that tell me not to.

And I dance for the first time since I danced with Dad.

I stop near the house to check my phone when it buzzes.

Smellope: *The house feels empty without you here.*

It catches me off guard and I can't move my feet. Dew dances around me, stopping when he sees my face lose its joy.

"What's wrong?" he asks.

"Nothing." But it's not nothing. "*Of course* she loves you," Dad would tell me when I questioned why he was leaving me with "her" again. It was last summer and I wasn't having it. No matter how much shit I gave him, he was adamant about me loving her or liking her or giving her a chance, or whatever.

"I didn't say anything about love," I'd quip. "She doesn't even *like* me."

"She does. You don't see all she does when you're not around."

"Like?" I'd press.

"She talks about you to her friends and makes sure she buys at least *three* boxes of Lucky Charms so you can pick out the marshmallows. And she hasn't thrown the flytrap in the trash. Yet."

"She tried. I dug PS back out. And three boxes is wrong. Six is the number. Not three. She knows and does whatever she wants anyway."

He'd scoff. "She wouldn't hurt you on purpose, honey. She's your family now, too."

"Nope."

"She needs you as much as you need her. You're both too stubborn to realize it. Besides, JJ and Kam will be there every summer waiting for your visit, like always. They aren't going anywhere."

"Yeah, *you* are," I'd argue tearfully. "You're the one who leaves. YOU."

"I'm . . . sorry," he'd say with a hand on mine. But he didn't say it like "I'm sorry to do this to you," it was more like "I'm sorry but I don't want to be here." I heard it in his voice and I felt it when he'd try to grab my hand because the touch didn't match the feeling in my gut.

"Dad, please don't go," I pleaded. "I feel like things will change. Something will happen."

With a sigh, he'd grab my poster and hold it between us. "What would Rosie do?"

"Roll up her sleeves and change a tire."

"I love that. I could use a tire change if you want to have at it."

"*Dad.*"

"I get it, kiddo. But hear me out. Before long, you'll be out of the house and off doing your own thing. Stick this out with Nell and Chris. She's not always very good at letting people in, but it's not intentional. She tries. That's where you and she are very similar. Remember that when I'm gone and you feel alone."

Hearing his voice in my head forces me to turn farther away from Dew and dancing and *free* to where I can retreat into my skin.

"Hey," Dew says. "Where'd you go just now?"

I blink the memories away. "Do you have anywhere to be?"

"Wherever my friend needs me to be," I don't want to smile, but I DEW.

I take him to my secret place in Ivy Springs—a weeping willow I stumbled upon near the river. We sit with our feet pointing toward the open sky with our backs against the trunk. The wind is a quiet whisper, blowing the willow moss like a gentle kiss.

"Dad," I say, looking to the sky. "This is Dew."

He looks over at me, in awe. I thank him for coming when he stops me.

"No, thank *you* for helping me see. Goodbye doesn't mean forever."

I suppose he's right.

◄◄ ►►| ►|| ■ ● DEW GD BRICKMAN
DURATION: 0:22

Friends or more: The YA contemporary (trope)
question of the century.

The buzz of the sunset's orange-glazed rays has become part of me. Forever printed in the echo chamber of my heart. The colors of the August Moon poster have come alive in the sky and I can feel them in me, with me, beside me. My parents.

"Find the things that scare you most and do them," my father says.

"Fear is a reminder you're alive," Mom says. "Blink and you'll miss everything life has to offer."

At the levee, I wish on planes and dream about what *could* be. The willow tree is about reflecting on the past, and how I came to be. The river could be a chance to understand the *now*. Of all the things that scare me, it's fear I fear the most. The way it pins me against a wall so I can't move or breathe. The way it tells me I can't do the things I know I can.

I will look fear in the eye, and this time, I won't blink.

NAIMA

I'm about to fall asleep when my phone buzzes.

DEW GD BRICKMAN: *I have a marvelous idea. Are you currently medicated?*

Me: *Wut*

DEW GD BRICKMAN: *In case of drowsiness. I'd like to avoid that.*

Me: *I'm not anything.*

Dew GD BRICKMAN: *Perfect. Meet me outside in 10 minutes.*

Me: *No*

DEW GD BRICKMAN: *I beg. It'll be a really cathartic event.*

Me: *It's not roller skating is it? That's the worst.*

DEW GD BRICKMAN: *No skates involved. But what a great fear to tackle in the future* ☺

Me: *You're annoying. See you in 10.*

I dress, and put on another coat of lipstick to boost any

lingering confidence. JJ and Kam are snuggled up on the couch. "Dew wants to show me something. Is it okay?"

They both smile, not even an inquisition. "Don't be long. It's getting late."

I head out through the front door to find him already standing there.

"Don't you have a girlfriend to hang out with or strangers to annoy? You can't spend all your free time with me. It's pathetic."

He smiles. "I'll take that as a compliment. Violet had previous plans and I have something I need your help with, just as I helped you."

"*Ugh*. Is this how our friendship's gonna be? Where it has to be fair and equal helping?"

"Yes."

"I don't love those conditions. What's this about?" I ask. Before he answers, he grabs me by the hand, ew, and pulls me down the sidewalk. We run down three streets before I stop him, out of breath. "What the hell? Can't you tell me first so I can tell you I don't wanna?"

"Sorry," he says, "no can DEW." He laughs. I don't. "I promise you no harm. Trust me?"

Trust. Trust. Trust. Trust. Trust. Trust.

The word feels foreign. But his eyes catch the moonlight. Two shining blips staring back at me. "Don't make me regret this."

He takes me to a familiar place—the levee, where we're seemingly the only people on earth. "I don't get it. Are we wishing on more planes? Going to the willow?"

"The answer's been here all along," he says. "The water."

"You're gonna have to give me more than that, man."

He pulls off his shoes and his socks. He begins to unbuckle his belt. I stop him. "*Whoa*, nope! What are you doing?"

"Don't panic—we're not skinny-dipping. I'm far too modest for that."

"Then what the hell? Put your clothes back on before someone sees."

He doesn't stop. He removes items faster. The shirt comes up over his head and the boy has abs—like genuine, defined abs against his bony frame. My eyeballs shoot out of their sockets at the gift he's been hiding. *Damn.*

"That's the thing," he huffs. "I've realized recently—since my recorder was destroyed—I don't much care what people think. I just want to live. Not merely be alive—*LIVE*."

"What does that have to do with the river?"

"We're jumping in the lake and swimming to the buoy."

I laugh. Loud. "You're out of your mind."

He pulls his pants down, lets them drop. His legs are twigs, barely fur covered. "Maybe I am, but you know what? Oh, well. This is me, Naima. I hope you'll change your mind because I envisioned this being more of a team-building exercise. Like I help you fight your fears and you help me fight mine."

Would you rather stand stark naked in front of the world, but emotionally protected, or be fully clothed and all your feelings in plain sight?

An airplane passes overhead and he stops. Our chins point up, both of us wishing. And suddenly I see him standing there, his tall, thin body frail under the stars. It's nearly the complete opposite of me. Something about it makes me feel at ease. I look around one last time—still no one—and decide to take another chance.

"I'm not taking my clothes off," I say. "And we better hurry before Officer Cane does his rounds."

"*Of course* you know his schedule."

"Get off my case." I reluctantly kick off my sneakers. "If you look at me weird, or touch me, or tell *anyone* about this, I'll end you."

"I have no doubt." He smiles and holds out a hand. I refuse it but together, we run into the water.

His arms fly through the air as he gasps. "I can't swim!" he shouts.

"Are you fucking kidding me?" I grab ahold of him and start to drag him to land but he resists.

"We *have* to get to the buoy."

I'm starting to see shadows of curious people, so to save time, I do what he asks, guiding him to the buoy, where he grabs ahold.

"*Why* do you need to touch the buoy?" I ask. We're quiet now, only the sound of waves gently crashing around us.

"I have a confession."

"*Jesus.* Now what?"

"When I sit along the levee, I'm not only wishing on airplanes. I'm also making a deal with this buoy."

"I don't get it."

"My parents were swerved off the road. Their car went into a river similar to this one. It struck a buoy. I've always wanted to touch the symbol of what took them from me. To show the universe it can't control me anymore. And I did it. Thanks to you, I did it."

The pain I feel over his loss is so similar to the pain of my own, my heart aches. "*You* did it."

He cries with laughter, an overwhelming pang of pride surging through. I splash him to ruin the moment, and he splashes back. We're loud and free and I've never felt more alive than in this moment. I don't ever want it to end.

The smell of apple butter permeates through the open kitchen window. I lift onto my heels from the back porch. I'm soaking wet with no justifiable explanation. Inside, JJ hums something choir-like, taking me back to my younger days when she'd comb through my wet hair, belting out along with a gospel record. Her voice is as powerful as ever, never quiet, never shrinking.

Kam sits at the table with his elbows propped. He's thumbing through another of JJ's books—*A Woman Is More Than Your Gaze: A Feminism Guide for Men*—and the floor where Dad's pieces fell has been swept clean.

I breeze through the door as if nothing happened. I mean, what else is there to do? They both stop what they're doing. "What happened to you?" JJ asks in a panic. She's grabbing all the kitchen towels to dry me off.

"I'm fine," I say. "I fell."

"Into a pool?" Kam asks.

"Good Lord, girl," JJ says. "I wasn't that wet during the swimming portion of my last triathlon."

"Can we pretend I'm not dripping all over the floor and skip this conversation altogether?"

With a smirk, JJ ushers me on to change my clothes. When I return, no one so much as looks up when I pull out the chair next to Kam—the one Dad had been in, but is now empty—and take a seat. The spot is cold, how I'd expect it to feel. Kam barely looks up from his page so as not to acknowledge me too much, as JJ's song never breaks from the chorus. A row of Lucky Charms boxes continues to line the table's edges. I've already sorted the marshmallows out of them and can't seem to toss the boxes into the trash heap. If it were with Nell, she'd already have taken them from me, before I'm ready. But JJ and Kam know to take my lead. They let me toss them on my time, when I'm ready. I know: high maintenance central. The strawberry cake Dew made still decorates the center of the table, only one piece cut, like a giant gaudy centerpiece.

JJ's song comes to an end, and suddenly, we are all still. The quiet after the storm. "I'll pretend I know nothing about the trespassers at the levee the news is talking about. Dew Brickman would never do anything so unlawful."

I slink into the chair. Kam finds my eyes with a smile as JJ pushes a small plate in front of me with a wink. I look down at the missing piece of Dew's strawberry cake, adorned with rainbow sprinkles. She swivels the plate so the cake's inside faces me. Apparently Dew GD Brickman is full of many surprises. Lucky Charms marshmallows are baked right into the center.

I want to be angry at JJ's apparent betrayal for spilling one of my weird secrets to an even weirder boy, but can't. I feel something else taking over instead; something indescribable. I've decided this is the second thing I like about him. The first, of course, is that he's probably the kindest, realest person I've ever met and I hate everything about it.

But don't tell him I said so. ← My new catchphrase, I guess.

⏮ ⏭ ▶❚ ■ ⬤   DEW GD BRICKMAN
DURATION: 4:25

Boy finds himself in hot (river) water, tries to climb out.

I wake later than usual to the smell of Stella's Sunday morning skillet breakfast, which consists mostly of vegetables and faux cheese.

"This one's for the blog so let me take a few photos first." She grabs her phone and adjusts the lighting, snapping a few shots before filling our plates.

"I wanted pancakes," Faith says, groggy-eyed.

"I'll find a pancake recipe for next weekend, okay?"

She grumbles, but ultimately eats what's in front of her. A speck of winged glitter is still drawn from her eyes, shimmering against the morning sunlight.

"Since I'm off today," Thomas says, "what do you say we do something together—as a family?"

Faith grunts again. "I'm *soooo* tired."

"I don't mean this minute."

"Fine." Her fork pierces the bits while I pretend to do the same.

"Food okay?" Stella worries.

"It's great."

She silently asks Thomas to step in with her gaze, a gentle nod of the head. He clears his throat. "If you don't feel up to family time, it's okay."

"That's not it."

"Stomach still bothering you?"

My heart, I think. "A little."

"Go lie down and we'll figure out our day later."

I clear my plate, a buzz from my pocket catching me before I go.

Violet: *Question: Did you and Naima go skinny-dipping last night? Ivy Springs is a small town. If you want to see other people, tell me. It's cool if you just want to be friends. Maybe it'd help my misaligned chakras and your graying aura? Just a thought.*

My finger levitates above the words, but freezes. I'm an idiot.

"Thomas," I say. He looks up, wide-eyed. "Can I talk to you about something?"

Stella pauses mid-chew.

"Of course." He follows me to my room, where I silently ask permission from the August Moon poster before continuing.

"What's up, buddy?" His plaid robe drags across the floor like a dance pirouette. It oddly reminds me of Dad twirling Mom in our apartment.

"I have a general question I'm not sure I know the answer to."

"Shoot."

"Say there's a boy who likes a girl, but decides to be friends with that girl, and starts dating another girl. But then, the first girl suddenly wants to spend more time with him, and he isn't sure how to feel about the new girl, or the first girl, because it's all too much. Has he done something wrong? Should he politely step aside from both to not cause any hurt feelings—especially his own?"

Thomas rubs his chin and takes a seat on the edge of my bed. "That's a tough one. If this boy has these concerns, it might signal something's not right and he shouldn't be with either girl."

"Oh." I look to the poster for moral support. It doesn't provide any.

"But I also think relationships are nuanced and each one deserves its own set of rules. The important thing to do—for this theoretical boy—is to talk to each girl and say how he's feeling. Without communication, it can all get tangled up pretty darn quick."

I nod, calculating the steps I need to take for all sides to end on a positive note.

"Anything else I can help with?"

"No." He stands, unsure of how long to linger, but obviously beaming with pride.

"It means a lot that you'd ask my opinion. I'm always here for you, Dew. *Always*." He offers a hug and closes the door behind him.

I think of the way Dad spoke of Mom. How he'd compare her to the sun. I think of Mom, how she compared me to the rarest of flowers. But August Moon compared love to the fire. It burns, it lights the way, but most of all, it inspires.

I know just what to do with my fire.

NAIMA

Morning sun streaks in through the sheer curtains covering the small window. I stare at the pile of letters on my floor.

"Breathe it in while you can," Dad would say as the sun arose each morning he was home. "My lungs are too tight," I'd argue.

"I didn't mean *literally*, Naima. In your soul," he'd continue, and I'd have to think about what it meant to feel something so deeply, it changed the way you saw the world. I could see it in his eyes sometimes; that he *did* breathe it in while he could.

Every day home with me, with us, while distracted by memories of war, he *tried* to be in the pocket of our conversations but often failed. Those are hard things to forget. We seemed to be happily distracted in each other's company and I liked it that way.

The warmth of the sun inches over my skin, and it's like I'm on fire; it's a sign—another *omen*. So, on a day where the loss of him will surround me as we set off balloons into the sky, I imagine the six red balloons in front of me. They hover above the ground, each reminding me of someone.

One red balloon prays like Nell. The *second* breathes like Dad. The *third* says a three-syllable word about me, like Dew. The *fourth* holds his favorite *Marine Dad* mug but can't seem to drink from it. The *fifth* refuses to leave my side even when I tell her I'm fine. And the *sixth* reflects back to me. They're all gathered in this weird, little circle offering support. I imagine tying them to my wrist and skipping on through the rest of my day, weightless. This feeling carries me through.

After we've all dressed, we pile into JJ's car and drive to the community park, where JJ abandons us to go to the 5K start line. We'll cheer her on from the non-exerciser section like I prefer. I've run with her and it's what I imagine punishment in hell to be.

Kam and I wave her off with good-luck kisses and fist bumps (not that she needs them), to go find two silver metallic markers— markers that others have used with their germ-ridden, grease-ball hands—at the dedication table so we can write something on our red balloons—the one request I made when JJ planned all of this—that we're to release at the conclusion of the race. The whole town seems to be here, and some from others places, too, all to say goodbye to Dad, and anyone they've loved and lost.

Kam scribbles on his balloon face, *You are my hero, son*, and grabs another for JJ. "Ready?"

I tell myself the marker is only slippery because of my hand, not because of someone else's sweat, and I write the only thing that feels right—*breathe*—and nod. Side by side, we take our red balloons to the finish line. Moments after the race is done, we'll listen to a dedication and set our balloons off into the sky, where they'll float past the clouds, out of the galaxy, and into Dad's arms.

One. Two. Three. Four. Five. Six.

JJ finishes the 5K in 23:01 in 98-degree weather, which gets her first place in her age group, and fourth overall. She's winded, but navigates through the line to receive her bottle of water, where we give her all the sweaty hugs.

"Not my best time, damn it," she says, frustrated.

She takes the balloon offering from Kam's fingers.

"You did awesome, like always," I tell her.

"Look at all those people struggling behind you." Kam points.

She takes a swig of water and we gather into the sea of balloons awaiting launch. JJ and Reverend Mills lead us in prayer, with an official blessing of the balloons. One by one, we let go of our strings. I watch mine fly high, bumping into others along the way. Over my shoulder, I see a familiar face—Dew—who has let go of two balloons. He's surrounded by his family; I leave him be, because just as I'm saying goodbye, he is, too. I wait a few beats, after the balloons have vanished into the atmosphere, before pulling my phone out.

Me: *It's hot AF*

DEW GD BRICKMAN: ☺ *Where art thou?*

Me: *To your right*

I pull my Ziploc out and chomp a few lucky marshmallows. He looks up from his screen and waves like I'm the first person he's recognized in his whole life. His tears are still wet on his cheeks. His feet stop just short of running into me and I don't know how to cut the sorrow out of our lives.

"Do you work today?" I ask.

"No, you?"

"No. What about Violet? Is she coming?"

He kicks his feet. "About that. I told her we'd probably work best as friends."

"Why?"

"I'd rather have friends I can count on than a summer romance that'll likely end. Besides, she's going to college soon. I don't want to hold her back."

"What'd she say about all this?"

"Her horoscope warned her 'something grim was on the horizon' so she was prepared. Luckily, she agreed and felt the same. We both fell into something neither of us was looking for. This way is best. For now."

"Very mature of you both. I'm impressed-ish."

Across the crowd, I'm distracted by a balloon still in the grips of someone's hands. My eyes squint and the face becomes clear. I redirect Dew's attention.

"Dodge," he murmurs. He moves toward him.

"What are you doing?" I try to hold him back, but there's a laser-like stare in his eye.

"I'm not quite sure. I just know I have to do this."

Confused, I follow, cracking my knuckles in case it's about to go down.

We approach. He's alone, and he's crying.

"Are you okay?" Dew asks.

Startled, Dodge jerks back. "Go away."

Dew is persistent. "I can't. I want to know who you are, why you're upset, but mostly, who this balloon is for."

When Dodge tries to walk away, I block him. "Fuck off," he replies.

Dew looks at him. "I let go of two balloons because my parents died. They're gone. It changed me. I don't even remember who I was before they left. So, please, kindly tell me who you're holding on to because I'm not going anywhere until you do."

After a long silence where I'm sure this kid's about to kill Dew, something else happens instead: Dodge looks away, eyes still wet, and lets us in. "My grandpa. He was . . . all I had. It's stupid; nevermind."

Dew rests a hand on his shoulder, guides his stare. "I hear you. You're not alone." I stand back to give them space. I'm about to interrupt with my own experiences when Dodge falls into Dew's chest and sobs. What's with this town and all the crying? Dew, unsure of what to do or how to react, gently pats the boy's back. He shushes him and tells him it's okay. That if he needs a friend, Dew will be that for him. I wait for Dodge to react, to spit in his face or worse. Instead, he composes himself, gratitude flashing across his features.

"When you're feeling blue," Dew tells him, "listen to August Moon, most notably, the song 'So Long.' It may help with those wounds. I know it helped with mine."

Dodge's frown lifts, gradually turning into a hint of a smile. "I will," he says. After a few moments of me trying to figure this situation the fuck out, the two agree on a friendship; a truce. They trade anecdotes on grief, shake hands, and start anew. Finally, Dodge lets his balloon float into the sky. He doesn't look up or wave goodbye or say a silent prayer, but his steps are a little lighter knowing he's been seen.

He is seen. He is seen. He is seen. He is seen. He is seen. He is seen.

"Well that was some shit," I say. "We live in eternal high school where there will always be the smart one, the pretty one, the outcast, the jock, and the bully. Sometimes we get lucky and they're all the same person. I really thought I had that assbag pegged."

"You're so cynical. And please don't call my new friend an assbag."

"I figured he'd push you away. It's easier."

"Easier, yes. Better? Not at all. I believe people evolve all the time. Maybe it's my mother's desire for everyone to be kind, or my dad's bottomless optimism, or maybe it's Stella and Thomas's belief that they could love me and I could love them back. The only thing consistent is change. We have to accept it or become our own enemies. Dodge is trying to navigate who he is without his most influential person. I can appreciate that feeling."

My features soften. "You give people too much credit. They're the worst."

"And you don't give them enough."

Our eyes lock, a smile rising on my face. "What's something that terrifies you?" I ask.

"Pardon?"

"Tell me one of your biggest fears. You've been helping me with things I'm afraid of. I want to help you with something other than the levee incident."

He looks up to the sky.

"Dying."

My heart sinks because it tops my own list. "Where are your parents buried?"

"Washington Park East in Indy."

He pauses to think on the words like it's the first time he's said them aloud.

"Hold on a sec." I scamper toward JJ and Kam, who are the center of the church group's conversation. With one tap, and a few whispers, JJ looks to Dew, and nods.

I grab his hand. "Do you have plans after this?"

"I'd have to ask."

"I want to take you somewhere."

"Where?"

"I need you to trust me."

I hate myself.

◄◄ ►► ►❚ ■ ● DEW GD BRICKMAN
DURATION: 3:00

*Top story: Saying goodbye is the hardest thing to
do, but local boy to try anyway.*

I sit quietly in the backseat of Joelle's car and remove my fedora.
The fabric feels different as my finger and thumb rub Dad's worn
space. Naima's eyes float out of the window, chasing trees and
yellow cornfields along the way. Her fingers delicately tap in
rhythm against the ridge between the handle and the door as if
counting spaces between objects or time, or possibly the thoughts
in her head.

The wheels roll along, my thoughts drifting to all the final
words Mom and Dad ever said. How the difference between life
and death is the fear in between, how life is unpredictable, and
beautiful, and messy, and painful, but there's no better plot twist
than living it, through the fear. That the unknown is the thing
we need to experience to feel alive, and if we aren't chasing the
fear, we're not living.

I don't want to merely live—I want to *feel* alive.

There's a cemetery, Washington Park East, on the edge of Indianapolis, near the city limits. Not far from where I lived *before,* on an old street that contains the ghosts of memory in which
I dwell. The streets along the way are part of me. The way they
curve and bend. We pass the ice cream trailer that pops up every
summer in the gas station parking lot three blocks from our
apartment building. Even at this speed, an imprint of Dad
counting change on the silver counter flashes through. He loved
the frozen ice, raspberry, but I loved our time together—time
that can never be again. There were the late night revelries between alleyways with August Moon blaring or the occasional
drum circle with Dad on his old *djembe* while Mom crooned to
the sway of hands in the damp summer air. I miss that; I miss
them.

Naima doesn't tell me where we're headed until it's too late. Until the backseat has become familiar with the shape of me. Part of me knew. The part that's desperate to reconcile the greatest loss of my existence. I clench my body, my fedora crushed between my thighs, until finally, she grabs ahold of my hand and says, "I hate germs so GD much," and I instantly unknot. I spend the rest of the drive wondering what I'll say, while she's likely wondering when she can release my germs from her grip.

Forty-eight long, uncomfortable minutes later, we arrive. Naima lets my hand drop. She rubs the sweat dry against her leggings with a look of disgust.

"Thank you," I say.

"Don't mention it," she says. "Seriously—don't *ever* mention it."

Joelle leans over her seat and hands me a small piece of scratch paper. There's a rough sketch of blocks lined in rows, with number/letter combinations. She points to the second block in the third row, 37B. I'd know that drawn block anywhere, no matter how much time has, or hasn't, passed.

"I got the information from your parents," Joelle says. "And I called for instructions on how to find the plots. Should be right over . . . ," she cranes her neck, checking the paper, "there." She points to a long row of graying headstones, interwoven with the occasional metal marker for those not afforded the luxury of a granite headstone. My *abuela* has a marker, one that had been mowed over nearly every visit. Mom would complain, they would fix it, and it would happen again. My parents decided then, no matter how difficult it might be to save the money, they wanted to be worth more than a mowed-down metal marker. They wanted to be seen, remembered; and yet, their only son hasn't yet been able to visit long enough to say goodbye.

My finger rests on the door handle. I have everything I need— what's stopping me? I've painted a line from me to them. My living body to their shared stone block. Naima huffs, exiting abruptly. She appears on the outside of my window and swings the door open. I hesitate still.

She offers her hand. "Don't get used to this or anything."

I look up, as much fear in my eyes as ever, and instead of adding to the snark, she rips the paper from my hand and gently pulls me from my spot. "Come on," she whispers. "You can do this."

I let her guide me across the rows of the dead. Names covered in lawn clippings and dead flower petals. Respects lost in crumbled dirt that's blown from the storms. Everyone here was someone else's *something*. My parents have left me for this new family of the fallen.

Naima's pace slows. My steps trickle to a stop, slightly behind her.

"Here," she says, letting go.

But I'm afraid. To step out from her shadow and see their names is to remember losing them. Though if Dad were to ever chime in on my thoughts he'd likely say, "Isn't that what you've done anyway?"

I edge past her and kneel at the base of the stone's ledge where DIAZ is highlighted beneath the cloud-eclipsed sun. Naima kneels, too.

"Take your time," she says.

There are no trinkets, because our family has gone and spread into different parts of the world or passed on to greet them in the sky. I can't say how long it's been since anyone's knelt in front of them, or spoken to them, or even thought of them. Except me. I wonder if they've been waiting, and if so, if I'm forgiven for letting fear prevail.

"Hi," I tell them.

Naima bows her head.

"I'm sorry I haven't visited. The truth is, I'm still not ready. But I'm learning there's never a good time to say goodbye. And that I can't let the past dictate the future, or I'll only ever be alive, not living."

I lay my dented fedora on the grass. An offering.

Naima picks it up and rests it on top of my head. "He'd want you to have it," she says with wet eyes.

I nod, and adjust the rim so my fingers touch the places Dad's did, just as an old August Moon melody rings between my ears— "Let You Go." One last wisp of memory appears before me, just beyond the small headstone where the grass meets concrete. Mom and Dad's hands tie together as they tower over me. Just as their colors sharpen into near-complete versions of their living selves, they break into particles that scatter with the wind. Maybe it's my imagination conjuring the ghostly image to make this visit easier than it is. Or maybe it really is them letting me know it's time to move on, without them. The song says to let someone go, you have to find a way to say the thing that hurts the most. I feel it now; it's time.

I pinch my eyes tight. I don't need six wishes, six chances to say goodbye, like Naima. I only need one, and it can never come true.

"Goodbye," I whisper, hoping it's enough.

"Goodbye," Naima echoes.

NAIMA

Days have passed since the balloon release. I'm sitting on the back porch stoop, making a new list of fears to conquer while simultaneously wondering where the deflated balloon bodies landed. Nell's SUV crawls into the drive. The tires screech, lulling to a stop, and of course she parks at a cockeyed angle. Immediately I want to run to her, shove her from the driver's seat into the rocks, and straighten the hell out of that chop job, but as I watch her outline through the window, a cloud of blue (Violet would call it an aura or some kind of neuro-electromagnetic healing energy bullshit) hangs heavy. She doesn't need to be in full view for me to feel the lingering pain of Dad's absence. It's all she reminds me of now.

Now. Now. Now. Now. Now. Now.

I inhale deeply, as Dad suggested in one of his letters. These days, Dew and I practice the exercises from opposite sides of the fence to make it less weird. We tried face-to-face but all I could focus on was what his face looked like when his eyes closed. It reminded me of taking his kissing virginity and the spit germs and what his lips felt like (*ew*), and I couldn't stop myself from saying "virginity" aloud six sharp times. He laughed at first, but his discomfort was obvious because—*hello*—I was uncomfortable saying it. From then on, we decided the fence holes would be our special friend-zone space but not for deep breathing. There's no pressure and it lets me decide how much space I need between us. I should tell you this whole scenario is helping with my anxiety, or whatever, but I don't want to admit that just yet. Maybe I'm afraid to let go because there's comfort in the panic.

Would you rather let a black hole swallow you up or find a way to deal with your shit?

The twelve o'clock church bells ring as Nell (finally) emerges from the car. Her steps are slow but more confident than last time. Her hair has clumped into matted strands, and her face has hollowed a bit, but her posture is as ballerina tall as ever, square with the invisible wall still painted between us.

Would you rather hold hands with someone you don't like for an hour or maintain uncomfortable eye contact for a day? Because this feels a little like both, and neither is great.

"Naima," she says, clutching her giant suitcase purse, "how are you?"

"Fine," I say. She examines me harder, forcing a confession. "I mean, you know. *Not* fine, but whatever."

"Same," she says. "It's good to see you. You look great."

"Thanks. You, too."

We hold the thread connecting us, right here in the open sky. It's loosened up a bit, but the weak spots are more evident now that we've had some distance. I'm just glad boring-ass Christian decided to fly in for the service with his dad but not to stay here with us or I'd be majorly less patient.

One. Two. Three. Four. Five. Six.

The time lags, stops completely, until JJ and Kam break our thread into segments before I can say something inappropriate about the way her ankles cave in those shoes. There's obviously not enough to support her gait (something I learned watching a documentary on running form), so her legs collapse from the weight of her. Even with her slender frame (and all those juice fasts), she can't hide those hips. I know because I've got them, too (and flaunt them, BTW).

"Welcome," JJ says through her hug. Nell's arms squeeze tight.

"Can you help me carry a few things?" she asks Kam.

"Already on it." He sprints to the car like we're timing him. Dew watches through the hole—his one big eye taking us all in—and I jerk my head to signal that he should mind his own damn business, but the eye stays. I guess I don't mind as much anymore. It's become our thing; being our full-on weirdo selves without apology (as if I'd ever). He's not some nuisance, but a compassionate, kind being who cares whether or not my stars die off and plummet into the stratosphere. Don't you dare tell him I said that, or I'll deny. Kam jogs back, breathless, holding two large boxes. Nell stops him, taking one for me to see.

"Found these at the base of your bed—*after* I scraped off all that gum."

My shoeboxes of marshmallows in all their sugary glory are tightly packed in a way only I could. I guess I was wrong about Nell. *Ugh.*

"Thanks," I say casually. I let six seconds of this new nonchalant attitude pass before ripping the box away from her weak fingers. I don't care how much yoga she does—those things can't hold on to shit. I cram the box into my chest and silently thank the General Mills leprechaun forever and ever and ever and ever and ever and ever and ever. It feels like a hug and I think I'm smiling but I'm not sure because it's not the most familiar feeling. When I pry my eyes open, Dew's thumb is lifted over the top of the fence as if to say, "Good for you, old chum," so I turn away to love my marshmallows in peace, because I hate him but also not that much anymore, maybe, but this is my moment.

"And this." Nell pulls something from the second box I never thought I'd see again: PS—my flytrap. She's weathered and sad-looking, but aren't we all? The more I look, she's actually kind of dead. I mean, again, aren't we all?

"One last thing." She digs through the boxes, pulling free my memory box from Dover. Her hands spread open with the box in the center. It's our steeple, our holy grail of loss. The very sight takes me back to the sound of those boots, marching Dad's transfer case toward the van's open doors.

"You didn't dig this up from the backyard." It's not a question. Reluctant, she nods.

"That's so morbid." I decide I like this about her.

"Cleaned it out for you. Couldn't leave it buried."

Instead of letting her sulk, I decide to raise her an unexpected gesture—I hug her (WHO AM I?). Our bodies touch lightly, avoiding the snug comfort of what a hug *should* be, and not only is it supremely awkward, but it also triggers something I don't expect: acceptance. Mom is gone. She's never been part of my life, except in the ways I imagine her to be. But Nell is *here*. She's been here for years, playing her own sacrificial role in Dad's absence. And now that he's really gone—our most important thread—she doesn't have to be. Perhaps this is what love is. Or something. Why did it take me so long to feel this?

"JJ said you got a package. From Ray."

I can't tell if she's happy or sad. "I did."

"It was the letters, wasn't it—the ones you returned?"

"How did you know?"

"He mentioned holding on to them." She squeezes harder, as if she's only just realized these things about me, too. I open my eyes to see Kam's arm around JJ. They look on, proud but clearly filled with sorrow. The four of us hold a new thread. One that is only ours.

It all feels as normal as it possibly can. Except for Dew's eye that has returned to the fence hole (I'm watching you, *Dewd*).

But then again,

> This is my new normal now
> > And it really isn't so bad
> > > Except for the
> > > > Missing my father part.
> > > > > That will never change.

During the parade, Dew and I count the seconds together. He's learning how to control his loss of time to be fully present in the moments. But he's teaching me to let some of those seconds pass without fearing I've lost something bigger. We wave our small, patriotic flags in unison, grateful for the sacrifices made but reflective of what they mean. To me, to every other grieving family, and to the country. I'm allowed to be me (whatever that means) because of what Dad has given. It's a hard truth but a very, very good truth.

The parade is brief, led by the mayor, who attended Dad's service a couple months back. By the time it's over, we've found our places in the chairs that are lined in rows. The scene is eerily like Dad's funeral procession.

"Breathe," Dew says, sensing my nerves.

I'm called up to the podium to speak, something I decided to be necessary after all. The view is wide and open, with a lookout to the lush greenery at City Hall's side. Dozens of mournful faces look up at me, phones are held high, tissues hang from pockets, and the instant my hands hit the podium's cool metal ledge, it feels like I've been smashed by several two-ton walls. I want to tell everyone to look away, to put their phones down, to not be here at all. My breaths are shaky, and in this god-awful heat, I'm suddenly rethinking my silk camisole after sweating the shape of a lumpy potato through the front of it. I told you not to trust silk.

I think back to Dad's letter on public speaking (he knew me too well) and how to overcome the anxiety. Dr. Tao told me to visualize the beach, but that only worked until I imagined a shark biting my face off. When she gave me the worry stone to rub, I laughed (really hard) because, just, no. Nice try. There's also a technique called "grounding," where I'm supposed to close my eyes and state facts ("the air is warm, the cement is rough, my stomach is on the verge of puking breakfast"), but this turned into a game of "What offensive thing can I say next?" like "Your bangs are way harsh," and she didn't get that I was serious (because I was). These things work for some; I have never been "some."

The faces stare hard at the potato stain on my cami. To comfort myself, I do this thing with my lips where I blow the air out and make my lips roll and it looks stupid but I really can't bring myself to care because it makes me feel better. After a few passing grunts and stray coughs, I pull up my phone, and instead of speaking, I do the very thing Dad hinted at (the very thing Dew would do) (ha—*dew do*). *FOCUS, IMA!*

JJ and Kam hold resistance signs in the crowd. I made them to commemorate this event (CHOOSE LIFE, DAD!). I press Play from a memo I'd pre-recorded, thanks to Dew, so I wouldn't flub my one chance to say goodbye properly.

▶ "Rise for something you believe in or fade with those in fear . . . those are the words my father instilled in me from an early age. . . ."

❚❚ You can hear the click from where I'd paused after the initial recording. I'm an amateur. Seconds later, when I try to resume, the song "Naima" plays instead. Apparently I never actually got the rest of my thoughtful speech on the damn memo. I could argue the logical: that I did this on purpose to divert my emotions *again*. And the illogical: Dad did it. You decide. The burden of proof lies with the guilty party and I object—this thesis is inadmissible because my medication has me obsessed with old episodes of *Law & Order* (it reruns on TNT). Basically, the verdict is, my damn speech got erased, or something, and in its place is music, but this is such a Naima thing to happen and Dad would understand.

I go with it, watching the eyes in the crowd embark on a journey of emotions. From confusion to laughter, to the tears I hoped were from the music and not how I screwed this up. I try not to make direct eye contact with anyone.

They are alive.

They are alive.

They are alive.

They are alive.

They are alive.

I am not.

When Nell's eyes catch mine, I shift my attention quickly. Count the worn parts of the podium, and divots in the grass beyond. I count the clouds burning into the wind, and the number of times Nell pulls another wad of tissues from her suitcase purse. When I attempt to turn the song off, I accidentally change it to another, high-octane dance song instead. Some kind of electronic dance music (EDM) and I have *no* idea how it got there, I swear. Then, and it would *only* happen to me, the GD screen freezes. So now, we're all in this pool of grief, saying goodbye to a man who sacrificed his life for our country while the mood tells us we're to dance out our emotions with glow sticks. I swear Kam's toes are tapping. I'm not mad about it. Dad wouldn't be either.

When Mayor Klein manages to move things forward, he officially dedicates this day—the Fourth of July—to Dad, and all others who've sacrificed their lives for our freedom and to those still fighting. We bow in silence to honor him, and them, and I feel the pang of missing him. *So hard.*

I hasten to make my exit, but Dad's old friend, Captain

Lewis from the police department, refuses to let me leave without folding me tight into him first. I don't want him to, but kinda-sorta do, so I let him. He smells like memories. As soon as he lets go, I feel an ache and crave for more hugs than I've had in years. It's as if I've lived in an alternate universe void of feeling and suddenly been shoved into one saturated with it. I never knew how much I needed it, until this moment. With a gruff whisper, he tells me he's proud, and that Dad would be, too. Maybe it shouldn't mean so much to me but it cements what Dad's sacrifice means for me, for everyone.

At some point, the service concludes. Ironically, I've lost track of time. JJ and Kam fumble as they carry Dad's urn. JJ carefully slides open the top. Nell pours a sprinkle of ashes in one seamless trip around the cherry tree seedling. JJ and Kam do the same. Together, they cover the area with more loose dirt, lingering over the finality. We'll be separating the remains between two other, smaller urns: one for Nell, and one for me.

"I was going to keep the ashes," Nell said, "but I realized how selfish that would be. Against his wishes. He'd have wanted me to make sure you got a piece of him. Maybe you can sit your urn next to the new flytrap seedling I ordered. So PS has company."

I feel my face brighten. "Perfect."

"I'll have it all set up in your bedroom at the new place I found in Albany. For when you come home. How does that sound?"

Home.

Home.

Home.

Home.

Home.

Home.

"I hoped you might change your mind and come live with me in August. I know it's weird without your dad, but will you think about it, Naima? We can go to the grief support group. Find a way to move on, together." Her *think about* and *together* feel like a plea of desperation. Maybe to hold on to the last piece of Dad she has. But with Dad gone, is that still my *home*? I'm legally obliged to Nell, I think, but if I have the choice, would I choose *her*?

I look to Kam with his pleated pants, JJ with her crystal earrings, and Dew with his plaid suspenders he's not wearing ironically. Is this *home*? It's old and new and confusing, but also makes me feel alive in ways I didn't think possible. But also, not. Neither place feels right but what will?

Would I rather live with Nell through graduation, where we'll wait for a man who won't return, or stay with JJ and Kam where it's the exact same feeling?

Out of the clear blue sky, my phone plays "Naima" again.
Or maybe it's in my head. *
Regardless, I think I know what I have to do.
it's definitely in my head

⏮ ⏭ ⏯ ⏹ ⏺ DEW GD BRICKMAN
DURATION: 4:05

BREAKING NEWS: Word just in that Marshmallow the Second has died. The circumstances are still unknown at this time.

The time is noon EST.

The church bells ring like usual, even during the daunting task of school registration. I'm learning that time doesn't have to be my enemy; it can be my ally, a beacon. There are few things you can count on in life ("death and taxes" is the joke, but I'd like to state that I can also count on Big Foot saying "sweet sauce" or "Ridic City"). The bells are a permanent reminder of what we can sink our feet into. For instance, today I'm officially seventeen. I suppose I can sink my feet into the very real fact that not only am I alive, I'm finally learning to *live* in some form. "Hands in the air at the top of a roller coaster and throttling down in a moment of glory" kind of living. I'm learning that, when it comes to grief, healing doesn't come with one singular breakthrough, but a series of them. I have to practice feeling okay, but if it means sewing up just one wound, I will do so.

Stella and Thomas are on each side of me as we tour the K–12 school I'll become a part of my junior year. Faith, an emerging fifth grader, navigates the halls in front of us, having found her people in her wrestling teammates. However, because it's a county-wide team, only two attend this school, but two friends is far better than none. As the unspoken leader of her pack, she now radiates a confidence the three of us had struggled to help her find.

"Do you need help finding your teachers?" Stella asks.

Faith doesn't answer, scooting off with only a wave of her hand. Her feather-embroidered denim jacket that brags THE CONNIPTION is all we see as she rounds the corner to make her mark, on her terms, with the three of us quietly supporting from behind. I smile. Right now, I'm okay; *we're* okay. I wouldn't have said as much a couple years back, but now, it's a wonderful place to be.

Violet: *Today's horoscope says Jupiter is pushing forward so anything is possible. Happy wanderings and happiest of birthdays to one of the coolest friends a girl can have*

Me: *But I can't be, if you are, in fact, the coolest (and thanks)*

When I slip my phone away, I reflect on how much has happened. What started as a confusing, desolate headspace soon became inflated with the fire of being alive; a feeling I hadn't had since before my parents passed. Dr. Peterson is pleased with the way I've learned to finally deal with my grief, hoping whatever sparked the changes has become part of my regular life, indefinitely. I don't tell her it was, in part, meeting Naima. She'd just try to convince me that no person is responsible for our own healing. I'd be remiss in saying Naima *didn't* give me a blueprint, not unlike my own. She saw the wounded places in herself, and connected with the ones in me, and together, we're finding our way.

"Did you go?" I ask from the hole in the fence when Naima shouts my name a bit later.

"Decided to drop out, change my name to Marshmallow, and run marathons with JJ."

"Naima."

"*Some* of us have to work, you know. Violet—my new frenemy for no good reason, who I have nothing in common with—says hi. We're headed to the open house in a few. She said she had nothing better to do, which I'll take as a compliment?"

"Together? Wow. You're making great progress with this friend thing."

"*Ugh.* Don't make it sound so nice. Gross."

"What do I owe this pleasure?"

She pushes a long tube through the hole that nearly pokes me in the eye.

"What's this?"

"Open it."

I flip the cap from the cardboard end and pull out a rolled-up laminated poster. My fingers quickly smooth the length of it out, to see coordinates and a title—a *name.*

RA 21h 30m 6s Dec "-5° 21' 33.3"

Constellation DIAZ

"I named a star after you, so stop wishing on the damn planes," she says.

I drop the tube, and the poster, and pieces of my heart. Through the hole, I may not see her face in its entirety, but I feel the warmth she tries so hard to conceal.

"Is it . . . okay?" she asks.

I hold back tears. "It's my . . . identity."

"Is that good or?"

I shove my eye into the hole, blinking tears. "It's *everything.*"

Her eyes soften. I've made her smile. "I get it now. *You're* the plot twist, *Dewd*. I guess this friend thing is off the trial basis. We're permanent."

"I would love nothing more."

"Why can't all guys be *this* cool, seriously?"

"All guys *aren't* cool. But all my parents raised me to be."

"I'm starting to understand. Plus, I technically took your kissing virginity, so there's that."

"Technically." I smile, too.

"Ready?" JJ shouts from the car.

"One sec," she shouts in return.

"Is that Dew?" JJ asks.

"Yep."

"Happy birthday, honey. I hope it's a great day."

"Thank you, Joelle," I yell.

"Welp," Naima interjects. "Later, chump."

I remain until their doors close, and their car vanishes from view. Like holding this place somehow magically cements my place in the world. Stella and Thomas have seen me. Faith has seen me. Joelle and Kam have seen me. Violet has seen me. And now, the most complex soul I've ever crossed paths with sees me, too. It's a pretty good day to be Dew GD Brickman, no matter what lies in my past or what's to come in the future.

Inside, Stella hovers over the countertop, icing a cake. She pauses to snap photos for her blog, scribbling a few notes in the small notebook nestled beside it. Thomas counts a package of candles, and Faith leads me to the table, where there's a gift waiting.

"Open it," she says with a grin. "I helped pick it out. You better love it."

"Is it wrestling related?"

Her lips purse. "That's *my* thing."

"Just checking." My fingers can't unwrap fast enough, eyes peering into the small box to find a new friend, for a new beginning: an MP3 recorder, extra sturdy. As Stella and Thomas gather around with my most favorite cake, minus the main ingredient— for good fortune—I decide it's best to find new ways to fill in my empty spaces, in this new chapter I've been given, where I'm surrounded by others who very much care to step into my shoes, to peel back my layers.

My eyes are alight, but there's more. An envelope with four tickets to an August Moon show. Time stops, all of us in our respective positions until I find a full breath; until my hearts picks up its tempo again. I look to Thomas, whose arm is wrapped snug around Stella. They're surrounded by a cloud of hope.

"Is this okay?" Stella asks. Her voice is soft, almost afraid to disappoint me.

I shove my chair from the table and leap into their arms. There aren't words suitable enough to thank them for what they've given me. Not only today, but all the days. Instead, I sing the very song Joelle streamed through their house one fateful day, the song Stella's hummed through the kitchen many times over— the song my mother would sing to me on this day to celebrate me—and within a few lines, the three of them join in to the words of "So Long." I have come full circle.

I have been reborn.

We soak in the closeness until we've finished the song. Then, we eat cake. We trade stories. We remember where we came from and give thanks for where we've landed. As the day settles, I find myself in the quiet of my room, reflecting on all that's happened, the good and the bad. With my fedora snug against my head, and Dad always with me, I pick up my new MP3 recorder. The only thing left to do is give my new mechanical friend a name in remembrance of how my mother lovingly referred to me. Something only she would say. I gaze at the August Moon tickets and the name comes in a flash.

My Darling.

A DYING STAR

Though her dad had been overseas for almost a year before his death, Naima couldn't help but wonder what would've happened if her mother hadn't died all those years ago. Would her dad still have left? Or would having someone *like Naima* force him away regardless? Two questions, no answers. She needed another plan. Plans are good. They're solid. You can count on them; rely on them, point by point. Naima likes that—knowing what comes next before it's in front of you.

Five hundred thirty-nine days before, after a lot of consideration, Naima planned to take her own life. Five hundred thirty-nine days before, her attempt failed. That was the beauty of her plan. She didn't *want* to die; it was an imperfect, highly problematic plan, but she wanted to give her father a reason to stay, however misguided.

Stay. Stay. Stay. Stay. Stay. Stay.

What Naima didn't know was that 743 miles away, there was another who could relate. The day Naima's grandparents, JJ and Kam, got news of Ray's death, an antique kettle couldn't be heard through their incessant wailing. And Dew GD Brickman—who hadn't yet earned his name—snuck in to pull the kettle off the stovetop, quietly leaving after. He knew it wasn't his place. But once Naima came to town, it was the only place he could imagine. Two constellations connected by one falling star: Staff Sergeant Raymond Rodriguez.

NAIMA

Today, it's not only Dew's birthday, but Dad's. Weird, right? Don't you dare call it kismet. In nine days, I'll start my senior year of high school, where I'll inevitably avoid everyone in my path (except Dew, I guess) so as not to make any new attachments in this temporary phase of life. *Everything* is temporary, really. I'm learning to grasp how to make the most of the moments before they become the past. I'm not about to wax poetic because I don't have all the answers, and I'm a frickin' long way from feeling healed, but I'm trying. There's a divine purpose tied into *every* decision I make, good or bad (whatever the hell that is); at least, that's what Dad said in the final letter.

Final. Final. Final. Final. Final. Final.

On this day, I take a few moments to myself, wondering what he'd have said if we had the chance to talk in the weeks before his death, and I remember the missed call. Did he know it'd be the last one? After six deep breaths, I listen to the last saved voicemail I've avoided, only now realizing, I've feared it for no reason. Probably wasn't even intended—a butt-dial in the desert if there ever was one; a perfect summation of the relationship we shared.

Voicemail

Dad

cell
May 22 at 1:14 AM

Transcription Beta

"[indecipherable]" [call ends]

▶ 0:00 |▬▬▬▬▬▬▬▬▬▬▬▬▬▬▬▬▬▬▬▬▬▬| -0:03

Speaker   **Call Back**   **Delete**

Would you rather live a long life where absolutely nothing of interest ever happens, or a short one where all the terrifying but exhilarating things do?

That question is the very thing I need to find out. I'll discover new therapies and medications—ones that work for me—because I accept I can't live this particular way anymore. I'm ready to let go. *I think.*

Think. Think. Think. Think. Think. Think.

After having six red, biodegradable balloons filled with helium for the last time this summer, Dew, JJ, Kam, and Nell join me as I release each wish into the sky. The 5k run's balloon release was fine enough, but these six balloons have deeper, more personal meanings attached. They represent the six goodbyes I never said to Dad. That's not something I could let go of in a crowd of strangers; Dad would understand that more than anyone. Just as how my tics change without notice, so does my heart. Dew's right—life *is* messy and I suppose this would be another plot twist in the version of mine. Maybe *I'm* a cliché trope, a generic one at that. Ask me if I care.

At the final balloon, I let out a held breath and release the strings from my grip. Hiccup, who JJ's tortured into a yellow doggie sundress and bonnet, nips at the backs of my heels. I lean over and boop his snout, which appears to disable the canine god's malfunction.

The corners of my mouth tug upward when I glimpse a shiny penny nearby. My fingers grasp the copper between them, and from that empty place inside, a full smile bursts up out of me. Maybe I don't know *exactly* what I'll do with my whole life. If I'll be brave enough to join the military, like Dad. Or support from afar, like Kam or Nell. I don't know if I'll be a political and educational pioneer, like JJ, or one who sacrifices her life for her child, like Mom. Maybe I'll never fully release a breath in the same way again. But there's no shame in figuring it out my way, on my terms. *Whatthehellever* that means.

I look up to the parting clouds and decide to buck everything I'd *normally* do the moment the noon church bells sing. I'm ready to let go.

THE TRUTH ABOUT FLOAT

FLOAT isn't an acronym meant *only* for service members. It's not even a real acronym. In fact, it has little to do with a silver box carried by a cargo plane from an overseas war. *Fallen Loved Ones Awaiting Transfer* is all of us broken by distance, emotional or physical. Even if our loved ones are alive. We're not in motion when they're gone, fighting, staying alive, dying; we're here, waiting, always waiting. *We're* the fallen, the cherry blossom petals, forgotten. *We're* the FLOAT wondering how to move forward with, *or without,* them, in a life that only moves forward.

Life goes in all sorts of directions, even when we're bound by pain. So maybe despite all your efforts to be away from everything that hurts you or scares you or leaves you feeling lost, this moment is exactly where you're meant to be.

Until you find a
　New balloon,
　　With new strings
　　　You can grab on to.
　　　　Where you can FLOAT like a butterfly
　　　　　Up into the clouds.
Until you find
Where you belong.

Voicemail

Naima

cell
August 23 at 5:05 AM

Transcription Beta

"I'm sorry it's taken so long for me to call you back. I've been afraid. It was wasted time. There's nothing I hate more. *Hate. Hate. Hate. Hate. Hate. Hate.* Maybe you can hear me, maybe not. Maybe I'll never be okay without you. *I don't know. I don't know. I don't know. I don't know. I don't know. I don't know.* There's a plane above me. I'm gonna pretend it's you, my star. Forever floating over to light the way through my darkest nights. [sigh] I should've said it more when you were alive, but thank you. For always seeing me. For loving me, even at my most unlovable. It's because of you I'm here at all. Take care of Mom [indecipherable]. *Goodbye.*"

▶ 0:00 |▬▬▬▬▬▬▬▬▬▬▬▬▬▬▬▬▬▬▬▬▬ -1:03

Speaker   **Call Back**   **Delete**

ACKNOWLEDGMENTS

Six Goodbyes underwent multiple full revisions. That means I've undergone multiple semi-breakdowns. No, but really. In the midst of telling Naima and Dew's stories, I found myself bound to my own mental illnesses, even hospitalized. I say this so all of you suffering in silence know: I hear you, I see you; I *am* you. Never be afraid to state your truth, state it loud. Until the stigmas disintegrate into nothing you cannot shrink. I wouldn't be here without the care and support of solid therapists who help me work through traumas, medication to "keep me level," as Naima would say, and a slew of family and friends, who, quite literally, pick me up off the floor when I feel I can't go on. You all took a page from Alejandra's book of verbs by stepping into my metaphorical shoes, peeling back my layers, and treating me with compassion and kindness when I felt most unworthy. I may not be here if it weren't for the love and acceptance, as I am, flaws and all. For that, I'm eternally grateful.

With that said, I want to thank my biological father, Matt. While I never had the chance to say my six goodbyes, I do in my mind and heart, every single day. Naima's empty longing and identity struggles are "gifts" my father's absence left in me. They may never disappear, but sometimes I think they're not meant to; they're reminders of who I am, and where my roots bind. In case he's listening, thank you, Matt, and *goodbye goodbye goodbye goodbye goodbye goodbye.*

Thank you to my brother, Jacob, and Dad, Jay, along with all veterans who've served our country and consulted on this project. You're far braver than me. And for my freedom, six thankyous could never be enough. *Never never never never never never.*

Along the same lines, thank you to those fostering any of the hundreds of thousands of children in the foster care system, and especially those who've adopted thereafter. Cyndi and Jesse Swafford, you've set the example and the world needs more of you. All children deserve a place they belong, a place they are loved, and a place they, too, are accepted as they are.

Mom, Kathy, thank you for standing by my side—especially over the last few years. I can't think of another human I've been closer with, trusted more, or who lifted me up most. I never say it enough, but thank you. You're more like Gram than you realize, and that is everything. And thank you to Randy, for being a father to me all these years.

Speaking of, I miss you, Gram; *come back come back come back come back come back come back.*

Of course, this book wouldn't be in your hands without my amazing editor, Vicki Lame. Through the many *many many many many many many* drafts and edits and corrections—and OMG WILL IT EVER END WITH THIS BOOK—I'm so thankful you didn't give up on me, that you ever believed in me in the first place with *Birdie & Bash*. You're the baddest, raddest, mofo (with just the right amount of optimistic sparkle) I've ever met. Also, hi to Troy. Meow.

Alongside Vicki, thank you to the whole Wednesday Books Team, which includes DJ DeSmyter, Dana Aprigliano, Sarah Bonamino, Jennie Conway, Kerri Resnick, Anna Gorovoy, Jeremy Pink, Janna Dokos, and Karen Richardson.

To Brent Taylor, my agent, who's been in my corner long before we *finally* teamed up. You're absolutely my North Star. No matter what I've gone through, I thank you for being there with boundless support and encouragement. Also, thank you again to Bethany Buck (previously at Greenburger) who sold *Six Goodbyes* along with *Birdie & Bash*, all the agents I had before Brent (Dan Mandel, Jackie Lindert, and Joanna Volpe), and every single person who read any part of this work, or any other. To Winans (hi, Taylor; ILY) for giving me all the writing fuel I could ever need (a lot), my ridiculous cats, Kitty, Feathers, & Milo Ventimeowlia. Because, why not? Meow again. To Jonathan Fletcher Faust. You've inspired something big between these pages. I'll leave it to you to figure out what.

To Erik—love is a verb. Love is patient; love is kind; love never fails. May we set the example our children will follow.

And finally, to my children, Lilliana and Sullivan. My darlings, it is you I breathe for, live for. May you wish on all the airplanes and dying stars, may those wishes come true, and may you never, ever, for a single second, doubt how amazing you are. Momma loves you from the earth to the sky, in this galaxy and all others, infinitely.

To everyone else, thank you for reading.

Without you,

There is no me.

Well, there is,

But not between the pages

That help pay

My endless therapy bills.